DutyBound

LIGHT WINGS EPIC VOL. 1

Mark A. Alvarez II

ISBN: 978-1-953865-10-6 (Paperback)
ISBN: 978-1-953865-11-3 (eBook)
ISBN: 978-1-953865-12-0 (Hardback)
Library of Congress Control Number: 2021902676

Any references to historical events, real people, or real places are used fictitiously. Names, characters, and places are products of the author's imagination.

Books Fluent
3014 Dauphine Street
New Orleans, LA

70117

For my teachers, who taught me the value of believing in
one's self. Missy, Pam, Samantha, Sara, and Aurora, this
one's for you . . .

Prologue

Today was a day of tragedy, though most did not know it.

Now, it was a dark and cloudless night. Not one sound broke throughout the grand white city of Moz, situated within the valley of a vast mountain range, sparkling like a diamond. Not a single ray of light could shed an ounce of joy upon the city, for it was already condemned by the haze that shrouded it. The mist hovered in the silence of the night, stagnant with the suffering of the land that lay below it. All the while, the people of Moz rested, unaware that all they held most dear teetered on the brink of ruin.

"Oh," Ara sighed as she sat alone in a muddled study at the base of a broad window. Her face flushed as her eyes scanned over a piece of parchment. Her irises, like embers, were so round and passionate, glistening almost red as she eagerly inspected the letter her beloved had left for her. But in that moment, as she realized what had happened, her eyes began to quiver, becoming trapped within garnet walls of fear. After everything they had faced, Stello had abandoned her, leaving their family broken.

Dearest Ara,

Not long ago, I started feeling it again. Do you remember? The strengthening cold and bitter skies were only signs of its return. I can never forget the pain of Frailty's War. I bear this burden of recalling the horror, and still, it pains me to know even you hold that, my dear.

Unfortunately, I must tell you that soon we will not be safe. The fog has begun to grow thick, and wrath-filled winds blow from the north where Pinea lies, building their empire with envy and hatred toward our sovereign nation. Though we won our place of power here in Moz, I can only say it came at a grave price, one that will plague our world if the bonds of our sins are not destroyed. It is critical that we protect what good is left in this world and amend the wrongs of the past.

I fear the worst for our family and would never forgive myself if I waited for its return. Thus, it is here in a place of faith that I tell you I must leave Moz to seek out its source, and see to it that this force is driven to where it can no longer threaten us. But at all costs, please, remain in Moz and wait.

With utmost importance, take care of sweet Lucia so that she grows into a bold and passionate maiden whose prayers are determined enough to protect and preserve us. I do promise to make it back to you someday. My love shall be with you both. Always.

Stello Sanoon

Ara grasped her blouse. This deepening wound tore at her chest as though she knew, this whole time, that it would be here that her heart would break.

"Lady Ara," called her loyal maid, Amelia, so struck with concern that the wrinkles in her forehead seemed to suddenly age her ten years. In her eyes was a clinging intuition.

Ara sensed her concern as if the maid already knew, but spoke anyway. "He's gone."

"The master?" asked the maid.

"Stello."

"My lady," Amelia said with grief before bringing her eyes back to Ara.

There was a lull as they both thought. The maid's stare grew distant as Ara let out a faint whimper, breaking the still silence.

Finally, Amelia asked, "May I ask why the master left?"

Ara's insides shuddered. "He fears of . . . " She hesitated, looking at the letter, fully dazed and unable to grasp the idea of its true meaning. It was as if something hid beneath his words, something he was not telling her. Memories flashed through her mind. Her chest tightened. *It couldn't still be out there.*

It was her prayers that had saved them. It was her strength, her power that had defeated it in the first place. Could it still exist somewhere, outside the reach of man? "He fears of its return." She felt the warmth of her tears beneath her eyes once more while the maid's face paled, her own fears apparent in this revelation. The war was supposed to be over. Amelia wanted to release tears of her own. But still she held an unchanging sternness of stone, something unbreakable. She had to show a strong sense of obligation and duty, no matter the adversity. She had to be strong for the lady, even though she could not be strong for herself.

"Lady Ara, I'm terribly sorry . . . Lucia—" Her concern for the child shone within the sparkles of her green eyes as she uttered her name. "Should I go to her?"

Ara looked up at her, her amber eyes still wet with tears. Despite the circumstances, she released a slight smile remembering her daughter in that moment. "Yes, please. Thank you."

Amelia bowed before leaving Ara alone in the reticence of her fractured thoughts.

Ara looked down from the window and upon the rigid streets

below, focusing on the mist rising over the horizon. She lay a hand upon the cold glass and wondered what her dear Stello had been thinking. Why would he place this burden on himself, when it was *her* power that had weakened the evil? Shouldn't this have been her burden to bear?

She grimaced and bit her lip, as if trying to make it bleed. Her woe turned to anger, causing her pain to tighten as the emotions converged. The thought of raising their daughter and carrying their province alone felt like a mightier burden than whatever quest Stello was chasing. She gave out an indignant roar, slamming her palm against the window. "Stello, why have you done this?! Must you leave us alone? I can't do this without you . . . how can I?"

Almost immediately as her hand pressed against the glass, the moonlight broke through the heavy clouds, blasting through the fog and into the window. A distant glimmer of light reflected off something lying on Stello's desk. She walked over to it, following the light as it sparkled beneath the cover of a cloth. Wrapped in silk was a silver chain. At its base was something white—a divinely cut pendant. Attached was a small scroll with a message written in freshly laid ink, just like the letter: "For Lucia, when she is of age. Take care of this, for she will need it."

Ara stared, dazzled by the diamond's beauty. From its side came tiny silver wings, angelically stylized with feathers on its ends—such perfection. She wrapped it in the silk and gripped the gift as she brought it to her chest. In that moment, her heart felt whole again, her pain forgotten and her grief absolved, lifted from her while the pendant left something better in its place: faith. Ara smiled, releasing a faint whisper into the moonlight. "Oh, Stello."

CHAPTER ONE

The Memento

I t had been seventeen years since the master of Moz left his province venturing forth into the farthest regions of Terestria in search of a redemption he would not find.

The morning was crisp and splendent as the spring brought in what appeared to be an early summer. The sunlight radiated down toward the grand Sanoon Manor in the city's northern district, drifting in softly through an immense stained glass window and into a sanctuary where, head bowed and beautiful, a girl of eighteen prayed within its brilliance. The girl was Lucia Sanoon, the sole heir and high maiden of Moz, daughter of the now-reigning Lady Ara who had taken the province after her husband, Master Stello, had undertaken a mission of peace to the north. This was her home, a mansion of white marble and glass. Pillars and engaged columns supported a vast basilica connecting the front of the manor to a balcony that was elevated by a wide staircase at its far end.

Lucia stood proudly before the altar with her eyes closed. She was shrouded in layers of golden and white cloth that flowed elegantly over her slender body. The long, loose sleeves of her blouse dangled at her elbows as her arms rose out from them. Her hands met at her chest, clenching together as she prayed. Her hair fell past her shoulders to just above her waist like waves of wholesome honey smelling of a light rose perfume.

No one could deny her charm, for she was the most beautiful maiden to ever grace the halls of Sanoon Manor. Her large eyes had been shaped with grace, narrowing at their corners like autumn almonds, and her lips were sculpted with such a serene purity that her smile brought joy to all who witnessed it. She was gently kissed by the heaven's light, giving her fair complexion a soft olive tone, as it often showed on the brightest of days. There was innocence in the way she stood, something untainted and untouched, but still bold and as blessed as could be. And in her hair was a band, well crafted, yet so delicate that it seemed to hover like a halo over her head—dove white, with feathers shaped onto the silver lining of its exterior. She wore a short skirt high above her knee-length boots, decorated in the traditional Mozian style with cross-stitched gold lacing that complemented the bow tied at the back of her waist.

She opened her eyes and looked at the window, fascinated by its spiraling colored panels with the familiar gold and violet as well as magenta and sky blue. Like always, this comforted her—bathing in the light. Lucia lowered her golden eyes as if to begin another prayer when she was startled by the call of her name.

"Lucia!"

She saw no one, but knew well to respond quickly. She rolled her eyes annoyed by this sudden intrusion on her thoughts. The tiresome expectations of her mother wore Lucia down sometimes. However, her mother had always told her that, like all things, even faith must be exercised. There was a reason for everything. *Duty above all else.* Lucia reached out to the altar toward a piece of parchment. With a quill, she scribbled something down before shouting, "Coming!"

She grasped the sheet and hurried into a wide hallway, crossing a narrow bridge and making her way down a staircase leading to the lower levels of the mansion. The ceiling above her was covered with frescoes containing representations of the divine spirits and creators of the world—the forces of light and darkness. Simple yet mighty, these all-powerful elements of matter and spirit cultivated the existence of time and space, allowing life to thrive. With light came the heavens and all living things, while with darkness came the earth and the essence of mortality itself: death.

These were their guardians, their creators, and were very much like gods—or so she thought. Inscribed in the ancient texts of the Sanoon library were tomes honoring the creation of the forces themselves, but nothing that described their purpose in creating the world Lucia lived in. That knowledge was thought to have long since been lost with time.

She took the stairs to the front of her home, a cathedral within a garden of neatly trimmed hedges and marble statues. Lucia felt faint, fatigued by her anxiety. *What could Mother want this time?* The maiden quickened her step, worrying as she often did and bolting past her mother's favorite mural, a mosaic depicting an alluring seraph emerging from golden light. At the tips of its feathered white wings, strips of bright opal cascaded like water flowing to the base of its frame.

Waiting for her, dressed in gray as usual, was Amelia, her loyal and devoted maid whom she had known for as long as she could remember—always the same and as firm and frozen as the marble around them. For years, Amelia had been the most respected serv-ant within the manor and had fulfilled her role as Lucia's second mother, caretaker, and tutor. Amelia had also taken her place as Lady Ara's right-hand advisor and best friend. Amelia's wisdom was never to be mistaken. Lucia could not think of a moment when she had given her faulty advice.

Amelia bowed her head as Lucia approached with graceful steps, her own anticipation building, making Lucia wary of what she was walking into. She carried a deep intuition but ignored it.

"Good day, High Maiden. Your mother has requested to see you."

Lucia smiled and tipped her head forward in response. Her headband glistened beneath the light of the high windows. "Thank you, Amelia. Where is she?"

Amelia chuckled before replying with a wide grin. "Your father's study."

Lucia gave a puzzled look. "But that place has been locked for ages. I don't think it's been opened since Father left." She shrugged, brushing her cheek to keep her hair from falling into her face. "I recall trying to get in as a child, but I never could manage to."

"Of course, but your mother does have the key."

"Right. Indeed, she does," Lucia mumbled.

Amelia tilted her head and crossed her arms as she stared at the maiden with suspicion. "Where were you?"

"Ah . . . " Lucia parted her lips, tossing back her hair and pointing a finger behind her. "The sanctuary. I was writing."

"Another song, I hope. Your hymns always prove to be the holiest, bringing about the most bountiful of harvests." Amelia smiled again and bowed before patting Lucia's shoulder. "Well take care. Your mother is waiting for you. If you need me, I'll be tending to the garden."

"Goodbye, Amelia." Lucia widened her lips before waving and bowing her head. She rushed back to the stairs and took the flight leading to the manor's west wing.

*   *   *

The study was guarded by two pompous, ruby-colored doors each with its own golden handle. Lucia gave a small push. The rush of stagnant air caught in her hair as her eyes searched inside. She crept into a neatly shelved room. Canvases adorned the walls sheltered with secrets. The colors were so heated and vibrant, displaying a variety of landscapes within each frame. As she moved forward, she noticed how each painting waned becoming so different than the one before it. The style of each subsequent painting became gloomier and darker until, at the edge of the study, a frame was filled with only black and white strokes—incomplete, as if the artist never returned to finish it.

The shelves held many books, scrolls, and parchments all covered in dust and worn by years of lying dormant. As Lucia continued on, the temperature seemingly dropped. A chill enveloped her, coiling about and bringing her goosebumps. Her nerves shook in this place. It was as if the room was haunted by a ghost she could not see, someone or something she did not know.

She closed her eyes and released a slow breath, trying to control her emotions. She did not like how she could sense the world changing around her within the fabric of time itself. It was incredibly intoxicating as reality shifted. She could feel her future itself now heading toward a different path.

Since childhood, Lucia had presented an unmistakable intuition so significant that it frightened those who knew her. Her nightmares mirrored disasters that would strike the everyday lives of her people, such as storms and droughts or even riots that would break out within Southern Moz from time to time. Her mother called it a "gift of the light," a reward for her unbreakable faith granted only to the chosen. Lucia's judgment was pristine—a blessing and, at times, a curse.

Now, it was as if she knew too much. She sensed something

looming—a calm before the storm. This premonition held something so grim in its feeling. Lifeless and cold, so cruel and hateful. It was terrifying. Lucia had felt it as soon as she made her way into the study. It moved into her heart as if it was coming home to stay. Things from here on out, she realized in that moment, would never be the same.

Across the study, her mother stood waiting, staring out the window with her fingers pressed against the glass. She turned to her daughter, her face glowing with excitement. But her eyes reflected a distinct distance within them. The lady's gown was crimson, her favorite color, and fit loosely over her wrists. Her hands clenched something shimmering. "Lucy, aren't they lovely?" She perked up as she looked at the paintings around them.

Lucia smiled, her eyes focusing again on her mother's hands. Within them was a ball of silver silk cloth. It was odd. Her eyes drew to it immediately, almost as if it was the cause of the commotion happening in her mind. Lucia shook it off. "Absolutely," she responded politely, covering up her sudden chill and trying to ease it asleep. She simpered, hoping it would distract her mother from her sudden tension.

"Lucia . . . " Ara paused, moving her gaze to the canvases surrounding them. She breathed a sigh before saying, "This place has been locked for seventeen years."

"I know," Lucia said, looking around. "This was Father's study."

"Yes." Ara sighed again at the memory. "Seventeen years ago on this day, your father left us. It was a dismal day for our family. I know growing up without your father has been especially tough on you, but he knew the day would come when you would learn to rule. You have grown since then. You are now of age."

"I suppose I have," Lucia said, looking away from her mother's mulling gaze. She felt a slight bit sarcastic. All of this sounded so familiar. She had only been eighteen for half a year, but why was she here? Why was she *now* hearing the story she'd heard over and over before, here in the depths of a study that had lain in silence for so long? Why must she be here where he lived then?

For years, the mere idea of her father leaving tore at her, but not without creating something stronger in the process. For some time she could hardly bear the thought of it—her father deserting her family. Tears would form at his mention, and she would withdraw into a state of self-loathing. It was, at one point in time, the easiest way to break her down. But since she had grown, Lucia had finally become distant and numb to the memory. She often hated her mother for not truly understanding that.

Still, the idea of not knowing her father troubled her. Yet, it was in not knowing where she found a particular sense of freedom, despite not having much of it. She could define herself within the boundaries of her own self-expectations, and imagine a life for herself outside of what her mother wanted. That was only half of who she was. The other half was left to interpretation, free for her to choose.

But now, in her father's long-dormant study, she questioned the freedom she had in composing her own story. Here, a part of who she was awakened as she peered into the paintings and within herself. Lucia recognized a passion for art, something she did not share with her mother who was more or less consumed by the duty and expectation of their nobility, favoring practicality over desire. Yet here, something deeper finally found its way to the surface.

Scattered along the walls was the sensitivity her mother so boldly opposed. Lucia wondered if this was because of him, this man she did not know. Did he leave these qualities embedded inside her? Despite how her mother felt, Lucia longed to be independent of her status in Moz and truly come into her own, leading a life she wanted. Being high maiden meant she was to be bright and dignified, to portray herself with honor and nothing less. So this bothered her, the inability to make her life what she wished.

Sometimes, she could imagine herself doing something far different, often dreaming of places she had never seen and wondering if they truly existed. Why care for thousands of people who knew nothing of what she valued? And what of their own ideals, their own dreams and agendas? How could she rule them all? There was no way for her to know all of their needs and intentions. From what she knew, she was hardly ready. Age did not change that, no matter what her mother said.

"Your father left something for you those many years ago. And now it's time for you to have it, to wear as you rule." Ara held out the cloth, her pale hands inching toward Lucia's.

Lucia accepted it from her mother, examined it, and gingerly pulled a chain from the cloth. She gasped as she traced the silver lining with her finger, feeling the cold of its touch transfer and, oddly enough, fill her warmly. "He left this for me?" she asked in disbelief, gazing at the silver that was now shimmering into her eyes.

Ara nodded. "It resembles your beauty." She touched Lucia's shoulder softly as she took the winged pendant and wrapped it around Lucia's neck. "It's elegant, isn't it? As if it was made just for you."

"I'm honored," Lucia said as she looked up to Ara, who was beaming more than before.

"I suppose you'll be wearing this to the banquet tomorrow night?" The lady stared deeply into the pendant as she asked.

"A banquet?" Lucia turned to her mother, confused but not completely surprised. It was just like her mother to stage another celebration to get into the good graces of the people. "What for?"

"Why, I thought we'd commemorate the twentieth anniversary of the war's end. Moz has been through so much, and as the governors of this province we have an obligation to our people to show them that prosperity does exist."

Lucia nodded softly as her mother kissed her head. Gently, she receded.

"What's this?" Ara asked, spotting the scroll in Lucia's hand.

"It's nothing," said Lucia, casting it aside. "Another prayer I've been writing. A hymn for the light."

Lady Ara was intrigued. "Oh really? Can I hear it?"

Lucia blushed. "I couldn't. Not right now." She bit her lip and then smirked. "Although, I do think it's really good. My best yet."

Ara's eyes narrowed. "I would like to ask something of you."

"What?"

"That glimmer I just saw. That sparkle in your eye." Ara placed a finger to her chin for a moment as the thought was fresh. "I want to ask you for your courage. Being the high maiden is by no means easy. Being lady can nearly break me at times. Lucia, I am aware of its burden, and I know that it just being the two of us has left you without an understanding of your true abilities. But you must be confident."

Lucia's confusion magnified further as her thoughts shifted toward the unexpected. "What do you mean?"

"Lucia, I have total faith in you as my heir, and you have portrayed yourself with elegance, beauty, and grace. I believe, now, that you are ready to show the province and the world what you really are inside. After all, it is your birthright." Ara smiled, watching her daughter's eyes sparkle above the diamond wings around her neck. "At the banquet tomorrow night, I would like you to share one of your hymns with the people of Moz, and let it be *their* anthem—a symbol of growth, prosperity, and hope. Let it be a reminder of what is good in the world. As you're the legitimate heir to the throne of Sanoon, your song will surely move and inspire them. It will be historic. Why not let their voices join you?"

"You want me to sing at the banquet?" Lucia asked, her voice nearly cracking. "To everyone?"

"Yes, to your people." Ara nodded. She raised a finger. "But I want you to be yourself. Don't worry about what they will think of you, my dear. You are beautiful and good inside. I'm certain that you'll gain the people's affection, and most of all their trust."

Lucia's heart fluttered. Was her mother really saying this to her? Was she really telling her that this was time to be herself, and to step up and take her true place as heir? Lucia couldn't contain her excitement, nor could she decipher it from the nervousness that consumed her. She would sing during her first address. "You really think I can do it? Bring the nation together with my song?"

"Of course. I can sense it within you, Lucy—an aspiration to lead. You will do great things for Terestria."

Lucia looked away, clenching the scroll in her hand. The moment she walked through those ruby doors, her life would change. She felt strange trying to imagine herself in front of all those people, her people—as the center of their world, her voice theirs. Trusting her mother, and even deep down wanting it herself, she accepted. "Thank you, Mother. I won't fail you. I'll make this something the people will remember."

Ara laughed and clapped her hands together. "I'm so happy that you're excited. Praise the light." She took a deep breath and looked back to Lucia, who was caressing the wings of the pendant with the tips of her middle and forefinger. "Don't worry, dear. This is for the best."

"Yes, Mother. Thank you."

Lucia followed her mother out of the study and, parting, walked through the halls with the weight of her pendant accentuating her gait. The color of the maroon carpet rose up through it, making it twinkle a pale magenta in the light. It was alluring with its changing refractions. She pondered whether or not her father imagined her wearing it, as if he would have known who she'd grow to be. She tried to shift her mind, avoiding the thought as she always did. She had never known him, and to her he was just a ghost—a haunting and in many ways unwanted presence that disrupted her world. To her he was hopeless, a lost cause. He would never return. Lucia knew this—her intuition told her so.

But now, she had this opportunity to take control and show the people of Moz that she loved the very person she constantly hid from them. It would be her time to rise and unify the people to a cause more familiar than her own. Her mother was right. There was something within her she could not understand just yet, a power she had yet to tap into. The light had chosen her for this purpose, to rule and bring balance to the realms. The moment the pendant had wrapped around her neck, she felt the essence of her reality transform, determining her future. Lucia was unique, and now she was bestowed with this mission, to use her words and her song to move her people into a new age.

However, something inside her still doubted. Something about this seemed too good; as if it were a dream, a fantasy. She had felt it in her father's study and had not forgotten how it clung to her. That gripping intuition still hovered in the currents. Although this was to be a banquet to honor the values of prosperity, Lucia sensed disaster in the midst. Her thoughts whispered chaos all from within the calm of a heavy storm.

CHAPTER TWO

A Stretch of Faith

Lucia looked beyond the altar and into the stained glass behind it. She blinked as the light seeped through and hit the pendant at the base of her neck causing it to shine. The colors were spiraling as usual, mixing into the sunlight. She felt the warmth, accepting the triumphant beauty that absorbed into her gaze, motivating her. She took her quill before unraveling her scroll, then traced the sheet with her eyes, breathing deeply, trying to recall the melody within the words . . . its rhythm.

Lucia often found herself here. Whenever she was away from her studies and not serving beside her mother during one of her briefings or social gatherings, she often retreated to this sanctuary. Here she could be herself, away from the pressure that constantly coiled about her life—the stinging expectations of diplomacy.

Usually when she was with her mother "honing her judgment," as her mother would say, Lucia attempted to bring herself back here—her mind daydreaming, lost in thought. Her prayers and hymns eased her heart more than anything else, even more than the thoughts of her father returning.

Lucia giggled to herself, humored by her own reluctance. Even if only for small instants at a time, she could escape the reality of her lonely life beneath the light of this window. But maybe things could be different now that this opportunity to lead had been proposed. She could start to use her place of power to make it as it should be—the way she'd always wanted.

She looked at the small wings again, admiring the pendant thoroughly before placing it at her chest. It had four symbols carved into a small diamond that was cut to perfection as if chiseled by the elite artisans of Argania—or better even. It exhibited a strange essence, a foreign force that drew questions from within her mind along with memories, all of which linked to create a tight chain that clashed, sounding an echo of a faint whisper she could not understand. Why was even *this* a reminder of him? Her imagination ran rampant.

The symbols lay at each of the diamond's four points, and as Lucia looked up to the window, she noticed the same symbols within the glass. She exhaled, trying to release the emptiness that suddenly clenched her. She walked, entranced, to touch them and draw in their meaning with her fingertips. So many emotions stirred uncontrollably inside her, and it was as if her anxiety was slowly magnifying. She continued to study the symbols, something telling her that it would be too painful to resist. It seemed to lie in the whispers—the faint thoughts within distant memories, and some wisdom she did not know.

She shook her head and stepped away. "What am I doing?" she asked aloud. She drew a breath and tried to calm her thoughts, feeling her blood flow into her eyes, her sweat about to break. Lucia looked at the symbols and touched them once more. Stepping back, she knelt down and prayed, subdued and almost afraid. A sudden feeling overtook her, hovering inside. She felt nothing else, sensed nothing else—a clinging intuition as if her emotions had been channeled into something inside her so tangible and so real, yet fragile enough to disappear.

The emotions clanged together and collected around her heart, making it heavy. Why was the pendant doing this to her? It seemed to drain energy from her as the silent whispers of her prayers left her lips. "Why me? Why place me here? What purpose do I have? Guide me please. Show me what to believe. Who am I?" Her voice cracked. *Not again*, she thought, holding her breath. "I just want to know . . . why?"

The light from the window dimmed as she continued alone at the altar, trying to understand, hoping that her prayers would be answered. At times, it seemed like she was only speaking to herself. But not today. This was different. As she whispered, a response came from within her. A sense of conviction rooted to her subconscious thoughts.

"Lucia," a voice echoed from behind her.

Lucia's eyes flickered open. Her gaze softened. She failed to notice that time had passed well past the evening. She rose as Ara, wearing her nightgown, walked to her side, tilted her head, and looked up into her face as Lucia tried to hide behind her own hair.

"My dear, how long have you been here? Is something wrong?" Ara asked firmly, so as to hide the worry in her voice.

"Mother, I'm . . . " Her voice quivered as she spoke. "I'm so sorry. I must have drifted to sleep at the altar," she lied, trying to hide the obvious anguish inside her, the torrents amplifying. Something was not alright. Still, her head was fuzzy; her thoughts were fiery, caught in a storm of lightning she had never experienced before.

Energy collided within her.

"You need your rest for tomorrow's banquet. Why is it that you're so weary?" Ara asked. "You should go to bed."

Lucia held the pendant with her fingers. "I am awfully tired." She tried to get up and rush past her mother, but Ara caught her shoulder and turned her daughter to face her, penetrating with her amber eyes.

"You're troubled."

"No," Lucia said, trying to force a smile and move on. But Ara's grip tightened. Lucia rolled her eyes as she looked back to her mother. "Can I go?"

Ara didn't say a word. Instead, she looked down at Lucia's neck and touched the pendant. "Sometimes you frighten me, Lucia."

"And why's that, Mother?"

Ara's face was firm. Lucia could tell she was thinking of something. She feared her mother when she was like this. It made her eyes shudder, because she knew her mother was judging her. She had experienced it often.

"I don't know if you can handle the power bestowed on you."

Lucia narrowed her eyes. "Mother, what power? I'm fine. Can I go now?" She hesitated before adding, "Please?"

Ara lowered her eyes, which brought Lucia off her toes. Maybe now she could escape her.

"Do you believe that you are ready for this?"

"I'm actually excited. I can't imagine what it'll be like. My hopes are high." She burst easily into false enthusiasm.

Ara closed her eyes and shook her head. "No, my dear. I mean, are you ready for the world to know what you stand for?"

Lucia clenched her teeth. What could her mother be getting at with this? It irritated her when her mother picked at her—prying, attempting to analyze and understand every intention, every instance of weakness that Lucia showed. "The thing about that is

. . . the world doesn't know me yet. My title as high maiden is all they've ever known. And, even if I do this, I still have some doubt that they might never know who I truly am."

"Do *you* know who you are?"

Lucia pulled her arm back slowly, knowing better than to provoke her mother with a sudden jerk, although she most definitely wanted to yank it away. "What kind of question is that?" Lucia asked, forcing a playful tone into her voice. "Of course I do."

Ara sighed and rested a hand over her heart. "It will be critical that you know yourself before you can fully understand your kingdom, or even the world. In order to protect what is close to you, you must protect yourself. Remember that, Lucia. This song should uphold your values. Keep them close. This will be your first address as high maiden, and depending on how it's received"—Ara took a step forward, facing the sanctuary doors, leaving Lucia confused by the brief speech—"it could very well be your last. Goodnight, Lucia."

Lucia rushed out of the sanctuary, trying not to think any longer. Her mother's words only rattled her senses more, echoing beyond even where they were before. She staggered and nearly tripped on the stairs as she placed a hand to her face.

She burst into her room and ruffled her hair, tearing the bright white band before tossing it into the chest at the end of her bed. She changed into her nightgown and slid into the golden cloth that hung over her bed eagerly as her body weakened. *What is wrong with me?* she thought. *This pendant . . . those symbols. I must be coming down with something.* She took a deep breath. "And then my mother. Why can't I rid myself of this . . . " She whispered as the weariness of her prayers pulled her lids down, "feeling."

Then, as if she was fully exhausted after all, she fell into a deep sleep, one that calmed her thoughts in an instant. Her breath softened and grew silent as she drifted deeper into her rest, and into a dream. This dream would be the deepest and most restful she would have for a long time.

*   *   *

Lucia awoke to the morning glow across her face. The familiar sound of bells rang from the east facade as she sat up, her body stretching comfortably alert. She pushed back her hair as she rose from her bed, feeling her tresses drape behind her. She bent down and pulled out her band, which she had gravely missed, and put it back in its rightful place. She smiled, turning to the full-length, gold-framed mirror at the end of the room, and stared back at her reflection as if she had never seen it before.

Lucia looked completely changed. Something about her seemed to have jumped through time, filling her to the peak of her youth. And there, still around her neck, those silver wings—so beautiful, so divine—sparkling in the sunlight as she caressed them and let out a breath. She hurriedly dragged herself over and opened the wardrobe. Her anxiety looming over the onset of the day's festivities, she pulled out too many outfits, unable to decide what would look most elegant (as her mother would put it), or more "herself." In the back of her mind was the thought that she couldn't avoid this. She could not quit, no matter what. The song was to be sung. Her hymn was to be an anthem for her people to cherish. She had some idea what to say, but still, her nerves built up inside. She remembered her mother's words from the day before and let out a faint whimper.

"The people will love me," Lucia assured herself even as she tried to stop the tiny chatter in her mouth. "They will believe in me as long as I believe in myself." She looked back at her reflection, releasing her anxiety as the pendant glimmered beneath her neck. She saw a hint of a sparkle and then a strand of light. "They will adore me," Lucia said suddenly, grasping that positivity as if she had to persuade even herself. "I can do this." She looked back at the wardrobe, examining it before moving her eyes back to the mirror, releasing the pressures within her mind. "I just need to—" Lucia could not finish her sentence. What if she was only lying to herself? What if she really knew nothing? But . . . of course she did—she had to. It was just like her to let pessimism overtake her. Her mother believed in her, so why shouldn't she? "I will do this. I *must* do this," she concluded. She smiled at her pendant. It seemed to go beautifully with every gown she held up to her chest.

Lucia moved over to her desk and withdrew a blank piece of parchment. Her mind clouded over with a shower of thoughts as she tried to evoke the right words to portray herself with. Virtues that would represent her people.

It was like she had forgotten the previous night and the weariness that had consumed her after speaking to her mother in the study. The lingering intuition—the cold grip—had left her now, and she was excited. Perhaps a party was exactly what she needed— meeting people, socializing amongst the nobles, and hearing all the latest news. There would be a feast and music to captivate the masses. Her mother had the most delectable and rich taste in sweets, and the baker in Moz, fortunately for her, made the finest pastries, soft and creamy. Lucia loved thinking about them.

Though the food was delicious, Lucia's favorite part of any party was the music, and she looked forward to it. The sounds of the orchestra would make her body react on its own. Her heart would flare to the rhythms, and she usually felt impassioned and inspired as the music moved through her, turning her body into a doll, a vessel for its own design. Her dance was so light, like a feather—too graceful, some would say, but Lucia knew no judgment.

"Good morning, High Maiden," Amelia said from behind.

Lucia looked up from her desk, her bright eyes shining as sunlight seeped in from the window. Surprised and quite possibly a tad bit confused, Lucia managed to uttered the words, "How do you do?" Lucia looked back to the mirror and then down to the blank piece of parchment. She bit her lip, worrisome.

"Your mother informed me of your presentation this evening. She is adamant that you be prepared." Amelia paced behind Lucia.

Lucia lowered her eyes further. "Adamant, you say? I still haven't found the words to sing."

"What of the many hymns you've already written?" Amelia rested her hand on top of Lucia's head. "Your prayers have always been so pure. I'm sure any would do."

"But this one is supposed to be different," Lucia said. She struggled to find the words, as if she was unable to grasp why she had lost her voice now. "This song is for my people."

Amelia traced her fingers through the honey waves of Lucia's hair. "I'm sure it'll come to you, dear. You must remember that this is for more than just your people. This is for *you*." She glanced toward the door. "Why don't you write somewhere you are more comfortable?" She smiled. "Where you'll find some musings." Her right palm found its way to the redwood surface of Lucia's desk and dropped a bronze key.

Lucia gazed in awe, reaching for it. She hesitated as it called out to her, whispering an echo of something cold. "This opens Father's study."

Amelia nodded. "It is yours now, a reward for your devotion to Moz and faith in the light. Your mother believes that it would be what your father would have wanted. It is now your rightful place."

Lucia's eyes were drawn to the mirror. She looked into her own eyes as they emptied and became hollow. She lost herself, as the light of the pendant enticed her, tugging at her curiosity. It was returning—that dreadful feeling. The sunlight faded, dimming her window. It was suddenly as if time froze. There it was, heavy on her desk, this omen, and all she could do was lose herself to her own thoughts. A warning stood stagnant in the air. She would have to choose her words wisely. Her call to power was not what it seemed; she sensed something darker beneath the surface.

She grasped the key, looking back at Amelia. "I'll bring honor to his name," Lucia said, forcing a smile. She resented the thought, *Oh sweet father, Master Stello Sanoon.*

* * *

Night came quickly, ushering in a starless night. The clouds reflected only the light of the great torch that radiated upward like a beacon from the central grounds of Manor Sanoon. A young knight stood in the garden, watching as carriages came from far and wide. His armor was shiny and new, and his chest was curtained with the protection of the Sanoon family crest—the seraph, elaborately detailed on plates of untarnished metal. He held a great sword at his side, its hilt firmly within his grasp. His grip loosened as his attention turned to the lady approaching him.

"Lady Ara." The knight removed his helmet from his head and bowed, letting his thick red hair fall to the sides of his face.

Humbled, Ara slowed her step. "Lieutenant Angelo Sarf. Please, there is no need for formalities." She tilted her head before curtseying. "Welcome to Manor Sanoon."

"I am honored to be here, milady." His eyes were earthy, as green as emeralds, filled with enthusiasm, calm and collected. He had been summoned here by the lady herself, chosen for a task he would hold alone. The reason he had been chosen was unclear, but his focus and alertness showed in the way he stood.

"General Arthur Plight has spoken very highly of you," said the lady. "You should thank him for his recommendation. He claims you were the swiftest of his young recruits," she teased.

"Thank you, milady. I am grateful to hear such praise." He smiled graciously, honored by her words. Moved, he asserted himself straighter than before, with a newfound confidence. "So, what service is due for my lady on such an occasion?"

Ara nodded. "Well, of course. What I ask of you is not much, but it is very important." She looked out onto the horizon as more and more people made their way to the manor grounds, crowding about its gates so as to catch a glimpse of the event inside. "Tonight is a special evening for my dear Lucia. The high maiden is to make her first address to the province, singing a hymn she wrote in honor of the war's end. I would like for it to go accordingly, without the slightest error. I'm sure it will be splendid; but just in case, I would like for you to watch over her and act as her bodyguard and protector. This feast is to commemorate peace, but there might still be those who wish to harm her."

"Harm the high maiden?" Angelo asked, his eyes growing stern. "Who would dare?"

"The war's end was not brought about by negotiations. It was brought about by force. There are still some who might not think it ended the way it should have. Not many sympathize with Pinea, as our family has. We show mercy, as any honorable leader would, but I can't help but wonder how many were angered when we called a truce after so much was lost."

"The war was an atrocity. It brought destruction to both provinces. When you decided to end the bloodshed, you saved so many lives. The people know that. I remember."

"But some may not agree. Everyone is different, Lieutenant." Ara tilted her head. "Tell me, where are you from?"

"My family came way of Gracile, but I was raised in South Moz, milady."

"Do you love this country?" she asked firmly.

"I pledged my life to serve it. Of course, I do."

"Then you must understand: it is dire that we eliminate the ties that bind us to our sins. Grief festers the darkest parts of hearts.

Loss brings about hate, anger, and all that comes with it. The truce has brought on a peace to quell this darkness; but never doubt, the darkness does still live. It lives within each of us. And though the war is over, those who have lost and not forgiven are among us. We must stay safe, by acknowledging that not everyone is good." Ara dropped her gaze as her thoughts turned distant. It was as if Stello had spoken through her. These words did not feel like her own. Her own heart became heavy as it was enveloped by a sensation of great discomfort with the sudden resurgence of the memory of her lost husband. "Do you understand?" she stammered.

Angelo was not sure, but he could not refuse her. "You have my word. No harm will come to the high maiden. She has my protection."

A grin surfaced as Ara came back to herself, abandoning her thoughts of distant fears. "Thank you, Lieutenant Sarf. Now, if you could please find Lucia and escort her to the grand ballroom. I will be announcing the commencement of the feast shortly."

"Yes, Lady Ara. Right away." Angelo bowed his head one final time before rushing past Ara and toward the manor, his green eyes fixed on the light of the torch.

* * *

Lucia was nervous, her hands shaking. She had rehearsed it over and over in her mind, hoping it would be enough. *What if I forget?* she thought. *Don't be so stupid.*

Pacing within the sanctuary, she clasped her hands together. "Please, light, don't fail me. I need you. Grant me the strength to do what I must do. My duty is your command." Her gown was flowing, shimmering a pale yellow beneath the lantern light.

"High Maiden," she heard from behind her. Angelo stood in the doorway.

Lucia turned to him.

"Good evening," he said.

"Likewise. Can I help you?"

Angelo came closer, passing through the pews and facing Lucia at the altar, his armor rattling. "Your mother asked that I escort you to the grand ballroom. The feast's about to begin." His eyes read through the expression on her face. "Nervous, are you?"

"Quite," Lucia said with a slight laugh. "I've not experienced anything like this before. I don't think I've ever been this petrified."

"I don't think I've ever met someone so afraid of a good time." Angelo provoked her playfully.

Lucia withdrew herself into a jovial facade, appearing cheerful. "Well, I suppose I'll just have to brace myself."

"For dire consequences . . . " His eyes sparkled. "Don't worry, Maiden. Just have fun."

Lucia held out her hand to the knight. "Pleased to meet you—" She was about to ask for his name when he interrupted.

"Lieutenant Angelo Sarf. The honor is mine." He grasped her fingers as he tilted his head toward the door. "Shall we?"

CHAPTER THREE

Duty's Bane

The gates of the manor were flooded with lights as multitudes of people traveled the roads. It took about a sixteenth of the Mozian military to securely lay passage for the relatively minuscule number of nobles invited to the party, as waves of commoners gathered there, ever hopeful. To witness a moment of luxury beyond this threshold gave their lives purpose—to celebrate the lives they did not live.

"You don't suppose we can get in without an invitation do you, Leo?" asked a young man standing at the gate. He was rebellious in nature, a fact made clear by the way his blond hair stood on end, untamed. Beside him was his best friend.

A man of twenty, Sir Leocadio Feral of Pinea—the province north of Moz—stared upward into the torchlight atop the hill, his lapis eyes fixed beyond the saturating crowds and on a mission concrete within his mind. His purpose far outweighed that of those who surrounded him. Destiny called his name. He pulled a small scroll from his vest pocket. Staring at the seal, he recognized the crest, the winged woman peering back at him. His blue eyes turned cold.

"This will get us in," he said, moving his dark brown hair from his face.

"Don't you think they'd notice a Feral at a Sanoon party? Your families have been at war for generations." Leo's friend was Sebastien Bono, whom he had known since they were very young. Though they had different upbringings, they shared a common connection that made them more like brothers.

Leo stepped past Bono and toward the manor. "It doesn't matter. This is business."

Bono's gaze tightened. "When you asked me to come along on this trip, I thought we were going to cause some trouble." He crossed his arms, smirking. "If I had known this was going to be about business, I probably would have stayed home."

"Oh, you'll have your fun." Leo smirked back. "There are lots of lovely ladies waiting inside."

"I sure hope so," Bono scoffed. "What's that scroll about anyways?"

Leo lowered his eyes, hesitating. He relaxed, dropping his guard. His wall melted down. "It's a message."

"Oh really?" Bono shrugged. "Sounds boring. For who? The lady herself?"

Leo shook his head. "The high maiden."

"Ah. I didn't know Moz had one of those. Who's the message from?"

That's when Leo's eyes hit absolute zero. His stare was blank. The words seeped from his lips as a faint echo, almost as if it were to fade away hopelessly without ever being heard. "Stello Sanoon."

* * *

Lucia's heart was fluttering within the silence of the west wing of the manor. Though she was excited, she could not keep her mind from making its own assumptions. It was in her nature to be so critical, wary of every move. She often wondered if this was her mother's way of thinking cultivated deep inside her, combatting the openness she often felt while praying.

Angelo led the way with short strides ahead of her. Casually, he glanced back to her, slowing to give the high maiden time to gather her thoughts. He smiled, noticing her eyes widen as they approached the threshold arch of the grand ballroom. The dark parts of her eyes tightened as they were enveloped in brightness.

The grand ballroom was flooded with the light of sparkling, multicolored lanterns rising upward among many marble pillars. At the center of the concentric structure, of stone and stunning clear stained glass, were rising steps where a large orchestra played. At its base a choir sang harmoniously, in sync with the dancers circling about under the twinkling lights. The walls were decorated with banners, two more prominent than the rest. On the left, embroidered in white and gold stitching, was the holy seraph with its sword and scales held high. And on the right, stitched in silver on a blue background, was the winged lion roaring as it broke free from the chains binding its feet. Traditionally, these symbols carried with them the legacy of the names associated with them, but today they represented something more than that. They signified the two nations to which these families had brought peace: Moz and Pinea.

"It's absolutely stunning," Lucia whispered in awe.

"A bit much?" asked the knight.

"You don't know my mother," Lucia said with a sly smile. "She's always had a tendency to overdo things." The pendant glistened beneath her neck, sparkling under the torches, its light dancing as they made their way across the ballroom and to the edge, beside one of the great marble pillars that surrounded the center stage.

The knight bowed his head, extending a hand outward. "Go on, milady. Enjoy yourself. I'll stand guard here until your mother makes the announcement. If there is any need for my service, I will be quick to come to your aid."

"Thank you," Lucia said before looking reluctantly back toward the crowd. "I suppose I'll take a look around until then."

"These are your guests. I'm sure they will adore your company."

Lucia nodded, the pendant drawing the gaze of the knight as it shone. "Of course." She noticed how his eyes were locked, entranced by the diamond, as if he were oblivious to her words. She turned her body, blocking his sight until he could shake his head.

"I apologize. That pendant is quite remarkable. I've never seen anything like it. The craftsmanship looks foreign. I wonder where it's from."

"Oh, it was a gift from my mother—or my father really. I don't know where it's from." She touched the center of the diamond with the tip of her finger, gently pressing against its hard surface. "But it is beautiful."

Lucia waved softly to the knight and made her way across the ballroom, her mind weary from rehearsing her song. She sighed, thinking of its words, trying hard not to forget. She had spent the past few hours isolated in her father's study. Though she made sure to spend the time she needed preparing for, quite possibly, one the most important moments of her life as high maiden, her thoughts had wandered in the solace of Stello's study. She was taken with his artwork, by the passion within the strokes of paint, drawing from them the inspiration she needed to find the words to sing. Staring upward across the ballroom, Lucia watched as the luminous glass windows opened to expose the clouded night sky, the moon filtering through and reflecting its light onto the garden below. Her eyes hovered for a moment as someone took notice from a distance.

"Excuse me," came from behind her.

She turned to face a young man, not much older than she was. She blinked wildly, taken with his charm as his blue eyes met hers for just a moment before he directed them toward the window. He was handsome, his posture straight like a proud lion. His chest was broad. He crossed his arms and eventually smiled at her as if he at first had trouble finding his words. His gaze fell back to hers as she bit her bottom lip, unsure of what the stranger wanted.

"I noticed you from across the ballroom. I was hoping a lovely lady like yourself could be of some help and provide me with a bit of direction."

Lucia grinned politely. "My pleasure. How can I help?"

He blinked twice just to be sure, but he was not mistaken. The pendant about her neck was just as his father had described it. Looking into it nearly blinded him, as he had said it would, sending a chill down his spine. In his heart, he hoped the stories were not true, but in his bones he knew they were—just as his father had warned the moment that scroll appeared on his desk. "The lady, is she around?"

Lucia took a moment to look around them before replying. Her mother was nowhere to be found. "I'm not sure. Mother should be somewhere around here. It's unlike her to leave her company unattended. But, then again, she's a very busy lady." Lucia noticed the hilt of a silver dagger at his waist as she inspected his body. The metal was sculpted in the shape of a lion's head. The etching of silver chains ran down its sides. Her eyes met the sheath, where her eyes fell upon the crest etched to its side. Her mouth dropped open, but before she could say anything, Leo spoke.

"So, you are the high maiden," he said, stepping forward and placing his hands over hers. He shook them roughly before Lucia pulled back, her discomfort obvious. "Lucia, is it?"

"Yes," she whispered crossly, her brows tense as she struggled to speak. "And you . . ." She shook her head, her discomfort turning to disgust. "Did you really think I wouldn't recognize an agent of Pinea in my own home? How did you—"

"Please. Such prejudice is uncalled for," Leo shouted over her, yet quietly enough for no one to notice. He placed a hand to his chest. "You didn't even allow me to introduce myself."

"And why would I? You shouldn't be here."

"Maiden, it is important that we speak. I mean no ill will. I promise."

Lucia took a deep breath as Angelo charged to her side. "Is everything alright here?" He placed a hand to the hilt of his broadsword. "High Maiden, are you okay?"

Lucia hesitated, looking into Leo's sapphire eyes. They pleaded with her silently, holding so much restraint within them. "Yes. I'm fine. Could we have a moment?"

The knight nodded his head, accepting her request and heading back to his post across the way.

Lucia groaned. Never in her life had she imagined she would find herself here, speaking to someone from the land that had brought war to her own so long ago, and on the day of her first address.

"Who are you?" she asked sharply.

"Watch your tone." Leo half smiled, crossing his arms again, his body tense. "Isn't this party supposed to be about peace across two nations? That's no way to treat a high-born guest." He rolled his eyes, testing Lucia's patience. "My name is Leocadio Feral."

Feral. The name struck a chord within Lucia's mind as she remembered the tales. "As in, the son of Sigranole Feral, master of Pinea?" She softened her voice. He was right. Her predisposition was unwarranted at the moment, no matter how much she didn't trust him; he was deserving of her respect. "My mother has spoken of you before. She told me that our families haven't met since the treaty was signed, on this day twenty years ago. It was never in the fine print, but it was implied that we were never to speak ever again." Lucia's heart sank as a shudder ran its course through her body. "If my mother sees I'm talking to you . . . " She worried as her mind flooded with contradictions. None of this made any sense to her. "How did you make it past the guards? Don't they know who you are?" Her body chilled. The sounds of the music drowned into the pounding of her own blood pulsing through her head. She felt a slight faintness similar to the night before, that grim feeling overtaking her again.

Leo breathed out as he relaxed, remembering his mission. "How could they if they have never seen my face?" He reached into his vest pocket and pulled from it a scroll with a golden seal. "I told them I was a page, nothing more, meant to deliver this"—he held out the scroll to Lucia—"to you."

Lucia's head tilted in confusion as she looked to the piece of parchment, wondering why a letter would come all this way from so far north. She recognized the seal almost immediately. "That is my family's crest."

An uproar of applause thundered across the ballroom as servants, dressed gallantly in gold and blue gowns, poured in single file from the threshold and circled the guests carrying silver platters of exquisite sweets, cheeses, and meats for them to enjoy. Lucia saw her mother—smiling as she waved gracefully to the crowd—enter among the servants, followed by Amelia. Lucia couldn't have thought of a worse time to see her mother; not while she felt this way, as if a darkness had befallen her mind. What was this deepening intuition? She watched as her mother crossed the crowds and met with Angelo Sarf then looked in Lucia's direction, her eyes wandering to catch a glimpse of her daughter. Lucia pulled her head from view before saying, "I've got to go."

Leo reached forward, touching her shoulder as she turned. "Please," he said, holding the scroll up to her. "Take this with you, and read it in private."

Lucia's eyes found the seal again, and her heart sank. A sense of dread emitted from it, a feeling of hopelessness and despair. In her heart, she knew nothing good would come from this but, obliged to honor the messenger, she took the scroll into her hands and rubbed the seal with her fingers. "Goodbye." She parted from him and made her way across the ballroom to meet her mother, leaving Leo to tend to his own worries.

"That was tense," Bono said, approaching Leo from the rear, holding in his hands a variety of pastries and chocolates. "She's out of your league, Sir Leo . . . . Boy, she's a pretty little lady, isn't she?"

"She could feel it too," Leo said, his voice almost a whisper.

"Feel what?" Bono asked, his mouth full, before taking another bite of iced lemon cake.

"The fear. It was as if she knew—even though it's unlikely."

Bono shrugged, wiped his mouth, and wrapped an arm around his best friend. "Our generation has always been in the dark. I'm sure the maiden was confused and perhaps more afraid of what her mother would think if she had seen her speaking with you. All of this is speculation anyways. Her father has always been a loon."

"I used to think so too, but"—Leo watched from afar as Lucia approached her mother—"that was before I saw those wings around her neck."

*   *   *

"You look so beautiful, my darling! What a day this is!" Ara shouted, embracing Lucia, who smiled reluctantly.

"Yes it is." Lucia held the crested scroll at her waist. She lowered her eyes, confused about what to say. Lucia wanted to be truthful, but she could feel a fear running deep within of what she did not know. These thoughts whispered beneath the surface of her own rationality. She could not grasp her words without struggling. "I'm rather anxious."

"Oh," Ara whispered, reaching forward to hug Lucia, her embrace tight. "I have complete faith in you. You will do well." She broke from her and held on to her daughter's shoulders while looking into her face with care. "The people will love you." Ara moved a hand to Lucia's cheek.

"I hope so," Lucia sighed, tightening her grip on the parchment in her hands. She tried her hardest to release the negativity now gripping her with an iron hold. She exhaled. "I'm so nervous." She let her face fall into her fingers. "I really do hope this song is enough."

Ara smiled. "You'll do fine. I'm so proud of your preparation. Determination suits you. Don't worry, my dear. If you'd like, we can wait till the very end of the night for you to sing your song, just to give you more time to relax and practice."

At this moment, Lucia couldn't resist the urge to speak. She stammered, overtaken by a peculiar impulse. "No, let's do it now." She could hardly believe what she was saying, but it came as a reflex, a deep-rooted defense mechanism triggered by the anguish inside. What better way to confront this feeling than as she did in her everyday life? If there was anything that could comfort her, especially from this pain she felt but didn't understand, it would be her song—her prayer to the light.

Her mother, white with shock, released a cry of joy, almost squealing, "Lucia, are you sure? I told you to take your time."

Lucia shook her head. Though she doubted herself now more than ever, she didn't wish to spoil her mother's excitement, and thought it would only be right to stand by her decision, even though it seemed almost as if she hadn't made it herself. "No, Mother. I'm ready."

Ara bowed her head, pleased by her daughter's wishes. "Lieutenant," she called, "once I make her formal introduction, could you please escort Lucia to the center of the ballroom?" Her eyes sparkled as she spoke. "The high maiden would like to make her address."

"Of course, milady."

Ara made her way across the ballroom. Each step was as slow as the pace of Lucia's beating heart. It was an eternity before the lady stood at its center, beneath the orchestra and rising platforms. She raised a hand, calling the attention of her guests. The music faded and the chatter fell flat as the eyes of the crowd were directed toward her. Leo and Bono, too, peered from afar, Leo's stomach turning as his eyes wandered over to Lucia, whose fingers quivered against the scroll in her hands.

"My friends," Ara said, her voice echoing about the chamber. The people listened attentively, eager to catch every word the lady had to say. She took a deep breath and continued, "Thank you for joining me here on this day: our twentieth anniversary of peace. Not long ago, our great nation was ravaged by a war unlike any Terestria had ever seen, one brought on by an unwarranted rivalry. However, justice prevailed—our nobility obliged by a duty to its people. The foundations of this peace, brought upon the calling of the land, were set to bring an end to the bloodshed that plagued not only one nation's people with suffering, but two. Man is not intended to bring about the end of its own, for the light did not create life so that it could destroy itself.

"Though countless lives were lost to this war, the light has not forgotten the plight of those who served us. Their names will forever lie in honor upon our houses, written in blood. It is for this reason that the nobility of Moz must do right by its people and honor those who died by also honoring those who now live and stand before us. It is our duty and promise to you to preserve this peace—so that no life shall ever be lost in vain, not ever again. Moz's redemption depends upon this truth.

"Knowing this, I stand before you as lady of Moz to lead this nation into a prosperity that will last beyond my years. I am blessed to introduce to you, with a heart of profound faith, a legacy that promises peace for ages to come. One where diplomacy will someday reign with a new name: Lucia Sanoon."

A sudden silence overtook the great room as Lucia felt cornered by a thousand eyes. Ara stood smiling, reaching out to her daughter who could only feel her heart sinking into itself. Lucia closed her eyes as she firmly held onto the scroll Leo had given her. She rushed forward, with Angelo close behind her, looking forward while trying to block out the many gazes that followed her. She could still feel it—the stagnant dread, dormant beneath the soles of her feet. Her mother's words, as moving as they were, could not mend this fear that had embedded itself within Lucia's heart and mind. The fear of a broken promise.

As Lucia approached the center of the ballroom, she held her head down almost as if she were ashamed of the applause and shouts of her name; but as she looked up and into the lights overhead, she sensed the anticipation in the air. So many people were waiting to hear her voice. Her mother was waiting, too. Now was not the time to let her emotions get the best of her.

Leo watched with one hand clutching the hilt of his dagger, his heart fluttering as sweat ran down the side of his face.

Lucia stood, blinking wildly as her mind sought the words to say.

"Nobles of Moz. My name is Lucia Sanoon. I am humbled to stand here before you to offer what my mother has promised . . . prosperity. The light has granted me a calling for which I must extend my gratitude; for fate has brought me here today, as your high maiden, to right the wrongs of this history of war and offer you a new right and claim to the light. Justly, I pledge to serve all the people of Moz, and it is with this song I pray that the light grants me its favor so that I may accomplish the destiny it has ordained for me."

Lucia's chest rose as the air filled her. She opened her eyes, staring outside the windows of the ballroom watching the light of the moon fade behind the brightening clouds. A storm was coming, but the people did not take notice, for this moment was Lucia's alone. Feeling the chills of the orchestra's melody rise into the air, she parted her lips so that her voice would be carried to those so willing to listen.

So long, I have waited for your love.
So long, I have waited for you.
When I've lost my light, what am I to do?
All I feel is emptiness,
In the embrace of this darkness.
Is it my fate to know such grace,
When I cannot see your face?
Can I find hope in what I have lost,
Or do I wait?

So long, I have waited for the day.
So long, I have waited for the faith,
In what I might find someday.
No matter the fate, good or bad.
This is where I stand.

So long, I have waited for that hope.
So long, I have waited for that ray,
For the sun to shine on my face,
With the love and the hope I have yet to find.
I must continue to believe that someday,

I will find my place.

So long as I can look up to the sky,
I will continue to try.
So long as the sun shines bright,
I will look to find you by my side.
Oh so I pray.
Someday.

The echoes of her voice fell to silence among the crowd. Entranced within her song, Lucia blinked before taking her right hand up to her neck. She clasped the pendant as it radiated beneath her fingers. For a moment, it was as if she had cleared her head. The words of her song had made her thoughts painless, but as soon as it came to an end the chatter and noise crept back in, growing louder than before. Lucia thought, at first, that her eyes had failed her as the torchlight dimmed and the air turned crisp. A wintry breeze seeped through the far window, blasting into the ballroom and stinging the skin of those it touched. Eerily, Lucia spoke." Thank you."

"That was brilliant," Bono said, clapping his hands together as the crowd erupted in applause. "Damn good. Don't you think, Sir Leo?" Bono turned to his friend, whose eyes were fixed on the window.

Leo watched carefully, moving his hand to the hilt of his dagger. "Don't you feel that?" he asked, slowly pulling it from its sheath as frost traced onto the metal. He darted his eyes to the maiden as the crowd continued to cheer and chant her name.

Lady Ara was smiling alongside Angelo Sarf, who was clapping happily, just as Lucia's head became light and hazy. The window slammed shut as the air pulled in, forcing it closed and shattering its glass into a million pieces. Time stood still as the screams of the guests within Sanoon Manor, as loud as they were, faded from

Lucia's perception as she swayed. Outside, the storm rumbled as hail formed and fell from lightning-filled skies. The bolts were unusual as they streaked across the sky, leaving violet trails in the wake of thunder and making the sky appear darker than it ever had been.

Lucia felt faint as the torchlights gave into the gusts of the blizzard that ran overhead. As shards of the glass window lifted into the air with every sinister quake of the sudden storm tempest, they brushed past the panicked crowd of Moz's elite; and a scarlet flurry, like a mist, filled the air. Lucia could not break from her trance, immobilized by this descent into darkness, afraid while watching as the window darkened in the eclipse of a shadow emerging from the haze of a clouded sky. She could barely make out the faint glow of something shining beneath her line of sight as her energy and perception left her, ushering in an unforgettable and ghastly silence.

CHAPTER FOUR

The Harbinger

Lucia was befuddled as she broke from dormancy. Anguish rose from her stomach. She gathered her senses, gasping for air as if suffocating, her body bursting with confusion as the reality of her situation settled in. She rose from the floor, bringing a hand to her face to wipe the blood from her cheek. Horrified, she watched the crimson drip from her nose and onto the floor. Slowly, she realized something terrible had happened, something she could not recall.

Suddenly, she saw that she was no longer in the ballroom with her mother or her noble guests, but was instead lying on the ground between the pews of the sanctuary—her domain. She could not explain why she was there, lying on the floor. But she somehow knew it wasn't a dream, even though it felt like a nightmare she'd had once before.

Afraid to move or make a sound, she searched her thoughts to figure out what had happened. She had been at the center of the ballroom, where she sang her hymn before the storm sounded. There were screams, and a sudden darkness. She didn't know where her mother was now, or why she was covered in blood, but Lucia did sense that this was all so very real. She sobbed silently, her head throbbing, before noticing that, at the base of the altar within the glare of the distant candlelight, there was a scroll stamped with a familiar gold seal. That's when she remembered. "The message."

Lucia picked herself up and walked to the altar as the sound of thunder echoed from outside the manor. Rain fell against the stained glass window just as a chill fell upon her. She grabbed the scroll and held it between her fingertips. Whispers of dread filled her thoughts as she broke the seal and unrolled the piece of parchment. "My Dear Lucia," she read aloud before letting her eyes scramble and fall to the page.

> *By now, I fear the worst has befallen our province. As you read these words, I hope that you are safe. The world will not be for long. My mission has failed, and I have failed you. There is no way to stop the flow of time that has cursed us so, and I am sorry that this destiny must fall to you.*
>
> *Our fates are written and cast within the stone—the stone of our salvation and our only beacon of hope. Make haste for the North, for the darkness is not far behind. Moz can no longer protect you. You must protect yourself and trust in the light. The answers lie in the virtues that you seek, those you must have dreamed of. Time is short, and you must leave your life behind if you do hope to survive.*
>
> *My sweet daughter, whom I miss with each passing day, I truly wish this duty wasn't your own, but you must be strong and follow your faith. The struggle has just begun, and the covenant is broken.*
>
> *Stello Sanoon*

The candles over the altar were bright and heavy. Lucia felt the creep, like a silent echo, starting inside her head and slowly flowing from her lips. Hoping that the spirits would guide her and show her how to do right, she prayed to the light. "Stello Sanoon," she whispered, "so he is *alive*." To hear her own words say that brought tears to her eyes. For so long, she had attempted to forget this man, one whose face she did not remember but whose absence haunted her every day. The guilt pierced her core like a blade slicing through. She brought her hands to her stomach, tightening them around the parchment as tears ran down her face. "What is happening?" she cried. "Why me?"

There was an unsettling silence. Only the sound of the descending showers sprinkled from above as a vibration brought the candlelight into a quiver, dancing in the darkness. As the candles dimmed, a familiar chill filled the air. Lucia looked up slowly as the air bit at her chest, striking her heart with bitterness, draining her mind of everything that once knew bliss. It spread like a poison, paralyzing her with a type of anguish she hoped she would never have to feel again. It felt black, empty, and cold; perhaps like death. It intensified within her—the fear—as if she sensed it coming. Something closing in from behind.

Lucia moved her gaze to the altar as the faint candlelight extinguished. All she could see was the smoke rising in the light, streaming from the stained glass. Behind her, the door swept closed as if all the air was pulled from the sanctuary leaving behind a vacuum that absorbed all light. Startled, Lucia spun, leaning against the altar. Her eyes darted around the room as she realized that she wasn't alone. The darkness around her thickened, as the light from the window faded. Her eyes seemed to be playing tricks on her, and she was cautious. Never had she experienced something like this before. Never had her intuition felt so right—but she was hoping that she was wrong.

Lucia backed up against the altar, using it to support her as the room darkened in the diminishing light of the stained glass window. Eventually, she saw nothing, and heard only the storm outside along with the pounding of her own heart and the occasional roar of thunder that only seemed to make the sky darker.

The sweat on her brow froze when she heard its growl.

Something was there. There had to be something within the shadows. She wasn't feeling something that didn't exist. The fear was undeniable and, thinking of her father's warning, Lucia knew that none of this was imaginary.

She sought out its presence as it watched her, with its scarlet eyes. Its breath was colder than ice. Her own breath hung ahead of her as lightning flashed, finally revealing the monstrosity.

"Impossible," she whispered as she stared into the shadows, watching as dark matter swarmed out from them, consuming the walls around her. From the dark matter formed the gigantic wings of the demon—solidified by the shadows into a muscular-shaped form. Its skin was slate, with claws at the tips of its fingers extending into silver blades. Its face became visible within a faint glow—a grin filled with fangs. It hovered as the dark matter formed gigantic horns that arched toward Lucia, stretching into life while emitting a wretched stench from a foul and icy chuckle. Lucia struggled to find the source of a scream, but choked as the beast's feet touched the ground and armor formed around its exterior like an onyx shell. A mist surrounded the being, a haze that spewed from the backs of its wings, filling the air and coating the inside of Lucia lungs, making it hard to breathe. She moved farther back, watching the mist thicken and spread out before her, collecting into orbs of matter that absorbed the light still sparkling at the base of her neck. What was this? Trapped within the terror of this nightmare, she clasped a hand around the pendant and prayed.

The beast laughed, broadening its palm, its claws glistening as light streamed from Lucia's fist. Swiftly, the monster slashed upward toward Lucia, causing her to cower backward as she prayed. Her eyes filled with tears. "I've got you now," it bellowed. "You're all mine." And with one great push of its powerful wings it sent Lucia falling backward.

Lucia caught herself with her free palm and knelt before the altar as the monster closed its fist, summoning dark matter to form beneath her feet. The earth cracked open and fell apart beneath her as the stone floor dissolved away and turned into a tar-like substance, pulling her in. And it was then that she screamed.

In agony, she called out, hoping someone would hear her. But the shadows grew, pulling on her. She struggled as she cried, "Help me! Someone, please! Mother!" The frost of a tear formed on her cheek. The darkness crept up her torso as she felt her lungs collapsing, her energy draining. "Please," she spoke in prayer, her head faint. "Please, redeem me of this fate. Forgive me of my sins. Accept me as I plead. Destroy this darkness!" She attempted to close her eyes but was immobilized, forced to look at the abomination as it moved its large and hideous feet toward her. Closing in, its eyes fixated on the light beneath Lucia's fingers, it breathed heavily, snarling as it lowered its face to her as she trembled.

Lucia's eyes quivered as she abandoned hope and gave herself to the monster.

"Witness *true* darkness," it whispered in a silent echo. "We have returned, believe this. Your rituals could never keep us apart. Surrender your light. Your words are no longer strong enough to stop us."

"What?" Lucia uttered, feeling her sanity break from reality and into delusion. Her heart popped and jumped as her spirit pulled away from this monster, while her body remained motionless. "No!" she cried as her mind was consumed by fear. Beneath the surface of her tormented thoughts, she sought out something to cling to. With each moment she found a new reason to surrender, facing a fate far worse than a quick death. The dark being consumed everything around her like dark flames from a distant world. But as fear overtook her, her thoughts collapsed behind something she did not know and a face she did not remember. In that moment, holding on to this image in her head, she found the strength to pray, not out of the fear of what she faced in the darkness of the sanctuary, but in hope that she may someday see this face of whom she did not know. In that instant, the light recognized her plight, summoning forth its blessing and streaming brightly beneath the cracks of her fist. Her vision blurred as she absorbed every bit of light she could into her fist before it burst open and revealed her pendant—beaming with divine light.

Lucia, struck with disbelief, felt the monster's hold loosen and shatter as the light caused the beast to shield its eyes with its claws. The pendant pulsed within a spectrum of colors. The light was magenta, then violet, then a stunning blue before changing into a brilliant yellow, shining almost gold. The symbols on the stained glass window behind her glowed as the window came to life. The outline of the divine being's wings rose from within the window as Lucia watched, astounded by the power she had awoken.

The dark monster hissed and roared as it flapped its wings violently. The flames of the candles burst to life, sending the light spiraling into the pendant, which only brightened before releasing threads that spun around Lucia and into the window. The panels of glass quaked as the light filled them, making them appear to be on fire. Light erupted from the window in multiple streams, dazzling around Lucia, bouncing in heavy sparks and colliding with the pendant, which shot an array of beams into the darkness. Lucia was in shock, frozen, as she became warm again and the darkness receded from her. The monster twirled into the altar, knocking the candles onto the ground and setting the pews ablaze. The heat intensified as smoke filled the air. The monster reached once more toward Lucia. "Leave me alone!" she yelled, waving her hand as light shot from her palm, causing the beast to fly backward into the flames.

"You dare use its power?" the beast snarled. "No matter. Its light is not strong enough to defeat us. Not now. Not ever."

What was this power surging through her body? This strength was incredible, and it filled Lucia with emotion. Her thoughts homed in on the words of the message: "Time is short, and you must leave your life behind if you do hope to survive." Though she felt more invincible than ever, she knew there was truth in this. What if she was not strong enough, even with this new power?

"Go," it whispered within her mind. The pendant, so radiant, seemed to invade her thoughts with each plea. "Protect the light. Protect us." She looked toward the far door; the manor was being consumed in flames. As the beast growled and tore at the debris that surrounded it, light burst around the door, pulling it open. "Go!"

Lucia caught her breath and agreed, without the slightest feeling of doubt. She ran toward the door, looking back to watch the darkness take flight and smash through the wall and into the corridor, roaring as it pursued her. The manor was dark ahead, but the flames moved quickly, feeding upon the tapestries and golden-framed artwork along the walls.

With the beast not far behind, Lucia made her way to the study, her mind set on escaping even as she watched her home being destroyed. As she pushed through the ruby-red doors, the chill of the darkness closed in behind her despite the inferno rising up and through the mansion. Quickly, she moved her father's desk to block the door as she thought of a plan. She raced to the window and lifted her hand against it instinctively. She closed her eyes, praying silently as the tips of her fingers filled the window with light, causing it to shatter. She hurried through, climbing onto the ledge outside as the rain poured overhead.

Lightning zipped through the sky, dark in its appearance. Instead of emitting its own light, as lightning should, the streaks were black and absent of all light, absorbing any light surrounding it instead. The darkness burst through the doorway, knocking back the desk with ease and tearing the ruby doors off their hinges before releasing its revolting mist, catching the coming inferno and igniting the gallery in dark purple flames. The air was still cold as it went through and toward the window. Lucia released a faint whimper as she let herself dangle and drop into the garden. She fell into the bushes as the darkness shot through the window, flying into the storm above just before fire burst from the window.

Lucia could only watch in despair as her home became a shadow of what it once was, falling into itself as the stone lost its strength and crumbled the foundation her family had built. Boulders of marble crashed down, and Lucia's heart stopped.

"Mother!" she cried out as the stone fell toward her. She raised her hands to shield herself from the eruption of fiery brimstone, but was distracted by her sudden worry. "Mother—I have to save her." But slowly, she felt it again, the power within whispering.

"This is not your fight. If you stay, she will die. Where there is light, darkness will surely follow."

Lucia took a deep breath, realizing what that must mean. She could not bear the thought of losing her mother, though she felt as if she already had. But there, amid the storm, was an echo of a promise, one that meant her mother would survive. Though it seemed unlikely as the blaze destroyed her childhood home, the force promised her so, and in that moment, she believed it to be true.

Glancing into the fiery essence of all she once knew, perhaps for the last time, Lucia sobbed before turning and dashing far away, taking to the city's streets. She kept running as far away from her home as she could, afraid for her life and fearful of her future. As she gained more and more distance, she rushed past people who looked at her as if she were insane. She was panicked, moving non-stop. It took some time for the people to notice what was happening. Once they did, Lucia was almost shocked at how oblivious they were, these people on the outside—watching as the high-borns burned beneath the white-hot rubble of Sanoon Manor.

But Lucia couldn't think about that right now. She didn't know where she was going, but the pendant guided her, pulling her along the streets with this familiar intuition, ever stronger. But before long, her legs grew tired. She would have to stop eventually. How could she travel so far on foot? Slowly, she came to a stop. She collapsed onto her knees, panting heavily. "Why?" she whispered to the pendant, feeling heavy tears fall from her eyes. "Why me?"

A gentle hand fell onto her shoulder. Afraid, she whipped around as if it were the force that stalked her, but instead she found a set of sapphire eyes staring back, comforting her immediately. It was then that she sensed the promise in the power that had saved her. "You . . ." Lucia said, feeling her heartbeat deepen and her head spin as she fell into his arms.

The warmth of his embrace filled her as she whimpered, burying her head into his chest. He was real and as alive as she was. At that moment, she knew her faith would not lie. Though it felt as if her world was falling apart and her life was being stripped from her, Lucia found solace as Leo held her tightly, his grief masked by the rain as tears streamed down his face.

Fleeing Fate

Smog fell upon the streets and a dense discord spread. Sanoon Manor's sudden destruction sent terrifying shockwaves amongst the people. The darkened sky brought about an eerie silence. The stench of decay rose within the cinder and smoke of the fire. Ashes showered down over the city and everyone raced toward their homes, desperate for safety.

Leo's arms tensed with worry. His muscled body remained still, stiff, as if he were in some sort of shock.

Lucia's heart was fluttering as she squeezed her eyes shut. She gathered her strength and pulled back to look at Leo. She saw a struggle in his eyes, with an azure reticence.

Leo held himself together, though he did not desire to. He was just as afraid as these people, if not more. He looked away for a moment as if he needed some time to think, but eventually found words. "Are you hurt?"

Lucia shook her head. She raised a hand to her chest and took the pendant into her fingers. "How did you . . . " She paused as memories of the monstrosity ran their course within her mind, darkening her heart and making it flutter more than it already was. "H-how did you escape? Why are you here?" She shuddered.

"I could ask you the same question." Leo lowered his eyes, breathing heavily as he attempted to speak over the sounds of the pouring rain. "But it seems I may already know the answer. After all, my father told me."

"You know"—Lucia tightened her fist around the jewel—"about this?" She opened her hand to reveal the diamond as it twinkled in the refracted light of the faraway blaze.

The glimmer of its light shone a brilliance that Leo could not forget. He nodded. "Those are the Light Wings. I'm certain."

A shiver ran through Lucia, elevating her senses as she heard the name for the first time. "The what?" she asked, almost as if she craved to hear the name one more time before being satisfied.

"The Light Wings, an ancient relic spoken of only in legend. For eons, its existence was thought only to be a myth, a part of a legend no one ever dreamed was true," Leo said, detached, as his thoughts lay adrift. "It is said that, once those wings appeared, the world would fall to ruin one province at a time, and Terestria would no longer be safe."

His somber eyes looked up into hers as Lucia tried to grasp the reality of what he was trying to tell her.

"The final days are approaching—the very end of the world," he finished.

Lucia brought a hand to her mouth as a great weight fell upon her chest. In that instant, she remembered her father's message. She patted herself down, only to realize she must have dropped the parchment during her escape from the beast. "The letter." *Could it possibly be true?* "It warned that it would not be safe here. My father . . . " Lucia shuddered. "He told me to leave and not return, but then"—the weight of the pendant seemed heavier around her neck—"I was attacked."

Leo's own face hardened, rife with anger. "As was I. The entire ballroom was slaughtered." His eyes quivered as he spoke, his voice nearly shattering as he lowered it. "The moment you finished your song, the torches blew out and all went dark. The air became unbearably cold and I heard screaming. I started to run, shouting to find my friend, when I slipped on some blood and was knocked unconscious. It was the stench of burning flesh that woke me. Somehow, I had survived and was able to make it here. By some holy chance, I was able to find you. Although, much of it is a haze. I don't quite remember how I did. I just knew."

Lucia could hardly breathe. "If what you speak is true, then my mother—she would be dead." Her fist clenched around the pendant. "And it's *not* true!"

"It's unlikely anyone survived," Leo said grimly. "I'm sorry."

But Lucia knew deep in her heart that this was not the case. There was a promise to be kept. A whisper of doubt within her mind told her so. "I must go. Whatever that beast was, it will be searching, and I can't be here when it finds me." The maiden bowed her head, her eyes brooding. "No one else has to die."

Leo was confused by her words. "You really believe she's alive, do you?"

Lucia set a finger on top of the pendant. "It told me so. It promised to keep her safe as long as I fled."

"It speaks to you?"

"Not exactly. It doesn't work like that. It's more like it invades my thoughts. Somehow, I know. I feel"—Lucia closed her eyes, listening to the beat of the radiant light as it intertwined with her spirit, clasping her faith and bringing a warmth only her mother could give—"its conviction." She pushed past Leo, her eyes welling up with tears as they fixed on the flaming manor.

Leo caught her by the arm, bringing her to a stop. "You aren't traveling alone. Do you even know where you're going?"

"I don't," Lucia said honestly, emotion ripe within her voice. "But the note said to head north."

"To Pinea." Leo said, stepping beside her and placing a hand on her shoulder. "Come with me, and speak to my father. Surely he will be able to tell you more than I can. After all, it was he who told me the real source of this prophecy."

"What source?"

The lightning flashed overhead, the rain of the storm stinging to the touch. Leo wiped his face to utter the name. "Stello."

The name lingered in the air, causing Lucia's mind to wander for a moment.

Leo strode ahead. "I have some horses stabled near the northern gate of the city border. We can take them to Pinea."

Lucia lowered her head, accepting the fate so carefully laid before her like a hand of cards in a game she had never played. She knew she had no choice. If her father had truly started this, Lucia would have to end it. "I have never left Moz before, nor have I ever ridden a horse, but if you could please help me find out what my father has to do with all this and why all this is happening to me, I would be most grateful."

"Of course. You have my word and my protection."

Lucia nodded her head and, oddly enough, found herself smiling. Despite feeling as if the world was hurdling closer and closer to its end, she was also excited. Never in her simplest or most profound dreams had she thought she would be given the chance to discover what really happened to her father—especially not with a member of the Feral family, or even alone. She stepped one weary foot ahead of the other, finding comfort in moving forward. "Let's go."

* * *

After some time traveling through the vacant traumatized streets of the marble city, the Mozian gates materialized before them, and Lucia's stomach burned.

Leo took a moment to check on Lucia, peering back at her with his dark blue eyes, attempting to reassure the high maiden. Her face displayed an undeniable anxiety.

Lucia was afraid. She felt it following her, refusing to show itself, perhaps waiting for the right time to strike. She moved forward, placing her hand into Leo's, which made her feel slightly safer as they approached the stables. She clenched his hand tightly, hoping he wouldn't slip away.

They came upon a broad, strong black stallion with white spots. Its saddle was plated with silver and blue steel, the Feral crest hidden beneath a gray cloak. Leo took the cloak and threw it over Lucia's shoulders before untying the horse. "Here. I'll help you up," he said, holding out his hand.

Lucia took his hand and stuck her foot into one of the stirrups. She stepped up and threw her legs over the horse, struggling not to slip. The roar of thunder startled the horse, but Lucia managed to maintain her grip. "What about you?" she asked as he placed the reins in her hands.

Leo pointed to a brown mare in a stable across from her. Its saddle was adorned with green-tinted iron. "I'll be riding my friend's horse."

There was something lying beneath Leo's tempered gaze, a splitting reservation Lucia could not ignore. She rested her hand over his, squeezing it slightly, comforting him. "Was your friend with you when it happened?"

Leo blinked wildly and swallowed hard, trying to push back the memory of blond-haired Sebastien Bono in his mind. "A lot has happened so fast," he said. He walked to Bono's horse, hopped on, and gave the mare a swift kick, prompting it to move forward.

"Watch me." He pulled in his rein, guiding the horse toward Lucia. She mimicked him, pulling back with a kick, prompting the horse to move toward Leo. "That's it. It's not so hard, is it?"

"No," Lucia said, pushing a free hand into the stallion's mane. Somehow, it felt as if she had done this before, the instinct stemming from the mysterious power around her neck. The memories of eons past seemed to be filled within it—memories of who or what, she was not certain, but she was aware of the connection. She sensed the emotions of the horse entering her fingertips and immediately understood that he was scared. "He knows that something's not right. He can sense it too."

"Let us hurry, then. The northern border is heavily secured, so keep your hood up at all times. We don't need the military believing the high maiden is trying to escape."

"But I am," Lucia said, disgraced by her words.

"Don't think about that," Leo shouted, reassuring her. "Think about your mission. They don't need to think you ran away. You know what you're setting out to do, and that's all that matters. You're doing the right thing."

But Lucia could not believe that herself. She could hardly believe anything anymore. This reality was not her life. She knew only the marble walls of a luxurious manor, nothing more. Some might wonder why she was fleeing her home, her mother, her obligation, and most of all her name. But right now, even Lucia was confused. All she knew was that her duty lay beyond the gates ahead.

As they pressed forward, past the heavy traffic of the many civilians who refused to stay in the royal-ridden city, she worried she was making a horrible decision. No matter what the Light Wings told her, leaving her people now defied all she had been taught. She could not justify it, not within herself, despite knowing she had to. Lucia found herself in a familiar place, thinking just like her father had the day he left Sanoon Manor. She only hoped to return soon enough to right the wrong of leaving her mother behind, hoping her father had felt the same. Once she knew more about the force that brought so much chaos into her life, maybe then she would understand.

The two managed to make it through the gates where the guards laid passage easily to all those who sought refuge away from the terror within the city. The fear was imminent, and controlling the hysteria of a public who watched so helplessly as their beloved governors were eradicated within the blaze was more than impossible. And it was unnecessary, given it appeared there was no one left to rule them.

Lucia looked back to the high walls of the city, watching as they faded farther and farther away. Ahead of them was nothing but wet, decaying fields of earth melting in the darkness of the storm. The lightning strikes that fell onto the plains brought a shadow that destroyed all the life in the land. It was unnatural, and forced a stench into the air neither Lucia nor Leo could forget. *Has the land always smelled of death?* Lucia wondered. How could she even know what death smelled like? Tears streamed down her face.

"Did my father have a good reason to leave?" Lucia asked. "After all this time, couldn't he have just waited so he could have protected us?"

"He had a good reason, I'm sure," Leo said to her. "Our families have history, and he sought our help. It was my father who denied him. Who knows what would've happened if he hadn't? Your father might have come home to you."

"Probably so," she said, wiping her cheek. "What do you know about my father?"

"He arrived in Pinea sometime after the war ended, probably a couple of years or so after, claiming he had information about a coming attack on Pinea. It had seemed so unlikely at the time, and the provinces weren't on good terms. After the signing of the Tranquility Treaty, my father said that Stello had taken something very dear from him, something he could not forget nor forgive. It's for that reason, I believe, that my father turned him away."

Leo kicked his horse, darting ahead as Lucia became more anxious. She followed closely behind him, trying to remain focused on riding, but her thoughts left her with many questions.

"Once we make it to Pinea safely, my father will tell you what you need to know. He will have no choice after seeing"—Leo hesitated—"that around your neck."

They rode long into the night as the showers eased. To the east were mountains that looked so weak, worn by the heavy rain brought on by the dark forces acting against them. Lucia heard the cries of the land within her thoughts, sensing its anguish. The land hated this night, wrought by the storm that corrupted it. But surely, as with all nights, it drifted to its end as they rode. An aurora of bright colors rose over the mountaintops, casting away the storms and swirling into perfect patterns, cleansing the land as it was bathed in light. Lucia swore she could see the land green as the light flowed down onto it. She sensed the praise it gave to the light. They rode into the fields as beauty bloomed from the newly drawn sunlight. *Is it always like this? So vibrant and animated?* Lucia knew this could not be true. The land could not be *that* alive. But it was, for now.

The gusts of the sweet smelling summer air pushed upward and to the north, where in the distance, Lucia noticed the fields rise and transform into hills covered by flowers of many bright colors. She reached down and let the petals caress her fingertips as she breathed in their scent, taking in the serenity of this moment—experiencing something new.

Leo smirked. "These are the Pinean hills, the site of the final battle twenty years ago."

Lucia blinked her eyes, seeing sudden flashes like distant, dark lightning, almost as if Leo's words themselves triggered something within her. "War, bloodthirst, and pain," she whispered, touching her head as images of swords clashing and blood splashing through piles of corpses swarmed into it. Her head swelled with brand new memories, evoking a wail of pain from her body.

At that moment, Lucia lost her grip on the reins. She was faint as she fell forward, clenching the horse's mane. It squealed in agony, shooting upward and almost sending Lucia backward and onto the ground.

Leo retreated with his horse. "Easy," he called to her, the sound of his command instantly bringing the mare to a stop.

Lucia regained her composure and sat up. She held her head in her hands, trying hard not to sob.

"Lucia?" he said, jumping from his horse and coming quickly to her side, shaking her. "Lucia."

She shook her head as tears fell from her eyes. As hard as she tried, there was no denying the energy of the place. Though it was beautiful, it lay corrupted by the war of the past. For a moment, she was possessed and forced to hear the cries of the dead and to absolve the grief of the lives that were lost there, taking on their pain herself. It was the most agonizing thing she had ever experienced, yet surprisingly, as her sight returned, Lucia felt an air of peace rising into the breeze despite feeling weaker than before. Her mind returned to the present.

"I'm sorry. I don't . . . " she whispered. "I don't know what's happening to me."

Leo looked into her golden eyes, trying to understand what she must be feeling. His eyes were drawn to the pendant. With each passing moment, her burden became greater and far grander. The world was calling out to her for its salvation, and the more she ventured off, the more it took from her and the vessel of light around her neck to rid itself of the darkness that tainted it. A ball of panic rose in his throat, but Leo swallowed it down as he watched Lucia pant and then become herself again.

"Just hold on tight, focus, and rest," Leo said hesitantly, keeping his voice low while he ran a finger carefully along the side of her face. "Everything will be alright." He took her hand in his, squeezing it gently as she calmly laid her head upon her horse, falling to sleep almost immediately, too weak to hold herself up. Leo gave out a great sigh, taking a rope and tying her horse to his. He watched her closely while he fastened the knots, trying to imagine what she must be dreaming in the midst of all her suffering. "I suppose we'll take it slow the rest of the way." Lucia was the most beautiful maiden he had ever laid his eyes on, and from what he could tell, far too good to deserve this. What was the purpose of the Light Wings in making this savior that his father spoke so highly of? To what end did they hope she'd sacrifice to achieve their mission? Leo could not bear to think of it.

Lucia sniffed and exhaled as Leo placed a damp blanket around her head. He jumped atop his horse and kicked it softly so they could continue their journey over the Pinean hills.

She lay slumped forward on the stallion, dreaming, unable to fully release the emotions that consumed her. It all started with the war—or was the world condemned long before even then? Something within her was changing, transforming and making her all too different. There had always been a part of her that she did not know, and ever since this jeweled relic came into her life, the memento of her father was becoming amplified, drawing itself forcefully to the surface. Whatever it was, it was devouring and manipulating her conscience. The sin that surrounded her was so obvious and easy to read in all she witnessed now, and it felt as if the world was turning against itself. Despite being hidden for so long, it was impossible to turn away from; now exposed.

The Light Wings drew out the truth, cultivating and sharpening her judgment, all beyond her knowledge and in the necessity of creating a champion of justice and virtue. That was the power of the Light Wings. To take and reform was their purpose, to right what was wrong and make things as they were truly meant to be. Perhaps Lucia was born to rule after all.

Her eyes flickered open, her strength returning. She pulled herself up and stretched, looking into the sky and far off twilight, finally awake yet still fearing the night. "I . . . " she mumbled. "I don't understand why I'm here."

Leo turned back in surprise, almost startled by the sound of her voice. He had been riding in silence for some time and did not expect her to awaken until nightfall. He smiled as she yawned. "Our families have their secrets. It's not your fault that you've been left in the dark. Every secret holds its purpose."

"And that is precisely the reason I can't fight this," Lucia said, breathing deeply. "I don't know how to. My mother told me nothing, and my father"—her gaze wandered as she brought her fingers to her chest—"wasn't there."

"And so," Leo said, his confidence beaming. He kicked his horse, prompting it to go faster as Lucia took the reins and followed behind him. "That doesn't have to stop you from finding the truth. Isn't that what this journey is about anyways?"

Leo was right.

"According to my father, seventeen years ago Stello Sanoon came to Pinea, traumatized and disoriented, pleading for help. He went on and on about a coming threat, one that would destroy Pinea and maybe the world if we did not heed his words. I don't know much about what was spoken between them, but he asked for my father's aid." Leo paused. "And my father sent him away." He released a soft cough.

Lucia's eyes lit as her brow tightened. "Why would my father lie?"

"My father did not trust him, not after the war and what he'd lost. Pinea was left in a depression, and the people were barely starting to rebuild. For all he knew, Stello's plea could have been an attempt to remove my father from his seat of power and deprive Pinea of its leadership so that Moz could invade and acquire whatever resources Pinea had left. My father simply refused the journey due to his obligations." He looked back at the pendant. "But most peculiar of all, Stello spoke of a legend, about a source of power linked to the very origins of this world."

Lucia tightened her hand around the Light Wings pulsing within her fingers. The pressure under her neck was like a heavy weight on her chest.

Leo continued. "And the world's last chance to redeem itself. Truthfully, my father didn't believe him. After all, this was mere hearsay and legend, but by the time that letter arrived, my father had changed."

Lucia squirmed at the words that chilled the air, prickling her skin. "Will Pinea be safe?"

Leo swallowed before replying, unsure of exactly how to answer her question. His response was far from what he wanted to accept, but it was sincere. "After what I saw in Moz, I don't believe anywhere is safe. Not even home."

Lucia's eyes fell to the jewel below. It sparkled in the brightening moonlight as a wave of sorrow filled her.

"I'm so sorry, Lucia." Leo's guilt collected in his chest. He hated causing her this pain, even if it was with the truth. To him, she was fragile and needed his help. She needed someone. Lucia had lost everything so quickly, too swiftly. She could be on the brink of an emotional collapse for all he knew. Leo felt it coming like a storm; a typhoon of empathy. For now, the air would be calm and flowers would bloom across these hills, but soon, just as the frost of winter began to blow over them, there would be chaos at bay. He pointed into the distance, to the large black onyx of the gate ahead of them. "Pinea is just beyond there."

Lucia didn't bother to look, instead fixing her gaze on the mountains to the west. She was studying them, wondering what might lie beyond. She had been praying for a solution for some time now, for some kind of answer to this nightmare she couldn't wake up from. And for some reason, as she analyzed the rigid silver cliffs rising just over the horizon, Lucia sensed something call out to her like a bird in song just before they reached the gates.

The guards opened the gates with no hesitation, greeting Leo as they approached. "Sir Leocadio, welcome home," said one of the guards, biting from an apple as he studied the maiden in front of him. "Is she with you?"

There was a pause. Leo looked back to Lucia, who bowed her head in silence as the guards tried to get a better look at her face. He nodded.

"Another girl," grunted an older guard with a scratch of his head. "Oh, the triviality of young men. You never cease to amaze me, Sir Leo. Best think twice before taking that one home, especially at this time of night. You know how your father is."

It seemed wrong to speak. The two shuffled in quietly, leaving the horrors they had witnessed behind them in their silence. Leo's heart still ached over the loss of his friend.

As they moved past the outer walls, Lucia missed Moz even more as she ventured into this strange place. But she was so easily taken in by the fascinations of this brand new city. Pinea, as strange as it was, reminded her so much of her own home, though different. The black stone of the walls surrounding her stretched high upward, so much like the white marble within her own city. The roads were paved with sandstone, and the grass was as green as she had ever seen. But as much as she tried to grasp the similarities, this place did not feel like home. Lucia did not feel safe. Her patience was confined to whatever Leo and his father could offer her. She bit her wrist and felt the pain, reminded this was no dream.

"Mozians aren't too welcome here either, unfortunately. But don't worry. As long as your identity is hidden and you're under our protection, no one will harm you."

Lucia stared off into the torchlight, her gaze hollow. "It's not the Pineans I fear." She glanced toward a pub where a crowd of people were making their leave, laughing gleefully as if they, too, were celebrating the war's end just as her people had been when the nobles met their demise. Most of them looked just like the denizens of her own great city. She could not understand why such a rivalry existed between two cities so alike in the first place. What event could spark so much anger? What could birth such wrath? Could the strife of war really create something so vain? The price of their lives should be worth more than the cause of such bloodshed. Lucia imagined children waving so happily, jumping and playing. She could almost see them reaching out to her horse. *No one should have to die.* The people in Pinea were living just as her people were far from here. They were all human.

There were some striking features Lucia had never seen before, though, of course, she hadn't ventured far from the ground of her own manor until now. Here, she could appreciate the architecture, so pristine and untarnished by chaos. The buildings stood tall, like stone pillars, and were made of onyx, circular in shape. Whatever lay inside was a mystery, but surely they were alluring within the moonlight. The small houses and dwellings of the townspeople convened at the base of the towers, aligned and spreading along curving streets that circled around open fields, with an enormous lake at the center. A large bridge, fairly ancient and made of thick brown granite, linked the surrounding city. Crossing the bridge made Lucia's heart jump as they traversed over the beautiful spar-kling waters below. The waters were so clear that she could see the vegetation sway beneath them while schools of fish darted around, plucking at their leaves.

Daisies and wildflowers bloomed along the path leading up a hill to pointed silver gates. Leo looked back, checking on Lucia as she approached, looking off into the distance. "Don't be so afraid," he said. "This is home." He brought a free hand to his waist, clenching the hilt of his dagger protectively before hopping off his horse.

"How did you learn to fight?" she asked, eying the blade.

Leo laughed. "I am not a high maiden, Lucia. Here in Pinea, men of my rank are taught to fight for their country." He moved forward and pulled a key ring from his side. After a moment, he inserted a black key into the gate and it opened. "I trained with the Pinean military for most of my life. General Tyton started my training at nine years old."

Lucia tried to remember all her mother had taught her through-out the many years of her life. Teachings of the faith, the centu-ries-old wisdom of the masters and ladies who reigned before her, and the long-standing history of her country came to mind, but nothing else. She was taught to pray and to believe in the light's hand in building her country. The light was the creator of nations, and the darkness their destroyer. Somehow, those teachings of faith started to make more sense now. Not as if they hadn't before, but now there lay something different within this knowledge, a deeper meaning she had not yet grasped. Lucia needed to know, her hunger growing as she pondered. The answers she sought with every question brought a burning, unnatural desire she could not rid herself of—one that would change her forever.

They continued into the vast garden, bigger than her garden at home and better maintained, at that.

"It's crucial for nobles to know how to defend themselves, especially in a world where our enemies lie at every turn. You mustn't be so naive to think you will always be safe. For every name lies a cost and a burden to live up to," Leo continued.

"Could you teach me to defend myself?" Lucia asked, as if she already knew she would have to sooner or later. It would be for her own benefit. After seeing that demon, she did not know exactly what to do about it. Even with the Light Wings around her neck, she did not feel strong enough. "If things really are going to get as bad as you say they are," she said, clenching her reins, "I'll need to know how to fight." Lucia looked away, her attempt to stay strong failing to hold. "Better than before."

Leo waved to the guards as they stopped in front of the grand mansion. It was elegant and immense, its memorable walkways and gardens covered with gigantic, bold black statues. The winged lions stood proudly within their chains, like fierce guardians staring through vast reaches of time and space, ready to strike down any foe that crossed them. "Welcome to Chateau Feral."

His home appeared more like a fortress protected by these stone colossi. The chateau was built to exhibit both strength and power. Leo dismounted, holding out his hand.

Lucia took it and studied the air of the place, picking up the sweet dianthus.

"You're right, I might as well prepare you for what I fear might be the worst period of your entire life. By the looks of it, you could really use a lesson. But then again"—he flicked at the wings around her neck as he strode up the steps toward the mansion's double doors—"maybe not."

Lucia could not interpret the gesture, distracted by her own revelations as she stared into the monumental structure lying before her. Eventually, she would have to fight. One day, she would see the monster and feel the wrap of the darkness' coil. Nothing frightened her more than the grip of the beast's shadow. Nothing made her feel more helpless than the embrace of the darkest touch. Lucia paced up the steps as Leo waited in front of the large wooden doors. "Do you think this will be easy?" she asked sarcastically.

"I'm just saying, those wings around your neck are a facade of innocent beauty. Perhaps just as much as you." Leo smiled. "There's more than meets the eye."

"They did save my life," she added before Leo could say anything else. True, Lucia did not understand the power of the jewel, nor how it had worked in those dire moments in her sanctuary, but she knew one thing: she did not want to rely on them alone. She had to depend on herself, just as she always had. Even if something horrible were to happen again, Lucia had to find her own strength. Stello may have left this for her, knowing that its power could indeed protect her, but that was all he had ever done. After all those years of solitude, holed up inside her manor, Lucia wanted nothing more than to trust in herself. "But I don't want them to again. I will need to fight for myself."

"If you insist, High Maiden," Leo said, opening the door.

Lucia gave him a quick glare as she stepped in. "Could you not call me that? Please." A sudden sadness trickled over her heart, as if she were no longer worthy of her title. She lowered her eyes. Leo closed the door behind them; she jumped slightly as the slam echoed through the decorative main hall. The sophisticated corridor was adorned with portraits on both sides. As they walked along the soft carpet, the ceiling opened into a large dome. A chandelier hung from the ceiling as candlelit torches circled the large room, reflecting an array of multicolored sparkles around them. At its center was a prodigious staircase, so wide it made Lucia dizzy following its spiral upward. She put her hand to her lips, gasping with admiration. "Leo, you live here?"

"It's not that special," he smirked, puffing out his chest as if she would not notice his boasting.

She stared around the staircase, tracing it as it branched off like a tree made of silver and stone connecting to the many levels of the northern, eastern, and western wings. Leo had led her to the first step, but Lucia peered back, pausing before taking it—a sudden chill breathing through her hair. *Please, do not be close,* she thought to herself, knocking the intuition back deep within her mind. Lucia traced her fingers over the gold rail, watching it sparkle like amber flames beneath her fingers. As they climbed the staircase, she examined the portraits and paintings overhead. The dome was covered with frescoes similar to those in her own home, those of the spirits. However, one stood out amongst the rest, prominent in its unfamiliarity. Lucia had seen nothing like it before. There were two beings, one pure white and divine while the other a dark violet and electric mixed with deepening black. "Leo, is that supposed to look like that?" She wrinkled her nose.

"I believe so. Those are the greater forces of Terestria, the creators. They gave it life and gave us the heavens with night and day."

"I know that," Lucia said, slightly annoyed. "I've just never seen them depicted like that. Like they're converging together."

Until now, Lucia had lived in a limited world that knew little of how it came to be. The story of Terestria's origin was not clear to her. She wondered where all this knowledge lay. Where was the proof that the story she'd been told all her life was the right one? Not within the Sanoon archives; but perhaps she could find something in the library of Moz's prestigious Sky University. Lucia was eager to know the truth. She stood staring as Leo stepped a little ahead of her.

He looked back. "This way, Lucia."

She nodded before following him upward. Leo stepped off one of the branches and pointed to a lone, dark hallway farthest to the corner.

"Where exactly are you taking me?" she asked, pushing her hair behind her ear.

Leo smiled back at her. "The balcony. I thought we could wait there and enjoy the view. My father will be looking for us once he hears word of my arrival. It'd be best to be somewhere he can easily find us."

"Oh," Lucia said, rather relieved that she would be able to continue absorbing the atmosphere of the Feral estate. She squinted in the dark as she noticed the corridor was very narrow, tightening her between the walls. Her heartbeat deepened as they moved forward in the fading light. In these shadows, she sensed the faint chill of danger following closely behind. With it came the innate fear boiling to the top of her skin, overflowing inside her head. Leo was ahead of her a good distance, where she could barely see him. Lucia quickened her step, reaching for his hand while almost slipping. She thrust her fingers into his and breathed her terror away, regaining control over her mind.

Leo's voice rose. "Are you okay?"

"Yes," she said, clasping his hand tighter. Lucia pushed back her hair. The thoughts descended as she was gripped by the sudden tension. Her heartbeat slowed as she saw the door at the end of the corridor. Holding her breath and feeling her free hand touch the wings on her neck, she watched Leo reach for the door and push it open. She coughed, relaxing herself as she hurried Leo through the doorway toward the moonlight.

"You looked as if you couldn't breathe." Leo worried as Lucia caught her breath. "Why were you holding your breath?"

She placed her hands on her knees for a moment, breathing shallowly before rising up. "No, that hallway was so tight. The lack of light was playing some sort of game with my head."

"It is late. You're probably tired from the journey. You're imagining things. There was plenty of space in that hallway."

Lucia patted at her skirt, still breathing heavily. "Let us wait now. I would really just like to rest and think for a bit." She brushed past him, neglecting his gaze while looking out onto the broad marble balcony. Her attention shifted to the center, where a peculiar stone structure stood. It was a circle of tall pillars that connected at the top. Vines grew along them, over lengthy carvings of broad flames, and at its center was a glass pyramid inside a cut bowl of water. The water flowed down the pyramid as an array of colors emerged from it. Lucia's mouth dropped open as she got close to it. The fountain was so beautiful. She bent over, staring at her reflection, seeing she had dried and still retained her beauty despite the storm. She waved her hand over the water of many colors. She placed a finger into the water and watched the ripples obstruct the figure below. A childish grin spread across her face. The water amused her.

Breaking her focus, and annoying her a bit, Leo grasped her free hand and pulled her to the end of the balcony, where the breeze tousled her hair and brushed her face. Beyond them rolled the great Pinean hills, covered in countless flowers. Their colors stretched across the hills like paint atop a canvas, reflecting in the moonlight.

Lucia looked back to Leo, who studied the rising hills solemnly with his bold blue eyes. She appreciated him and all he had done for her. For the first time, she truly admired him—just as she had his home, with its brilliant stone structures and many works of art. It brought a warm sensation within her as she smiled.

Lucia relaxed her shoulders a bit and took in the moment as she peered at the hills and beyond into the sky. It was almost as if, in that moment, she could forget everything. But just as she found peace within herself, an air of regret loomed, reminding her of how far off she really was from what she was supposed to be searching for, this place she did not know. Lucia wondered how Moz might be by now, and thought about how she'd been drawn away from there—about her mother, the massacre, and her utter failure to protect what she held most dear. The embarrassment overtook her, and she still felt her shame. How could she lead her people if she could not even protect them? How could she receive their love when she allowed so many to be slaughtered and burned? Did she deserve it? Their forgiveness. Why was this happening? Lucia's sadness showed in her eyes.

Leo moved closer to her as she tried not to cry, tears dripping down her cheeks. Lucia had always wanted more than her privileged, Mozian lifestyle; but not like this, not by force. Just as Leo enfolded her in his arms, the sound of distant footsteps emerged from behind them. Instinctively, Lucia parted from Leo, turning to face the figure slowly approaching them. He was an older, gray-eyed man. His hair was a familiar shade of dark brown, touched with silver at the sides. He looked aged by years of stress and worry, as you can imagine any ruler would be. He wore a dark blue robe, and his chin was covered with gray stubble. Lucia immediately assumed that he was the master of this place: Sigranole Feral.

"Leo, is she"—the master's eyes widened as he saw the familiar features on her face—"Lucia Sanoon?"

"Father." Leo's brows tightened with worry, overtaken by his father's expression, as if he had never seen his father so afraid. He looked at Lucia, staring at her necklace. He lowered his gaze, signaling the old man to look for himself.

Sigranole flinched back as if struck by a great blow of pain.

Lucia stood in confusion, still not knowing the meaning of why she was there, being alienated at a glance, all while trying to embrace the idea of being stalked by something she barely understood.

"Stello's prophecy . . . . It's true." Sigranole stared at her neck, breathing heavily. Turning from her and toward his son, his face was transparent. "That *pendant*, he really did find that pendant." He looked at the pair and, his voice filled with sheer terror said, "Those are the Light Wings."

CHAPTER SIX

Revelations of Fear

"Preposterous!" Sigranole exclaimed, his mouth quivering as his voice carried into the swaying hills behind them. "The wings were just a myth." His body trembled as he held his head in his hands.

Lucia looked outward, her eyes troubled. She did not know what to make of his reaction. Shame cast its shower over her and then beneath a wave of uncertainty. "What exactly are you afraid of?" she asked, clenching the pendant in her fist, haunted by the constant echo of "why?" within her head. "The Light Wings, or the darkness set out to destroy us?" She stepped back, emotion overtaking her body, the Light Wings pleading with her. "Please, tell me." Lucia's eyes grew moist as a ball of grief formed at the base of her throat.

Leo looked at her and then back to his father, who was still trying to grasp the answers to Lucia's questions. Immediately, Leo saw that his father was afraid, and even though he himself barely understood the power his father spoke of, he still saw how low the wings draped from Lucia's neck, as if heavy with burden. He walked forward and placed a gentle hand on Lucia's shoulder as she let go of the knot in her throat.

Sigranole took a step toward them as a gentle wind carried in a chill from the north. "There is much to discuss, so much to prepare for. The peril that shall start from this—it has all been foreseen." He then looked to his son as Leo held on to Lucia. "I am Sigranole Feral," he finally addressed her, properly introducing himself, "the master of Pinea. I'm sorry that we must meet under these circumstances. However, now I know the truth. And you, my dear, are the key to saving us all. Please, follow me." Sigranole glanced toward his son, nodding his head slowly as if he were signaling him somehow, almost as if they had rehearsed this before her arrival.

Lucia quivered. The chill deepened, running through the hall and causing her chest to tighten. The longer they waited, the closer it felt. The darkness that had presented itself in Moz was not far behind. It could have even been there already, invisible and watching them closely. Lucia sensed it in the shadows lurking, hidden, waiting.

They were led back to the stairway and to the far left wing of the mansion. Lucia stayed silent, paying close attention to Sigranole, who walked strangely through the halls slouching forward and raising his hand occasionally to pinch the bridge of his nose. His eyes were surrounded by dark, cloud-like circles. His skin took on the image of ash and gloom, while his cheeks sank into his face with dread. *An invalid,* she thought, turning her head away sadly.

Sigranole glanced backward at her for a few moments, staring deeply into the pendant. *How could this have happened? Will things be as bad as they say they will be?*

Lucia looked down at the angelic wings. *Of course they will.*

Lucia pondered whether she would ever wake from this dream. The nightmare of this cold, dark destiny had gripped her into an ever-growing sadness that felt eternal. Slowly, the woe of reality settled in and she began to understand that it was not her father who had chosen this fate for her.

Eventually, Leo opened the doors ahead of them and Lucia stepped into a lengthy library. The basilica was composed of panels of stained glass supported by arches that crossed over many layers of bookcases. Dozens of ladders and staircases scaled upward beneath a gigantic rose window. Cut like a diamond, it beamed down light from outside and reflected it through a network of mirror-like pillars that lit the walkways surrounding them. Leo's eyes sparkled as they walked farther into the corridor. Never would he tire of this library. Just like this place, his own memories here were profound and monumental. As they stood in silence, Leo honored his domain with a quaint smile, breathing deeply to absorb its ambience.

"These mirrors are so efficient. I could imagine how they make reading much easier," Lucia said, jumping ahead of Leo and onto the stairs. She ran her hand over one of the pillars, feeling its smoothness while bathing in its light. It rotated slightly, moving the light toward her and into the Light Wings. She gasped as the light lit the stained glass and refracted colored light toward her, filling her with a new electric energy.

"They were innovated to light even at night. The angle can catch the moonlight and some starlight, believe it or not. I could spend hours here." Leo proudly pointed to the window above them. "I can't imagine any place more peaceful."

"I don't know about that," Lucia said, smiling politely as she admired the sparkling light glistening up the platform. "The sanctuary back home was my favorite place." She bowed her head as the images of flames nearly brought tears to her eyes. She shook it off before looking back to the pillars and wondering if she could see her reflection in their light. Instead, she found numerous reliefs of lions cut along the stone's reflective surface. Lucia placed a finger to her lips. "And at night, do they always work? I mean, the moon doesn't always shine."

"When it doesn't, we do use candlelight." Leo pulled Lucia forward and onto the top step while bringing her closer to him.

Lucia's hand fell on his chest, where she felt the warmth of his heartbeat. She pulled back and blushed. She rushed past the stairs after Sigranole. Keeping her hands clasped together, she stepped softly over the royal blue carpet, following it. She looked back as Leo followed behind her, his hand sliding along the rail.

Leo watched his father cross in front of them, preoccupied. Sigranole held a worn leatherbound book below his disoriented face. The book was brown, its cover fragile with age. His eyes moved wildly about its yellow pages as if searching for something important. "Never in the seventeen years had I regretted my decision, but now I think it is the worst I've ever made."

Lucia held her breath as the weight fell back onto her shoulders. The pressure built within her, pushing up against her chest as her hands tingled with blood flow. Here it came, a fraction of the truth, like a wave ready to crash.

"The force was thought to have been destroyed in the war. The chief elder of the Carist tribe had warned us, telling us that the force was legendary. His knowledge was not to be mistaken. However, when it faded away, it felt as if it would never return. No one could feel its presence. But now, it seems that your father's prophecies are coming true. The Light Wings are indeed here." Sigranole pointed at the page and huffed. Then, suddenly overtaken by anger, he threw the book out over the stairs. The pages rained from its spine, falling down the levels like snow caught in still air, drifting in the light. He grunted as he drew back his wrath, hiding his face in his palms.

Lucia did not understand—how could she? How could so much agony derive from something so beautiful? She caressed the pendant and then walked forward. "What exactly are the Light Wings?" She doubted her decision to ask, dreading the truth no matter what it was, yet she longed for answers. The pendant was powerful, its influence intoxicating. If Lucia hoped to survive, she would need to know what the relic was capable of. She did not want to lose control.

Sigranole looked up to her and tried to breathe. "The Light Wings are fabled among Terestria, spoken of only in ancient mythology." He could not find his words easily, stammering as if he himself could not fully believe what he was saying.

Lucia could not blame him.

He continued. "They were created by the light as a means to call upon the creator if the world was to face the perils of the other—darkness. The pendant holds the essence of all that is good in our world, the power of life's virtue. It is said to be so pure that it can cleanse away any sin and shine an unbreakable light through any darkness. Its beacon can shatter all that is evil. Its purpose: sanctification."

"But that does not explain why you should fear this." Lucia lowered her head. "If the Light Wings are holy or divine, why fear anything at all?"

"The Carist chief speaks of a balance that exists in Terestria beyond our understanding. Legend states that the Light Wings would emerge into the known world once that balance was threatened, but only would they . . . " Sigranole hesitated while realizing the truth in his own words. He shuddered.

"Keep going."

"Find their master if the balance were broken. For once the balance is gone, the savior will be needed to restore balance to the world, using the power of the Light Wings."

"The savior?" Lucia asked quietly, touching her lips with the tips of her fingers.

"You."

Lucia stepped back, shaking her head fiercely. "No," she said, her heart sinking. "That can't be true. I am no savior. I cannot—" She questioned her ability to lead her own people. How could she be the savior of all humanity, or life for that matter?

"Lucia, the Light Wings found their way to *you*, the only one destined to control their powers. They chose you for a reason. You are the only one capable of holding the light that dwells within them. Your faith is strong, the strongest of anyone."

"They couldn't have chosen me!" she shouted. "My father left this for me. *He* chose me. Not fate or destiny, but my father." Lucia could hardly believe this. It could not be true, but then how could she explain what had happened at the manor, the light that had flashed right in front of her from within the pendant. She cowered at the thought of all of this. Lucia did not want to accept it, but the truth was wrapped around her neck. Sigranole was right, and her father was too. Yet still, she doubted. How could she be the savior, when her faith was fractured?

"I believe not." Sigranole placed a hand on his temple. "Your father knew more—things no one would. Not even the Carist chief, the proclaimed keeper of knowledge. Stello could see the future. How? I cannot say." He broke eye contact as he continued. "But everything has come to pass. He spoke of your arrival with those wings around your neck. His prophecies didn't end there either. The rest are disasters waiting to happen . . . " Somehow, Sigranole's voice became more powerful with every word as a bitter fierceness rumbled beneath a roar. "Disasters beyond our control. Outside the mortal reach of man!"

Lucia could not fathom these words, nor could she ignore them. With every ounce of her will, she sought to reject them, but was bound completely. This was not the role her mother had worked so hard to prepare her for. She knew her faith was strong, but not strong enough to hold and use this power. Lucia knew not even the proper ways to defend herself. The chime of a bell echoed inside her head, the call of destiny ringing as she slipped into another fate shift. Her future was changing right before her eyes.

"Lucia, your father believed in you," Leo said.

Lucia looked into his sapphire eyes as her face flushed with heat and emotion.

"Where could he have found them? Not there . . . " Sigranole asked slowly, his voice cold and still. "He spoke of catastrophes across the entire world. Across every province, a dark age of sin is about to begin."

"But"—Lucia stumbled on her words—"did my father know I would be attacked?"

"Attacked by what?"

"In the sanctuary back in Moz, this monstrosity confronted me. Shadows covered every wall, swarming about. They clung to me like a gripping cold, and I was trapped until light emerged from the pendant as if from nowhere. It helped me escape, and I ran as far as I could from there. The Light Wings protected me, but my home was destroyed." Lucia shuddered as a chill ran down her back from the memories frozen within her mind. "It follows me. I can still feel it watching within the shadows. I can sense it even here." She bowed her head as guilt filled her heart as if making it moisten with thick, red blood. "And it has my mother within its clutches."

Sigranole pinched his nose, swallowing hard as his eyes

moistened. "It is as I feared. The darkness has returned. Lucia, this world will no longer be a safe place for anyone." He paced forward, pointing to the stairs. "We must hurry in our preparations. Do not worry, I will send word to Moz and let them know you're safe. Let's hope word reaches your mother in time."

"You can't," Lucia shuddered. "The nobles are dead. I don't even know who's in charge anymore. The city fends for itself."

Sigranole's eyes went blank. "You mean Ara . . . she's gone?"

"It's unlikely she survived," Leo said, "but Lucia believes she's still alive. She may be out there somewhere." He tried to choose the right words, not wanting to cause Lucia any more suffering, knowing her burden to be too great. "Still, send word."

Sigranole was caught in a daze, but soon nodded. "Right, my son."

"You must brace yourself," Leo said to Lucia.

Lucia's face was void as the words left her lips, "For what?" She blinked. "Another war?"

"Worse." Sigranole hurried to the front of the library, stopping only for a moment to stare up and out into the moonlight above them. "Cherish these moments. They won't last long."

"Nothing lasts forever," Leo said. "Not even peace."

"Lucia, your father was here, and I shunned him in disbelief because I had not trusted his motives. Our provinces had been rivals. To me, he had taken my honor, my pride, and all that was dear to me. I thought his words were nothing more than a feign to form a false allegiance, but I see now those words have become his prophecy." Sigranole blew out a deep breath. "And still, I'm left with nothing but memories."

"What am I supposed to do?!" Lucia stomped her foot. Her patience was thinning just as her blood began to heat to a boil. "All of these prophecies, regrets, and cries for help are getting us nowhere. Tell me, what exactly are we fighting, and how do we defeat it?"

The two men stopped in their tracks, shocked by her voice. Its firmness still echoed about the chamber.

She continued, "We don't have time to loathe, grieve, or sulk in our self-pity. I'm scared, and I don't think we're going to win. Not like this."

Sigranole turned to her as Leo approached from behind. Sigranole had one more secret he was willing to tell, a lead for attempting to prevent what he still, like Lucia, hoped was nothing more than a strange nightmare. There was nothing he wanted more than to neglect the truth and to deny the darkness ever existed, but as Lucia's words hung over them he remembered. "I do know where your father was headed," he said, his voice bold. "He had mentioned that the opening act in this calamity would fall soon, so he was going to seek guidance in Aldric, from the Carist chief—Talon Renon."

Lucia's heart bumped upward. "Aldric, the land of scholars?"

"Aldric lies on the cliffs to the west, past the Pinean hills and beyond the southern forest border. That is where Stello's prophecy continues. The Carist tribe, for eons, have been the keepers of knowledge. The chief elder is trusted with many secrets, many of which have been lost through the ages. He alone could possibly tell you how this all started and, more importantly, how to bring an end to it. Seek out Talon and plead that he share his secrets with you. They should prove to be most useful."

For a moment, it was as if the weight lifted, giving Lucia the chance to breathe. A glimmer of hope seemed to shine within her eyes and she brought her hands to her chest.

"This darkness will spread. The balance that once protected Terestria is gone. Life as we know it will cease to exist with each passing day as the people will be left unprotected and subject to their own corruption. Sin shall reign." Sigranole touched her shoulder and turned to his son. "Leo, you will assist her to Aldric until you both find a way to stop Stello's prophecies."

Leo nodded, touching the dagger at his side.

"Lucia, that force you witnessed will do anything to tear those wings from your neck. With the balance broken, it will grow stronger as it feeds on the sins of men, and will destroy everything." Sigranole's eyes looked into hers as the light within them faded. "Pray, my dear. Summon the will to fight and stop at nothing until the darkness threatens the world no more. Do what your father couldn't do. Save the world. I beg of you."

A ball of terror built up in Lucia's throat again. She couldn't ease the tension rising within her. She still couldn't make anything of the cards that lay before her, but she understood one thing— she had to make a move. Though, she felt more cursed and weak than blessed and powerful. She wanted to break down, to weep, but she couldn't. Her body was numb, torn by the sudden burden that fell onto her. She was once the beautiful high maiden of Moz, and now she was something more, or maybe even less—but ultimately something she never wanted to be. Even so, a sense of duty rose from inside as if a piece of her mother was still there with her. For some reason, the word *balance* meant everything.

"This was not the first time it emerged. I should have seen this coming. Why do you think we fear it so much? It was born from our sin, this darkness," Sigranole shared. "The war twenty years ago gave birth to something just as you described. During the last battle of the war, Pinea and Moz were locked in conflict. Blood stained the outskirts of the hills when it rose from the earth, shrouding the heavens and blocking out the sun. It stormed over us, killing thousands of soldiers from both sides, until a woman came before the beast, kneeling as the dark mass rose as a heavy gust. She stood with her hands to the heavens, pleading and praying loudly for all to hear. Oddly, as the people joined together to pray, the force subsided. It weakened as light broke through the clouds. No longer fighting but praying together as one, the people followed this woman as she led them into song. Their rage had turned to faith, and I cannot tell you why or how, but their faith manifested itself, summoning a light that drove away the force."

Lucia and Leo were dazed as he told his tale. Why had they not known this? Why had Pinea and Moz remained enemies still, if this were true? How many sides were there to this story? It was not at all how Lucia had imagined it to be. It was all lies.

Sigranole continued, "After it disappeared, we noticed the price of our bloodshed, of our hate and our pride. We saw what it caused. That day, we witnessed a darkness neither province could define. It left a scar upon our cities, and after we had lost so much, I had no choice but to sign the Treaty of Tranquility surrendering on my behalf only to prevent something like that from happening again. The Carist chief explained to us the consequence of Frailty's War, but somehow balance was seemingly retained. Though most of our own history is lost, the ancient tribe holds what is left within their records, but all that remains is a heavy mystery to us. The tribe will guard their secrets, and at first they will not trust you. Even I, being of nobility, could not convince them to share what they know—but *you* will have to. You will have no choice. I never forgave Moz, for taking the glory and for bringing such chaos into our world at that time. But I thought it was over, and as part of the treaty we swore to keep the truth from the people, and even you. We could not let them know of the beast we had seen. We could not speak of a war that started over sin, only of peace and of what had ended. Such things should only exist in myth, but now it has returned, and by the looks of it, the legend speaks of only worse to come."

"But who defines the truth when it remains so hidden right before our eyes," Leo said quietly. "To whom does the final judgment lie?"

Sigranole's eyes found Lucia.

"But if our history is all but a hidden secret," she asked, "who are we to call such things myths? No one knows for sure. Every story could be part of a larger one. That's the story we need to find, the one that started it all." Lucia's heart eased as she let go of the unknown and tried to accept the world for what it truly was, one big mystery.

"I promise you, if you follow your father's trail and seek out this man Talon, you will find the answers you need. I'm sorry for rejecting your father, and for feeling such anger toward your family, but now it is I who comes to you pleading. You hold the key to banishing this darkness, and you must redeem us from the chaos that will soon fall onto the world. Please, Lucia. This is something you *must* do."

Lucia glanced up into the light above and felt its warmth falling onto her face. *Duty above all else.* How much longer would this last? She didn't desire to feel anything less than the warmth of the coming dawn, the beginning of something grand, of something beautiful. So, she couldn't refuse. How could she? This was her duty.

Lucia looked over to Leo, who stood nobly by her side, upright and strong. Of course he'd protect her.

"I'm sorry. That is all I can tell you. The rest is merely history. Seek the rest of the knowledge on your own. The Carist surely hold the hope we need."

Lucia let out a small puff of air and stared directly into Sigranole's eyes as something shifted within her. "I'm going to Aldric. I'm going to find Talon and figure out how to stop this." She touched the pendant. "I will go, and maybe find my father along the way, to face him. There is so much I need to know. About everything. I have so many questions."

"Well, at least you won't be alone," Leo said, patting her shoulder, straightening then looking to his father. He grinned softly and Lucia smiled back, touching his hand with her fingertips.

"That's the spirit," Sigranole said as he embraced both of them. Then he whispered, "I will forever be indebted to you. I'll send word to Moz immediately and make sure our provinces work together. This bond will be sacred."

"Ending the rivalry?" Lucia asked gleefully.

"Forever," Leo responded in place of his father, his eyes beaming with delight.

"There's an even greater rivalry to worry about, a rivalry worse than this. In order to restore peace, we have to end it completely." As the old man spoke, it was as if his words breathed new life into him. The youth of his past returned to his eyes as he placed his faith in the coming generation. "Rest tonight, for the morning will be here very soon and we wouldn't want you to be weary on your journey. It will be long and perilous, but please, under all circumstances, stay faithful and attempt to enjoy what little you have. Even if it's as simple as each other's company." He smiled at the two as he parted from them. "Please take care of each other." Sigranole's eyes swelled as he looked at his son.

"Wait, there is still something I don't quite understand," Lucia interrupted. "If that was how the war ended, how did my mother and father come to power in Moz so quickly? What of their victory and ascension? I thought they were heroes."

Sigranole smiled. "She was." He looked up into the light as it streamed from the window above them. "It was your mother who started that prayer long ago."

Lucia touched the pendant, feeling her heart grow blue. For some time, she'd thought so ill of her mother and her expectations. She never would have thought her mother could be so selfless. Except, then again, she was the most powerful woman she knew. Lucia prayed she was safe.

"Come, Lucia." Leo gave her a slight nudge. "I'll show you to your quarters."

She grinned a bit, but withdrew her smile and looked away from the light. She followed Leo into the vast hallway and back toward the center of the chateau, her mind wandering. *Father, you seem to have left this burden to me. You placed it long before I even knew how to pray, and now that I know why you truly left our family, I can only think of one thing: when will I ever see home again?*

Is mother truly safe? I might not live to ever know. I'm actually more afraid than I can show, and it's more than I can bear. I'm petrified. Seeing that beast and feeling its strength has left me more than afraid. In its presence, I felt nothing more than a gripping and cold emptiness, something so dark and corrupted I could imagine death to be better. It was the most terrifying thing I have ever witnessed. Even with something as divine as the Light Wings wrapped around my neck, I will never forget the terror . . . .

* * *

Lucia was settling into the room, thinking heavily on what she would do once she reached Aldric. She wasn't too sure how to even contact this man that Sigranole spoke of. Maybe she wouldn't find him. But she knew if all else failed, she would seek out the answer one way or another. The Light Wings told her that, softly between each heartbeat. A light warmth within her heart pointed like a compass toward Aldric, her father's last known destination.

Sigranole had shown her his letter to Moz, signed and sealed, which explained the situation in full detail. Hopefully, sending word to Moz was better than sending none at all, no matter how ridiculous it might sound considering the known circumstances.

She sat on her bed, soft and silky and filled with down atop carved redwood. Lucia brushed her hands over the familiar bold carvings. She held her breath, trying to repress the memory of that night, remembering that chill yet again, the emptiness that played like an omen over and over inside her head. She peered through the window at the end of the room. Pinea was doubtlessly a beautiful city. The bright hills reflected a colored sunset over the onyx buildings, and Lucia again tried to understand why her nation would fight against such a place. The same values she upheld for her own homeland were the same as Leo's. What set them apart? Frailty's War? She thought of what he had said, about the secrets and the hidden history the ancient tribes knew, the stories they kept. Could the answer really lie out there somewhere, destined for her to discover it?

She tossed her hair from her face as she examined the pendant around her neck. *What exactly do I pray for?* Faith was like any other virtue to Lucia. Just as she had studied as a child, her memories struck a spark within her mind. *Even I, being of nobility, could not convince them to share what they know—but you will have to.* Those words lay heavily on her shoulders. She knew there was faith, because "nobility was to be of virtue," as her tutors had told her over the years. Growing up in her sanctuary, she was raised to pray within it and partake in the blessings and rituals passed on to her. She never fully understood where the power of her prayers came from, but she had always known it was there, just as the light surely was. Prayer and faith were virtues, virtues she had grown to honor and obey. There was no reason, no purpose, to why she had to pray. But she did anyways. It was almost as if all of her praying, her writing, her singing had groomed her toward this one great sacrifice. The expectations she held herself up to her entire life were nothing compared to this moment. The sudden rush of mystery surrounded her, drowning her in the secrets of the forgotten world, the world she had never known. What else was to the story—the story of how their origins had been scattered? There might be a hidden purpose cut across time. That wisdom and truth must hold an even greater power. If she could learn the true nature of this world, she might find the way to stop the evil threatening to consume it.

She heard a knock at the doorway. Slowly, Lucia glanced backwards, her fingers placed upon the edge of the bedroom window. Leo stood leaning against the edge of the doorway. His arms were crossed, and his sapphire eyes fixed on Lucia's pendant, which was glowing vibrantly.

"He really urges us to go to Aldric," he said. "He thinks if we can convince the Carist chief of what's happening, the chief might let us in on the secret to defeating the darkness."

Lucia bit her lip as she played with the tip of her hair. She scoffed. "I don't even know how to fight. I'm nowhere near ready. It's all just too much." She moved to her bed, sitting down, her hands in her lap. Leo stepped in front of her.

He took her hands and helped her to her feet. He smiled. "You're afraid you are rushing into this, aren't you?"

Lucia shook her head as she widened her eyes. "It's not just that. It's just I don't know how I can survive this. My life has never been so—"

"Complicated." Leo finished for her.

"So, you noticed." Lucia said, smiling.

"How could I not? Your worry is so obvious. Have you always been so sheltered?"

"What do you mean?" Lucia asked, standing and pushing past him, unsure of what to make of his words. She peered out the window for a brief second and then quickly turned back to Leo.

"You have an interesting way of seeing the world," Leo said, smiling as the light from the dusk streamed in from behind Lucia. "Every detail. Every touch. Every smell. Everything you see affects you differently."

Lucia's cheeks pulled back as she studied Leo's laugh. "And to think I was just a maiden with a title to live up to. My mother always sought to live a life of perfection, which also meant protection. I couldn't ever leave her side. She always told me that I was blessed with duty above all things. Since I was a child, I wondered what those words meant. 'Duty above all else.' But now, it's quite easy to understand. This is exactly what she was preparing me for, except I didn't see it." Her voice started to crack as her body started to tremble. "It's as if she wanted me to experience all of Terestria at once for the first time. As if seeing the world wasn't my right if left otherwise. Free will is such an illusion."

"But everyone has the right to make their own decisions anyway. You're speaking as if you have no choice. No matter what, there will always be a choice. Its either this or that. There is no avoiding it. You chose to leave that manor. You chose to come here. You chose to do what you felt was right. If you believe in the choices you've made, you control your own destiny."

"But that's the thing . . . I didn't choose. I was told what to do, just like I always am." Lucia's anxious heart pushed up against her chest. "How could I turn away from this? Who would? When the light binds you."

"That's why it had to choose the most faithful. It needed someone like you. Someone to uphold the duty it's bestowed upon you."

"My mother always use to say that. 'The light needs you. Not just someone. You.' There is no choice. There is no free will in that."

"If there wasn't free will, there would be no corruption. Why would the light want to bring this on itself? Hey, I'm sorry, but we still choose. Even you. Our choices are based on what we believe. But—" Leo retreated to the door. "Free will is what makes us human."

Lucia could see that. But it was also the people's choices that corrupted the world. She didn't want to be seen as that difficult.

So, Lucia kept her thoughts to herself. But somehow Leo was able to read them perfectly. Lucia's glare was piercing. Her emotion was so withheld, so focused, and concentrated into her line of sight. One look at her eyes, and they'd tell Leo more than her words ever could.

"Don't worry about time. Father is preparing our journey, and he said we could have all day tomorrow to get ready if we want. Our *choice*." Leo teased. With his hand, he brushed his hair out of his face. "So that means we're training."

Lucia blinked, almost taken by the young sir's charms, but she nodded, hoping the certainty in his voice would prove true. "I'm looking forward to it." She pulled her hair behind her slender shoulders and it fell back like a fiery rain. Like honey, it dripped through her fingers. "Thank you, Leo."

Turning, and with a slight wave of his hand, Leo left Lucia alone with her thoughts once again.

Looking back out the window as the light caught her and made her dress sparkle like topaz, she took the band from her head and looked at it, trying to remember the day she got it. Her mother gave it to her when she turned seventeen. It had a stunning outline of gold and ivory with delicate silver feathers along its edge. Lucia held it to her chest, remembering her mother's gentle face, her amber eyes, and her soft voice, assertive like any noble but not as careless as some of them. A tear fell from her eye, and she quickly wiped it away. A promise is a promise. She fled to keep her mother safe. So, the light that had led her here—the light that led her to Leo and closer to the end—was like fate. But to Lucia, it felt like something darker and quite the opposite. Her morals did not even rationalize her choices now. She tried to shake away the feeling of defying her very nature, but found herself obsessing even more. Lucia rose from the bed and lowered her head as she brought her hands to her chest. "Dear light . . ."

CHAPTER SEVEN

Phantasms of Pride

Sigranole was alone, deep within his study. The fireplace before his desk blazed forth a scarlet light across the surfaces of many ornate black bookcases and the colors of two decorative golden-framed paintings. He held a rather large glass, and into it he poured a thick wine of dark maroon. Its scent flooded the room, and as he drank from his glass he moved his hands over parchments and open books, all so old. His eyes blurred as his mind spun endlessly. The age had yellowed into the pages and cracked the leather of the spines. The markings within them were crimson, and they formed not any common language but more symbols, runes of ancient times. He placed a finger over them, tracing the pages, absorbing each image. "Leo," he said as the door clicked behind him.

"Father," Leo said, approaching the desk.

"Where is Lucia?" Sigranole asked sipping from his glass.

"Bathing," he said awkwardly.

Sigranole rose and turned to his son, who stood firmly before his father.

Leo asked, "Are you sure you'd like me to leave Pinea?"

Sigranole took a sip of wine before setting down his glass. He looked back up to Leo, whose face looked more woeful than a stormy day. "Leo, you must stay with her."

"But, Father, I can't leave you. Not if this is all true." Leo had done his best to maintain a tough exterior in front of Lucia, but here alone with his father, his gaze could not contain his true feelings. The inner boy, not the man he was coming to be, spoke instead.

"It is not yours to say. This is what fate has decided. It has all played out this way because of fate."

"It's not fate, Father. It's because I chose to honor your wishes, because I chose to believe you, but don't I have a choice?" Leo lowered his gaze.

Sigranole put a hand to his son's shoulder and lifted Leo's chin with his finger. "No," he said coldly. "The history of the world has been written already. We must follow it"—he moved a hand over the books again—"just as it has been written." His eyes broadened and shifted to Leo. "You must make sure she reaches Aldric at all costs, my son." He staggered forward a bit.

Leo nodded.

"You must not let her stray. Instead, you must guide her. Show her the will to fight, just as I've shown you." He looked down and then back up to Leo as the color fell from his face. He became ghastly pale as if he were being choked by fear. "Home will always be with you. I will be, too, as long as you remember what you stand for. Please." Sigranole's eyes narrowed while his voice softened. "Don't forget."

"Father, what do you mean?" Leo looked to the wine and caught his father as he stumbled into him. Sigranole drifted from consciousness as his breathing became a series of heavy snores. Leo smirked with a shake of his head. He pulled his father over his shoulder and reached for the door with a disapproving groan. "You need to stop drinking so much."

* * *

The night was eerie as Pinea lay dormant within its darkness, waiting. The air was growing colder, and the wind becoming sharp. The amber colored curtains blew softly as the wind seeped through a small opening at the base of a window inside Lucia's chamber. The chill of the air fell over her as she lay silently in the security of her soft, warm bed. Despite the comfort, she was restless. She tossed and turned. The waves of her hair hovered in a flurry as she was thrown around in a fit of fear. All night, she was plagued by nightmares accompanied by a strange presence, perhaps an omen of something to come. It was coming . . . the thing she was most afraid of. A nightmare.

Lucia was standing atop a large hill overlooking the black city as it stood undisturbed beneath a clouded sky. Random spurts of lightning dimly lit the streets within the night as a cold shower descended upon it. She sensed something in the air, an ominous feeling, rife with deceit as the images played their course within her mind. A little girl with a kite in hand darted from behind her, the kite flying high on the winds of the coming storm. A strange panic emerged from inside Lucia as she reached out to the girl. "No, that's dangerous. Please, come back!" she yelled. She sprinted toward the girl, who was laughing in the rain as she disappeared into the city. Lucia reached the bottom of the hill and watched as the girl faded into the streets, which were murky and uglier than she remembered. She walked along the cracked pavement, feeling the earth rumble as a quake of thunder clapped overhead.

Lucia heard the laughter again. The girl was standing at the end of an alleyway with her kite at her feet, covered in mud. Lucia stepped toward her as the thunder rumbled. The girl was drenched, but still smiling in the darkness of the alley. As Lucia approached her, it seemed as if the figure of the young girl faded again. Eventually, only the lightning would reveal her form, until suddenly she disappeared and Lucia was left alone in blackness.

Lucia heard her own breathing under the falling rain. Each drop that fell upon her skin brought with it a deep chill that felt so real. Was this truly a dream? A large rattle caused Lucia to fall back startled and slip in the mud. She caught herself as she fell backward, and from her neck a light glowed, illuminating her surroundings. The realm was dark, and the sky was hidden within the dense fog. The buildings were rugged and broken up like they had been abandoned for some time, so worn that moss and vegetation had overtaken them as if they had lain dormant for centuries. *Pinea.*

A faint whisper came from the shadows. "Darkness will be everywhere."

A knot formed in Lucia's throat as her hand reached for the pendant around her neck. "What are you?"

"I am the essence of your pride, the very source of the fear you feel inside. I am your insecurity. I am your weakness." The echo of this whisper bounced all around her, almost as if a million voices spoke at once. "I am the destroyer of men, a darkness within themselves, a bane you call 'sin.'"

"You're the darkness," Lucia said.

A distorted cluster of laughs spilled from the shadows. "A part of it. I'm pleased to finally meet the savior of light. Nigh is my turn to draw blood."

The rain fell like needles as it froze in the sudden chill of the air. Lucia turned hastily back the way she came, only to crash to the ground as the street iced over. She grunted while trying to pull herself up, looking ahead as the little girl stared down at her, her blonde curls drenched. Lucia spotted something forming behind the girl, a hooded figure with scarlet eyes, burning with a pale aura. Its cloak filled the air, absorbing the light around it as it slowly approached the girl. Long, tentacle-like appendages spewed from beneath its hood and reached toward the girl as Lucia watched in horror. Her scream was caught in her throat as the beast hissed.

"Look out!" Lucia screamed, holding out her hand. A light pulsated from the Light Wings, flowing through her and into her palm. From it shot a light so brilliant it sent out a blast that turned the surrounding ice into vapor while tossing up the phantom with white-hot fire. Lucia sprinted forward and picked up the girl as the figure rose into the air and dissipated into a cloud of smoke.

A deep fog encompassed them, and the monster was inside her head. "You cannot escape me. I live inside you, within your darkest nightmares."

"Show yourself," Lucia said, "or leave me alone!"

"Your fear will make you reckless!" It snarled in the shadows, with its many voices. "Your confidence shall fail you when you least expect it, and when it does, I will be waiting."

"Stop it. Get away from me. Let me go!" Lucia's scream evoked a pillar of light from her chest, causing a volley to shoot into the sky and erupt into light. From the pendant, a wave of light burst through the city, tearing through the shadows and engulfing the buildings in flames. "No," she said, dropping the girl suddenly as she screamed in agony, burning in the light Lucia had summoned. The girl's body was enveloped in white fire, squirming as she reached out toward Lucia in pain. "This isn't real. This isn't real," Lucia cried, holding her head in her hands.

"You are responsible for their pain. You are what's most

dangerous. Your power will consume you and all you hold most dear, just as pride will consume this city."

The figure manifested itself overhead, floating above the burning city as Lucia became dizzy from the heat. Buildings began to crumble and fall as her strength left her. She collapsed in the smoke, coughing and wheezing as she tried to pull herself to her feet. The buildings toppled down and over her, trapping Lucia under the burning rubble. *Why does this feel so real? It's only a dream. Isn't it?*

Slowly, the dread pulled her into darkness and shot her back into the reality of her chamber, only to realize that the same figure she had seen in her dream was hovering there above her, so close to her face that she could see the light of her pendant being drained into its hood. She tried to move but was bound to her bed, incapacitated by the terror of the nightmare.

*   *   *

The sound of screaming woke Leo, causing a jolt in his gut. He gasped for air as he moved upright and panicked. He went for his door, tumbling as he called to her. "Lucia, I'm coming!" *What could be happening?* He thought about tearing the door open. *Has it found us?* The corridor was empty as the lightning seeped from the windows, illuminating it. Leo was still bleary as he took careful steps. He could no longer hear it, the screaming that had woken him, but instead the whistle of the wind from outside the walls of his home came beneath a wake of thunder, sending a chill into the halls and frightening him. A haunting presence loomed in the air as the walls distorted, changing miraculously in the shudder of the lightning as if Leo were falling in and out of one of his darkest dreams. The walls became grotesque, peeling with decay and overrun with moss, but then in the distant flashes, they alternated between normal and disarray.

The illusion nearly broke him, disturbing his sanity as he

cowered backward. "No." His heart sank as its voice seeped into his mind, planting its seed within his thoughts. "Father . . . " He ran back and past his room, his heart beating with every step as he raced toward Sigranole's quarters. The walls were still changing around him, though he did not notice. He kept his eyes fixed on his destination at the far end of the hall, determined to find his father alive and well. But thorns emerged from the walls and in his mind, coiling around his deepest fears.

His shadow stretched out, far in front of him, extending within the light of the storm outside. He watched it rise from the floor and run ahead of him like a doppelganger, a vision of himself. Leo slowed, observing as his shadow reached for the door to his father's chamber. "I must be dreaming," he said softly. "This can't be."

His doppelgänger turned the handle while reaching for his knife, pulling it from its sheath as he pushed his way inside. "What is going on?" Leo watched as the door closed and the lock latched from inside. "No!" he shouted, running to and rattling the door. His blood heated beneath his skin as the walls changed yet again. Blood rained down from above the door and onto his hands. Leo cried as he brought his trembling hands to his face, staining his cheeks crimson. He slammed his fist against the door, his fears alive, breathing. "Father, please, open the door!" At that moment, he heard it click. A breath of relief left his chest as he pushed through the door, finally open, only to have the air ripped from his throat as his father wobbled toward him from across the room and collapsed with his hand over his neck, gasping as blood spurted from it. Leo's eyes widened, the terror seeping in. He watched as Sigranole turned to face his killer, the boy he had raised and loved, looming as a shadow over him with his dagger dripping red.

"Leo, please," he tried to say as the heavy flow of blood ran over his tongue.

"Goodbye, Father," the shadow whispered, his voice sounding exactly like Leo's, with its eyes a glaring purple. With one fell swoop, the dagger fell into Sigranole's chest, and a scream echoed in all directions through the halls.

"Papa!" Leo fell to his knees and crawled toward his father, the shadow brushing past him to dissolve into its true form. The figure's laughter filled the room, roaring from its hood as it peered backward with its pale red eyes. It dissipated as Leo pulled Sigranole into his lap and rocked while tears burst from beneath his blue eyes. "Papa, stay with me, I beg of you. Please! Somebody, help me!" Leo wrapped his fingers around the hilt of his dagger and tugged it from his father's chest as he called out in agony. "Somebody, please!" Sigranole's eyes stared blankly upward, and the sound of his last struggling breath hissed through the silence. "Father . . . " Leo uttered, his lips trembling. Within his eyes, his walls fractured. Cracks splintered, chipping at his psyche. "Father!"

"Leo—" There in the doorway, Lucia stood shocked. Her hand dropped from her mouth as she watched Leo sob over his father's corpse. "Sigranole," she whispered. "It's not real. This is another nightmare." She came to Leo and put her arms on his shoulders as he let out another agonizing scream.

Wrapped in woe, he shouted, his temper flaring within his roar, "Get off of me! Leave me in peace!"

"Leo," Lucia said, pulling backward. "It's found us. The darkness is here."

"I saw it. I saw it happen." Leo stuttered, "It—it was me. I . . . I did it. I . . . I killed him." He hunched over his father's body and cradled him as Lucia looked at the dagger lying covered in Sigranole's blood.

"What do you mean you killed him?" Lucia asked, confused. "You couldn't have."

Leo cried. "It was me. Or at least, it looked like me. It had my dagger, and it thrust into his heart. I felt it. My heart stopped beating." Leo was shaking. "I could feel his fear. He knew he was going to die." Leo's voice roared and echoed through the chateau. "I saw it in his eyes!"

"It was not you. The darkness is messing with your head."

"But my dagger . . . " Leo put a free hand over the silver hilt as his conscience riddled with guilt.

Suddenly, the sound of a stampede came from the distance. Men shouted, rushing through the halls. "Hurry, to the master's quarters! The master's in danger!"

"This was its plan," Lucia said, realizing now exactly what the phantom had done. This wasn't merely a murder. It was a set up. "We have to go." She pulled on Leo's arm, but he was stiff, frozen by his despair, unable to let go of the boy he once was. "Leo, get up!"

"I can't leave him, not like this."

"The guards will come for you. They will have your head once they find him murdered."

Leo's eyes wandered. His emotion lay adrift. "So be it."

Lucia felt a blow to her chest as her face flushed. "They'll find you with me and think Moz has something to do with it. This is what it wanted. It wants the provinces at each other's throat. You have to come with me. We have to flee. Now!" She fell beside him, desperate for him to understand. "Leo, please. Your father had a mission for us, remember?"

Leo shut his eyes, letting his tears stream down and drop onto his father's pale face. He closed his father's eyes, remembering the promise he had made. "Did he die thinking it was truly me? Does he know I love him?"

Lucia shook her head and pleaded, "I'm not sure, but if we stay here, we won't be able to avenge him. So many people will die, including us."

Leo turned his head and grabbed his dagger, the one that killed his father. He wiped it clean and stowed it in his sheath. His eyes hardened as he contained himself, calling to whatever light was left within his mind. "Goodbye, Papa." He rose and turned to the door.

Lucia grabbed his hand before hugging him. "Let's go."

They took their leave. Sigranole lay within the silence, his life taken in cold blood. His light diminished in the storm and swept into the night, deep within a dream. As they fled, avoiding the guards and with heavy hearts, burdened by the horror they had witnessed, Leo brought them to a secret passageway beneath the chateau, accessed through the library. They hurried through the crypts, the very place Leo would not get to see his father buried, emerging on the surface of a graveyard within a dark forest. He closed the door to the passage and used a candlestick from the base of a broken headstone to hold the handles together, buying them some time as they prepared to leave Pinea behind.

Lucia wondered what Leo must have been feeling. Just like her, he was forced from his home, but worse, he'd lost his father. He had watched him die. She observed how it pained him to turn away and take the blame, but he had no choice. The Light Wings had not only cursed her in this process, but had also brought an unimaginable grief upon the only person she thought she had left; and that, too, was another burden to bear. Who else had to die for this mission to be met? What more must the world sacrifice to protect her?

"It'll be a long journey to Aldric. We better stop at the nearest town and get supplies. We won't make it without any food or water," Leo said.

"But we don't have any money," Lucia worried.

"Well, if word doesn't travel fast, I'll use my name to get us what we need. The neighboring villages are loyal to the Feral line. They will greet us with good intentions." Leo removed his bloodstained shirt. He walked quickly to a nearby spring where he dipped his shirt and scrubbed as much of his father's blood off its gentle fabric as he could. "Keep quiet about your heritage, just until we make it out of the Pinean territory."

"Of course." It was eating at her, watching Leo this way. His muscles tightening as he continued to scrub his blood-stained shirt so wildly. Eventually, she could hardly tell there was any blood on it at all. She looked away as Leo turned and threw his shirt around his shoulders, leaving it open. Was he broken?

When the darkness had released Lucia from her bed earlier that night, she had no idea what it was after. She had thought it was only hunting her—but now she knew. The darkness had a taste for sadistic and cruel torture. It was fond of playing games and causing suffering beyond anything she had ever seen. Lucia looked away as she spoke, unable to grasp the reality of it. "I'm so sorry. I know this must hurt you. I can only imagine."

Leo remained silent for a few moments, his eyes hollow as he looked ahead into the forest. "Let's hurry, before the rest of the world knows my father's dead."

Lucia nodded as Leo passed in front of her. She followed closely behind him, her stomach rumbling as the dawn sprinkled light in through the trees of the vast forest. The night had been long, the darkest it had ever been, and it seemed as if things would only grow worse.

CHAPTER EIGHT

Light's Folly

What little joy she had in seeing the world had been drained from her now. Leo's faith, too, was tragically broken. How could their world become this? Why would their lives take this turn? Was it fate that their minds were left so mangled and torn? What was there to gain from all this?

The duo made their way from the woods and to the top of a rocky hill. It was not long before they could see the destruction. The smell of ash and decay rose into the air, darkening the sky. Lucia gasped as she stared across to the broken city, now shrouded by smoke and burning in the distance.

Leo's eyes turned to stone. He clenched his fists as he watched Pinea's walls crumble and his fortress fall, his heart pounding as his anger swelled.

Lucia placed a hand atop the Light Wings, remembering the dream she had of the burning black city. Had her nightmare been an omen all this time, or was it *she* who had brought the blaze?

Though there was this guilt buried deep within her, like a secret she had to hide, Lucia knew the phantom had done this. The darkness wrought this misfortune.

"This is terrible." Lucia tried to hide the shame in her voice. "In my dream, I saw it burning just like this. Except—" Lucia sighed before confessing. "I was the one who caused it. I had lost control."

Leo shook his head, his expression almost blank. "You didn't do this," Leo said, his voice long and low. He lowered his eyes, using every ounce of will he had to contain his emotions. He lifted his eyes, staring toward Pinea in the distance. "One day, we will destroy the darkness. I will not rest until we rid Terestria of this plague. I swear it." Leo turned away from the chaos, his chest broad. He wiped away his tears while holding his composure and building his strength, changing suddenly.

There was something fierce within his gaze, something Lucia could not quite understand. Was he angry, or sad? What was once so apparent became hidden, behind an impenetrable wall, like a dam holding back a sea of emotion. It must've taken an incredible amount of will for Leo to hold back how he truly felt.

At that moment, Leo wanted nothing more than to be reckless. Flashbacks to his childhood, his training with the other boys in the courtyard, scrambling atop the grass with blood dripping across his knuckles, the memories filled his head. Anger. Wrath. Pride. That wasn't him anymore, it couldn't be. He had more self-control than that, but in this moment he wanted nothing more than to fight, to face the force that killed his father and show it he was not afraid. But he couldn't. He was not strong enough— at least not yet.

* * *

As they proceeded onward, each knew the journey would change them. Loss had become too common, and grief more certain. They stopped at a nearby village for supplies. Lucia waited patiently at a crossroads as the sun began to set, shining a magenta haze over the horizon. Her worry only increased as night approached. They had been traveling for some time, and there was no telling if word of Pinea's doom had yet reached the outskirts, but Lucia held on to hope. It was frightening enough running from a malevolent force that could strike at any moment, but it was even more so running from Leo's fellow countrymen as fugitives. Leo's name would be tainted by his father's blood, and no sane person would believe him when he told them of the things he saw that dreadful night. Lucia bowed her head, growing paranoid.

"Come on, Leo." She saw him scurrying toward her. He was newly dressed, wearing a dark blue jacket over a pristine gray tunic. *Something suitable for traveling north*, Lucia thought, looking then to her own southern clothing. She sighed. Leo had a large brown sack cast over his shoulder, beneath which she noticed a quiver of arrows.

Leo held up a bow and handed it to her. "Do you like it?"

Lucia looked confused, dangling the bow from her fingers. "What's this for?"

"It's for you. It'll come in handy when we run low on food. I thought I'd teach you how to hunt." Leo smiled. "Not to mention, if we run into any enemies on the way up to Aldric. It makes for a good weapon."

"I've never . . ."

Leo moved toward her and placed a hand on her forearm. His eyes met hers, somber at the gesture. Something hovered over her skin as she held her breath. "I'll show you." He raised his hand to the side of her face and caressed her cheek with his thumb as Lucia's sight almost failed her.

She knew he was hurting. So was she, but in that moment, there was something else building up between them. Lucia blinked, clearing her throat as she broke away from him. "Thank you, Leo.

I really do appreciate you." She found it hard to breathe. Her face was a bright red, like a ruby shining in the sun. Leo seemed to chuckle a bit before taking the quiver from his back and handing it to Lucia.

"Is there something I could change into?" Lucia asked, pulling the quiver over her shoulder.

"Oh," Leo said, almost as if he'd forgotten. He dropped the sack and pulled from it a parcel. "I hope it's of your taste. The clothes are a bit heavier than I think you are used to, but traveling north and into the mountains, it's due to get colder."

"Great. I suppose I'll have to wait until I have some proper cover to get into these."

"I wouldn't be opposed to you changing now." Leo shrugged his shoulders. "It would save us some time, and after all, there's nobody around."

Lucia smiled before pushing the parcel into his chest. "No one except for you. So, I'll wait."

Leo laughed, making his way in front of her. "As you wish, High Maiden."

*　*　*

As they made their way toward Aldric, night fell quickly, filled with long periods of silence. The night brought with it a heavy mist that hovered over the hills as they moved past and into a low valley filled with dying flowers. Leo thought about his city, wondering if the towering walls of shattered stone smoked, knowing that now they were far behind. After what seemed to be an eternity, at a quarter past midnight, the flowers led to a path that crept further into the fog.

The path narrowed as the hills rose around them, making the valley seem as if they were falling into the brush, sinking lower as they moved onward. More time had passed. It seemed as if they would never reach the edge of the forest. But as they continued, the flowers turned into vines, and the vines into heavy bushes, until finally they were surrounded by trees within the depths of the dark forest. It seemed they had found some way into the forested mountain, the dimension transformed right before their very eyes.

"The Pinea hills are so different now," Lucia started, pushing the vines from her face. She pulled a hood over her head to prevent the branches from snagging her hair as the two made their way through the woods. The clothes Leo had brought her had since made the journey more comfortable. Her cloak was chestnut, draping down her back, protecting her from the chill of the night, while her brown leather stockings protected her legs from the thorns and the stray twigs that would scratch her as she walked through the high grass. Her beige vest hugged a yellow blouse, protecting her torso from anything that might try to pierce her, just as the soles of her boots protected her feet from any sharp rocks she might step on.

"The forest serves as the border between Pinea and Aldric. Once we're through here, we'll be within the Aldric region," Leo said, peering backwards and squinting to get a better look at Lucia as she hurried behind him. "It gets darker from here on, so I'd stay close." Leo cut the bush ahead of them with his dagger.

Lucia watched as streams of moonlight dripped from the canopies of the forest, casting large shadows over them, freezing Lucia's heart and causing her hands to tremble. The darkness had her right where it wanted her, within the doubts and fears of this ghastly, mysterious forest. She whimpered, reaching for the pendant like she always did to find its comforting glow. Lucia's eyes hovered briefly, peering beyond the trees and into her mind. She nearly lost herself within it, before the sound of Leo's voice snapped her back into reality.

"The farther we go, the more the hills grow. They twist and

change as they become more like mountains. It's like a labyrinth."

"Is this your way of saying we're lost?" Lucia peered forward, understanding what he meant as the path split off around them into a network of different paths—a forest maze made to confuse and deter anyone from crossing. She realized that even the landscape could deceive you, turn against you, betray you. What web of secrets did this forest hold? What was it protecting? "Do you even know where you're going?"

"I've never actually made a trip to Aldric, but it is said that if you stay to the center and don't let yourself get distracted by the paths that present themselves, you'll make it through in no time." Leo scoffed. "I know it's just hearsay, but—" His voice became shaky and light as the chill of a thousand needles bristled over his skin.

There was a crackle of decay beneath each of their steps, and the forest thickened around them. The light of the sky thinned and the air became a tense mass of cold stench. The earth softened below them, drawing their feet deeper into the soil as if it meant to devour them. The forest itself seemed alive. It *was* alive. All was connected within the trees, the soil, and the very roots themselves. It was as if every leaf was an eye watching them, their prey, as they pressed through.

Leo finally continued, breaking the silence as they made their way down a steep hill. "It's all I've got. Is it just me or does the forest feel angry to you?"

Lucia nodded, huddling behind Leo. "Yes. It's strange, but not as far-fetched as it sounds. You feel it too?"

Leo peered back at her as she grabbed onto his shirt.

"Leo, it's as if I can feel the land's anguish, and right now, something's wrong." The forest was speaking to her, whispering softly beneath the tense moist air, words she could not understand but feel. It wanted her to know the pain it was in as the darkness consumed it. The Light Wings drew in the emotions of the forest, feeding them to Lucia's mind, and filling her with its many thoughts. So many thoughts, warning her of something—coming. Something terrible. "No," Lucia muttered, holding on to Leo as she held in a building urge to shriek. She lay her face to his back, feeling as the terror returned just as the forest's remaining light disappeared. It was nearly black. All Lucia heard were the sounds of her own footsteps. She shivered as nyctophobia—a fear of the night—pinched her insides.

Leo attempted to keep a pure focus on the central path ahead of them, but even he felt his fear collecting. He was not too sure he could keep himself on the right path, or even protect Lucia when the time came. Not in this blackness. But he paid attention to every action he made, no matter how difficult. Though he struggled to breathe himself, his will drew from within, anchoring onto something and helping him establish a sense of control. Every decision he made was crucial, and for Lucia's sake, he had to make the right ones. Fortunately for him, this made things easier. It was in that moment of recognizing this truth that Leo realized she was all that mattered to him. He looked back, barely seeing the outline of her hair through the faint glow of the Light Wings around her neck. He recognized it in her gentle face—the tense worry, the horror, and most of all, how every single sound that echoed around them tore at her psyche, nearly destroying her. There was no other way. He had to free her from the chains of fate's embrace.

"Are you alright?" Leo asked. His calm, deep voice broke through the tense moist air of the forest.

"Are you really asking me that?" Lucia asked, with her eyes as low as her voice.

"You're worrying me."

"Am I?" Lucia asked, parting a bit from him. She did not want to become a burden. The weight around her neck was heavy enough for her to bear on her own; there was no reason drag him down with her. Not after he'd lost so much. She did not want to cause any more pain or bring about any more destruction. She thought of Pinea and imagined all who had already died. In that moment, she prayed for peace—peace of mind. "I'm sorry."

Leo's eyebrows tilted. The words seeped in a bit and played around in Leo's mind, burning through his emotions like wildfire. There was nothing for her to be sorry for. Everything he did, everything he would do, was for her now, irrevocably so. He hesitated before uttering the words, almost weary of saying them. "I care. I—I care about you." He pushed forward and slid his dagger into its sheath. Leo couldn't determine why he couldn't stop thinking about her, or how she felt about everything happening to her, or how she felt about him or the things that were happening to him. His mind was racing in circles, chasing a far-off fantasy.

It bugged him. How vulnerable and melancholy she was, just as he hid beneath his woes within the depths his own sorrows. He couldn't ignore the way Lucia made him feel. There was something about the way she carried herself, something within her reason, that drew him magnetically toward her. Lucia lived with a sincerity that made her appear to be fragile and weak; but no, Lucia's weakness was her very strength. The desire to stay true to how she felt bound him, making it hard for him to hide his own emotions, to keep his cool as he was known to do. Leo bit his lip as he turned to his side and watched Lucia walk, her head down. He wrapped his hand over hers, sliding his fingers through her soft hands, but Lucia pulled away, crossing her arms, hiding her hands. It was like she didn't want to him to touch her. She was keeping her distance. This confused him even more, and he bowed his head in disappointment, feeling as though he had failed.

Lucia locked her gaze. She was hearing the whispers in her head now, the silent thoughts that invaded her subconscious. The echoes magnified the longer she wore the pendant. The more she prayed to the light, the easier it became to hear the Light Wings. If she prayed long enough, she could understand them. The words became clearer, as if they somehow connected her to another world, within a separate plane of existence. Within every passing moment, their power surged. And even more so in the darkness.

In the past, each new experience had confused Lucia more than the last; but as they ventured forth, she became more familiar with the Light Wings' hold over her, and the wisdom that they shared. They brought upon this sense of security, as if the echoes whispered some sort of assurance as she gave in to them. They promised her safety despite the circumstances, despite the pain she felt, the pain she would feel. Lucia could not deny that she was indeed bound—bound to the Light Wings and their purpose. This was a burden she alone had to bear. But maybe she could someday be free? The Light Wings dangled this thought within her mind, sending something electric through her hands and onto her fingertips. "Hope, it lies ahead of you." Lucia did not know what to make of the voice, but she did not question it. Hope was ahead of them. The answer, and her freedom, lay just outside these hills. She just had to believe.

Suddenly, Leo saw something in the distance. It was a light at the end of a long tunnel, a bright gate that broke through the green far off in front of them.

Lucia's chest pulled toward the threshold as if the Light Wings longed for the daylight to fall within their clear white diamond and be filled with its grace once more. The Light Wings desired to feel and reflect, but more importantly to feed upon light and all its power. Lucia clenched the pendant as her breath was abruptly taken from her. The Light Wings' anguish broke through her psyche, sending a sharp shrill as she fell to her knees. *What is this?* Lucia thought desperately as she pulled herself up. The Light

Wings flickered as a pain cut through her chest. She groaned a bit, silently, unable to relax as her life was seemingly pulled from her. The loud ringing then rose higher inside her head, and all she could do was hold her breath as she tried to force it to slumber, but the pendant was too strong.

It became clear that the Light Wings were depleting her of her strength to fuel their own. Deprived of the light, they sought their master even at the expense of Lucia's life force. Lucia had no choice. She had to run—or die. She threw Leo aside and bolted ahead of him, but the light was still too distant.

Leo fell onto a knee but caught himself. He jerked his head upward as Lucia stumbled into the high grass far in front of him, struggling to climb uphill. "Lucia, what are you doing now?" he asked through his teeth biting down, his canines sharp, as he prevented himself from losing his temper. He looked ahead of her as he worked to pull his thoughts together. "Are you mad?" he shouted, racing after her, trying to keep a close eye on her and observing for any immediate danger nearby. He hurried behind, hoping she would signal to him that she was indeed all right; but as he paced up toward her, the tense air chilled, condensing the humidity of the forest air, bringing forth a heavy mist closing in behind them. Leo's hair stood on end as it rippled like a wave through his back. He could almost hear it, the demented snicker of the phantom approaching them.

At that moment, his worst fears came to present as the fog swirled about. The danger did not lie ahead but rather behind them. He quickened the pace, running at full speed, trying not to trip over the vines and roots of the trees as he jumped ahead. "Lucia, move! Keep going," he yelled from behind her as the voice echoed through the forest.

Lucia couldn't hear Leo's words. All she could hear was that painful ringing as the very essence of her life was being sucked from her chest. She couldn't focus on anything but reaching the end of this damned forest. It was consuming every breath, every ounce of energy she had. She had to reach that light. Her adrenaline was pumping, causing her body to move in ways it never had. The Light Wings took full control. This speed and strength had never existed before and came as if from nowhere. As incredible as it was, it still pained her and starved her of her own energy. She hungered. She had to reach the sunlight before the last of her light was depleted.

Leo heard it now, the darkness ruffling behind them. The sudden growl of wolves emitted through the air as they rose from the ground and poured out from the shades of the forest and into the vast meadow, their eyes glowing like embers within the mist. They flooded from the heavy density of the trees, shrouded by the shadows that created them with their garnet eyes set on the maiden, so helpless and vulnerable ahead of them. They brushed past Leo and towards her and her alone, to the flickering light. He struggled, unable to keep up, the beasts were too fast. They had a power far beyond his own mortal strength, and as they continuously poured around him, he watched as the nightmare gripped him.

Leo did not cower. He refused to bend to the will of the force that was driven by fear. It would not break him, not again and not like this. He pulled forth his silver dagger and darted forward, lunging downward, slashing at the beasts and tearing his knife into the tar-like dark flesh of the darkness' illusions. However, the metal of his blade would only split the darkness in two and, with one quick roar, transformed it into a pillar that wrapped around Leo's arm and tossed him. The darkness reformed to pursue Lucia once more. He clashed into a far tree, stunned when his skull cracked against its bark. He tumble forward, landing face down. He wearily opened his eyes, trying hard to regain his sight, and only managed to yell, "Lucia, they're behind you!"

Lucia's senses were overloaded as the Light Wings pierced into her heart. The pain sprouted upward like the pull of a knife stuck in her ribs. With its power overwhelming, she couldn't control it, couldn't stop it from consuming her. Her will was no longer her own. Her eyes began to sparkle, glittering a bright gold. She must surrender herself to the Light Wings. It was her only choice. "Stop resisting," they said as they flickered brightly and emitted strikes of white lightning around her. They catapulted Lucia into the air, throwing her forward, her eyes now glowing intensely.

Leo watched as Lucia propelled into the air, her chest sprouting a huge light that seemed to peel and pull from her body. She fell forward with a thud as the light pulsed through the forest, shattering the waves of beasts emerging from it. They dissolved like shattering stained glass into sparks of many colors. Magenta, violet, cerulean, pale yellow—the orbs of light ascended upwards until there was nothing left.

Lucia's body was aching, burning. Her sight was blurring as each of her senses numbed. She had lost every ounce of what energy sent her forward, yet she still felt the pull, the thirst. The Light Wings had taken as much life as they could to protect themselves, but she needed to reach the end so she could feed on the light.

Leo rushed, his dark hair pulling back over his forehead. He nearly slid as he dropped to her side. Lucia struggled to catch her breath. He quickly scanned her for injuries but found nothing. She gulped for air, unable to speak, as Leo struggled to understand what was happening to her. "Lucia, what's wrong?" He panicked. "Please, tell me." His blue eyes teared as she shook. "What do I do?"

Lucia's energy continued to seep from her and into the dimming Light Wings. She felt it go as her body went cold. She was dying, or at the very least, she felt like she was; but the burning pull within her chest, the hunger, would not grant her even that mercy. The pendant continued to draw on her spirit, directing it toward the light. It was painful to speak. The words caught like thorns in her throat. Leo's tears dripped onto her face, merging with her own. "L—light . . ." She pointed her golden gaze toward the exit at the end as the sunlight seeped in.

At first, Leo could not fully comprehend what Lucia must be telling him; but he picked her up, thinking as much that he should get her away from the dangers of the forest. He held her limp, weary body in his arms. Her body was like a thread connected to her life, lingering in some sort of limbo, bound but far apart.

Leo hurried, his gaze shrewd. He couldn't lose her, the only person he had left, his reason for living. He could not imagine going on without her. The world would surely end with the darkness claiming the last piece of his sanity. Victorious.

He was not far from the opening, just feet away, as he jumped forward and into the light of the sun and clear hills vacant of forest. The sunlight fell over them, and he looked down to Lucia as it hit the Light Wings, sending out a brilliant force reflecting and absorbing the light while finally filling with life. Lucia's lungs gulped a heavy breath as her sight returned to her. She stared into Leo's precious jewel-like eyes, seeing how handsome he was, even with smears and smudges of dirt covering his face. Especially now, as Leo put her down and brushed his knuckles to the side of her face.

Lucia blinked wildly. She hunched on her side and placed a hand to her head as Leo kneeled next to her. She could not yet put into words what had happened, but when the light had touched the Light Wings, her body had returned to her. Her pain receded. It was instantaneous, as if somehow her life and the light were somehow connected, bound to the same place. The Light Wings could not live without the light, so they had nearly taken Lucia's life—but why? What was she missing? What did she not know?

"Leo, I don't understand." She hesitated, grabbing the wings around her neck. "It was so bizarre. I can't even explain what happened, or why even, not the slightest bit."

"Why did you run?" he asked, palpating her legs, still examining her for any injuries. He wanted to make sure she was okay. He had nearly lost her, and truthfully, there could be nothing more terrifying.

"I don't know," Lucia said, touching her head. "I felt this sudden pain, like hunger, consume me. It was overwhelming and caused me to act without thinking. I lost control. I needed to be in the light as if my life depended on it." She looked down. "The Light Wings panicked. Without the light, I could feel the pendant drain me as if it needed my life to power its own. It used my strength to defend itself but nearly killed me in the process, because it had no power left to use. It used mine instead."

Leo stared at her in puzzlement. "You could sense the danger, couldn't you? The darkness came in the form of wolves."

"No, I sensed nothing but the Light Wings' longing," Lucia said. "They tried to get me the closest to the light, so they took over completely. I felt so helpless."

"What was that power anyways? What power are you talking about? What power did it take from you?"

"My life . . . I could feel it drain, depleting with every moment. My life force was being used to sustain its light, because they had lost their own."

"So when the sunlight hit you, or the Light Wings, more specifically, they released you."

Lucia touched the diamond and sighed with a slight nod. "Precisely."

Leo's eyes widened as he shook his head. "It's just like the legend."

Lucia tilted her head, trying to recall the legend he spoke of. "I don't follow."

"The story of how light and darkness created the world." Leo thought hard, trying to bring the story together, making sense of it more than ever before. "It is said that the light created the heavens and all life, while darkness created the earth and death so that there would always be a balance. We live and die to be buried and return to the earth and allow our lives to cycle through it, in turn, bringing about the grass, the trees, and everything else."

Leo lowered his voice as he continued. "Life *is* light. It drew on your life because that's the closest thing it had to the light itself. And that's what the darkness is so eager to destroy. It brings death in order to thwart its rival, but the light refuses to lose. I bet that's why the Light Wings were created, to preserve the balance in case the darkness tried to overthrow it . . . . But how could the darkness grow so strong so quickly?"

"This is all a game, isn't it?" Lucia asked, her head fuzzy. "Our gods are playing with us."

"I know it can feel like that, but I think there's more to it." Leo looked to the sky. "This could have been the end of everything." He rose to his feet as the wind blew over the horizon.

The sun was setting, and Lucia was lucky to have arrived in the clearing of light before it had. This made her feel like her destiny relied on pure chance. What if Leo had not been there to bring her into the light? What if the sun had not been shining? Would the Light Wings have burst and let her die? Would they fail themselves? How could this be fate when there was a limit to the light's power, a limit to the life they had, and a *chance* they could lose? There was a limit set that Lucia had failed to even notice. She would have to be careful from now on because, just as the world depended on the wings, the wings depended on the savior to uphold their light. She could fall just as easily as the world could. "Hopefully, the Carists know the rest of the story."

Leo stared longingly toward Lucia, who now stared at the blue sea in the distance. "Lucia, you are everything Terestria needs. The world—" Leo hesitated. "*I* can't afford to lose you."

"That's the ocean?" Lucia asked almost as if she did not hear him. She did, but she decided then that it was better to pretend like she didn't.

"Yes, the Aldric Sea. Aldric lies left on the coast of the west bank. That is where the Carist tribe lives."

Lucia was touching her neck, saddened suddenly. Her emotions crumbled beneath the foundation of the new energy that filled her. "Leo, I don't want that to ever happen again. It mustn't."

"Can't you just take off the Light Wings before, so they don't drain you?"

Lucia hadn't considered that. The thought never crossed her mind. It could just be as simple as that, couldn't it? Maybe she could abandon the pendant right there. Couldn't she? She could take it off and throw it into the ocean and forget about it. Light knew, she wanted to. She reached behind her neck, beneath her hair, and searched for the latch that undid the chain. She turned the chain and felt no such thing. It was as if it had melted and disappeared completely. Lucia's hand felt and felt for it, but it was as if the chain was never meant to come off. "I can't. The latch, it's not there!"

"Impossible," Leo said, examining the chain behind her. But he, too, found no latch and no escape.

"What if I break it? I can still break it, right?" Lucia asked frantically, prepared to pull. But Leo jumped and grabbed her hand and pulled it down gently.

"No, Lucia. Don't be foolish. We need this."

"But," Lucia whined.

"It's too small to fit around your head. It seems as if you're stuck with it."

Lucia frowned and tilted her head with a stomp of her foot. "Why does this disappoint me?" She huffed at the beautiful piece of jewelry that had enslaved her. "There goes my freedom." She tugged, without Leo's approval, but the chain would not break no matter how hard she pulled. The pendant was bound to her neck. She was indeed stuck with it, just as Leo had said.

The weight of the world fell on her shoulders. She felt trapped and seemingly forever bound with this burden. She was supposed to feel something else, wasn't she? Honored, perhaps. But no. She felt nothing of the sort. This was no honor. This was a punishment. A conviction. Deep down, Lucia knew that despite not understanding why. Droplets began to form at the base of her golden eyes as Leo studied the chain at the back of her neck. The omen, as light and beautiful as it may be, was hers to deal with until the end.

CHAPTER NINE

Contempt of the Carist

Lucia paced behind Leo, her head tilted away from the setting sun, shielding her pale gaze from the magenta streaks of light bouncing off the ocean and onto the silver cliffs of the vast Aldric region. A heavy breeze was flowing through her hair, coming off the sands of the lower shores, and filling her nostrils with the rich smell of salt and sulfur. A lingering heartache persisted as she walked, deepening with every step, with the fear of the coming night.

Despite now knowing the destiny she was charged with, Lucia's fragile spirit had cracked, leaving her hope fiercely shattered into dust. What faith she had before was fading with each passing second. She had only begun to realize what she had lost. In mere moments, her home, her freedom, her life was stripped from her like bark from a tree. Her will was now bound to the pendant. Its fate sealed to her own. The Light Wings had taken everything from her. She thought back to her life in Moz, remembering how she felt then, restrained within the walls of her manor and bound by the claims of duty her mother had set. But now, she appreciated how fortunate she once was—how privileged she had been. Lucia was plagued by memories of all the things she took for granted. Because now she was a hostage, trapped within an open world of danger, bound by the lies and secrets of her father. At this moment, she'd rather be dead to be rid of the imminent sense of chaos. It lay deep inside her, strangling anything she had once found to be right. No longer could she trust the faith that had once led her. Everything she had lived for was nothing more than an object set to deceive, and for the first time in her life, Lucia thought how selfish the light must be. To ask so much of her, to forsake her as it did now. What was her father thinking, bequeathing this pendant to her?

As the sky darkened, a strange glow appeared in the distance. It broke eerily through the air, and Lucia watched as Leo moved toward it, desperately, unrelentingly. She couldn't make out Aldric's capital at first, but as they moved closer, it became clear that the city was growing, turning more monumental and standing tall beyond that of anything she had ever laid eyes upon. As they approached the capital from the south, the colossal structure of its gate rose from the ground like a mirage hovering over the edge of a cliff. The gate was made up of cylindrical pillars of silver and shining light—light that emitted powerfully, not by flame and not by mirrors as Lucia had seen in Pinea, but purely of bright, shimmering green light generated by something unseen.

They eventually found their way to a long trail of glowing structures that hummed with a strange sound. The trail led them to the edge of a gate that stood almost like a tower itself, topped with a gigantic bird statue that loomed over them with a condescending stare. Leo took Lucia's hand and hurried toward the guards, past the strange misshapen structures, and to the area's main threshold.

They stepped up a wide staircase and onto a platform covered with etchings of winged beasts. Light poured through the crevices beneath their feet as they walked. Where was the light coming from? Lucia couldn't help but wonder. The power itself seemed to rival that of the Light Wings, but she knew this couldn't be possible. The light had to come from somewhere, from a natural source. There was no other way.

Around them were many citizens sitting and conversing with each other. Their conversations were indistinguishable, for they spoke in a dialect Lucia did not know, but she somehow understood. Their bodies changed the moment their eyes met hers—how distrusting they were. The Carists lowered their voices as the outsiders made their way to the center of the platform.

Lucia noticed how unusually dressed the Carists were, growing tense as they stared her down. She had seen many odd fashions in her eighteen years, from the headmistress of Sky University—Professor Patricia, who had a very abnormal taste in exotic furs—to the very twig-like noble Sir Christopher Lyles of Eastern Villa, who anointed each of his robes with a layer of exquisite gemstones. But these Carists were beyond that. They were all dressed in beautiful armor, so unlike the armor of the Mozian and Pinian armed forces. Light and fit to their body, the armor featured silk robes that gracefully draped from their backs, like wings. There were symbols within their armor, carved very delicately along the glossy exterior of each plate.

The females had masks that covered their faces, detailed and decorated with a variety of colors to each resemble something different. Each mask was individual and unique. A young girl to

Lucia's left had a mask that resembled a violet-and-black butterfly, while another much farther ahead of her resembled some sort of aquatic creature with ravishing painted scales up the sides.

The sudden rush of this newfound culture sent Lucia's mind spiraling. She could not escape their gazes as the crowd moved forward, waiting to gain access to the city. It appeared that they had to check in with a series of guards, all dressed in this same fashion and standing at a row of altars. Everyone was waiting for their name to be recorded and their entry into the city to be permitted by the guards. The Carists were strict and set in ways that discouraged Lucia; but Leo remained assertive, keeping his eyes forward on the guards in front of him. His sapphire stare was fixed along with his determination to honor his father's wish. He sent a slight reassuring squeeze to Lucia's hand to appease her as her mind wandered deeper into worry.

To see how Aldric had prospered so far made Lucia wonder. What knowledge did Aldric use to leave both Pinea and Moz so far behind? Their innovations had made this bright city a marvelous emerald along the shore, a beacon for all mankind to envy, yet her own city was on the brink of discord. And within Leo's, people were surely suffering. A sudden flash of anger coursed inside her, building as her stomach knotted and her heart flared. How could this knowledge not be shared? To what lengths did the Carists hold their secrets? And why would these secrets be the very key to the survival of their world? What responsibility did Aldric share with the rest of Terestria's provinces as the threat of darkness loomed over them? Aldric had cast a shadow over them. If the Carists truly held the answer to what was happening, their negligence put the rest of the world at risk and sealed their fates.

If the Carists knew the truth, the blood of Moz and Pinea would be on their hands, for people had died for their arrogance and their inability to enlighten others. This was an injustice.

Lucia clamped her eyes shut as vengeful tears dripped from her lashes. A shroud of pain consumed her as she heard the cries of her dying people over and over again in her head. Her emotions were suddenly overwrought. Why was she feeling this? What was wrong with her?

Lucia attempted to drown her anguish, fearing that if someone spotted her weakness, it would only make it more real. For so long, this was what she'd been taught. Lucia could not be weak, no matter how painful things were. She had to force away the pain, not only for the light, but for her mother and for her people. *Duty above all else.* Lucia held to this undeniable expectation, one she felt she could never live up to. But now, she had no choice but to accept her destiny as the seeds of corruption became more apparent to her. And to all those who saw her, her conviction was clearly written across her face.

Leo had only begun to understand how this judgment confined Lucia, forcing her thoughts to take on what most people shouldn't. That was her duty, to face these worries with a heavy heart so that others wouldn't have to. He wanted to help Lucia, to show her how to quell the emotions raging inside her; but right now, he felt powerless. He, too, was frail by his own right. Perhaps because he also needed to find his own duty, his own sense of control.

"Next," called the guard, pointing to them with a gloved finger. Leo nodded and pulled Lucia along with him. "State your name, birth province, and class. After I record this, state your purpose."

"Leocadio Feral, sir of Pinea," he said.

The guard looked doubtfully toward Leo and then to Lucia. "And you?" he asked, tilting his head toward Lucia, who was distracted by his strange accent.

"I'm Lucia Sanoon." She hesitated and then said quietly, "High maiden of Moz."

The guard seemed to squint beneath his visor, staring dubiously, which had been shaped into an emerald-colored serpent with violet horns. "What kind of business do two young people, especially of your class, if that *is* your class, have here in Aldric?" He obviously had some sort of suspicion, but he wrote down their information anyway in a large metal-covered book that appeared to be very heavy. He hesitated, waiting for a response. "So?"

"We need to arrange a meeting with the chief elder immediately," Leo said. "However, I don't want to alarm anyone." He whispered it slowly, full of concern. "Both Moz and Pinea have been attacked."

The guard's eyes widened beneath his visor, and he stepped back. He swallowed, sweat forming along the side of his neck. "Attacked, you say?" He lowered his voice so no one could hear.

"Yes. By a destructive force beyond our understanding. My father claimed that the Carist chief, Talon Renon, might hold knowledge of what exactly the force might be and how we could stop it. We don't have much time. It is highly likely that Aldric could be next."

Lucia stayed quiet as they whispered. She looked around as the people took notice of their hushed conversation. There was a certain tension in the faces of the adults. But what made Lucia most uncomfortable was gazing into the faces of the children, who seemed so happy, oblivious to the peril they were in. Just by being here, Lucia brought danger upon them. She wore an omen of light beneath her neck, and she was in no way proud of what it stood for. Leo squeezed her hand, and Lucia looked up at him.

"Stand back," Leo said. "They are about to open the gate."

"What happened?" Lucia asked. "What did he say?"

"He is going to personally escort us to the main tower. He's actually the head of Aldric's defense squadron and assumes this to be some terrorist threat."

"Didn't you tell him about the Light Wings, or what Sigranole said about my father? This isn't the antic of some terrorists," Lucia said, shaking her head." It's something far worse."

"I know," Leo whispered back. "He wouldn't listen. They have their own information, but the people are unaware, and he prefers, as should we, not to cause a panic. But even so, he seems to lack insight on the matter himself. It's as if the chief elder withheld information from the military as well. He will only abide by the chief's command."

"For what reason would he lie to the people, with so much at risk?" Lucia blinked her eyes wildly.

"I haven't the slightest idea. The same way our parents, as governors, kept the information of the war from our people, we altered our own history into something believable, to assume control," Leo said. "Our people are liars too. We mustn't judge without looking at our own first."

"But this isn't our world. It's theirs: these forces, they aren't myth. The world belongs to them, and that's why we're no longer safe. That's our reality!"

"Shhh," Leo hissed. "We have to wait until we make it to the main tower. Talon will have to tell us one way or another."

"And if he doesn't believe us?"

Leo tossed his dark bangs to the side. "Then we prove it."

Lucia stepped back and clenched the diamond. She knew exactly what he meant, and it would involve her using the light again, despite it almost killing her before. But she had no choice, did she? This is what she would have to do. After all, the Light Wings were the key to saving Terestria. In the end, it was to be their salvation. Yet still, amongst these people, there was a budding hostility within this place, something unwelcoming. Lucia carried this intuition. Aldric did not *want* to be saved. It could not.

"When I was in the sanctuary back home, I felt so sure of everything. There was always something to believe in. Nothing made me feel safer than my faith. My mother had raised me to believe in the good of the world and to place my faith in it. As long as you held on to your faith in the light and all its gifts, your prayers would be answered. You would stand protected because your virtue would be your shield." She paused, feeling the next question echo through her mind. Sincerely, she asked as if it were the first time she had truly thought about it without being blind to the bias of what she thought she knew. "What happens when we die?"

Leo gave her a wild look, full of confusion. He relaxed his face and parted his lips as if to say something but retracted his words and thought again. "I'm not sure, but that is part of the story, isn't it? The legend about light and dark, life and death . . . ."

"Two forces created the world. One gave us life, and one gave us death, indoctrinating a balance that would exist for all time, but never did I ever think about what happens after that. We return to the earth, but then what?" She held out her hand and pointed at her chest. "What happens to our hearts? Where do our spirits go?"

"It is said to return to the creator to cycle through time. I never really understood it really; not beyond what my tutors taught me."

"The light created the heavens and life. The darkness created the earth and death, yet we do not know which creator we go back to. Who claims our souls? That which breathed our very lives into us, or that to which our bodies are sent after we die?"

Leo laughed and sent her another squeeze of the hand. "So inquisitive, yet so naive."

"Don't call me naive," Lucia said with a sigh. "I'm just thinking."

"I don't know all the answers either, Lucia. But if I must say, being a philosopher truly suits you." Leo smiled. "You really do think like a lady, you know."

"I'm hardly a lady yet," Lucia said. "I don't know these things, yet something tells me they are important." She bowed her head as her thoughts deepened. "I can't rule and know nothing. I can't expect anyone to lead their lives without some sort of knowledge of their own. We need to know the truth. With the truth comes our freedom."

Leo's grin widened. "And we will be free soon enough."

Leo's mood was contagious, causing Lucia's spirits to rise just a bit, pulling her from the depths of worry and into something more hopeful. She nudged the side of Leo's shoulder, while he leaned his head back onto hers with a chuckle. Lucia smiled too, distracted by Leo's charm. Her faith lifted from the depths of the anguish that bound her and into something bright. Despite losing his father and his home, Leo remained so carefree. How did he do it? How did he manage to escape the struggles of his grief and harbor his own despair? She looked up into the dark sky, examining the white studs that sparkled over the purple plane. And then she heard it, the echo of a thought that was not her own: "As long as there is light, there is hope."

"Hope?" she asked herself, as if there were more meaning to the word. "Why do you keep saying that word?"

"Saying what?" Leo asked.

Lucia straightened up and rubbed her cheek. "Uh . . . . It's nothing. Don't worry about it." *Here we go* she thought as she rolled her eyes. *I'm absolutely losing it.* Now she wasn't merely listening to voices inside her head, but she was actually starting to speak back to them, meeting her very own definition of insanity.

The Carist commander approached them, emitting a sort of arrogance that brought Leo a sense of intimidation, though he knew he had nothing to be afraid of. The Carists had information that they solely needed, and Leo was determined to get it, no matter the cost. The Carists would be foolish to try to harm them considering what was at stake. It was a fair bargain, he assumed, information in exchange for safety from the threat that could very well mean the end of them both.

"Come. I'll show you into the city." The guard's voice was emotionless, and rather loud.

Lucia gently squeezed Leo's forearm, and it was as if she could send her thoughts directly into his mind. *Something is wrong about this place.*

Somehow, Leo understood the words beneath the touch, feeling the same intuition blaze in the pit of his stomach. Something was indeed not right.

They were led to the large gate which flashed with light that leaked from the tiny carvings etched across it. A piercing roar rang out as the gate lowered into the earth. Lucia was eager to see what might lie beyond the threshold. Her anticipation built up, along with her fears, but she found relief in the light as it cloaked her. It was strong. Lucia knew this because it seeped into her pendant and filled her with its radiance. She just hoped she would be powerful enough to fight off whatever darkness might try to consume it.

The gate disappeared beneath the platform, and the sound of rushing water came from the distance. Lucia smelled the ocean as she followed Leo and the commander inside. The water lifted into the air, forming into a light mist, crisp with salt and cool to the touch. Lucia rubbed the moisture between her fingers.

A large network of rivers webbed throughout the city, shining blue like veins within the body. *Flowing light,* Lucia thought as she was tempted to kneel and dip her fingers into it. Each riverside was connected by a bridge, and alongside them were metallic buildings, similar in architecture but differing in size. The rivers separated the different sections of the city, creating what appeared to be a collection of various islands. As the buildings got smaller, they became more populated with people. It was not difficult to see how the city functioned. Aldric was divided by these rivers, with a marketplace and many groups of houses similar to the neighborhoods and districts in Moz. As they walked farther Lucia noticed what she had seen from behind the gate. Large lighted towers, massive in scale, were elevated over the destination of all the rivers flowing within the outer wall. There, all the waters fell into the sea, creating a massive waterfall hurling down onto the shores below.

The city floated along a cliff, dangling atop a clouded waterfall, powered by the water as it entered the towers and dropped below. *So strange*, Lucia thought. And there, at the edge of this cliff, existed the most lavish, marvelous, and elegant piece of all the architecture within the city walls. This building was cut of marble, coated with a shiny glaze that reflected the light, making it seem to glow itself. It was a column, fluted and tall, and its crown was a shimmering ember of citrine, emitting a strange incandescence of amber-colored flames. It stretched upward and stood at the highest point of the city, past where the rivers met, behind two long, stone bridges and atop a large arch-shaped island where the water fell from behind.

Lucia gasped as the citrine emitted a powerful blast of fire and smoke right before her eyes. She could feel the heat as she winced and shuddered as the flames dispersed. But soon, her senses fell back into reality, apart from the haze and illusion of her premonition. She held Leo's arm as the guard stopped, looking at the citrine crystal. Shining, still, and absolutely solid.

"Across the bridge is the Glass Tower. That is where the council will listen to your plea and determine their judgment."

"What judgment, a plea? What are we, on trial?" Leo asked with a hint of sarcasm. His eyes were now cold, burning through his icy blue stare.

"You asked for our help, remember?" The guard growled. "If your provinces are under attack, as you say they are, I would mind your tongue. After all the trouble they have caused amongst themselves in the past, I wouldn't doubt that they are the subject of their own folly. If terrorists are running amuck, trying to start another war between your nations, I'd much rather keep Aldric out of it.

"But still"—the guard approached Leo—"if Aldric is in any danger, we must defend our home, even from the likes of you and your pathetic wars. If you wish for our help, you must state reason enough to help you keep the peace. If not good enough, all you've accomplished is wasting the time of our grand council, and we will be more than happy to be rid of you. We take care of our own here. Our tribe has remained neutral for ages. It would shame us to help provinces bring dishonor upon themselves."

Leo twitched as his face flared red. He pulled his silver dagger from its sheath and grasped it within his fist. Lucia pushed between them. She exhaled as Leo panted, his rage apparent as his eyes blazed like blue fire.

"You're supposed to be an admiral of Aldric's defense squadron, yet I see nothing but a coward standing here before me. You bring shame to your own existence with your prejudices. You are not worthy of your title. You are not worthy enough to protect your own people, because you deny the truth. We didn't come here to ask for your damn help. We're here to save you!"

" Leo," Lucia said, quite surprised she'd have to be saying "behave yourself, please!" She broadened her shoulders between the men.

"I act only at the request of the council. Here, we are neutral unless our aid is absolutely necessary in protecting our city. It's most likely that no danger will come here. Our tribe is keen in both body and mind. We can defend ourselves. We won't act according to demands placed by two obviously disoriented youths." The guard scoffed at Lucia's troubled face, clearly apathetic. He was even less reactive to the piercing glare of Leo's sapphire stare. Something was indeed wrong, but it was not clear what. The guard had seemed so worried before, but once he passed the gate, he had entered into some sort of other facade. Why so careless to his duty? Why so repulsive of their plight? "All I can do is lead you here. You're on your own."

"Fine," Leo said, his tolerance wearing thin. "We can take care of ourselves. Why don't you make yourself useful and get lost before I grow tired of your presence and remove you myself?"

"Leo, this is not the time to be lashing out with threats." Lucia took a deep breath, contemplating the irony of the situation. Usually, she could not contain her emotions, but this time, it seemed as if Leo was on the verge of losing his temper and ruining any chance they had of making their case.

"If you could handle your own, you wouldn't be here. We have complete reason to distrust you and no reason to believe you." The guard turned from them and walked away.

Leo balled up his fist, his anger flowing red in his face. "That selfish pig," he said. "He *chooses* not to listen." He mocked. "Why can't he see how dire this is?"

There were no words that could justify the commander's actions, and Lucia couldn't help but feel slightly disappointed. Aldric was the land of scholars, and the Carists were longtime keepers of the knowledge they needed, yet the whole city seemed to be ignorant of the truth. The commander was so dim to the severity of the situation that he was incapable of garnering even the slightest grain of sympathy. It was apparent that he acted only as the council directed, not as a commander or leader of any kind. He was the epitome of a contradiction to the very definition of duty. To Lucia, he was a pawn, nothing more. It saddened her to think that Leo's words were perhaps true. This ignorance was shameful.

And all this made Lucia wonder if she was guilty of the same: taking orders in blind faith. In that regard, she could relate, yet the ways of the Carists were so different than her own. Lucia held firmly to this belief that there was something surely missing within Aldric's walls. If not duty, what else? To what standard, what virtue, did the Carists oblige themselves to? To that of man, or that of what could not be understood or explained?

The Carists did not see a threat coming, because they chose to ignore it. The threat was right in front of them, within their walls, despite believing otherwise. What they needed was an immediate defense to be put up around the city, not a justification for doing so. What more must they tell them? Two provinces were under attack, and still the Carists would deny them? The key to stopping this monstrosity could very well lay before them, but now it appeared as if it may be nearly impossible to get the tribe to cooperate. If the Carist commander was like this, there was no telling how the chief elder would be. And if he did not believe them, how could they protect Aldric at all—or anyone else?

Lucia thought of her father, who had been cast away. He probably had been treated all the same. This made Lucia feel even more that this was an impossible mission. She simply could not find the strength to say it.

"The city is in danger, Lucia. The darkness has taken Moz and Pinea. Yet still, the Carists have the nerve to consider rejecting us. He spoke like *we* were the problem, like *we* were the terrorists. We're not. Our people aren't—"

"Leo, don't work yourself up over this." Lucia took his hand in hers. "I know what he said hurt you. You've lost so much, but you haven't lost yourself. You know what you're here to do. So, do what you do best, and keep your cool." She was staring into

Leo's sapphire gaze when he smiled, appeased by the comfort of her touch.

He put a hand to her cheek and said, "Is that what you really think of me? You think I'm cool?"

Lucia smiled back at him. "Well, you've got a very distinctive temperament."

"It's just that"—Leo blinked as he tried to relax—"they act like they're so damn perfect and righteous. You don't need a reason to save someone, even from themselves. Why is it so hard to believe some things just happen in the world? There are things we can't explain. We have to accept that. They will lose everything just as we did. They are no different than us." He bowed his head. The Carists' greatest strength would bring about their downfall. It was their arrogance, their vanity, that made them weak. It shocked Leo how the most advanced tribe to ever exist within Terestria could be the most closed-minded and stubborn of them all. "They're heartless."

"Stop thinking like that." Lucia squeezed his hand. "Let's go find Talon."

"Do you think he will tell us what he knows?"

"That idiot was foolish," Lucia said. "I highly doubt the chief elder will be. I assure you. He'll listen. And if he doesn't, somebody else will. Have a little hope."

"Why so optimistic?" Leo asked, genuinely surprised.

Lucia had been struggling to accept her duty this entire journey. And now, it was as if she'd found something to hold onto. "Leo, the will of one man doesn't define that of an entire people. Someone will help us. I just know, okay?" She looked up at the bright citrine atop the tower, imagining the flames once more. The heat hit her face as a distant echo of a crackle of thunder came from afar. "Talon will have no choice but to see the truth." She lifted her palm, feeling the light tingle in the tips of her fingers.

"He won't say no."

Leo's eyes widened as the sparkles of light drifted up and into the atmosphere like fireflies.

"Remember what Sigranole said about Talon, the story of the darkness and how it rose from the bloodshed of Frailty's War? Maybe that's what he meant. The Carists know of this, and they blame us for what has befallen our people," Lucia said. "They judge us for what they know of us. They have no other perception."

Leo took a deep breath. "Judged for the sake of the knowledge they keep secret. And with their secrets, they control the fate of their people and the world." He trembled with disgust. The origins of the world had been reduced to secrets, and truth turned to myth, cultivating a lie that would provide power over the masses. Secrecy would destroy this city, and the Carists, too, would fault their own leaders.

Lucia's eyes widened, and suddenly it hit her like a heavy storm on a shore of shattered glass. Could it have been there all this time? Or was there something else she should be seeking? Within her kingdom was a place said to be of great knowledge and prestige, rumored to hold many secrets. But why had she not thought of this before? *Sky University.* She held her breath before releasing it softly, comforted by the sudden thought. It brought her a surge of excitement, but still she knew she could not go back there. She hoped maybe the light would let her, because there would be something she needed to retrieve, something she could not find here.

She enclosed her hand around the diamond, feeling its power. It was pulsing softly, like a heartbeat and very much alive. Something about this situation was menacing. It was quickening and sending a rush of defensive power through her body. It filled her hands, electrifying her. Lucia shook her head as her senses intensified, sharpening the feeling of the cold storm stinging her face. She felt it coming long before it even touched the shore, from within the walls of Aldric's fragile ego. The sky was dark with the night, and the stars were shining bright, yet something was coming from the sea, perhaps from its depths—a threat they could not see.

"Let's hurry," Lucia said. "We're running out of time."

CHAPTER TEN

Dove's Plight

They hustled toward the looming tower. The citrine crystal could not foresee the darkness that was coming, and the chief elder could not save them now despite all they had hoped for. However, it was precisely their hope that brought them to this tower of glistening marble. Lucia trekked up a wide staircase toward the tower's threshold, to a pair of seemingly impassable shiny granite doors. As she looked back at the ever-darkening sky, the stars disappeared behind the shadows of thickening clouds. Though the artificial light of the bright city reflected off the base of the overcast, Lucia knew it held no chance against the developing storm—the same storm that had fallen onto Pinea and cast it into flames.

She approached the doors and examined them with her hands, feeling the glossy exterior beneath her fingertips. The doors were stiff against her palms, but Lucia did not let that worry her. Slowly, she lifted up her fist and knocked her knuckles against the granite, letting the sound vibrate through the doors and echo behind it. Dust raised from underneath her feet, and she instinctively jumped backward. The doors opened inward to reveal the haze of a long-slanted staircase, one that wound upward into the unknown.

Lucia and Leo stepped warily inside, as if they were falling into a trap. They felt the unseen enemy watching them, sensing it from the shadows. Lucia tried to ignore this as her body was overcome with emotion. With deep breaths, she grounded herself by focusing on the present moment and the grand architecture that made up this wonder.

The tower's interior was astonishing. Lamps illuminated the doorway and hung from the walls as the staircase wrapped around to guide them through the massive cylindrical structure. As they pressed forward, the stairway led branched to platforms and hallways with distinct areas. Certainly there was some truth to its name: the Glass Tower. The tower appeared to be a web of stone and glass, with a clear view upward. The more they rose, the more their destination opened up to them, and all while the citrine high above them became more visible. Carist statues were stylized atop pedestals beside each doorway, watching the pair as they proceeded higher, their stares growing more ominous with each step. Lucia couldn't help but think of the place as some sort of museum.

Eventually, they came upon a platform that stretched from the chamber of the stairwell. It extended around them as the steps continued up, connecting to many bridges that further expanded the Carists' web of secrets. Leo stepped off, and Lucia followed, her eyes locked on the citrine at the very top sparkling overhead like a watchful eye. She still felt the heat of her vision from earlier that night on her face. The exploding crystal was still present within her mind. *Please, do not be true.*

The platform was the shape of a circle and had bookcases with many shelves, with ladders and bridges between them. They appeared to be in a library of sorts, filled with busy scholars. The Carists did not notice them at first. Many stood whispering at the base of the bookcases, while others sat at tables with their masks and visors buried deep within piles of multicolored tomes. Lucia watched as some ventured past the bridges to lifts that propelled them along the edge of the tower walls, off to some unknown place. It did not take long before they realized exactly what this place was, standing like a fortress of history. The knowledge they sought certainly existed here. The lead they needed was closer than they thought.

Finally, Lucia's eyes met with those of a girl reading at the edge of a bookcase. Her knuckles rested at the base of her chin as she snapped her book shut. For a moment, it was as if she hadn't seen Lucia at all, but as soon as Lucia looked away, she took notice. Lucia hid behind Leo's shoulder as the girl approached them with her book still wrapped in her grip. Lucia secured her band in place and touched the side of her face, her nerves shaking as the glare of the girl's platinum armor nearly blinded her. The metal was molded onto her shoulders like a pair of wings and connected to a fine-fitting breastplate tied into place with magenta ribbons. Her mask was gentle, covering only the top part of her face. It resembled that of a simple white dove, with a soft beak above her lips and bright pink patches on her cheeks. She was different from the rest of them. In her eyes was an undeniable interest that showed care and curiosity. Lucia's anxiety melted away as their eyes met again.

Lucia imagined the girl under the mask to be very beautiful. Her eyes were a stunning shade of aquamarine, and her blonde hair was tied into a stylish ponytail by a vivid pink ribbon that matched the ones dangling from the pieces of her armor.

She bowed before them, holding her book to her chest. "My deepest apologies. I was supposed to be at my post here, but I've been somewhat preoccupied today with my studies. I've been researching the history of Aldric's electricity. It's quite fascinating how much more efficient and innovative it has become over the centuries. Our current system is said to output nearly one hundred times more watts than that of our previous one. Remarkable, isn't it?" She flashed her teeth, smiling greatly while her sky blue eyes sparkled like an ocean beneath her mask. There was something mysterious within them. "I'm Luzanna," she said.

Lucia smiled, returning the bow. "I'm Lucia Sanoon, high maiden of Moz, and this is—"

Leo stepped forward and held out a hand to Luzanna, who took it and shook it softly. Leo smiled, turning on his charm as his eyes met with hers. "Leocadio Feral, sir of Pinea. But most call me Leo."

Luzanna tilted her head playfully as she took back her hand and wrapped her arms around her book. "Nice to meet you, good sir."

Lucia took a small step back, touching her head as if something was grinding inside it. She shook it off and put on a mask of her own, facing Luzanna with a simper.

Luzanna blinked her eyes. She noticed the pendant as it emitted a strange yet natural glow. "What a beautiful diamond," she said, leaning in for a closer look as Lucia flinched. "Oh," she said, stepping back, "it looks awfully familiar." She placed a finger to the beak of her mask. "It's as if I've seen it before. I just can't remember where at the moment."

Lucia jumped. "You've seen it?"

"Not with my own two eyes, of course. I've never seen it in person, but I think I've seen it in a book illustrated somewhere." She laughed. "I'm not keen to forget anything I read, especially when it's from the ancient archives. *Oh,* that must be it."

"Ancient archives?" Lucia asked. She perceived that this girl was important somehow. Luzanna was complex, inquisitive, and free-thinking, so unlike the commander they had met before. A positive energy emitted from her eyes. Who was she, exactly?

"Ah. Well, only the council is allowed to read the archives, but I have special access to them as part of my training. Everything else here is free to the public." Luzanna looked back to the many shelves behind her. "Pardon my distractions. I've been going on and on pondering such matters. There must be something I can help you with. No matter what you're studying, I'm sure I can point you in the right direction." She grinned. Obviously time wasn't an issue to her, but to them it was wearing thin.

"We are actually here to plead"—shame cast its shadow on Lucia's thoughts before she corrected herself with emphasis—"to inform the chief elder of the tragedies that have befallen the provinces of Moz and Pinea. We don't know much about what is going on, and we fear that whatever attacked them will soon be coming here. I don't wish to alarm you, but we all may be in danger."

Luzanna's eyes clearly lost their light as she heard that. "You can't be serious," she said flatly. "Nothing like that could ever befall Aldric. Aldric is the safest place in all of Terestria. Our technology surpasses all. Nothing can break through our walls."

Leo interjected. "This force is not of our world. It's been prophesied that the emergence of the Light Wings would signify the end of things as we know it. Darkness would roam until balance was restored." He crossed his arms, seizing the opportunity to probe her for information. "Surely, if you've truly read of the Light Wings someplace before, you would know something about this prophecy. Wouldn't you?"

Luzanna narrowed her eyes before lowering them to the ground. She was clearly conflicted as she softly replied, "I've been told that Aldric is not to meddle in the affairs of Moz or Pinea. They would say anything to have us forgive their transgressions. Their war nearly destroyed the entire world before, and"—she shook—"I'm just going to tell you now. The elder won't help you." She closed her eyes. "I'm sorry." She turned her head. "I really do wish *I* could, but my father simply wouldn't stand for it. I would never be able to continue my research."

"Your father?" Leo asked as a knot tightened within his chest.

At that moment, Luzanna smiled, almost as if she was surprised that they barely understood. "Talon Renon."

Leo gasped. "The chief elder."

Lucia's gaze fell as Leo's own widened in disbelief. Lucia frowned, accepting now the strict accusations placed against her people. All of this resentment stemmed from a firsthand account of war twenty years ago, one that sent ripples of distrust and deceit throughout the realms in the years that followed. Their war had set off a chain of events that would corrupt the powers of each province, allowing them to alter their own history and force their people to live within a world without knowing the very truth that could later save them. This city, like their own, was dependent on their governors—but how could their leaders protect them when they, too, denied the truth?

"Talon knows," Lucia said quietly, stepping forward. "Luzanna, your father knows of the peril we are in. I'm sure of it. If you could please take us to him, I'm sure I can convince him to tell us how to stop it. If he rejects us, he will have doomed us all!"

Luzanna lowered her eyes again, thinking. "My father is very old and stubborn. He's set in his ways. Even I struggle to change his mind from time to time. He doesn't take to new discoveries well, but if what you say is true, and I do nothing . . . I, too, will be responsible for destroying the future of my people."

Lucia sensed it then again, the tingling feeling inside her head.

Within Luzanna's words was something Lucia knew all too well: a call of duty. Perhaps they were not so different after all. Lucia took Luzanna's hand in hers. "Please, help us." Lucia smiled, but not without that gleam of compassion in her eyes. "There's not much time."

"Yes," Leo said in support. "Listen to Lucia. Together we can right the wrongs of our fathers. You, too, can do the same."

Luzanna glanced at the pendant. "I remember my father telling me years ago, about a man from Moz coming to warn him of a catastrophe that would befall the world. My father said the man was driven insane by the guilt that corrupted him, by the choices he made in his own life. I thought of it as some fable my father made up to remind me that the past would always be there to haunt us. That's why I have striven to walk this path every day of my life.

"But there is one thing that still troubles me, even to this day." Luzanna looked up, recalling the memory. "The man also said that my father would die and that our tribe's bloodline would fade into time. It chills me to think that could be true. This prophecy was supposed to be a lie, of course, created to absolve the guilt of some lunatic. It was supposed to be his own curse, not our own. How could that, of all things, be true?"

Lucia held her breath. "That sounds like one side of the story." Hearing the tale again brought tears to her eyes. After all this time, thinking about her father and what he'd done, she felt her grief seep through the shell encased around her heart.

"I know," Luzanna continued. "Often, I've thought why—why would he lie? I know it's unreal to think prophecies like such could come true. It's wise to be skeptical, but you're supposed to see the good in people and keep an open mind. Why call them hopeless or deny them when they actually believe the words they speak? Why not pray for them and hope, no matter who they are, that they find the peace they are looking for? He was trying to warn us in order to protect us, but instead my father rejected him. I know we might not be right all the time, but my father and most of us have a hard time admitting when we're wrong. If this prophecy is, in fact, true, I cannot stand idly by and allow my people to suffer."

Lucia touched the Light Wings, the radiance warming the tips of her fingers. She saw the shame in Luzanna's own eyes. "Your father may be keeping everyone away from the truth, but you—you're the hope of your people. My father's plight is your own. You just don't know it yet."

"Your father . . . ." Luzanna stepped back in shock, the fear rising within her.

"My father left Moz to seek the end of the same force that threatens our world now. He's the one who left a prophecy for Pinea, and I'm sure he left this prophecy for Aldric too. Just as your father rejected mine, so did his." Lucia gestured to Leo. "And not long ago, the darkness destroyed both our homes with fire." Lucia's eyes filled with tears as her voice tensed. "I'm sure it was my father you spoke of, and now I'm here pleading as he once did." She choked, clasping the Light Wings. "His prophecy is bound to happen unless you do something about it."

Luzanna put her hands to her chest, her eyes wet beneath her mask. The Carists around them took notice, rising up to look at the weeping dove.

"Are you saying your father was telling the truth?" Luzanna asked.

"Yes, nothing but the truth."

"Then that means—"

"It's coming," Leo said, walking between them and reaching to Luzanna's shoulder. "Please, take us to your father."

Luzanna shook her head and tossed Leo's arm from her side.

"Now," he commanded.

"No," she cried fiercely. "My father, he's going to . . . " She stepped back, wiping the tears from her mask. "He'll die!"

"He won't if we act," Lucia pleaded. "Please, Luzanna."

Luzanna blinked wildly as she considered. Suddenly, she picked up her eyes. "You will need proof. The council won't accept your plea without proof." She stepped forward, dropping her book on a nearby table, and gripping her hands together.

Lucia followed her, placing only a foot between her and the dove. "You said you've seen this somewhere, right?" She pointed to the pendant.

"Yes," Luzanna said softly, "in the ancient archives. I'm sure of it."

Lucia nodded, calming herself. She took Luzanna's hand and placed it over the pendant. "These are the Light Wings, a relic of ancient origin created solely for preserving the light and restoring balance to this world."

Luzanna's eyes focused on the light illuminating through her fingers. She retracted her hand slowly and touched the top of her head, a sudden rush of wisdom flowing through her mind. "The Light Wings, I remember." She panicked, breathing rapidly. Her hands shook as her armor rattled over her. "The vessel of virtue, born of the light. Those holy wings and cleanser of sin." She gasped as tears flooded her eyes. "Oh no!"

There it was, within Luzanna's eyes. Lucia saw it coming like a light from the end of a long dark tunnel: the truth.

Luzanna continued, "The age of corruption is signified by the coming of the Light Wings. It's said that during this time, the darkness would cross over into our realm to take back its creation and rid the light of its own. It would corrupt the land with sin, all so that the world would belong to the darkness forever. The darkness will come to reclaim the earth and bring about life's destruction, leaving the Light Wings no choice but to summon the light's virtue in order to thwart its rival."

Reclaim the earth and bring about life's destruction? Lucia thought as it all started falling into place. "You *do* know, and I'm sure your father knows even more. We must speak with him now. Your father has seen the darkness. He saw it in the heat of our war. He knows what's at stake, and we must go to him before it's too late. There must be a way we can stop it."

Lucia felt the relief in her chest as Luzanna's eyes filled with a new trust, a bond forged in hope. Luzanna took their hands, and Lucia felt the connection between the three of them, as if it were fate that they would someday come together, like it was destined to happen this way.

Lucia glanced up into the citrine and sensed the fire. "Please, let's save the world."

Luzanna nodded and pulled them behind her. "This way!" She led them to the edge of the tower and up a flight of stairs.

As they climbed, Lucia finally felt the pleasure of their progress. Everything had seemed so hopeless, but with Luzanna there was now a certainty that things would be alright, an optimism that felt unreal. It was strong, and like an aura, it shaped the core of Luzanna's being just as Leo's calmness and self-restraint shaped his. There was a clearness encased within her opal eyes, just as there was something shining within the coolness of Leo's eyes of sapphire.

Then, just as Lucia felt that hope once more, just as she felt it peak as they ran up those steps, something cold coiled itself around her, rushing blood to her face and sending a chill shuddering through her. She stared up into the vibrant citrine, her eyes drawn to it as the frost formed over it. "No," Lucia whispered, feeling the Light Wings vibrate with light. She held her head as the lamps around them burst into extinguishing flames one by one, exploding violently and plunging every space and corner of the tower into darkness.

Leo and Luzanna huddled around Lucia and the bleak light of the Light Wings as she dropped down, embracing the steps with her hands and sheltering her face away from the falling glass. She heard it shatter and fall around them, but oddly enough she could not tell from where.

"What's happening?" Luzanna cried out.

Lucia tried to yell but was overcome by a violent roar that shook the tower. It was a deafening and antagonizing sound, screeching over the screams of the Carists above and below.

Leo pulled the girls behind him, pushing them closer to the steps and standing protectively over them as the platform shook. He stared up into the citrine as an orange glow bled into the gray light of the sky, sending only remnants below. This brought fear into him as it seemed like the darkness was swallowing them whole. His fear of the blackening sky above grew, and he knew that the light would not last much longer. They were not fast enough. He grasped the glass rail of the stairs as the earth began to quake, pushing him forward against the railing. He tried to push away, his muscles tightening as his body was forced forward. How far up were they? Leo stared out into the growing darkness into the pitch black hole beneath them. He could not tell if it was real or merely a figment of his imagination, but he felt it pulling him in. His hands shook as he held on with all his might. "I can't . . ."

The glow of the Light Wings was faint, but Lucia made out Leo's struggling figure within its radiance. The tower was shaking violently as she tried to stand. She slipped a bit as she attempted to balance herself and reach for Leo. She was wobbling back and forth in the darkness as gusts of wind pulled her downward. The light of the citrine was falling and dissolving, mixing into the shadows that surrounded them. Lucia felt its warmth as it started to haze. The Light Wings dangled below her head like a single firefly, its light pulsating as they rocked. She had to do something. Whatever this was, it was drawing everything to the center. The tower was going to collapse in and on itself. They were going to be crushed within it. The darkness had never felt so strong before. It was almost as if it was being concentrated. Was only the tower feeling its impact? The city outside, was it safe?

Lucia could not be certain, but she knew the darkness was toying with them. Whatever it was doing would not end here, not so swiftly. The darkness knew no such mercy. A deep chuckle inside her head, a sinister laugh, erupted as images of glaring red eyes flashed within her mind: "Darkness will thrive. You won't survive it."

Suddenly there was another roar, and Lucia flew forward as a fierce force pushed up from beneath her. She tried to scream, but instead she inhaled a heavy gulp of unwanted air. Her sight blurred as panic gripped her mind, bleeding it dry. She saw Leo's face as he watched her fly over his head.

"Lucia!" he called while reaching toward her, losing his balance and falling backward to land next to a silent and unconscious Luzanna. There was a crack as his head hit the wall. It throbbed as he lifted it and searched for that glow, only to see it beneath the rail. Adrenaline burned through his blood as he scurried, hoping to see her. He crawled, reaching for the glow, until his hand met another on the shaking stone.

Lucia could hear her own heavy breathing as she fought to keep herself on the ledge. The tower trembled, and agonizing wails came from every direction. She was clutching the base of the stairway, trying not to slip into the darkness that was forcefully pulling her down. But the strength she was using wasn't her own.

Leo held onto her as he hugged the stone beneath him. He looked back, only to see a shimmer of platinum, motionless. He brought his eyes back to the glow, using it to guide his sight. What was all this? It was like gravity, but stronger. Colder, bitter, and more destructive. He clenched his teeth growling as he pulled Lucia with all his might, shifting his weight away from the darkness' strange power.

Lucia concentrated on the warmth of his hands, trying to keep her fragile mind from breaking. She wept, tightening her grip to pull herself up.

"Hold on," Leo whispered to himself as he pushed up against the stone with his feet. "Oh light, please. Give me strength!" he screamed, using the last of his power and pulling fiercely in a final effort, pushing his body up onto to his feet.

Lucia brought herself up, freeing herself from the hold of the being, from whatever grip it had on her, and without hesitation threw herself into Leo's arms, smashing her face against his chest.

Leo fell backward as she landed on top of him. Lucia's heart beat hard against his skin through his torn shirt. For a moment, there was a feeling of peace as his senses homed in on the sound of her breath. He was rushed with a sense of pride he had not felt in some time. He'd saved Lucia's life. Leo embraced her, almost as if he would never let her go. He wouldn't. He couldn't.

She pressed her face against his shoulder as the stairwell shook. Slowly, she raised her face to his ear. Leo listened intently, trying hard to hold on to every word.

She said, "It happens as it should. Be still."

Leo blinked, clueless, as the stairway trembled, unable to wrap his head around those cryptic words. Her voice was so soft and so calm. It wasn't like her at all. What did she mean? Did she mean to say that?

The stairway gave another quake, and Leo and the stairway began to crumble. Alert, he tried to rise, but Lucia lay tense and resistant on top of him, as if she were in a lock of some sort. She didn't move. She was frozen, hard like a diamond. Not even he could break through to her. "Lucia, move now!" he yelled, but it was no use. She lay there, dormant. "Lucia!" he cried as he struggled, the steps widening under him and loosening from the wall they were attached to. "No, Lucia, wake up!" he urged, but still she lay silent, wrapped around his body. The stairs dipped, the pull of the force tearing them from the wall. Her grip loosened as the steps shattered under them. Luzanna drifted into the air, while Lucia seemed to glide upward, as Leo, finally, fell into the darkness.

*   *   *

Lucia could not make out what she was seeing. There was no way of telling what it was. Thousands of lights shot over a dark plane like shooting stars crossing the night sky. She was hovering, floating as if her body were weightless; and motionless as she watched those shooting lights glide over her. She was numb and felt no semblance of pain. She merely existed, with the lights. As graceful as they were, they showered around her and Lucia felt no fear or suffering as they consumed her. Suddenly, a golden light illuminated. Drifting among the stars in the distance was a figure, like a sleeping angel, dressed in gold-and-white cloth and with hair like honey. *Is that me?* Lucia thought. The golden light rose from her other body, rising out of her chest and clinging to it as it was torn from her. The light was not white like the Light Wings, and surely it did not come from within them. This was somehow her own.

Lucia heard the echo of a gentle voice. "Light amongst fragile waves." What was this voice? What was it trying to tell her? "Sparkling softly as violet lays a blanket over an azure sky. As clear as the fuchsia rays drawn into the golden sun, silver flies, drawn here for a purpose—to serve with light and not dark shadow. Only with an intention renewed and cleansed for good can one bring what's right to aid this life." Lucia did not understand the words, so opaque. The gold grew, expelling over her body, drawing everything into it. Lucia's consciousness dissolved and swallowed her into the light as it overtook her and threw her back to reality.

*　*　*

"No! No, please come back!" Lucia struggled as her body materialized and her senses sharpened. She jerked forward as if her spirit had awakened itself rather than her own body. She was breathing heavily, brought back into a gray reality—this nightmare that was her life. The faint glow of a flickering lamp hovered overhead. Her sight was still hazy, and her body ached as she tried to move. Her stockings were torn and her chest was cut. Blood had dried over her blouse and it covered Lucia's hands, just as soot had the night her manor burned.

She looked around this dreadful place. The walls were worn brick, and the ground was moist dirt decaying with mold. Lucia covered her mouth and held in her breath. The wretched stench made it hard to breathe. Where was she? A drip of water fell from a crack in the ceiling over her. Immediately, she touched her neck, where the chain still embraced it. Lucia gave a sigh of relief and slowly went back to examining the room. Across from her was a wooden door, handle-less and rusted. This place was an abyss she could not escape from, a dungeon of despair. She had an idea of where she might be, but hoped it would not be so. She huddled close to a corner, trying to warm her wet body. She was soaked in sweat and her body trembled.

"Can this nightmare get any worse?" she whispered to herself, letting the words make it all the more real. She held her eyes shut, took in a breath, and remembered something her mother had taught her when she was a little girl. She embraced the silence and closed her eyes. She let go of the distractions and focused. *I'm in Moz, sitting in the garden on a rainy day.* She immediately felt a sense of being home run through her, almost as if she could open her eyes and be exactly where she said she was. She knew that was impossible, but she remembered what her mother had told her: "Faith is a powerful thing. With it, you can do anything, as long as it never breaks."

Lucia had faith that the place she remembered truly existed. Still, she hoped to return someday. She could not see it, but as long as she believed in that place, as long as she closed her eyes and imagined it in her mind, even if she wasn't there her home still existed deep within her heart. "Even for a moment, just let it all go, be home and feel happy."

She smiled with the memory, ignoring the doubt inside. She refused to let it consume her. The darkness would not win. It would not destroy what little faith she had left. Even in her agony, she still had this memory of home to hold on to. "As long as there is light, there is hope," she whispered to herself. "There has to be."

She leaned back against the wall, unsure of what the future had for her. Lucia prayed for a miracle. She laid her head back and held on to her memory, using it to fuel the light she felt inside. She did not notice, but the Light Wings were sparkling a soft pink. Though the events of that night did not seem to offer the slightest glimmer of hope, she would soon realize that her prayers carried more power than she ever thought they would.

CHAPTER ELEVEN

From Beneath

Luzanna's eyes flickered beneath the soft light of the sun as it draped in through a skylight that made up half the ceiling above her bedroom. Her face brushed against the smooth surface of her silk pillow as her eyes flicked open, her breathing slow and deep. Her mask lay beside her. Wearily, she rose from the bed as if she had escaped from some terrible dream. Though still lightheaded, she was strong enough to stand. Her senses sharpened into focus.

"Was it all a dream?" Luzanna whispered. She placed a hand over her mask, trying hard to remember everything that had happened. Suddenly, she noticed two figures observing her from the foot of her bed. Her mother was dressed in similar fashion but clothed in deep blue, with a mask of a prominent jay covering her face. And beside her, armored heavily in the orange of gallant flames, was Luzanna's father, sparkling in the sunlight beneath the window. His visor rose upward and curved over his head sharply. Atop were metallic feathers carved into the orange metal that hugged his upper face, and at the center of his forehead, placed within his visor, was the Elder Stone, glistening with its cascade of many colors. From his shoulder plates flowed multicolored ribbons that caped down his back.

"Luzanna, did they hurt you?" asked Ofelia, rushing towards her daughter. She brushed a hand to her Luzanna's face. The delicate touch was enough to draw the rest of Luzanna's wandering mind into reality.

Luzanna looked up at them as a sudden surge of pain rose in her left hand. "Ugh," she groaned.

Her mother grabbed the hand as it tightened and twisted.

"Didn't you both feel it? The quake that took the tower, where did it come from?" Luzanna asked. She panicked through the pain as her mother tried to relax her hand. "Mother, it's fine." She tore it from her mother's grasp. The pain dissipated a bit as she stretched her fingers, but it persisted there, burning to the tips. Luzanna knew this was not normal but chose to ignore it. "Father, tell me what happened."

Talon looked at his wife, who had understood Luzanna's sharp actions and receded to his side. "The tower was taken hostage by outsiders. Somehow, they were able to infiltrate the city, but we managed to capture and maintain them. The city is safe once more."

"Outsiders?" Luzanna asked, confused. She lowered her eyes, remembering the faint flashes of what happened, the sounds of the rubble falling from the tower and the sounds of shattering glass, those horrible screams. She could only imagine the blood, but still, she remembered the stench of it steaming through her nostrils as if it were still fresh, the smell of open flesh. She knew *exactly* how it had happened, exactly how her head had fallen to the wall, knocking her into darkness. He lied.

"Not long after the attack, gatekeepers from Pinea arrived and informed us of the calamity that befell their respective provinces. They told us of what that boy did to his father and of the girl he ran off with, the daughter of that fool! To think, after all this time and the mercy I shed, they'd return here to terrorize us.

"I can't help but partly blame myself. The boy has been taken into questioning, and the girl remains imprisoned for the time being. We are lucky they didn't cause more harm. They were both armed and very dangerous."

Luzanna hesitated, recalling the warmth of the light she had seen draped around the neck of the girl dressed in soft yellow. Behind her father at the foot of the door, she saw the very bow the girl carried on her back. "You don't mean Lucia and Leo, do you?" She flared up from the bed. "Father, you have it wrong. The gatekeepers have it wrong! They hurt no one. They came here to help us with the real threat."

"Nonsense, let's not take to such fantasies." Talon smiled and gave her mother a slight wave, signaling that he wanted to be alone with their daughter. She nodded and touched Luzanna's shoulder before heading to the door and out of their sight. "But I do have some questions for you as well, my dear."

Luzanna shuddered a bit as a small orb of sweat ran along the side of her face.

"We found you beside the other two, unconscious. Though their attack was one of suicide, I wasn't sure why you had been so close to them. What did they tell you if they did not try to hurt you as you say?" Talon crossed his arms and lowered his gaze from hers.

"Like I said, Father, they are not dangerous, nor are they radicals. I demand they be released this instant!" Luzanna stood firmly, her throbbing fist clenched. She refused to believe what her father said. "They aren't the real threat here," she whispered. "It was . . ."

Her throat swelled as she remembered the chill of its embrace and the coil of its touch as it gripped her spirit. The prophecy, was it coming true?

"Luzanna . . ." Talon hesitated, suddenly choking on his words as they tried to leave his lips. She saw it in his eyes, a flicker of fear, as if he had something hidden deep within his opaque gaze. "I know what you are trying to say." He nodded his head and let out a soft breath before staring back into her ocean-like eyes. The phoenix pointed to her hand before pacing to the side, still hesitant to speak.

"You do?" Luzanna looked away.

He nodded. He looked back at her and put a hand to his chest. "It breaks my heart that this day has come." He walked over and faced Luzanna, placing his hands over hers. "I never thought my own daughter would fall victim to this plague."

"Plague?" Luzanna asked softly.

Talon broke from her, stepping back and returning his hand to his chest. "Though you feel sympathy for them, Luzanna, you must forget them or you shall fall into sin as well. They are at fault."

The glare in her eyes rescinded. "What are you talking about?"

"Though they didn't mean harm, they still brought it into our province. Our kingdom fell victim to their sin," Talon said, his deep voice echoing through the silence with a heavy bellow.

Luzanna fell silent, waiting for the vibrations to calm before she tried to speak. "They brought *what*?"

"Luzanna, there are things in this world not meant for the rest of Terestria to know. Becoming master of this province comes the burden of this knowledge. You have always been a smart girl. You know wisdom has its price!"

His eyes closed behind his visor, releasing tears like her mother's, except Luzanna perceived more pain in them—somehow, she had gained a new perception. This fresh feeling came through her throbbing hand, so strong she could sense that her father was somehow corrupted by his own emotion. The truth he refused to speak, the truth he knew of all this time, was being cast aside and rejected.

He clenched his teeth. "Do you really think I hadn't seen those wings before?"

She gasped, nearly falling backward onto the bed. He knew. "Father, then surely you must know of the real threat. The darkness of legend, don't you remember?"

Talon nodded, stepping backward. "Yes, and also I remember that warning left so many years ago by that imbecile. The fall of this empire and the death of its king are all signified with the emergence of those wings." He turned his head away from Luzanna as her fear heightened.

"So surely you would help them, wouldn't you?" she asked.

Talon locked his gaze to her, showing nothing more than rage in his eyes. "Never," he whispered.

Luzanna released a whine of grief. "Why not?"

"Do you know what their war has brought into this world?" His voice held nothing more than burning venom that stung Luzanna's eyes, bringing only more pain into her heart. "*Their* sin has brought forth the very pure form of evil, sin incarnate."

"Father, their war is in the past. They aren't responsible for the sins of their ancestors."

"Luzanna," he cried. "You don't know what kind of omen this is, or of the consequences that shall be faced from here on. They are unbearable. And Sigranole"—Talon sounded hurt by this revelation—"my friend is dead, and presumably by his son's own hand. How could I forgive this?"

"Why call them dangerous radicals or terrorists when you know the truth, Father? Why do you lie as if you know nothing?" She tried to hold firm, but her emotions were tingling beneath her skin. "You're nothing more than a liar, to me and your own people. That itself is its own sin!" Luzanna's blood rushed to her chest, causing her heart to clatter beneath her chest plate. It sounded as if rain were falling within her head, making her lips flush bright red. "Tell me what is going on and why it is happening! Withholding the truth is just as bad as lying about it."

Talon looked wearily to his daughter, exhaling in disappointment and sadness. "I will not," he said, taking a step toward the door. "Because I will see to the destruction of those wings and the execution of those two for what they brought into this world. I'll do what I should have done to their parents so long ago. They will be punished for their crimes."

"Crimes they did not commit! No one is born guilty of their parents' crimes," Luzanna cried, throwing herself forward to grab her father's arm. "Please, Father, you can't control everything. You're going to make things worse. We have to let them help us or we will suffer a fate worse than death. The Light Wings are here to redeem us, not destroy us!"

Talon jerked his arm from her before sending a firm hand across her face. Luzanna fell backward and onto the floor. The moisture of her tears stung as they ran down the palm mark on her face. She looked at her father, who stood silently in front of the door. He turned his head to look back to Luzanna as she tried to tough through the pain. She held her cheek with her hand.

"This world is *built* on secrets, Luzanna. Don't you dare share what I spoke with you here today or I'm afraid you would have to suffer a fate just as they do." He glowered at his daughter, who only let out a wail of grief as he bolted out the door with a slam.

*　*　*

"Lucia," he mumbled, breaking from his sleep. "Lucia!" Leo was drifting from what seemed one world to the next. There was water. He saw it, water flowing under a violent storm. He stared across it from the shore, watching as the tide rose up and over his feet, cold as stinging ice.

As he stared into that sea, he knew exactly what it was: death. The water had turned black, a violet wave twisting upward like a serpent, glowing crimson at its tip. He could not explain what he was seeing or where he was. All he knew was that he needed to be afraid. He needed to fear the water, or possibly what lay beneath it.

"Get up!"

This is a terrible reality, he thought as his dream broke from his vision with the harsh blow of a foot into his stomach. Leo coughed and wheezed, gasping for air.

"Stop crying like a little girl and get up, you traitor!"

Leo made out the faint glow of gray and recognized dirt underneath him. His mind was still in a haze. He was surrounded by three guards, all garbed in armor and spitting on him as he struggled to raise his head. He was disoriented and confused as to why these men hated him, but something told him that they knew—they knew his father was dead. Instinctively, he reached for his side, where he touched the outline of his sheath. He searched for his dagger but, in a panic, realized it was gone.

"Looking for this?" a guard taunted, waving Leo's silver dagger in front of his face. "It looks pleasantly expensive. Custom made." He ran a finger along its edge and bent down over Leo, who was still struggling for air and in too much pain to move. "Don't you suppose this is the same blade he killed his father with?" He took the blade and slowly ran it over Leo's cheek. "What a shame it would be . . ."

Leo looked into his hateful eyes. He was a Carist, but obviously not a smart one, based on his looks and his lowly job as a prison guard. He was dirty, wrinkled, and balding quickly. Leo held his breath to avoid the stench of his decaying mouth.

The guard finally finished his threat. "If I had to run this into your chest because you refuse to listen. Just like you did your poor ol' dad." He released a vile laugh. "But honestly, prisoners like you make my job a lot more fun." He dragged the knife deeply across Leo's face.

Leo groaned, tightening his cheek as the warmth of his own blood flowed along it. He focused his gaze on the laughing guard as he rose. "You will"—he grunted through his teeth—"regret ever touching my face."

The guard made a face puckering out his lips and crossing his eyes. "Aw, did I hurt the poor pretty boy's face? I'm sorry." He laughed, his lips curving into a demonic smile. "Oh, that's gonna leave a scar. Too bad," he mocked.

Rage built up inside Leo. His hands wanted to rip the lips from the guard's face. He wanted the pleasure of hurting him, but something inside told him not to, to keep his cool. His rage retreated as he breathed, thinking only of Lucia and of finding where she might be. She was nowhere in sight, and he already sensed the danger they were in. He clenched his eyes shut, imagining what they might be doing to her. He gathered his strength, focusing it into the depth of his chest, feeling his ambition overshadow his heart. His drive and his light was found there.

"That's right, get up," bellowed another guard. He laughed before spitting in Leo's face, stinging the cut on his cheek.

Leo's sapphire eyes were heated almost in a trancelike state, burning fiercely with an unspoken emotion. He didn't blink as he wiped his face and looked blankly to the ground as the main guard forced him forward to the rusted cell door.

"Move," the guard demanded with a great push, knocking Leo to the ground.

Leo took in a deep breath as he shoved himself up from the earth, his eyes still glistening but now almost a bright violet, fusing with the red of his anger. Something crossed his mind as he felt the hopelessness of the situation. The stench of this prison and its flickering lamps could only mean they were underground someplace. Leo had no way of telling where, but at least he knew he had to be deliberate with his actions if he ever hoped to escape. He was reminded of the cold that was approaching, and even so, he heard the faint whispers of what he needed to do coming from a distance, calling from somewhere. There was still hope, as long as he believed there was, as long as he remained in control.

*   *   *

"How could he be so irrational? No logic could have come up with that conclusion. He must be running on nothing but fear." Luzanna was pacing her room, talking to herself, trying to understand what had just happened. She touched her face, flinching at the cold of her fingers. "He's"—she shut her eyes as she whispered—"never struck me before."

She looked up and into the light of the windows behind her bed. It was morning. The previous night had faded, and she now faced a new dilemma: preventing something far worse from coming in this night. She sensed its chill through her very armor, rattling with her body. She strode to the window, placed her hand on the glass, and looked out across her city. The grand kingdom, glorious and bright amid the sun's reflection, shined like a mirror. Her eyes widened as she took notice of the many Carists below her, all entering the tower and pulling carts of materials of stone, glass, and metal out of it like ants from a demolished anthill.

She looked away, shedding a tear as she remembered what she could from that night. The endless cold was agony, and the darkness was despair. It all had been true, and was foretold to only become much worse. She pulled her hand down and turned to her bed. On it lay her mask, artistically crafted and beautifully her own. She picked it up and observed it with her bright light eyes. Luzanna could hardly believe what her life had become so quickly, or bring herself to cope with and to understand why her father had taken to all this, or even more why he had threatened his own daughter. "What does he hope to accomplish?"

In her studies to become chief elder herself one day, she had learned many of the myths and fables concerning the tides of the world. She knew of the forces that created it, and of the balance that was preserved over the landscape; but for her entire life it was as if she'd been groomed to believe only part of the story. She had never known the whole truth. Though there were archives she had access to, she felt there was more than what she knew. There was knowledge lost, pieces of the puzzle gone, maybe even to her father.

"Does my father want to contaminate even that?" she asked herself, turning to the window. "Does he wish to disrupt that balance by destroying exactly what the light has bestowed upon this land in order to save it?" She looked back to her mask. "Does he want to shatter this world's last hope and worsen the balance that has already been broken?" She collapsed on the bed, letting a mixture of rage and sadness overtake her. "Why, Father? Why must you envy the fate of the rest of the world and not accept your own? Why can't you find hope in saving the world you'll leave behind, and where's your faith in me to lead? What hope is left for me or for your people when you think that *selfishly*?"

Her father wanted to destroy the Light Wings, and Luzanna knew it was because of Stello's warning. "The fall of an empire and the death of its king," she whispered. In destroying the wings, he would defy his own fate and hopefully save himself. Luzanna knew this. And if she were to defy him, what would come from that? She could not bear to even think of it. Her whole life, he had loved her and showed such faith in her decisions, teaching her the power of spirit, of mind and body, of light and darkness. But these forces that revolved around them, bestowing them with what they knew as Terestria, had now gone rogue. And her father was not meant to survive.

The pain in Luzanna's hand stung violently again. She tightened her fist and rose, holding it close to her chest. She could tolerate it, but still it annoyed her. It seemed to worsen the more she doubted. "I can't," she cried. She looked to the mask and touched the ribbon in her blonde hair. She took a deep breath, grabbed the mask, and put it to her face. She knelt down and pulled a case from beneath the bed. It was a long, rectangular wooden box made of glazed cypress, engraved with the symbols of the ancient language of the oldest Carist tribes. Slowly, as if she had never opened it before, she unlatched it and lifted its top. She looked down at the light crimson cloth. Then she picked up a small parchment and read the words written across it.

To our fair daughter Luzanna,

Our proud white dove, it brings us such joy to watch you grow. May this serve you well once you become chieftess. We hope you may never have to use it. Cherish it as a symbol of your wisdom as a scholar and strength as a warrior on this day of your sixteenth birthday.

Your loving parents,
Talon and Ofelia Renon

With that, she tore open the crimson to reveal a long silver spear headed with wide blades. The head was encrusted with gems of blue and pink scaling along the sides. She rose and stood proudly with it by her side. She lowered her gaze. "You hoped I'd never have to use this, and so had I. But I must keep faith in the future and hope for a better world. I will defend my country even if it's fated to be destroyed. I have the will to fight! And I'm sorry if it means I must strike you down—so be it."

She took the spear and, in a fury of speed, moved to her

bedroom door. Luzanna had her own objective, something within her. She knew what she needed to do. A light burning in her heart told her that she had to join Lucia and Leo before the true threat could snake its way through her father's own and stop his heart completely.

*　*　*

Lucia was hardly breathing. A slight stream of air lifted up into her as she sat against the far wall of the cell. The Light Wings were draining more than they should from her body, but she noticed how her wounds from the fall, the cuts and punctures, all healed quickly underneath the tatters of her blouse. She did not know what to feel or think just yet. The thought still lingered, the one that came from the pendant around her neck. The faint whispers told her, "Hope."

"What can I do?" she whispered to herself, shamed by how she had failed so much. The darkness had trapped her here, probably knowing she would end up there all along. Was it not fated to be so? Lucia was trapped within this gray, flickering reality. The light above would flash every now and again, as if it was meant to burst any moment and send her into a void of an even more painful life force drain, possibly something fatal. Here, she could feel how the dark shadows thickened as it shifted from bright to dark in the cell. Sooner or later, the darkness would find her, and she would have to face it. Her fear deepened, sending her heart into its own darkness—the abyss of her doubts. Lucia was afraid she would be lost forever.

She fixed her golden eyes on the dirt floor below. "Let me go," she whispered, feeling the cold trail of tears dripping onto her cheek. She placed her hands over the pendant, sheltering her eyes from its glow. "There is no hope." There was a hint of anger in her voice. She was tired of being told what to do. But most of all, she was tired of being told what to believe. "Do not forsake me," she called out, her voice echoing around her. She looked into the air, hoping to hear an answer from somewhere, but instead there was silence. Instantly, she withdrew herself with a whimper, falling back against the wall. She heard a scrape of metal and the door across from her slowly opened.

*　*　*

"Move, you imbecile," they spat, pushing Leo with the hilts of large lances.

Leo dragged his feet in front of them, keeping his head lowered as he walked down the corridor of the dungeon. Along its path of unsteady and flickering lamps were many cell doors. The shouts of prisoners, a mixture of criminals and lunatics, could be heard from outside. He wondered which one held Lucia, if she was even here. Leo was searching for a sign, any sign. He listened, hoping to hear the sound of her voice.

"You walk so slow," complained one of the guards behind him. "I wonder why this punk's got the chief so scared. Him? A terrorist? Humph." The guard nudged one of his comrades. "And to think this freak almost brought down the Glass Tower. But then again, what else could you expect from someone who'd commit patricide. You are truly the epitome of scum." He pushed Leo again, pointing to the far door at the end. "Get in there now!"

Leo growled under his breath, clenching his fist, but still understanding the accusations, pitying them for their ignorance.

"You know, I overheard the chief say he was only an accomplice," said the third guard. "The real terrorist is the Mozian girl. She was said to be holding some sort of powerful weapon."

The first guard laughed obnoxiously once more. "A girl? How pathetic." He kicked the back of Leo's leg, nearly sending him off his feet. Leo managed to take the blow without sacrificing his balance. "That girl probably has more balls than this kid ever will! His probably haven't even dropped yet."

Leo's face tightened as the guards laughed behind him. His eyes were hot as their laughing increased, echoing along the lengthy hallway for all to hear, drowning out any hope of hearing Lucia. The pit of his stomach burned and his hands shook. He somehow maintained the equilibrium within his body as he continued to move toward the door. *I must preserve my strength.*

"Oh, but it's a damn shame," the guard said in disappointment. "That girl was the prettiest thing I ever did see. Her beauty alone should warrant a pardon. It's a pity she has to die. But after all, she did set Pinea into a blaze with that weapon of hers. I heard the fire polluted the earth so much that it turned much of the ground to contaminated mush. Pinea's nothing more than a toxic wasteland now, with land so poisonous it's causing an uptick of incurable diseases. It's filled with plague. Not that it wasn't already. It did produce this brute."

"What?" Leo asked, and the guards stopped in surprise.

"Well, well, well, the boy speaks," said one of the guards before slapping Leo on the back.

Leo could not fight back his words anymore. The line had been crossed. He had heard enough lies, enough of the assumptions. It was time they heard the truth. "Don't touch me," he said through his teeth. His canines sharp and ready to draw blood.

"Oh, you think you have a say, do you?" The guard landed a blunt blow to Leo's nose with the end of his spear, knocking him to the ground.

"Do you think you can tell *us* what to do? You're our prisoner, remember?" asked the largest of the three guards.

He spat again into Leo's face; but Leo had spent his time gaining back his energy, waiting for the right moment to strike. With ease, Leo grabbed the guard's leg and pulled him under, tipping him onto the ground. The guard's visor flew from his face and cracked against one of the cell doors. The other guards stood shocked for a moment before attempting to retaliate. They pulled their spears before them, but Leo rose up from under them, pushing upward and grabbing the center of one spear before tearing it from the guard. Using the shaft to balance himself, he knocked over the balding guard with the end of it. He pulled backward, focusing his strength as he sent a firm fist into the visor of the skinniest guard, cracking through the front of it and impacting him with a force strong enough to push his head back, causing it to hit the wall behind him, staining the wall with his blood. All three guards lay on the ground, struggling to find a weapon of their own, but Leo was far too swift and skilled when it came to the art of fighting. All of his training suited this very moment. He had put them in their place.

"Who are you?" whispered a guard as he spat blood from his mouth.

"I'm Leocadio Feral, noble sir of Pinea. I thought you knew," Leo said proudly, panting as he wiped the sweat from his face. "Never would I allow my own country to be destroyed, nor would I do such a thing to yours! You should be ashamed of your ignorance. It has left you blinded from the truth." It had never felt this good to be this honest. "For a bunch of Carists, you lot are awfully stupid."

"Lies," bellowed the guards' leader. "Believe the elder. He knows all."

"Your elder lies," Leo roared, violently sending a swift kick to the guard's face. "Pieces of shit. Do you really think you're so fucking special disrespecting a high-born?" He knelt before the guards' leader. He took the head of a spear and used it to cut open the guards' cheek slowly, piercing through the skin. Quickly, he pulled it out. "Hurts doesn't it?" Leo asked, throwing the spear against the wall as blood oozed from the guard's face. "Fuck you," Leo said, spitting in his face, feeling the rush of adrenaline pumping as he grinned, his eyes shining.

"You're a monster," said the guard, wincing as his cheek moved. "Who would ever forgive you, after the things you've done. All this for a damn girl, you sadistic fuck."

Leo smirked, seeing a familiar silver glisten on the belt of the guard below him. He reached down and picked up his dagger. Leo felt pleasure in reuniting with his blade. He placed it on his fingers, feeling its edge. "Don't test me. I *know* monsters. You haven't seen what I've seen." Leo's eyes spaced. "I've been fighting my whole life, training to protect my land and my people. From what I see, I was brought up better than any of you. I was taught to think for myself, but you? You're too foolish to see that you are merely the elder's cronies. You're told what to believe and what to do, while he hoards the knowledge of what's outside this city and our world all so you will remain loyal to him, all so only *he* can protect you from the real threat!

"He promises you protection in exchange for your loyalty, using your fear and dependence against you, but look where it has you now—following orders to kill the very people trying to save you! That girl didn't cause this destruction. She holds the key to stopping it. But if I had it my way, I'd say none of you are worth saving." Leo knelt down, looking into the guard's angered eyes before dropping the tip of his blade into the top of the guard's left hand. The guard agonized as Leo twisted the tip with the dagger's silver handle. He pulled his knife upwards, releasing a splatter of blood. The guard screamed as his hand curled.

"Look at you all high and mighty," the guard wearily spoke, clasping his injured hand. "The Carist tribe has always prevailed. We reign supreme. We always have." The guard's voice remained as cruel as before, despite Leo's aggression.

"Not for long. Now tell me. Lucia, the girl you imprisoned, where is she?"

The guards all looked at each other, releasing a look of shame and then submission as if speaking with their expressions. As Leo loomed over them, dagger in hand, the guards knew they had no choice but to listen. The guard with the shattered visor nodded, tearing it from his face. "I'll take you to her."

Leo nodded in satisfaction, finally free from the rage that had consumed his spirit. He helped the guard up to his feet. The others wore looks of disgust as they lay there bleeding, beaten and defeated.

"You two will stay here, or I'll be piercing more than a cheek next time. Tell me—don't you wish you had your visor now?" Leo sneered, pointing his dagger between the eyes of the visorless guard. He distrusted them after all they had done to him, his mind fractured and seemingly split in two. He tried to ignore his rage and focus on Lucia, following her voice as it rang in his head. He had to find her before she lost her light once and for all. Leo pushed the guard forward, not hesitating to bring his dagger into menacing visibility. The guard shuddered as they abandoned the other two and retreated back into the prison.

It was not long before they had reached the far end of the passage, not too far from where Leo had originally been held. His heart beat faster as the guard fumbled to pull a chain of keys from his waist. They trembled within his grip. "Hurry up," Leo spat, nudging the tip of his blade into the guard's back. The guard sneered at him with a low growl. His eyes were foul with hatred. Slowly, the keys slid into the hole, turned, and clicked in the rust of the lock. Leo's spirit leapt from his body as he heard the latch of the lock break free from the door. He pulled it open, releasing a quick breeze of air.

"Lucia!"

* * *

The call of her name from Leo was magnetic, pulling her up the wall and bringing her senses into full awareness as she smelled the aroma of decay around her. The Light Wings pulsed vibrantly, aligning with her sudden emotions. In that moment, it was like she forgot where she was, like time itself completely stopped. It was as if the reality of the prison slipped away, only to leave raw emotion in its place. Her fears dissolved, and she found her strength again. Somehow she felt no danger and, instead, as her mind returned to her, she leaped forward into the warmth of Leo's embrace. "I can't believe you're here."

Leo held her as her body trembled.

"What happened?" she cried.

In that instant, the guard tore away and dashed back into the corridor ahead of them. He ran as if his life depended on it. Leo knew better than to trust him, but he was not disappointed. He had what he was after—what he needed to put his mind at ease— and that was all that mattered. All would be well in the end; or, perhaps it would not be. But either way, she was with him. With a deep breath and all his strength, he froze this moment into his mind, binding it into an abyss of secrets he would keep for himself away from the world, so that maybe, one day, he would get to feel this once more.

Slowly, with struggle, he pulled away from her. "We have to get out of here. The Carists believe we're responsible for destroying their tower," he whispered. "And they know about my father too. They think I murdered him."

Lucia cringed, nonresistant to the tremble that quaked through her. She brought up her hand and brushed it against Leo's cheek, feeling the blood wet on her fingers. She saw the pain in Leo's eyes as he tightened them above his bruised, bleeding nose. "They hurt you."

"You should see the other guys," Leo boasted. "They were going to hurt you too if I hadn't fought them off."

Lucia put a hand to her lips, staying silent but still looking deep into the oceans on his face. She could not explain it—that moment—like a haze, a fog of emotion she could not quite define. She had her doubts and fears, as well as her hopes and dreams. To her, those were clear now, but what she felt in this very moment was something unlike anything she had ever experienced. Despite his cool exterior, when it came to protecting her Leo was impulsive and reckless. It was as if he lost a part of himself—or gave it up all for the sake of making sure she was safe. He was devoted and selfless, willing to risk his own life for hers. Since they'd met, she watched his temperament change. His willingness to fight became stronger, and harder for him to control. And with that, something inside told her to resist.

"Lucia, we have to get you somewhere safe," Leo said. "There has to be a way to the surface. We can't stay down here when it comes. We'll be crushed."

Lucia's eyes narrowed, her sadness apparent. She shook her head. "Leo, listen. I don't want you to fight anymore. You have to save yourself."

Leo gave her a wild look, the same as always, just as confused. "Save myself?" Did she know what he just went through? What he did to save her? How could she be saying this?

Lucia shook her head again as her heart began to crack like lightning stretching across a bitter sky. "If I'm destined to win, I will. That is reason enough to save yourself. You can lead me up to the surface, but why not go back home, for your sake? You've already lost so much because of me. Who am I if I let you keep fighting? It's changing you."

Leo's lips quivered as he tried to speak. "Look, Lucia. What I did back there, I did for you. You wouldn't be out of that cell if I hadn't fought them off." Leo was desperate to explain. But a piece of him knew she was right. It was all a blur to him, but he was violent, vicious—brutal even. He'd lost himself in the heat of the moment and Lucia knew that without having witnessed it. Shame was plainly written across his face. "They were going to hurt you, Lucia." He sobbed as he nearly broke down.

Lucia let one tear slide, but shifted her head as if to hide it. "They wouldn't have been able to. You should know that. The Light Wings are with me. These men are not the enemy here." She tried hard not to cry, but she was in no way as good at containing her emotions as Leo was; or, at the very least, used to be. She held her breath before saying, "Your pride and passion are going to get you killed. At least in Pinea, you'll have a better reason to fight. You don't need to die for me." She clenched her fist as she fought back her own words. *Why am I doing this?* "You have a duty to yourself and to your homeland, but not to me. Fight for your people. *They* should be your priority." Lucia then pointed to the small pendant at her neck. "And this is mine."

Leo's cheeks flushed under his pale skin. "You can't be serious, Lucia." He took both her hands in his. "There is no home to go back to. The land's polluted and my people are dying. Out here, with you, I have a fighting chance. Don't you see? Following you, protecting you, that's my duty. That's my promise. I vowed. I can't turn back now."

She pulled away, pushed past him and turned sharply to face him. "But . . . you're losing yourself. You've forgotten where you've come from and who you're supposed to be." She placed a hand over her heart and felt a shock she did not expect. It seemed to leave her heart turned and tightened. "Leo, I can't—" She stopped herself as she peered into his sapphire blue eyes. "I can't be responsible for that. I just can't. Not if something happens to you. It doesn't matter if you end up alive or dead, you'll never be the same." Lucia bowed her head. "*I'll* never be the same."

There was a lull, a haunting silence. The tension was intoxicating, thick and strong, and concentrated like sharp acid.

"Fine," Leo said reluctantly, resting his hand on the hilt of his dagger. "I won't waste your time." He walked a good distance ahead of her before turning. "I'll lead you out, but from there"—he swallowed hard, holding back the tears in his own eyes—"we'll just see what happens."

Lucia's eyes swelled as they widened. She nodded. She could not believe at all what she had done, but she did not need to risk him losing anything more. All he had now was his life, after losing his family and his home. He needed to focus on finding that place again, a place to call his own, something to believe in. He did not need to lose whatever was left of himself. Not because of her. Not because of the Light Wings.

Lucia clenched the Light Wings, taking in a breath as her gaze darted ahead of her. She followed after Leo, quickening her step before reaching him. She grimaced in thought. If only Stello had left more for her, something other than a prophecy and a pendant—he could have left her something more, and better instruction.

Leo stopped suddenly, analyzing the corridor the best he could without looking back, without even casting the slightest glance toward Lucia. He did not want to see her. With every stare, he could not help but admire her. But right now, he did not want to admire her—he was angry about what she had said. He would follow her request, as much as it pained him. He would only lead her to the surface, and then leave her. It was what she wanted. But what would he do without her? How could he leave her to accomplish this task alone?

She was right about one thing. He would never be the same. He was changing, for better or for worse. He could not help but feel ashamed of what he done during his escape against the guards. Without Lucia, he was senseless. And he didn't know why. All he knew was that he wanted to stay by her side more than anything.

There had to be a way to show her that he needed to.

"Are you okay?" Lucia asked as Leo broke his trance.

He looked again to the walls and saw the blood stains in the dirt below his boots. "The guards," he said. "They're gone. They might have gone to inform Talon of our escape. It won't be long before they come for us."

Lucia drowned another spike of panic with a deep breath. The pendant pulsed slowly like a struggling heartbeat. The lights flickered above her, bringing her stomach into a twist with the duration of silence. She was not thinking fast enough. Something within her told her she didn't have much time. "Let's hurry."

Leo nodded in response, still hesitating to look back to her. Swiftly, they moved along the corridor, hearing nothing more than the sound of waves crashing over them. The world shivered as if it were afraid, releasing a light whimper into the air, jiggling it. The door out of the holding cells emerged from the shadows in the distance, while a small ring of light glowed around the pendant like a halo. The light reflected off the door as they approached it. Gently, Leo reached forward and pulled the handle, cracking the door free from the stone wall.

Lucia bit her lip with impatience but still stood warily behind Leo. The sense of impending danger only grew. She said, "Remember what I told you."

Leo bowed his head. "Is that even possible?"

Lucia didn't respond. Truthfully, she was not at all sure. She was very much afraid of what lay ahead and she didn't have all the answers she needed; but the Light Wings had saved her more than once. Even when she failed, the light redeemed her. She had to do what felt right, what felt fair. She had to let Leo serve his own duty while she served hers. He did not deserve this.

Leo did not wait for a reply. Instead, he passed through the door and moved up the steps, following them up the spiral stone staircase. Only by instinct did he glance behind him with his bright blue eyes to catch a glimpse of the girl following behind him.

She walked up, sad and beautiful, keeping her head lowered gracefully to the side. She brushed her gentle fingers along the stone, sensing it as the shadows watched them quiver. She was afraid.

Leo whispered to himself, deciding then. "I could never let you go."

CHAPTER TWELVE

The Trial of the Carists

"Father!" Luzanna yelled out in anger as she burst through two finely cut doors of cypress. Her eyes were burning with an intense glare, piercing through the haze of her own sad thoughts. She entered the vast arena, taking in the essence of the light as it fell onto her mask absorbing into the dove-white exterior and imbuing it with an intense vision, filled with hope. This was the training ground where she had worked all her life. For years, she held true to the philosophy of her tribe, honing her skills as a scholar and a warrior. To be strong in both body and mind was the highest honor of the Carists, the keepers of knowledge and guardians of secrets. Within this circular room, Luzanna knew in her heart that she would have no choice but to face her father, despite all she feared. In this room she would face the final test of her youth.

The light was unusually gray, dim beneath a drizzle of rain. Behind the glass of a gigantic dome, flashes of purple lightning crawled across the fabric of the darkening clouds. Luzanna's heartbeat deepened as the thunder roared. She paced across the marble floors, looking toward the large archway. She clenched her fists over the shaft of her polearm as her palms became slick with sweat. She held the spear high, weary of every step, as if she knew something terrible was coming on the horizon.

Atop a stone throne was Talon, armored in gold. The phoenix, seemingly powerful and wildly deranged, stared at his daughter. He rested his head in his hand as he lost himself within the chambers of his mind, as if consumed by something. Was it the darkness, his fear, or his own sin? Whatever it was, it was restless. Perhaps, it was a memory of a not-so-distant past.

Luzanna stepped into the fragmented light of the dome. The platinum of her armor radiated as the lightning flashed overhead. Her magenta ribbon seemed to tighten in her golden hair as Talon struggled to his feet, standing as proudly as any man of power would, except Luzanna could sense the darkness' hold on him. She tried not to exhibit the slightest ounce of weakness, though she was very much afraid. Still, her fear did not overshadow her conviction. She knew of all she hoped and fought for.

"You've come before me, my daughter, holding arms against your father? Do my eyes deceive me?"

Luzanna shook her head. "Father, you won't listen to me. What other choice do I have?" She pointed the tip of her spear forward. "You're *not* going to break the world's natural order. You're not going to kill her! She's the only one capable of destroying the darkness."

Talon stepped down from the throne, keeping a distance. He gave a half smile before pulling a short sword from his side. It was forged of gold-gilded steel, glistening a dark yellow, and was nearly as bright as the flames of his armor. Like the phoenix feather, bladed to the tip, it blazed. "You are so strong, Luzanna, but still you are naive to think you know what nature has intended for us. It is as it should be." He lowered his sword and turned from her, leaving her confused.

"As it should be?" Luzanna's hope drew anger from the pit of her chest. "Don't play with my head!" She ran forward, pointing the tip of her spear toward her father. Immediately, her tears flooded over her eyelids. They sparkled with sorrow, fueled by her despair. Shocked at her own actions, she pulled the spear away and fell to her knees as anger overtook her body. Luzanna had failed to see the lengths her faith had taken her—to the point she would have fought or even killed her own father. But she could not. She was not as heartless as the darkness wanted her to be, but she still had the urge to fight raging within her. She cried out, "Why don't you just kill me then? If you kill her, if you destroy the pendant, you're going to condemn me to a fate far worse than your sword could ever bring. I'd rather die rebelling against you than watch the world die for your mistake!"

Talon turned to her as she curled up on the floor. His face softened, free of tension and full of sympathy. "You hold firm to this belief, because such hope lies in your heart—a hope I cannot see, a hope I envy. I envy your ambition, the heart to die for a dream that might not be. Your youth, your vigor; the very life I had a part in creating has brought into this world something beautiful. You have the hope this world needs, the hope of a true leader. Something I may never know."

Luzanna looked up to her father, her anger dissolving, as if something inside understood his words. Her emotions swung as if on a pendulum.

He continued. "All has happened just as he predicted. The

prophecy is coming true. The girl has awoken the ancient spirits with her song, and she is now connected. Luzanna, you don't understand because you have not yet seen it. You have not yet seen the realm of the protectors."

"Father, you don't mean . . . " Luzanna said quietly, still on her knees, "Remena."

"It is your birthright to someday hold these secrets, just as I have. But never did I think you would have to face this, not this young. Stello once told me of what you would be destined for, of the greatness you would someday achieve, but he also told me of all the suffering you would endure because of it." Talon choked. "All without me by your side. I cast him away not because I feared death, Luzanna, but because I feared leaving you to face this darkness on your own. However, it is too late. My time has already come."

"Father, what do you mean? You *must* tell me."

"The girl has opened the door, one that was perhaps unlocked long ago but never fully pushed open. Like her mother, she holds a very special gift, one that connects her to their world." Talon sighed, taking a moment to remember his old friend. "Ara once sealed the darkness into place, but Lucia has done the opposite. She has given it a way in, and they are using her gift against her, all because the covenant is broken."

"The covenant? Father, I'm confused."

Talon smiled. "It's because you have to go for yourself and discover the truth. The darkness will not be sealed away again that easily. It is stronger now than it ever was before, fueled by the sins of those it devours. I thought that if I severed the connection, it might be forced away. But Stello, he knew her faith would not yet be strong enough to keep the sins at bay. Luzanna, please forgive me for not realizing this sooner. I deeply regret my actions and want nothing more than to see you fulfill the prophecy Stello has left. You must go and restore virtue to the world."

"But, Father, how can I do that? I know nothing of the world outside these walls."

Talon stepped down from his throne and approached his daughter as she kneeled before him. "You know what you must do, my dear. You must take on your pilgrimage and assume your role as chieftess. Become the keeper of knowledge, and I . . . " Talon closed his eyes as tears ran beneath his visor.

Luzanna looked into the sky as the storm raged. She saw the hint of green and sensed how the air chilled more with every breath.

"I will die protecting my country."

"No!" Luzanna cried. Her spear fell from her hands as she thrust her arms around her father and buried her face into his neck. "I won't let you go. I can't. Not now." How could she have ever come to terms with killing this man? The pain returned to her hand, burning with a white-hot fury. Why was she, too, changing?

Talon held his daughter, feeling his life within his hands. "Hold on to your dreams, my sweet. Fate needs you to survive past this. Take the girl with you to Remena. See to it that she realizes the truth. It is time that the world knows the whole story."

"Father, I won't let you die. You won't. I can change all this." She backed away to stare into her father's eyes. "I won't treat you like some lost cause! There is a future for both of us."

Talon smiled again. "For you, yes. But, I shouldn't have intervened. This is my sin. I must take responsibility." He lifted his hand and touched the top of his visor. He clasped the clear opal stone and pulled it from its place before putting it into Luzanna's stinging hand.

Instantly, the throbbing washed away. "The Elder Stone," Luzanna whispered as tears streamed.

"For generations, this stone has been a symbol of leadership within our tribe, and now it is yours. Hold on to it always, and let it be your strength. Always remember where you've come from. The blood of the Carist runs strong within you. In time it will fade, but the stories you will share, the history you will make will be enough to keep our lineage live and well."

"Oh, Father . . . "

"It's alright, Luzanna. Don't fear what you don't know. All knowledge comes with time. Go now to Lucia and see that she is taken to safety. I must gather the troops and prepare for battle. It won't be long now."

Luzanna could not believe what was happening. She stood, shocked by her father's sudden change of heart but somehow not surprised. Whatever she said, and whatever he had seen, had brought a kindness from deep within him. Though her hope managed to displace his fear through this last test of her own faith, Luzanna felt as if her world had changed forever.

*   *   *

"There they are!" Leo pushed Lucia back behind him as he held out his dagger.

Lucia gripped the pendant in her fist as her eyes traced the tips of their long-bladed spears.

The flock of men pushed forth from the front of the corridor. "Surrender now, or resist and regret it," one of them warned.

Her mind was spinning. There they were, in the midst of another battle, and she could not get the voices out of her head. She clenched her eyes shut and sensed the slight movements of Leo's muscles tightening as his eyes fully dilated like a lion locked on its prey. Lucia shook her head. "Seriously?"

Leo smiled softly. With ease he pounced, charging at the men. They took efforts trying to disarm and subdue him, but Leo's reflexes were too swift. No man could catch him. Lucia wondered how he learned to move as he did, as she watched him smash his fist against the visors of the Carist soldiers and slash toward them to get them off their feet. He sent his fists into the open spots of their armor and used the blade of his dagger to sweep low, sending them crashing to the floor. He leapt and took hold of one of their weapons, twirling it as he brought down two more men. As soon as he got his hands on any of their spears, he disarmed them and tossed their weapons out of arms reach.

All this fighting frightened Lucia, but there was no other choice. She realized there was a purpose to it all. It was time to act, and Lucia couldn't afford to lose. Fate had demonstrated its hold over them as the fighting subsided, leaving Leo in feral state. He was a fierce fighter. Stronger than she realized. Faster than any man she had ever seen. Better even than any of the military men guarding her capital. But Lucia worried. There had to be something fueling him. And if it was not his home, his duty, or Lucia herself, what was the root of all his fury? Why could he no longer contain it within himself?

With the pendant still in hand, she opened her heart and started her prayer. "Please, no more. Put an end to this. With your power, I ask of thee. Lend me the strength I need." And with that, the door opened once more, the connection to the other world. A surge overwhelmed her as the wings pulsed with light. Lucia opened her hand, releasing a bright flash. She lifted out her hand and, with a wave, shot an orb from the tips of her fingers and filled Leo's fists with a gallant, azure glow.

Charged with an unbelievable strength, Leo sent his foes flying backward. The force was unreal, unimaginable as the men shook and hit the back of the corridor, causing shockwaves to ripple through the air. Tapestries fell from the stone walls as they crumbled.

Leo's eyes were blazing with blue fire as the power faded from his fists. His eyes lowered towards his shaking hands, still tingling from the might of the light. The men lay defeated on the floor. Some were groaning, others unconscious or pretending to be, but surely sulking in their shame. Leo glanced toward Lucia, who was breathing almost as heavily as he was.

"I couldn't just stand by and watch," she said. "I had to do something."

"Well, I'm glad you did." Leo was curious as his anger miraculously subsided. He was almost laughing as the rush of adrenaline burned beneath his skin. " So you do have some fight in you after all."

"I suppose I do." Lucia stepped closer to Leo and brushed her arm against his, feeling the static spark as they touched. She closed her eyes, listening to the whispers of the Light Wings as if she knew they were warning her of what was to come. "There isn't much time. The worst has yet to come." Lucia glanced back towards Leo, unsure of who he was or of the person he had become. She couldn't help but empathize. She broke the tension with her voice as doom loomed. "I'm sure the tower has been secured with more guards by now. Our only hope is to fight our way through."

"I thought you didn't want to fight?"

"I didn't want *you* to fight," Lucia corrected. "But as for me"— she clutched the pendant—"the Light Wings have other plans." She paused. "Let's get going. We need to get out of here."

"What's with her?" Leo thought, muttering under his breath. He could not quite make out what exactly it was, but Lucia did not seem at all herself. Was *she* changing, too? No, this was different. It wasn't as if she were resisting as Leo was, straying far from the lessons he'd learned within his youth. Far from the person he was supposed to be. Lucia's transformation was nothing like his own. The more she used the pendant's power, the more the Light Wings changed her, grooming her, tailoring her like they would a doll. He tried to understand what it might be like, feeling all that power. He did feel it for a moment, but it was benevolent. One could even say calming. Very unlike the fighting he had grown used to. Where had all his anger gone? The more he tried to understand, the more lost he became. There was this heavy burden encased within Lucia's eyes, as if her spirit was weighed down, shackled. His eyes followed the arch of her collarbone and eventually met with the silver chain where it rested beneath her neck, bearing the entire weight of Terestria.

"Whatever it is you're worrying about, stop," Leo said, clenching his fist. "You underestimate its power and my own. If you think we can't do this, if you think *I* can't do this, then we've already lost the battle. Why give up?" He locked with her gaze. "We will protect you."

Lucia lowered her head as the shame washed over her. His words sank deep, cutting into her. As much as she hated to admit it, he was right. *The light has always protected me,* she thought. *And so has he.* Who was she to determine, to judge, to decide? After all, none of this was her choice. This path was already chosen for her. The light had blessed her with this purpose, and it chose him to be her guardian.

"Leo," Lucia said. She had trouble finding the words. In her quest for fairness, she now realized that she had been blinded. By what, she could not say, but the more she noticed his determination, it became all too apparent. She could not do this without him. "Thank you."

Leo blinked, nearly surprised by her words. "You're welcome."

A sense of security rose then, a mutual understanding of each other's strengths and purpose. It was clear that the two had begun to care for one another. Neither could bear to see the other in any pain, though there was no avoiding it. Alone, neither would get very far, but together in support of one another, they stood a chance to rise up against the trials they soon would face. If they ever hoped to survive, they had to work together as equals, and ultimately, as a team.

*   *   *

They hurried into a long corridor that wound around and turned into a stairwell. As they rose, the rooms became brighter and the hallways grew more elaborate. They were well on their way to the surface, and with each step it became clear that they were very close. They proceeded with caution, trying to stay hidden from the few Carist soldiers patrolling the area.

Lucia felt it like a tug at her heartstrings. The chill was within her blood, almost as if it were a part of her. "Wait!" Lucia stopped, pulling Leo behind a nearby bookcase. "Do you see it? There," she whispered as she pointed to an eerie glow of purple in the distance. It was less a glow and more a distortion of some sort, like anti-light or a ripple in space or time. It refracted and drew in the shine of the light around it, pulling apart the spectrum and shattering it in the depths of its growing blackness. As it spread, it dissolved all the matter it touched, turning it into shadow. "Is that . . . ?" Lucia's eyes quivered.

The distortion clung to the corners of the walls, seemingly building its strength as it absorbed and took in more of the light. The lanterns themselves flickered, and the air sharpened with frost as it grew dense around the force, tense with gravity. As the area darkened, the force became more powerful, transforming right before their eyes.

Lucia saw flames of the beast within her mind. The flames erupted as glass fell, and the image rose like a premonition, tossing her thoughts into hysteria. She watched it happening all once more. Her breath hovered as her body shook, each nerve falling into another waking nightmare. The force emitted a stench as it sprang to life. Lucia's body tingled as the base of her neck sparkled. Instinctively, her fingers came together as she took a deep breath.

The Light Wings pulled at her tendons as a master would its puppet, honing her focus as her eyes locked onto their target. She pushed past Leo as the puddle of dark radiance emitted a shriek so frightening it shook the sanity of all who heard it. "Watch out!" she screamed.

From the depths of the emptiness rose a scaly black tentacle. Like a serpent, it coiled upward, hissing loudly as an onyx blade cut from its end, glossy to the tip and oozing with black tar. The tentacle sprang, tossing its sharp blade at the bookcase, sending up a shower of papers and scrolls, obscuring their vision. Leo dropped to the ground, dodging the coil as it spun around. Lucia released her hands, sending a wave of light through the air, stunning the tail as it whipped back toward the portal through which it had entered.

"It nearly decapitated you!" she yelled at Leo, who was panting on one knee. She shook her head. "You've got to be more careful!"

"Don't you have something more important to worry about? Go, Lucia!" Leo yelled, his shining gaze fixated on the monster.

Lucia nodded, watching as the blade of the beast pointed down like a snake eying its prey. Lucia's body was trembling, but she knew not to hesitate. Leo was too weary from fighting—she had to do this on her own.

It sent out another relentless shriek, ripping through the shadows emitting from its body. The strength of the force was growing more powerful; but still, Lucia could tell this was only a fragment of its true form. The Light Wings pulsed vibrantly, calling her hand forward as the serpent sent another wave of power through the room.

The tentacles darted forward. Leo's panicked eyes glazed as he rushed toward Lucia.

Lucia's thoughts uttered a resonance of a prayer as light erupted from beneath her neck, shining as she brought her fingers to her temples. An understanding was beginning to spread through her. "These monsters. They are . . . manifestations."

"Lucia!" The blade was falling toward her, and it seemed as if Lucia did not notice, as if she chose not to. Leo watched in terror as Lucia closed her eyes, inviting the darkness in as she cloaked herself with light.

The pendant pulsed as a pair of diamond wings sprouted from Lucia's back, wrapping around and protecting her. They sparkled as the onyx clashed against their exterior, sending them flinching backward seething in the radiance of their own bright light. The wings shattered with a gigantic flash, sending thousands of flying shards of pulsating sparks shooting and tearing into the flesh of the beast. The tentacle screeched in pain, torn apart by what appeared to be an array of shooting stars as it disintegrated in a blaze of white flame.

"Lucia, are you alright?" Leo asked, watching as the smoke cleared and the light retreated back into the pendant. There she was, still standing.

Lucia could hardly believe it herself. She opened her eyes. "That was incredible." She held a hand to her chest, still feeling the power course through her. *Did I just . . .* Her eyes quivered as she thought, *I just fought back.* "I never thought my prayers could hold so much power." How did she become this? Somehow, her faith, the one thing she spent her entire life tempering, had become her weapon. Lucia was now far from the gentle maiden she once was, and more like the heroine Terestria had called her to be. "Is this really who I am?"

Leo could see now why the Light Wings had chosen her. Without the slightest hesitation or thought, he pulled her close and held on to her as he spoke. "When we first met, I swore to fight beside you and to follow your every decision. Even if at times they were unreasonable, I thought it was my duty to protect you, the golden rose of Moz. I never thought I'd be this proud to say it."

Lucia listened to his words as her emotions swelled.

Leo had only begun to understand that a supernatural faith had cursed her, for she embodied a divinity that she never asked for, one that would haunt her for the rest of her life. "But I see now, the burden you hold and the pain it has caused you." He lifted her chin and stared into her low, honey-streaked hazel eyes. "Just wait, I promise you. Once this is all over, we'll rebuild this world and you'll get to see it through different eyes. I'll show it to you, and all will be right, the way it should be. You won't be trapped within the grips of duty or darkness, but by the ways of the land blessed by the light that you, alone, have given it. Trust that one day, when this duty is finally done, you will find your dreams"—he lowered his head—"with me."

She wiped away her tears, took a step back, and muttered, "It won't be that easy." She turned from him, leaving Leo dazed. She could tell how he felt about her. After all, he had shown it quite enough, but there was no way she could allow him to sacrifice any more for her. There was only so much she could let happen before losing him completely. "We don't know how this will end. We don't know who will be left standing." Lucia paced past him, onward, her expression blank.

Leo hurried after her, his heart now heavy from Lucia's cold exterior. How could she turn so quickly? It was as if she was changing with each passing moment, becoming more distant and less herself. He could not think of the words to share, more than he already had, to get her to open her heart to him. Instead of letting it eat away at whatever was left of his broken heart, he decided to focus on the chaos at hand and the darkness that threatened to destroy them.

* * *

They finally came upon a lone door at the end of a poorly lit hallway. Lucia lifted a hand, using it to light the way as she reached for the door. Surprisingly, just as she was about to touch the knob, it burst open. Leo jumped backward, pulling Lucia behind him defensively and bracing for whatever was coming through. His eyes squinted, trying to make out the figure as it moved like a blur through the doorway.

Contrary to their initial expectations, they were warmly embraced by a familiar figure. Her voice pounded in their ears, vibrating with an energizing enthusiasm that left their hearts fluttering. "I found you! I actually found you! And you're okay!" Luzanna released them from her grip and clasped her hands together in joy. "My father ordered you to be released not long ago. Where have you been?"

"Released? You must be joking. Your men really roughed us up," Leo said disdainfully, the anger apparent as he pointed to the cut on his face. "Is this how you treat all your prisoners?"

"Leo, it's not her fault!" Lucia said. "Calm yourself."

"It's quite alright," Luzanna said, somehow understanding Leo's plight. "It was in no way easy convincing my father to release you. He wasn't nice about it either." She removed her mask from her face to reveal the large bruise across her face.

Leo gasped, his eyes somber with regret. "I'm sorry. I spoke out of turn."

"Don't worry about it," Luzanna smiled. "All that matters is that you're safe now."

Lucia brushed off her clothing. "So, did your father agree to help us?"

Luzanna nodded, pushing back her long blonde hair and placing her mask back on her face. "My father's briefing the military as we speak, preparing our weapons. There has been no sign of an imminent attack, not since the incident. But he's not taking any chances."

"Well, I'd trust your father's intuition on this one," Leo said while pointing to the pendant. It was pulsating. "The darkness is near. We were attacked by what appeared to be something of its lesser minions. Not far from where we standing now, actually. I'm sure the real monstrosity is a lot closer than we realize."

"He's right," Lucia said, raising her voice with utmost authority. "I can sense it. Whatever it is, it's not far. And"—Lucia shook her head, trying to release it from the dread seeping into her every thought—"there might be more of them. Whatever's coming, it doesn't feel the same as what I saw in Moz or Pinea. It's different altogether."

"So, you're saying there are three of these beasts?"

Lucia shook her head again. *Damn, this dread.* She thought. "No, there are four. At least, that's what the Light Wings are telling me."

"Well damn them all to hell!" Leo roared. "Let's hurry and find Talon before this gets worse than it has to." He pushed past Luzanna, whose eyes were low, seemingly drifting into the shadows.

"Luzanna . . . " Lucia reached out and touched her hands. "Everything is going to be okay, remember? You saved us. Because of you, there's hope."

Luzanna blinked. Somehow the words resonated with something in her heart. Her right hand tingled. The pain returned, but she forced it back as she brought a smile to her face. "Right, there is always hope."

"Exactly." Lucia looked to the doorway. Within moments, her face hardened as she realized that this would be her first real battle. She had never seen war before. When her mother spoke of it, it was just a story. But now, she was on the verge of witnessing its bloodlust firsthand. More people were going to die. *In order to maintain peace, one must be willing to sacrifice.* Her mother's words reverberated as her senses moved into critical overdrive. Every ounce of dark energy within the city was tuning into this power, a force deep within the depths of the earth. It was growing and heading closer and closer to the surface. She yanked Luzanna through the door. "Come on. It's coming!"

"The darkness?" Luzanna asked, the fear prematurely blooming in the core of her stomach.

"The very demise of Aldric would be that of its own folly," Lucia said, her words not her own.

Leo narrowed his sapphire eyes. Slowly, he withdrew his dagger as he hastened his stride. "Lucia, earlier you called these monsters 'manifestations.' Would you care to elaborate? We need to know what we're getting into here."

"Oh! You mean about the beasts and there being more than one?" Luzanna interjected, curiously. She obviously was eager to know herself.

"All linking to *one*," Lucia corrected. "There is one darkness. That is certain, but—" She heard the whispers. The secret knowledge flowed through her, given to her by the light itself. "The darkness has its remnants, its sins. That's what the phantom in Pinea called itself."

"Wait!" Luzanna stopped to catch her breath. "That's exactly what my father called it. He said 'the darkness is fueled by the sins of those it devours.' He also said that faith alone would not be able to keep the sins at bay, and that we needed to restore virtue to the world."

"That's a bit too cryptic, don't you think?" Leo asked. "He didn't by any chance tell you how we'd go about doing that, did he?"

"No, he didn't. But he said I'd learn more soon. After all of this." Luzanna blinked. "Honestly, I should've probed him for more information." She looked over to Lucia. "I'm sorry, Lucia. I was in shock."

"So what we're about to face is another one of these 'sins'?" Leo asked grimly. "And not the sin that destroyed your home or mine—but the incarnation of Aldric's own . . . sin?"

"Yes. They are the incarnations of our sin. Now that I remember, in Pinea the darkness called itself 'pride' and it said that we'd bring about our own destruction. That's why the war . . . " Lucia hesitated as she pieced together the story. "That's why the war ended as it did. The bloodshed and the malice manifested into its own sin, or many, and it terrified all those who witnessed it. That was the beginning of the end. That's when—"

After hearing Lucia's words, Luzanna's body shook with panic. "The covenant was broken," she whispered as her eyes went blank. "We have to find my father, right now. If what you say is true, if the prophecy is true . . . " Luzanna sobbed. "He will die! Can't you see? Your father foretold it. My tribe, my country, it will all be vanquished!"

"There is much more at stake here. All of Terestria is in danger," Leo said. "Aldric is only the beginning."

"Whatever's coming is strong. We can't let up for even a moment. I don't even think we can defeat it. Not at this point. Not if there are more than one," Lucia said.

"You don't think you can take them?" Leo asked. "The Light Wings are strong enough."

Lucia glared at him. "But they only act on their own."

"Only because you don't try to control them. They take over when you're in danger and at your most vulnerable. They sense what you're feeling and save you. Your emotional state is what draws their power. If you could control your emotions, you could control the Light Wings." Leo had learned by now that Lucia's weakness was indeed her strength. That sensitivity Lucia was ashamed of was the only thing that could save them.

Lucia's voice rose in her throat. "What if I don't *want* to control it? What if I don't want anything to do with it?" She stepped in front of Leo. "You don't understand how their power makes me feel." She moved back by Luzanna. "You never did!"

"Not this again," Leo said. He scoffed before nudging past the girls. "I'm growing tired of your negligence. I admit, you've grown since we met, but you still lack the sense of a true leader. You refuse to acknowledge your destiny, you forget the strength of your own voice, and you choose to accept what's right in front of you rather than what lies beneath. Your emotions don't make you weak, Lucia. Your naivety does.

"Since when have you forgotten that I had a voice too, that I've lost just as much as you have, if not more. Aren't I a noble with a duty just like your own? What makes us so different? I know my own strength. I have just as much of an obligation to this world as you do—and you know what?" He calmed himself and approached her slowly. "You would have never gotten this far without me. I was the one who saved you in that damned forest. I was the one who opened the door and released you from your cell before the Carist could have tortured, killed, or worse . . . .

"The way they talked about you . . . . Do you truly understand how you make *me* feel about the things I do? Who are you to judge and decide what actions another should take? You refuse to control the Light Wings because they are above you, but everything else is beneath you, isn't it? You like watching everyone bend over backwards and literally sacrifice their lives for you. Admit: you'd rather others make your choices for you!" Leo scoffed. "Free will is no illusion, Lucia. Not when you're so willing to reject it!"

Lucia stepped back, her heart sinking, almost breaking. She knew it was true, but she dared not admit it. However, there was something in his eyes still sympathetic. Tears welled up in her gaze. Since when had she become so selfish? Or was that simply who she was? Privileged. Special. Selfish. Far from perfect.

"I'm sorry," he said with a soft face, his impulsion melting away. "I don't know what's wrong with me."

"No," Lucia said, "*I'm* sorry. I wasn't aware of how much I had burdened you. I was consumed by my own self-pity. I simply forgot and disregarded everything you were going through. Well, not disregarded, but simplified and set aside. To think I didn't appreciate—"

"All is forgiven."

"Still, it doesn't change how I feel." Lucia sighed. "I admit, I fear its power. I fear how overwhelming and all-consuming it is. Every time I use it, a piece of it melds itself to me. I don't want to depend on it or anyone. That's how I really feel, but I'm afraid. More than anything, I fear the death that follows my every move." Lucia knew she couldn't tear the pendant from her neck. She was eternally bound to it. If she lost control would she be herself again?

Luzanna held back a sob. "So what are you going to do? We can't just let my people die."

Lucia knew the answer. It was dreaded, but it was the right one. Even if it defied fate, it was what they had to do. It would be difficult. Everything up to this point already had been, but it was not at all impossible, right? Not with hope by their side. Not with free will. Could she fight against the very nature of what her father had predicted? Could she break the curse once and for all? Could she choose a better outcome? "We are going to find your father and save him. It might not be what we are supposed to do, but it is the right thing to do. We must save him at all costs."

Luzanna's eyes lit up with optimism, and her body jumped with joy.

Then Lucia felt the despair as it coiled around her core. She sensed it coming, rising from the depths of a vast dark ocean. It broke free from the trenches of the deep, spewing from the chambers of the darkest shadows, and crept its way to the surface with its scarlet glare.

CHAPTER THIRTEEN

The Prey of the Serpent

Ceo was unsure how to feel about saving the man who had ordered Lucia to be killed. But he trusted Lucia's instinct. There was a strength blossoming from within her, one he knew would somehow find its way to the surface and save them all. He had to believe in her unyielding faith. After all, who was he to go against it? It was her faith that had gotten them this far, despite her reluctance to use her new power. It was her faith that had saved them over and over again. Her constant refusal to let the darkness take her had accomplished what no man could. It had solidified her resolve. It was fitting that she'd been chosen to hold the light. The light was all-powerful, but not without weakness. No despair was too great to shatter through its holy might, yet still, it was as fragile as Lucia was human. But, like the light, Lucia was seemingly incorruptible. That was why she chose to save Talon, the man who almost killed her.

Because she could do what Leo could not: forgive.

This was what Leo had come to accept. Lucia *believed* in all things. She believed the world could be a better place, despite seeing it only at its worst. And because she believed, she sacrificed. Was this why the Light Wings chose her to carry out their will? If this was true, he would have to push her. If they were to survive, she would have to face her limits. Even if she didn't want to, it would have to be her choice. Her sacrifice.

Though his pride was bruised and damaged, he would have to place his faith in Lucia. He would have to be as incorruptible as she was. No matter how angry he was at the men who sought the destruction of their very lives, or at the monster that had framed him and destroyed his kingdom, he could not let himself fall into the darkness of despair.

* * *

The three entered the main room of the tower. Lucia surveyed the area. It was dormant and seemingly frozen within ruin, yet there was no trace of anyone having been there. The last time they were there, Lucia had heard the screams. She had smelled the blood. But now, it was as if no one had died there. It looked as if the tower had been abandoned for some time.

Piles of rubble replaced the stairwells. The walls were fractured, scarred by the quake that had shaken them. The bookcases were broken and covered with a haze of dust. It made Lucia wonder: how long had she been sleeping?

Luzanna pointed to the citrine crystal above them as they crept over broken glass. Her eyes widened as the crystal darkened. A storm rumbled overhead, the thunder sending an ominous and threatening chill. This made Luzanna's heart jump once or twice. Lightning flashed, and a shock of terror struck a nerve in her body.

"We're running out of time," she said softly, her voice trembling as she fought the knot in her throat.

Lucia narrowed her eyes while tilting her head. "I sure hope not." She moistened her lips before following Luzanna further.

Leo hurried behind her, caressing the hilt of his dagger with deep anticipation. He sensed it too, the budding animosity, as if the air itself was tainted with negativity. It hung over his shoulders, pulling him down.

Luzanna led them to one lone surviving stairwell and instructed them to go forward. "Watch your step. I'm not sure how well this will hold, but the barracks are this way."

They hurried up, turning their steps into a full-force run as the lightning became louder, stronger. It wasn't long before the ground began to vibrate. Lucia's senses ached. She touched her forehead, slowing as the sound of a strange hissing rang in her ears. It hovered over her head nearly overwhelming her.

"Lucia, are you alright?" Leo asked, pulling her to his side. He noticed that her skin was lightly coated with sweat. Obviously, she was growing anxious. "You're burning up."

"I'm fine," Lucia said, nearly shaking the band out of her hair. She kept her eyes tight as the ringing painfully heightened, reaching pitches she never thought possible. She was breathing harder now, trying to suppress the sound, but it was encompassing her mind. Still, the harder she fought, the more the noise subsided. Eventually, the ringing faded. She was finally gaining some control over it. "It's approaching the city," she said, taking her hand off her head and staring straight forward with regained composure. "And I think"—she looked up at Leo with a heavy nod—"I know where it's going."

"Where?" Luzanna asked, pacing toward her nervously.

"The shore. It's coming from the sea," Lucia whispered. Luzanna's eyes drifted into a trepidation, and Lucia felt her heart halt with her step. It started again, the ringing. It slowly rose as Luzanna and Leo stood in their silence. The air was growing dense, and the only sounds were the roar of the storm and the patter of rain. Their breaths drifted from their mouths like puffs of smoke, and for a moment it was as if all time had frozen. "It's too late. It's here."

There was a lingering hesitation, one that possibly dragged out longer than it should have, but there was no helping it. The three of them realized that as much as they rushed, as much as they had tried to fight fate, nothing could change this reality.

The lights flickered around them. Luzanna's eyes welled with tears. "It really is too late," she cried. "We must hurry to my father! He must be in the elder's quarters." She started to bolt forward, but Lucia caught her arm, pulling her hand back.

"He isn't," Lucia said, closing her eyes. She saw the image within her mind. It was heavy and thick. She could hardly see past the darkness, but she could see the color of onyx and bright orange clashing in a thick fog of gray. "He's on the shore below the city already. He's attempting to fight off the darkness." She closed her eyes tighter as the image cleared. "Other Carists are with him. It's an army. They're fighting together and these . . . ." She saw them, the bodies of the serpents rising from the water with their blades. "There are so many of them. They're outnumbered and outmatched. Their weapons aren't working." Lucia heard her own emotion swell in her voice as the Light Wings leaked in the horrible vision of the beast's breath destroying the Aldric army's cannons. "Their efforts are futile. They're dying."

Luzanna shook her head wildly, letting the ribbons in her hair fling into the front of her mask and back. "No, they can't be. It won't win. My father knew his fate. They need to retreat right now!"

"Perhaps that's why he chose to fight," Leo said, his eyes broody.

"Better to die defending your homeland than to run from your fate and die anyways. Would you rather die a coward or a hero? I'm guessing he chose the latter." Leo took a step backward, down the stairs. "We must move the Light Wings from here. They need you on the beach."

Luzanna dropped like a weight to her knees. The clash of her armor rattled against the marble floor as she covered her mask with her hands in shock. She looked up to Lucia, almost pleading with her. "We can't just let him die! My father told me to hold on to my hope. I can't let those words die in vain! We must fight with him."

Lucia placed a hand over her heart, sharing Luzanna's pain as she stared into her deep sea gaze. Lucia had come here in search of Talon, and to rid him of his fate. She had sought to prove her destiny limitless, but it did indeed seem so hopeless. She couldn't possibly save Talon now, not with the darkness so near. Time was wearing thin, and Aldric was near its destruction. This was indeed its end, but as she looked into Luzanna's eyes she could not let go of the emotion hidden beneath her sorrow.

Lucia sighed in the peril of the forsaken tower as the earth shook with a heavy surge of thunder. She couldn't just abandon her mission now. She had to hold on to that hope. It was hope that would redeem them from this curse. With Luzanna's hope, Leo's resolve, and her own conviction, they could change fate. She just had to *believe*. "We'll go to the shore. It's the only way to change the course of this wretched prophecy. Leo, while I use the Light Wings to keep the darkness occupied, you need to take Luzanna to Talon and get the survivors to safety. Get as many people as you can and escape Aldric. No matter what, don't look back. I'll come find you when this is all over." Lucia bit her lip. Her mind was filled with thoughts, each eager to prove her worthy and able enough to hold this power. If only her mother knew how much she had changed. If she could only see how determined, how devoted she was. "Remember, duty above all else. There isn't much we can do, but we can save these people. Luzanna, we will save your people."

"Are you sure you can do this?" Leo asked with a glimmer of worry in his eyes.

Lucia wasn't confident, but nodded anyways.

He fought back the urge to tell her no. The thought of leaving her side right now pained him, but he understood. "Let's move."

*   *   *

The next moments were like a flash, passing a lot faster than expected. The earth was shaking violently by then, and screams and panic filled the city. It had become a hive of chaos. Buildings were collapsing as the ground crumbled. Sparks of purple lightning stretched across the sky as a stinging rain fell, dissolving the stone on which it touched. Lucia and the others were running from the tower as lightning struck at its top, hitting the citrine crystal and causing it to burst into flames. A gigantic explosion rumbled through the tower as each of its levels fell onto the next.

Lucia's gut turned. The citrine crystal exploded just as she had foreseen. How accurate were these visions—these prophecies? Was there any point to stopping them? Lucia pushed back the thought. She could not allow herself to think that way. She could not let go of hope.

They found their way onto the bridge ahead of the tower as it fell backward from the cliff. Like a slow nightmare, the chill of the air grew unbearably cold. The rain froze into stinging darts, piercing into their clothing. "It hurts so much," Leo cried as he noticed his skin coated with blood. This storm was meant to bring about suffering. It was not in its nature to deliver a quick death.

Winds ripped at Lucia's clothing and hair as they ran into the crumbling and crying city. She held on to her band, trying to keep it from flying from her head as she fixed her gaze out toward the sea. She could not see it yet, but she knew it was there. It was calling to her, hissing its false promises, its sinful wishes. They ran down to the edge of the cliff, anticipation building as they came upon it above the bloodstained sands of the Aldric shore.

It was there that they first witnessed the vengeful power of the serpent—a sight so chilling it burned deep into the back of Lucia's mind. Each of her senses flared into overdrive, ringing as her eyes widened at the glare of the enormous monstrosity. It was at least a hundred times larger than the demon in Moz, and so much larger than the phantom and its many forms. She could not determine which was more terrifying. And somehow, it could sense her approaching.

It stood tall, rising high from a pool of black tar that expanded across the surface of the ocean, absorbing all the light that met it. Its skin was pitch black, like that of the monsters they had seen within the tower. Were they monsters themselves, or merely a *part* of this one? The serpent of doom was writhing, horned and sharp-toothed. The horns curved beneath its blazing scarlet eyes—eyes like drops of blood painted on a black canvas.

Turning its enormous head towards Lucia, she was sure it shined a demented grin as it slowly approached the edge of the cliff. Lucia stood frozen, almost charmed by the snake's gaze. Lucia noticed how Luzanna's eyes went blank as she met the monster's.

"Come on," Luzanna cried, pulling Lucia back as the serpent darted and snapped at her.

They ran for their lives as the beast let out a deep roar, shaking the air. It chuckled as they dashed down toward the shore.

There was an intense surge as the serpent sent out a thick ripple of force from its body, knocking every person off their feet. It sent out another roar of laughter as its head rose over the city. "This is so much fun, watching you cower in *fear*," it hissed. "Your light is weaker than I thought."

"Hurry!" Leo commanded, jumping to his feet. He pulled

Lucia back as black-bladed tentacles sprang from their portals, like geysers, from the ground. "Move, now!" he screamed, forcing them to run faster.

The tentacles charged, homing in on Luzanna as she led them away from the cliff. The blades fell close behind her, barely missing.

The Light Wings were pulsating brilliantly as Lucia's emotion swelled yet again. The light radiated, glowing brighter and brighter as the darkness sent out another roar. The Light Wings were merging with her spirit, uniting with it and drawing on her pain. The pendant tugged at her chest, pinching at her spine. Her strength was building as she ran down the stone spiral steps along the city's outskirts. The shore materialized beneath her feet as her boots splashed on the bloodstained sand. And just as Lucia made out the bodies of the Carists in the distance, she felt Luzanna's heart break.

Luzanna snatched up a bloody spear from one of the fallen. She hurried onto the shore, and with a loud warlike yell she let out, "Faaather!"

Leo raced after Luzanna, giving Lucia a slight nod before leaving her side.

Lucia slowly took her position at the edge of the vast shore. It was low tide, as if the beast was drawing the water in. A thick cloud of dark matter hovered over the water's icy surface. At the base of the serpent was a mass of tentacles wrapping around each other like a nest of vipers. Lucia's intuition was correct. The tentacles connected to this monster. There weren't many monsters— just one hideous, demented source of temptation. The beast was another piece of the darkness, a spawn of a different sin. Just like the pride of Pinea, this sin was here to feed on the sins of the Carist.

Thousands of tentacles swarmed the beach. Their blades cut into the Carist soldiers, falling, impacting, missing, and impaling them as they struggled to stay in formation, firing their cannons and releasing their spears into the air. Lucia was afraid. There was no escaping the intensity of the anguish she felt, but as soon as those blood-red eyes found and fixed on her, she clenched her fists.

The serpent smiled before lowering its head into a sharp coil. "Don't you see? It's hopeless. You can't save them. They've all been corrupted. Their souls are stained by their delicious sin. Fighting me is no use when I exist in every heart. I feel every beat before it stops. I know every move before it's ever made."

Its words sent chills down her spine. Could it really have such power? To see into the hearts of men? What sin was this? "Who do you think you are?" Lucia flared as the wing flashed in anger. "You are not worthy to speak to me. I am your enemy, here to destroy you!"

It laughed, sending another heavy shock wave and knocking the army to its knees.

Lucia struggled to stay up, covering her face as the sand stormed around them. She looked in haste, trying to retain her sight of Luzanna and Leo, but she had lost them in a sea of running bodies.

"Don't bother looking. They're most likely dead."

Lucia glared back at the beast. "You're full of lies, aren't you?"

"Believe what you want, but your fragile light will burn out soon enough. They were right to abandon you, just as your father did. It makes for easy prey." The beast laughed once more, except this time as if it had a sense of pity. "You are weak." It lowered its glare. "Just . . . like . . . him."

Lucia's heart hardened. What could this sin know? It wasn't true. She was not weak. And her father . . . *Is it reading my thoughts? No, it couldn't live in every heart. Could it?* "What do you know? I'm here to fight! My friends fight. My father fights."

"You mean *fought*," hissed the serpent. "Because he's dead. Just like you soon will be."

"Shut up!"

"I assure you, your father died a coward's death. You know you've thought about it. How he abandoned you and your family. How he didn't deserve your love. I know because you covet. You covet your friends for how much their fathers loved them. *Their* fathers would die for them! One already has. The other, soon enough. But yours, a pity he was. It was a pleasure ripping him to shreds."

Its laughter shook through her mind, fragmenting it as her heart sank. *No . . . .* Her grief turned to agony as she realized it spoke the truth.

"They have and will. All fathers will die. Just like yours."

"No," Lucia cried, trying to hold back her tears. "What are you?"

"Isn't it obvious?" the serpent roared. "I am the corruption of your perception, the deceiver of your hope. I am your envy . . . the bane of your self-righteousness." *The deceiver of my hope . . . the corruption of my perception . . . the bane of my self-righteousness.* Lucia's thoughts were spiraling as she felt it deep within her heart. The coil of its tail wrapped around, and with the tip it pierced her.

"Lucia!"

Suddenly, Lucia's sight shattered as the pendant vibrated, sending ripples of light through the air. The beast cowered back, hissing as it sent another shock wave toward the shore. It almost had her.

She felt herself falling, almost as if its slithers were tempting her to give in to it. She felt as if her own heart had betrayed her as she'd listened to the serpent's words. There was some truth in all of it, but never had she ever taken it seriously. Not even her darkest inclinations could cause her to stray from her duty. Orders were orders. *Duty above all else.*

Lucia collected her thoughts, listening for the voice of the Light Wings. Slowly, they came to her, telling her what she must do. "Relax, my child. Let me guide you." And with that, Lucia was overcome by a wave of emotion.

At that moment, Lucia crossed her hands and lifted them above her head. She trusted in the light, letting it in. *Forgive me,* she thought as she cleared the doubt that sin had rooted within her subconscious. In that moment, she felt the spirit course through and her body tingled. The Light Wings glowed with a bright incandescence. It was blinding as it poured from Lucia's chest. The light pushed back over her body, coating her blouse and encasing her within a chrysalis of bright light. The light was dripping down her body and over her boots, merging with the fabric of her clothing and etching golden strands into it. "I grant you my protection," the Light Wings whispered as it charged her with holy might. The light traced up her arms, wrapping around her wrists and the palms of her hands until they were enveloped in its heavenly shine. Brilliant and serene, her hands emerged completely transformed, gloved in glorious gold; all while her body, too, changed.

Lucia's clothes, tattered by her journey, had been restored and imbued with a nearly invincible material. Her boots had become lighter than anything she had ever worn. They covered most of her legs and made her feel as if she were floating over the sand beneath her feet. Her blouse was composed of a decorative golden mail that draped over her shoulders. Like her boots, it was incredibly light. It had accents of opal, amethyst, and sapphire across its collar, and from its back a cloak fell below her waist. *What is this?* she thought, looking at her hands and then at herself. What had she become?

Both of her hands were covered with beautiful gloves bearing runes of many colors written across her knuckles. Lucia was not at all sure what they meant, but she felt as if they were somehow familiar. *Violet, magenta, blue, gold—haven't I seen these colors before?* She didn't have time to think much about it before the Light Wings entered her thoughts to explain the purpose of the gloves. "Lend these gloves your faith as you pray," they whispered from the pendant. "Fill them with your virtue, and use them to control your light."

Lucia looked at her hands, dazzled. She smiled as she felt the light's power within them.

The beast snarled, "Those cursed wings. They still are no match for sin—not without their virtue." It let out an echoing roar as Lucia clenched her fists.

"Enough of your games," Lucia called out, pointing her finger. "I will *end* you." It was just a split second before the tip of her finger began to shimmer. "Judgment is here!" she cried, letting go of a divine ray. It beamed through the air heading toward the monstrosity.

It didn't take long for the beast to pull back its tentacles, removing them from the beach and the heat of battle so it could use them for cover to absorb the blast.

But before it could reveal itself once more to counterattack, Lucia darted down the shore. She hovered lightly with each step, swiftly crossing over the coastline and gaining speed before she jumped into the fray and out of sight.

The beast snarled as it lost sight of her. "You can't hide from me!"

"Everyone, get into formation around me, quickly!" Lucia commanded as the mob of frightened Carists cowered away from her. "I am not your enemy. Together, we can win. Please, hurry up and get around me before it—"

There was a splash of blood as Lucia was knocked backward by a black force. Bodies of Carists flew through the air. Body parts fell all around her as she tumbled across the sand. Lucia turned to see an onyx blade pointing down at her.

"Found you."

"No!" she screamed, putting a hand over her face. The beast had her cornered.

"The stupidity. Shielding yourself with mere mortals. Is this the best the Light Wings could come up with? I was hoping for more of a fight."

Suddenly, there was a flash of blue as silver clashed with the darkness. Red-hot sparks flew as Leo emerged from behind Lucia holding a dagger stained with dark, dripping ooze. This was the blood of the beast, black like tar. "Lucia, are you okay?" He hurried to pull her to her feet. His careful eyes never lost sight of the serpent. He held her close as he took his position beside her. "So this is it, huh?" he asked, almost gleefully. "We're really fighting this—thing."

The tentacles started to rise, climbing up high and over the cliffs. Eventually, they sped up and shot into the thundering clouds and disappeared. In the distance, Lucia watched the head of the serpent. Something about its gaze looked annoyed. Was it actually starting to worry? She couldn't know for sure, but she knew it was planning another attack, a big one. She had to think fast. She couldn't be caught off guard again. This time, she needed a plan of her own. Up to this point, everything had been pure luck. The Light Wings had acted on impulse, but this time she would control the outcome.

She let her eyes wander a bit before she caught sight of gold in the distance. Talon, armed with a spear, walked through shallow water. He was moving in close, pointing his spear directly at the head of the beast. Was he getting ready to throw it? *There is no way he can reach it!* Luzanna was running toward him as he arched his hand back and, with one swift release, sent the spear flying freely through the air. It soared, catching speed as a sudden gust blew from behind. Blessed by the light, his spear shot directly into the beast. *He actually did it.*

Lucia stuck out a glowing hand, seeing the opportunity to change the tides of the battle. *We can win this!* She focused her faith into the spear, filling it with light. And then, like a bolt of lightning, light erupted from the blade of the spear building and flaring into the sky within a pillar of white-hot fire. There was a burst of magenta sparks as the fiery pillar shattered the beast's right horn to pieces.

The beast of sin wailed in pain as Luzanna grasped her father's hand and withdrew him backward, toward what was left of the Carist army. "Father, are you crazy?" she asked frantically. "Why are you still fighting? We need to save everyone. I need to save you!"

"No, Luzanna, you need to live. Trust me, this is my destiny." He tried to break free from her hands. "You must go now and take who you can to safety."

"But she can save you. She will save us all. Please. I can't let you die!"

"Luzanna, I have served my purpose. I must do what I can to defend my kingdom and ensure you live to serve yours. I'm placing my hope in you!" he shouted.

His eyes swelled with overwhelming compassion as he looked into Luzanna's tearful stare. "I love you, my sweet dove. I will always be with you." Talon tore off his visor, exposing his fury. He pushed back his silver hair as he kissed the beak of Luzanna's mask. With one last touch to his daughter's shoulder, and one last look, he flew toward the sea with his armor glistening with gallant flames.

"Father!" Luzanna cried. She watched as he took up a bloody spear.

Lucia, with a quick flourish of her hand, sent a light into the spear as Talon skillfully threw it toward the face of the beast. The light guided the spear through the air, bursting into white flames as it met with the neck of the monster.

Leo ran to Luzanna and held her back at her shoulders as she tried to dash toward her father. "Can't you see?" Leo told her. "He's the only one who can do this. He's the only one who can hit the beast! Look." Leo pointed his finger toward her father as the warrior took up another spear and sent it hurling into the air. He turned Luzanna around, looking into her broken eyes. "Talon is strong. If he fights with Lucia, we might win this. So please, do what he says and help the others. Your mother needs you. Your people need you! Focus on saving them while *we* focus on saving him. He's fighting for you, Luzanna. He's fighting for all of us."

Luzanna bowed her head as Leo touched her face. She clenched her fist, trying to contain her emotions. Then she moved her tearful gaze away from the battle, knowing he was right. Her father was strong. She couldn't think of anyone better to fight alongside Lucia, but there was this terrible aching in her heart.

Leo pleaded, "Please, go."

Luzanna swallowed hard and took in a deep breath. Reluctantly, she nodded before turning on her heel and running toward the remaining Aldric army.

The sky filled with dark purple lightning. Suddenly, there was a large quake. It stretched across the sky as blades fell like rain. They fell faster than a single thought could cross the mind. Lucia brought up her hand in a panic, sending up the flare of two bright pillars. *Nothing beats the speed of light,* Lucia thought. The light shot toward the heavens and brought a series of multicolored pops that tore through the blades off the tentacles, radiating and reflecting as they bounced and merged into each other like a brilliant cosmic display. Their black skin caught fire within the light's white inferno, dissolving them into ash. The beast wailed in anger and agony as his tentacles burned away. It growled before fixing its sight on Lucia.

Its plan had been foiled, and it was angry. Lucia could see that within its deep crimson gaze, but soon the monster smiled at her. This made her stomach turn and knot beneath her chilled skin. *What can it possibly be planning now? Is this all just one big game?* If it was, Lucia didn't know the rules. Either way, she was committed to beating it this time. She would fight her fate no longer. This was her duty. Duty above all else.

Luzanna was ushering her tribe through the stone stairwell, away from the chaos and hopefully to safety. She still worried about her father and the others, but knew she needed to honor Talon's wishes. She had an obligation to her people. And he had placed his faith in her to protect them. She would not fail them. She couldn't. Luzanna looked down to the beach from the top of the cliff, watching as they fought. She unclenched her fist, revealing the Elder Stone in the palm of her hand. *Father, I will be your hope.* And with one tearful nod, she placed the Elder Stone into the groove between the eyes of her mask, clicking it into its rightful place.

Leo, Lucia, and Talon were left alone with the monstrosity as it slithered, trying to regain its strength. Lucia knew she had weakened it greatly by destroying its bladed limbs. Yet still, it was only a matter of time before it regained them. The matter at the base of the beast was churning, readying for another attack. Now or never, they had to execute. This might be their last shot to win and change the course of the prophecy forever. Lucia looked to Leo as she pointed to Talon. "Take him while it's weak. We made a promise to Luzanna. If Talon survives, my father's prophecy won't come true. We can change everything."

"But what if you can't?" Leo asked. "What if you're not strong enough?"

"I *am* strong enough!" she yelled. "Trust me. At the very least, I can drive it away. I won't be able to destroy it, not in my current form, but I can see that Aldric survives. We can save them!" She looked into the sapphire of Leo's eyes. "Please."

Leo could not find the words, but instead nodded in agreement. He ran to Talon as Talon gazed, almost frozen, at the beast.

"Chief, we must take you to safety. Lucia has weakened it enough. We need to get you out of here and put this prophecy to rest."

"You're wrong, you know." Talon groaned weakly. "You won't be able to change the course of Stello's prophecies. The light drives a hard bargain. Its word is its contract." Talon coughed and wheezed.

Leo saw that the beast was not the only thing that was weakened.

"That's how we got here in the first place. The covenant . . . it's broken."

"The covenant?" Leo asked.

Talon stared back at Leo with wide eyes. They seemed far gone, afraid, and lost with pain. The words that then came from his mouth chilled Leo to his core. "This is only the beginning."

"Please," Leo said, still winded. "Let's go before it regains its strength."

Talon hesitated, looking toward Lucia. Her eyes were dead-locked on the beast. For over twenty-five years, Talon had kept this knowledge a secret. There was no way anyone could have known the things Stello did. No one could have been so precise or so accurate. No one could have predicted what the future would hold for these three youths. No one could have foreseen the trials they would face—none except Stello. But how? How could he have known all this?

"Her father, he knew things . . . horrible things. How? I can't say, but there has to be some sort of connection between him and the protectors." Talon coughed again. "You're all so young. It'd be hard for you to understand why I kept this knowledge a secret for as long as I did. It was my duty to the protectors to ensure that the knowledge would be safe. All so that balance could remain."

With those words, it all seemed to fit into place. Talon smiled to himself. "I think I see it now," he continued, "the part I'm supposed to play in all this." He picked up another spear and took one last breath, holding it deep within his chest. "Please, take care of her," he said softly to Leo before he blasted toward the beast.

Leo's eyes widened as he reached out to grab Talon. "No!" he shouted.

But it was too late. Talon dashed and threw the spear at full force into the beastly mass. With its great smile, it released a storm of blades from beneath the water.

Lucia gasped as the blades shot toward Talon. How long had those weapons been in hiding? There was no way to tell for certain, but this was the trick to the monster's grin. This was how it would win.

The tentacles caught Talon, gripping him tightly before dragging him through the water and into the air. Leo watched in horror as they wrapped around his body.

Talon didn't struggle. Wearily, he let out a few words as the serpent tightened its grip and blood fell from the corner of his mouth. "Stello, dear friend, I'm sorry."

Lucia collapsed in despair, falling into the sand as the serpent held Talon in front of its face. There was nothing she could do. Even if he tried to escape, even if they made a run for it, the monster had hidden its weapons under the water. It was waiting for her to try to defy her father's prophecy, toying with her. *How could it have known?* She had been deceived by the beast and her own beliefs. Her heart tightened as she cried out agony.

The tentacles continued to coil around Talon's body just like a serpent before devouring its prey. They pointed inward with their bladed tips, and the blades pushed forward and into the crevices of its many tails, impaling Talon within the beast's grip. They came from all directions, each blade meticulously placed into the knot around Talon's body. The beast watched playfully as Talon's blood dripped into the water. Talon was shaking, seemingly choking, consumed with pain. The serpent chuckled as it positioned its last blade and gave its tentacles one quick turn, spiraling Talon's body loose with the blades still intact. There was a shower of blood as the blades turned and shredded Talon to pieces.

Lucia turned away and screamed, letting her voice reflect her terror as the scarlet shower stained the water a deep crimson. In her swelling sorrow, Lucia felt the Light Wings beat with emotion. Diamond wings sprouted from her back, shooting sparks into the sky, and her hands vibrated, emitting a gallant orange fire. The sparks enlarged, exploding brighter and higher as they trailed over the blood-red dead and up around the darkness, enveloping it in light and white clouds of heat. The light shot up into the storm of violet lightning overhead, towering into the sky and parting the clouds as the beast was engulfed in the fire of Lucia's rage.

It roared in its own pain as Lucia fell to the ground. "You will pay for what you have done. I will not forget! I will not forgive! I will show no mercy!" She was levitating as she poured every ounce of her pain into her hand. Her eyes shined as a halo formed behind her head. And with one final wave of raw emotion, she pushed with all her might sending a tempest of radiant energy toward the beast, which rippled through it causing it to squirm and wither.

It let out another pain-filled roar as it began to slowly submerge into the depths of the sea. "You think you have proven victorious, but you are wrong." It lowered its head. "At what cost did you decide to use your precious light?" it asked with a distorted groan. "You have learned nothing! This world belongs to us. As four— we'll break you. We'll destroy all virtue. You will know *true* sin."

A large rumbling came from deep within the earth. Lucia

watched her step as her feet hit the ground. She hurried to Leo, holding him close as she looked up toward the cliff. "Something's coming up from underneath," she said while trying to hold her balance. She heard the ground splitting as the cliff began to cave in, and a violet ray of intense electricity shot up from beneath the city and into the sky.

It vibrated a pillar of dark matter through the city, sending a pulse of dark fire through it. The anti-light swarmed, sending lightning through each building and spewing ashes in its wake. The entire cliff erupted and the earth swallowed the city, pulling everything around it in.

Leo was panting heavily, his body in shock.

Lucia held her breath and covered her mouth as tears streamed from her eyes. "Luzanna," she whispered as she lowered her fingers.

In a panic, they bolted toward the stone staircase. There was nothing they could do to escape the sense of dread escalating within their hearts. The catastrophe they fought so hard to prevent had happened, just as predicted. Talon was dead, just as the prophecy had foretold; the city destroyed and void of life.

There was nothing they could do. Fate would, for now, remain unbroken.

CHAPTER FOURTEEN

Cosing Hope

No one could have survived a blast like that, Lucia thought as she stepped into the ruins of Aldric. Its walls were torn, its buildings crumbled, reduced to rubble and ash. The once bright and prosperous nation, blessed by the grace of its knowledge, was now broken. The city, for some time, had shone brilliantly, like a lone star hovering over a silent sea. But now, in the smoke of this long-fated battle, that glow was replaced by the diminishing gleam of a dying pit of fire. The age of the Carist was no more, and the power of its light was gone.

Lucia stopped to search the ruins. She couldn't prevent the stench of the decaying earth from entering her nostrils. It was like Pinea all over again—perhaps even worse. There wasn't a trace of surviving life around them, no sign that anyone was alive. The smoke scalded her eyes as she covered her mouth. *How could I let this happen? I was supposed to save them,* she thought. *This can't be real.* But it was. If it wasn't, she would wake up at home, safe and away from the burden of saving a dying world. It would be nothing but a horrible nightmare. But, as fate would have it, this was her reality, her life, and now her duty. There was no running from destiny. She was neither anointed nor cursed, but rather trapped.

It taunted her, the omen around her neck; forcing her to realize that no matter how hard she tried, she could not escape its call-to-arms. There was no life to live—only decay, ruin, ash, and suffering. Just as her father had predicted, there was no escaping the destruction of these great nations. No matter where she went, the darkness would follow, ready to condemn the very ground she walked upon.

Leo stood beside Lucia as the tears in her eyes sparkled. Her pulse quickened as he took her hand. They walked farther into the devastation, watching the ashes still fall from the sky. The sight was mortifying, causing Leo's blood to cool. What the beast left served no other purpose beyond frightening all who had witnessed the bitter scene. The blood ran thick across the ground, boiling on the crust of the heated earth beneath scattered bodies and broken lances. As they walked deeper, the sky darkened from the smoke collecting and hanging overhead.

This was a testament to the power of sin and its hold over all men's lives. If they could not save one, how could they expect to save them all? Despite the circumstances laid out in this hellish blur, Lucia prayed that her home would never know despair such as this. She prayed for no worse than what it had already experienced.

As they approached the city's center, Lucia was overtaken by a peculiar sensation. Tingles ran down the base of her neck, over her body, and into the tips of her fingers. She took a heavy breath before clasping a hand over the pendant.

"What is it?" Leo asked. He secured his grip on her hand.

"There is still life here." Lucia gazed out into the flat wasteland of ashes. She watched the embers crumble beneath the sole of her boot and listened to the sizzle in the air, trying to isolate the source of the lingering intuition. "I don't know how, but I almost feel her holding her breath. I can hear her cries." She clenched the Light Wings, focusing her senses as she whispered. She stepped forward toward what was left of the city gate, the threshold where they had first crossed into this mystical fortress.

"Where are we going?" Leo asked. He looked around, noticing the landscape changed. Overnight, the sky had darkened, and rolling green hills beyond the cliffs had changed into dying fields of tattered brown vegetation.

Lucia pushed past the heavy rocks, casting them from each other. She dug into the wall of the gate with her hands. "Well"—she stepped back and stared at the rubble with irritation—"if anyone survived, they would have to be outside the city by now. Luzanna . . . " Lucia closed her eyes and listened within her heart. "She's alive."

Leo's eyes widened. "Are you sure?"

Lucia took another deep breath. She held out her hand and focused her sadness into her glove. With a heavy force, it expelled light into the rubble, causing it to explode into sparks of light, leaving an open way for them to cross.

"I'm certain," Lucia said with a breath of relief. "I can sense it. The Light Wings want me to find her." She walked forward with ease, holding out her hand. *Is my father ever wrong?* Lucia couldn't help but thinking. He expected great things from Luzanna . . . . Her fate—her future, too—was eternally bound.

Unknowingly, she brushed the top of Leo's shoulder as she crossed beside him. This sent his eyes darting to the glove. The brilliant gold gleamed against Lucia's sun-kissed skin. Something had noticeably changed in her. There was a glimmer of strength that he had not yet seen in the time he had known her. And there was a deep focus in her golden irises, a strong will emerging from her fractured spirit. Her long lashes lined the wide almond shape of her eyes as they glistened with sympathetic tears that were filled with restraint. So much depth lay within those eyes, so much reason.

Lucia saw no signs of life immediately, but still sensed it in her mind. Hope tugged at her neck. The pendant pulled her, even in its motionlessness, like it was after something, longing to find her. *Life and light,* she thought. *They are connected.* She tied the ends together. Understanding the rules of their existence was the core to the mystery of their journey. It wasn't as if she had a choice. She had to contemplate this far-gone fantasy. But this was no illusion. She let out a deep sigh as she followed the internal piercing in her neck.

It wasn't long before, in the distance, Lucia saw the glimmer of metal beneath the canopy of a dying tree. Her soft, silent cry echoed in the void as the stone turned into grass. She pointed out into the field ahead of them and then, with an unexpected push, ran to her—the glimmer of shining metal hunched over, rocking in the distance. Lucia stopped herself. Leo put a hand to his lips as he picked up her mask and clenched his eyes shut, looking away as the girl grieved.

Lucia called, "Luzanna . . . "

Luzanna's bare face, round and pale, was facing down as her thick golden hair fell over her shoulders, draping over her breast-plate. Tears rained from her sea-colored eyes. She hugged the body of someone Lucia herself could not recognize, but it wasn't difficult to tell who this was. The features were all too prominent, all too similar to the girl who held her. A trail of blood pooled in the grass and mixed with the muddy earth. Lucia understood now that the only life she felt was Luzanna herself. Every breath and every cry was hers alone.

"We nearly made it," Luzanna cried while trying hard not to swallow the words. "But as we reached the gate, the blast caught the others, and my mother"—she choked as the words dug into the walls of her throat—"shielded me with herself. I pulled her from the ruins and brought her to safety. I tried to save her, but . . . " Luzanna collapsed into a massive moan, holding on to her mother's body.

Leo held his breath as the tears formed in his own eyes. "Talon . . . ?"

At that moment, there was no way to tell if she was unsurprised or simply frozen by her grief, but Luzanna knew. "Father's dead." Her eyes met with theirs. Like an owl, she stared into almost nothing, entranced and broken as her eyes melted into misery.

"I'm so sorry," Lucia said. "We tried—I tried, but it wasn't enough."

Luzanna stopped her. "It's as I feared it would be, inevitable. That's what separates myth from prophecy. Prophecies *always* come true." She let out another sob as she looked down at her mother, Ofelia Renon. "I want her to know peace. I hope they all do." Her chest tightened with her breath, and her vision blurred with her thoughts. She tightened her hands and shut her eyes, begging for the pain to stop. "It's all gone. Everything I've ever known has been taken from me. I'm alone, I'm scared, and . . . a part of me wishes I could have died with them."

Leo's eyes softened. He stepped toward Luzanna and lowered next to her. Lucia did the same. And there, shoulder to shoulder, they mourned with her. They cried with her. They hoped with her, praying for peace.

"We have to end this. There can't be more. I know there will be, but there just can't . . . " Luzanna's pale skin, so fair before, flushed to a light scarlet. With heavy fists, she lashed, slamming an armored hand into the ground. "How could anyone survive this? The world won't—" She shook her head fiercely. Her anguish surged as her mind fractured.

Lucia placed a warm hand on Luzanna's ice-cold face. She felt her sadness. Her pain was seemingly infinite, her suffering endless. Lucia thought of her own mother and the words echoing from the day she left her home. *I cannot lose her,* she remembered thinking. Lucia lowered her golden eyes, focusing on this memory, wrapping and enveloping its light before sending it into her hand and into Luzanna. The light was warm as it coursed through her body, calming her blood flow and allowing her mind to be free from the overflow of despair.

"Talon was very brave," Lucia said. "He was a warrior, a chief, and a father. He fought to the end and did it all to honor you. And your mother—she did the same. I know this hurts, but they loved you, Luzanna. Their legacy lives on through you." Lucia prayed silently, sending another wave of calming light into Luzanna's body and mind. With a series of reassuring thoughts, it brought her out of the wrath and sudden hatred.

Luzanna's feelings burst into warmth, and the chills of fear and sorrow seemed to almost leave her completely. She flinched backward, her eyes drawing toward Leo's as he held out her mask. She caressed it before taking it into her hands, grasping it as a sad cry echoed across the sky and soft water fell upon them. It was not heavy, nor cold, but soft and breezy. It was as if the world itself was consumed with grief. The sky grayed and the clouds descended, blanketing heavily over the terrain as Luzanna fell back to her mother's side.

Lucia held out her hand, and Leo was quick to take it into his own. She gazed into his crystal-blue eyes. They turned dark as a heavy glaze coated his lashes. There was guilt within them, a despair she knew too well. The air tensed as the sounds of thunder built overhead, almost as if it were warning them.

Lucia didn't know what to do. She clenched Leo's hand, expelling another wave of warmth from her palm to ease the torment shrouding his soul. She sent in the light with an image of many colors, those of the bright petals of flowers floating amongst the soft winds of the Pinean hills, as well as the aroma that came with it. Though it might feel as if his home and title were stripped from him, they still existed. That was all that mattered. Somehow, he would get his home back.

His hand loosened around hers as his eyes shut and his breathing calmed. Lucia smiled softly at the revelation of her newfound power. To absolve the pain of others—what a truly selfless gift, yet still a heavy burden to take on all of these emotions on her own. Even in the depths of these feelings, she couldn't bring herself to express them, not like she used to. She looked into the distance, into nothing, as a numbness overcame her. The Light Wings could cleanse them of their troubles, but it could not expel her own. And in absorbing their grief, Lucia's heart only hardened while her mind sharpened. This pain, she could not forget it. Her sadness was transforming. What was once doubt and fear became something entirely different.

"How are we supposed to stop this?" Luzanna asked, letting out a cold breath and seeing it hang in the air.

"We don't know," Lucia said. "That's why we sought out Talon. Sigranole told us your father would know, but now . . . " She wiped the rain from her cheek.

"His secrets died with him." Leo finished her thought as a shade of guilt covered his face. "I wish I had done more to protect him."

Luzanna touched the side of her mother's face before rising to her feet. She let out one more breath, to collect herself. Then, with ease, she took the mask and placed it on her face. And with one swift movement, she took the magenta ribbons and tied them into her hair, securing the mask. Her tone steadied with resolve. "His secrets did not die with him. They were never his secrets to begin with." She turned to face Lucia. From her pocket, she pulled forth the Elder Stone. It shimmered in her fingers like a cinder with magenta streaks. She secured it into the center groove of her mask, on top of her forehead, where it seemingly enlightened and brought her into a higher state, empowered by the wisdom of her ancestors.

"What do you mean?" Lucia asked.

"In the training grounds, when I confronted my father, he told me that it was my birthright to someday hold these secrets. They would come with my ascension as chieftess of my tribe. The only way to learn them is through the sacred pilgrimage to the realm of the protectors, Remena."

"Remena?" Leo scoffed. "I thought that place was only a legend, the kind of place heard of in fairy tales."

"I remember," Lucia said quietly, recalling a memory from her childhood. "Amelia used to tell me stories about these people called the 'children of light.' She told me they had once existed long ago, born to preserve the balance of nature. They were supposedly the first generation of humans to live in Terestria." She turned to Luzanna. "These people—they truly existed?"

"Yes," Luzanna said. "I believe so, and I think they still do." She tried to remember the final conversation she had with her father. "My father said that you opened a door, Lucia. With some power, you established a connection." She held back tears, maintaining her focus as her father's words left her lips. "And the darkness is now using that power to stay connected to this world."

"*My* power? You mean the Light Wings?"

"No," Luzanna said. She paused to analyze the details of Talon's testimony. "It's a power passed on from your mother. In all the history I've researched and studied, there's never been a record of a human being born with any supernatural abilities, not like those of the Light Wings or otherwise. Any sort of special abilities were spoken of in the context of fiction. Or, at least that's what I believed it to be . . . . But the protectors of legend, they were said to be direct descendants of the light. They were themselves created solely for the purpose of worshipping it and, like you said, preserving the balance between the light and the darkness, nature itself. And to do so, they were given powers not of this world. I know we've all heard stories, but what if it's true? What if the protectors do exist . . . and you, Lucia"—Luzanna tilted her head—"are one of them."

Lucia shook her head. "That couldn't be possible. My mother was born and raised in Moz. Our house has held power for centuries. Granted, my grandfather never bore a son and my mother was given the throne. If her family was from Remena, I would know."

"But your abilities, Lucia," Leo interjected. "Can you say for certain they all came from the Light Wings? Have there been signs before of you doing things you can't explain?"

Lucia began to sweat. Her stomach churned as she remembered every premonition, every intuition, every thought that ever came true. "I . . . " Lucia closed her eyes, exhaling before she managed to speak. "My mother called my intuition the light's blessing. It was a gift for my faithfulness to it. I've always had visions. Ever since I was a little girl, I could somehow predict events, droughts, storms, natural disasters, or conflicts within the city. My mother— she was adamant about me honing this gift so I could better serve the province. That's why I spent so much time in the sanctuary, always praying. Because faith, like all things, must be exercised."

"But these visions, how are they connected to the darkness? Lucia didn't see *this* coming," Leo said to Luzanna.

Lucia interrupted. "No, but I could feel it. Death . . . it clung to them—the Light Wings." Lucia recalled the moment she first laid eyes on the silk they were wrapped in. She remembered the exact moment her entire world changed.

"But that still doesn't answer my question," Leo said. "How do we know for certain that the power Lucia has inherited is the same power bestowed on the protectors? How do we know it's connected to the darkness?"

"It's true. My mother never spoke of having a power of her own. Just prayer—she firmly believed in it. She always said that prayer would ward off evil. Just as she experienced in Frailty's War."

"And my father said your faith would not be strong enough to keep the darkness at bay, not yet anyway." Luzanna thought a moment. "I'm trying to make sense of all this. But it's hard to put the details together when there is still so much we don't know." She recalled her father's words. "'She awoke the ancient spirits with her song, and now she is connected.'"

"My song?" Lucia clasped the pendant with her hand, stepping back as Luzanna's words seeped in. "That's how . . . that's when this all started. How would you know that? You weren't even there!"

Luzanna blinked. "Well isn't it obvious? It's because your father knew. Everything he foretold is coming true—every fate, every destiny. It's as if he wrote it himself."

"And that's a detail you're just going to overlook?" Leo asked with wide eyes. "Lucia has the gift of intuition, an ability to foresee, or from what we know, *feel* the outcome of future events. If it's not her mother who passed on the ability, it was Stello."

This was all too much for Lucia to process. She struggled to breathe. Everything fell silent as her thoughts began to isolate. These pieces of herself, those she had once interpreted so blissfully, were now under scrutiny. With each passing moment, they closed in on the truth, and for some reason this terrified her. "I never knew much about him. My mother spoke nothing intimate of him, only of his nobility and devotion to Moz and its well-being. I always thought he left us, abandoned us . . . or died on his mission for peace, a mission that he failed."

"Well, Leo's right. That simply can't be overlooked. What if this gift of 'intuition' isn't intuition at all? What if your visions, your premonitions, are prophecies as well? You can't ignore that the two are in fact similar, Lucia, not right now. It can't be a mere coincidence. You're clairvoyant."

"Clair—what now?" Leo asked scratching his head.

For the first time in a while, Luzanna smiled. "Clairvoyant is a word used to describe someone with extrasensory perception."

Leo gave his wild look, still confused. Luzanna shook her head.

Lucia blinked hard. "I know there might be some truth to what you're saying, Luzanna. I shouldn't overlook or deny the truth. Every detail is far too important to ignore. But this whole damn world revolves around me right now, and I can't do anything to free myself from it. Can you imagine what that must feel like?" She turned from them as anger pulsed through her chest. Her head pounded as her thoughts pumped in and out of her head like the blood in her heart. "Damn it," she whispered, as the thoughts seeped in. Famished, she craved the truth more than anything, yet she didn't know what she feared more: the truth or the darkness surrounding it.

"There is one other thing my father mentioned." Luzanna tapped her beak with the tip of her finger. "He said that when the darkness emerged years ago, your mother used her power to seal it away. Yours, on the other hand, is being used as a gateway to our world. If this is true, then I'm certain we can find a way to use Lucia's power to cut off her connection to it."

"And how do you suppose we go about doing that?" Leo asked. "Can't you see Lucia's had enough? She needs her strength."

"Then what do we do? Wait?" Luzanna crossed her arms.

"We've analyzed the facts and taken into consideration every move made up to now. If we have any chance of defeating the darkness, we have to—"

"We?" Leo interrupted in frustration. "When has it ever been 'we'?"

Luzanna gasped.

Lucia looked back to them, feeling the sting of Leo's words where Luzanna's mother was still dead within their sight. Immediately, Lucia stepped forward and, with a push of her hand, sent a wave of light toward Leo, knocking him off his feet and into the bark of the tree in the distance. With a loud smack, he cracked into it and fell to the ground as the air left his body.

"Luzanna, I'm sorry," Lucia said. "Don't listen to him. We'll go with you to Remena and fulfill your sacred pilgrimage. Surely there is more to the story of the protectors and their gifts." Lucia's stern look dissolved into a comforting smile. "And I know that's what your parents would have wanted for you, to learn the truth." She clenched the Light Wings in her fist. "You're stuck with us. Right, Leo?"

Luzanna blinked slowly before looking to Leo, who struggled to get to his knees. "I guess she's strong enough," she said slowly. "Thank you, Lucia."

Lucia walked over to Leo and held out her hand. "Are you going to get up?"

Leo grunted, taking her hand and bringing himself to his feet, catching his breath. "I'm sorry, Luzanna," he said softly, unable to make eye contact with her. "I spoke out of turn. I should have . . ." He hesitated, raising his sapphire gaze. "Shown more restraint."

"No offense taken. Apology accepted." Luzanna walked toward them and, with her two arms, took them both in. "We'll figure this out. I know we will."

Lucia saw the sympathy form in Leo's eyes. She knew, even if

Leo didn't agree with them, he was wrong for pushing Luzanna away. After all, they were all one another had left. Lucia had once felt she had to do this all alone, but these two had shown her that this was a lot larger than her. Perhaps, if it was true, she'd learn more about her father and his connection to all this. Despite everything, there was something exciting about it, learning more about who she was and about this power she held deep inside. Whether it was from the Light Wings or some ancient bloodline, it made her stronger. She simply had to believe, even if it changed the way she saw herself completely.

Lucia sighed. "So where is Remena, anyway?"

"To the west, I believe, past the marshlands. The marshes aren't the prettiest of places, but I don't think it'd take longer than a couple days to get through it," Luzanna said.

Lucia said, "We'll go on this pilgrimage together, the three of us, for Luzanna and for Terestria. Talon did say that Luzanna would learn many things there, and so can we. Who knows what might be there? It might be the key to saving the world."

"And if it isn't?" Leo asked with an awkward smile.

"Let's just hope it is," Luzanna said, containing a distinctive optimism in her aqua-green eyes.

Lucia smiled so big that her eyes narrowed into mere slits on her face. Something welled up inside her like a bubble floating to the surface of a murky pond. The warmth of friendship emitted between them as the burden lifted off her. She wasn't alone, even when she felt she was—as she did when she had almost forced Leo to leave her. It was different now, and somehow, she'd changed. The gloves that pressed so snugly against her skin seemed to bring light not only into the lives of those around her, but into her own as well.

CHAPTER FIFTEEN

Rites of Passage

It took three days to reach the marshlands west of Aldric. The journey to Remena had not been an easy one, and was referred to as a "pilgrimage" for many reasons. Luzanna was quick to explain the way to the ancient and sacred land, but as the land changed, it became more and more apparent that the route they had chosen was in no way going to be forgiving.

The path itself made Lucia loathe walking, even more than she already did, especially as the storm hung over her head, drizzling and matting her hair beneath her white band. She had thought the journey to Aldric from Pinea was a tough one; one that nearly killed her, if she remembered correctly. The memory was still fresh in her mind, the terrible and uncontrollable pain that consumed her and drained her body as she was pushed through the forest against her will. It was all too clear. She remembered how her muscles and bones had fought for every ounce of control as her body seemingly tossed itself toward the light outside of that dark and ominous forest. It was terrifying. But here, as the days passed and the weather worsened, she felt dread. Whatever she was walking into scared her more than whatever they had faced in the past. Even if they had yet to lay their eyes upon it, she knew. The darkness was still out there, watching beneath her shadow.

Still, traveling with Leo and Luzanna made things a lot easier for Lucia to deal with. Luzanna's optimism was a bright contrast to Leo's brooding and serious nature. It was oddly energizing. Luzanna often broke out in spontaneous narratives of their travels. Lucia couldn't tell if she was speaking aloud or merely trying to be funny, but it was amusing to say the least. Luzanna enjoyed examining the ever-changing landscapes. She nearly shrieked when they saw a rare mountain eagle perched along a rugged cliff near one of their campsites. "Do you know what that is?" she asked. "It's an Aldrician mountain eagle! They almost went extinct two decades ago when a strange plague swept through the mountains here. So many plants and animals died. My father had researchers out here for months trying to figure out the cause of the outbreak, but no one could manage to figure it out. To this day, it remains a mystery."

Lucia smiled, looking up at the multicolored bird. Its feathers were shimmery, even in the dull light of their campfire. "It's beautiful, Luzanna." She dropped her gaze, staring into the fire, her thoughts running again. "You sure do know a lot. I can't say I've studied as much as you."

Luzanna chuckled, "My father used to say that I was going to be the most innovative chief Aldric ever had because of my imagination." Grief swept over her again. It had been coming in waves for some time, and by now she was used to it, mostly desensitized to the thought of her father passing. "But surely none of the research done in Aldric could come close in comparison to that of Sky University, Lucia. My father was to send me there to study upon my eighteenth birthday, but I suppose that dream is lost now."

Despite her appearance, Luzanna was quite young. She had just turned sixteen three months prior to Lucia and Leo's arrival in Aldric. This made her two years younger than Lucia and four years younger than Leo. However, she was wise beyond her years, which could be expected due to her capacity as an intellectual, causing her to seem more mature than her age indicated.

"Don't talk like that, Luzanna. After all this, I promise, I'll have you personally admitted. I am the high maiden of Moz, after all. I've met the headmistress on many occasions. You'd be a fine addition to the academy."

Luzanna sighed. "That would be all swell and dandy, Lucia, but I'm chieftess now. I can't change that. I'll have to return to Aldric and rebuild what I have lost and rule my people."

"What people?" Leo asked. "No offense, Luzanna, but your home is gone. I'm not saying this to hurt you; but as a person of reason, you can understand that you're going to have to move on. You can rebuild in time, but for now, it's okay to take care of yourself. Your land will be there when you are ready to get back to it."

Luzanna sighed again. "I do appreciate your honesty, but I don't want to think that way. My home still exists, destroyed or not. In memory, in my past, it still exists. And sure enough, it exists somewhere in my future too, just as these prophecies were written. It is my duty to build Aldric anew." She lifted her hand and pointed a finger to her forehead. There, the Elder Stone sparkled in the flame light. "I'm the elder now, and it is my sworn duty to call the Carists home."

Hearing Luzanna speak made Lucia think of her mother. "Duty above all else." She smiled as she heard the words. "That's my family's motto. In a way, I suppose that applies to all of us."

Leo scoffed. "Not me. Not anymore. My people want me dead."

"Because they don't know the truth," Lucia refuted. "You didn't kill your father. The darkness did, and soon they will see that. When word gets back about Aldric, they'll change their minds."

"How do you know that word will even get back? That monster might have taken out whatever messenger Pinea sent to Moz and destroyed whatever chance we had to clear our names. As far as we know, they'll think we're the ones who set the city ablaze. They'll blame us just like they did in Aldric."

"Two people could not cause that much destruction. Not alone. There is no way. It's not like you had an army with you." Luzanna shook her head. "Could you try to be a little more positive? Everything you're saying sounds like acts of wars are being committed, and thinking like that is only going to have more people turn against each other."

Leo looked blankly into the distance. Lucia saw the resistance in his eyes about to break. His chin quivered as he wiped his eyes. He hopped up and left the campsite, his footsteps heavy until he disappeared deep into the marshland. The girls glanced at each other. Luzanna dropped her head as Lucia hopped up and chased after him.

She slowed her pace as Leo stopped beneath a dying tree. It was slumped away from a dry patch and hung precariously over the moist waters of the marsh. Leo sat alone at its base, sending a short glance backward toward Lucia. She sat next to him, wondering what he might be thinking. "Are you alright?" she asked carefully, putting a hand over his. "What she said—she means well. We just want you to be strong, okay?"

"Am I not"—a couple tears left his eyes—"strong?"

Lucia got up and crouched in front of him. Leo hung his head and looked away from her. He didn't want her to see him like this. Usually he was good at controlling his emotions, but lately it had become all the more difficult. As his faith began to break, that part of him that he had once trained so frequently for battle dissolved. There was no winning this battle within himself.

"Of course you are. You're the strongest person I know." Lucia placed her hands on his knees as she bowed her head. "You know, you're way stronger than I am. I don't know what I would have done if I ever saw my mother die the way your father did. I don't know how I would have felt if she had died the way Talon or Ofelia did either." Lucia closed her eyes, searching for the right words to say. She was tempted to use the light to bring about his healing, but deep down, she felt that would have been a cheat. There was something she needed to say, something he deserved to hear from her own mouth. "I know I was harsh before, believing I had to do this on my own. I said some things, things that hurt you. And I admit, I took you for granted. Everything you've done, I'm extremely grateful for. The truth is that *I've* been selfish. I've lost the least of the three of us, and I . . . I wish so much that I knew then what I know now. If I was strong enough, if I had used the power even just a little bit more, things could be different." Lucia didn't notice it, but tears were flowing from her eyes. "I'm sorry, Leo. Deeply, I am. So please, don't lose yourself . . . because I need you."

Leo's eyebrows tensed up as his eyes narrowed. "There is something different about you. You've changed. I mean, I think I have too, but you have the most. If anything, you've grown so sage. Far from the naive girl I once knew." Leo paused and looked away for a moment, trying to contain his feelings, but his strength was gone. Whatever Lucia remembered, whatever she saw in him, it was gone. "You see, you're special, Lucia."

Lucia bowed her head doubtfully.

"I mean it. Ever since the first moment I saw you, I could tell." Leo sighed softly as Lucia looked up to him. "I knew I had to save you. I was only meant to deliver that letter to you, but as soon as things started to fall apart—that was my only instinct, making sure you were safe. I don't know why I felt that way, considering our family's history, but I did and still do. The world is not safe, and it's out of control. Terestria is on the brink of ruin, and all I can think about is saving it." Leo blinked as his guard broke even more. "And not because the world is ending, but because you deserve to see it as I once did—as I see *you*, full of light." He lifted his hand and brushed his thumb against the side of her hand. He watched it closely as he spoke. "My whole life, I always had this edge, this advantage over everything. And now I don't, not when I'm with you. I'm not in control."

"Why?" Lucia asked, tilting her head to get a glimpse of his face. Leo looked up to her, meeting her gaze. His expression surprised her.

"Because when I'm with you, I'm weak. My desire to protect you, to put your life before my own—that is all that drives me, nothing else. If anything were ever to happen to you . . . "

Lucia was speechless. She quite literally could not find the words to say.

"Journeying with you, it has made me question everything. My plans for my future, my hopes and dreams—they mean nothing without you." Leo looked into her eyes, the gold that sparkled in the moonlight. In her eyes, he saw his own reflecting blue, both combining into a dark green. There was a long pause. The silence echoed, and only the sound of their heavy heartbeats made it through. Only they existed. His arms reached forward and grasped her soft gloved hands. Slowly, he lifted his body, bringing Lucia up with him. "I'm losing control because I *want* you." He placed his arms around her waist as he moved his face toward hers. Gently, as their noses touched, he pressed forward and laid his lips on hers.

A flutter of sudden warmth swarmed the two, and Lucia felt her heart deepen more than it ever had before. She rested her hands on Leo's shoulders as she moved closer to him. Everything she was feeling, every emotion, was dialed into this moment, and it was as if she had forgotten all about the danger they were in. Leo held on to her as he broke the kiss, withdrawing a slow breath as he stared into her eyes. She didn't know what to say or do, but inside, she could no longer deny what she wanted.

"I . . ." Lucia mumbled. She lowered her face and touched her lips with the tips of her fingers as she still felt him there, the memory of their kiss still fresh. Leo's eyes shifted as she let out a soft breath. A shimmer of tingles ran down her skin like a short winter breeze. He lowered his hands, brushing the sides of her arms. He took her hand and brought it to his chest, and she felt his heartbeat beneath his chest. Somehow her own began to take on a new rhythm, one renewed and aligned with his.

"I love you," Leo whispered.

Lucia could not speak as the words lingered inside her head, which was racing. Without thinking, she moved closer to him. She needed to feel it again. Her lips locked with his as he closed his eyes and brought a hand to her face.

As the two separated, Lucia wondered if this was love. She remained speechless. Her expression was a cross between embarrassment and euphoria, or perhaps a combination of both, but she couldn't stop feeling it, this attraction that bound their hearts.

"Lucia," Leo whispered. "Are you okay?"

Lucia laughed as she attempted to process what had just happened. "Yes, I'm great. It's just . . ." She smiled at Leo. "That was my first kiss."

"Oh, really?" Leo clenched his teeth, blushing as he shrugged. "I'm sorry. I should have—"

Lucia shook her head. "No. Don't be. It was nice."

"Nice?" Leo asked bashfully.

"Yes," Lucia said, looking up with a sly smile. "It was." She giggled a bit as Leo shrugged and rubbed the back of his head.

He took her hand and rubbed his thumb into the center of her palm, feeling the soft cloth of the glove rub against his skin.

"I was surprised," she said.

"So was I." Leo took her other hand and held them both close. "When you kissed me back."

"In a way," Lucia said, thinking, "I'm kind of glad, but in a lot of ways, I'm afraid."

"Afraid of what?" he asked softly.

Lucia wrapped her arms around his shoulders and laid her head on one of them. "Of losing you."

"You wouldn't. I'm not going anywhere." Leo pressed his face against her. "I promise. I'll never leave."

"Well, promise me also . . ." The Light Wings emitted a vibrant violet glow. "When it comes down to it, let me do the saving." She stepped back as the Light Wings pulsed between them, as if they had their own words to say. "Don't die for me."

Leo blinked as the light of the wings entered his eyes. He nodded, grasping the message. "Yes, High Maiden. Your word is my command." He then stepped closer to Lucia as the Light Wings brightened. He held her waist as she tilted her head, smiling beneath their kiss.

This was the happiest she had ever felt, there within Leo's arms.

* * *

It's arguable whether Luzanna noticed that something had changed between Leo and Lucia. When the two made their way back to camp, she went about acting just as she always had, seemingly oblivious to it. But there were moments when she caught Leo glancing toward Lucia, smiling more than he had before.

"So I'm guessing you're feeling a lot better now?" Luzanna asked Leo. His mood was evidently elevated. The darkness in his eyes had faded, after all.

"Yes," he said quickly before lying back on the ground. He placed his head on his hands and looked into the starlight, and into the not-so-distant past. "A lot better."

"Well good, I'm glad." Luzanna set her attention on Lucia, whose gaze was locked onto the fire. "And you? How are you feeling?"

Lucia let out a deep breath before uttering a word. "I'm alright, Luzanna. Thanks for asking."

"Everyone's okay, then?"

"Yup," Lucia and Leo replied in unison.

Luzanna nodded in satisfaction. "That's good."

The three of them sat in silence for a while. Leo was drifting to sleep. Luzanna yawned as her weariness started to come over her. Lucia was still wide awake, her thoughts twisting and turning. Luzanna laid on her side, and soon her breath deepened as she also drifted to sleep.

Only the crackle of the fire echoed throughout the misty void. Lucia looked up and into the starlit sky. She held her hands out toward the warmth of the fire. It was peaceful. She would have never expected the night to be like this, and oddly, it brought a sense of bliss. She took a moment to appreciate it, this strange feeling. She took in the silence, apart from the whistling of the reeds and buzzing of the fireflies that surrounded them. Since she had left Moz, she hadn't been able to truly enjoy the places she visited. Her worries often split her focus, leaving her lost in thoughts of the future and the past. She could barely remember a time when she remained fully in the present moment. Now, there was something changing inside her. Despite everything, she felt more alive.

It was unfortunate that this moment was to be short-lived, as Lucia's intuition soon brought a chill to her spine. Her selfless revelation and peace were suddenly disrupted as her chest began to cave at its center and the light of the wings started to grow.

Something wasn't right. Lucia's heartbeat hastened as gusts of wind brought in a heavy fog. It was thickening before her eyes, growing denser in the distance as if nature itself was warning her. She rose slowly, looking directly into the sky as the fog ascended, nearly covering the entire sky. The air, once crisp, stung as it entered her body and left her breath hanging in front of her face. "No," Lucia uttered as the light of the moon and stars became completely blocked. A burst of heavy wind came from the west, casting their fire aside and leaving them in the darkness of the night. Only the incandescence of the pendant remained as the fog darkened, turning into shadow and absorbing all the light that touched it.

Soon, the fog gathered, drawing up closer to the sky overhead. There were sparks of purple and black lightning within the mist as the shape of wings formed. The body of the beast could be seen in the haze. Its humanlike figure and black slated body became clearer with each passing second. Lucia's eyes widened, her voice leaving her as it had the first time she laid eyes on the demon. With its wings, it brought down a loud tempest that shook Leo and Luzanna awake. And then, as it opened its scarlet-red eyes, the shadows collected, absorbing into its black wings.

"Oh no—" Lucia realized its intentions as it arched backward. "Watch out!" she said as the demon's wings emitted a dark energy. And with one more great flap, a wave of black lightning filled the air rushing toward them. Lucia raced forward and, with a spin of her hand, sent out a wave of her own that spread and extinguished the lightning, turning it into particles of anti-light.

The demon growled. "I see you've grown fond of the Light Wings' power. How does it feel, being the light's mindless puppet?"

Lucia stepped back, holding up her hands. "Luzanna, Leo, get up and move now!"

The shadow held up its dark claws. Anti-light spiraled up from the center of its body, covering it with slate-black armor. Its gauntlets were sharp, and its claws were surrounded by a dark aura. Its horns spiraled downward from atop its head, as the last bit of shadows collected to form the final pieces of the beast.

Luzanna was on her knees when she first laid eyes on it. She froze as the air was stripped of its warmth and thrown into an icey blizzard. The moist waters of the marsh started to frost over as Leo rose to his feet, his blue eyes now purple with rage.

The demon appeared to grow in size as its dark wings stretched outward, sending another heavy gust toward them. They flapped, lifting the beast upward. The dark aura seeped from it, pouring from its feet and spreading across the ground.

It was impossible to tell why the demon had chosen to show itself here. They were not in a city, nor surrounded by people to mercilessly slaughter. What dubious intentions would it have in the middle of nowhere and with them alone in the night? Lucia tried to attune herself to its thoughts, listening for the Light Wings' words, yet she heard nothing but the nonsense of her own mind.

The demon rose high above, taking flight. Lucia stepped forward as it lifted higher, her spirit breaking through the fear and intensifying in anger. "I remember you," she said as her clenched fists pulsed. "You burned down my home. You killed my people."

The beast sent out an unworldly and deep chuckle as it looked at its newly formed body in amusement. "Yes. And my strength grows with each death of the light's precious life. My brothers have done well . . . ." It set its fiery gaze onto Leo and Luzanna, who both stood silently behind Lucia. "Ruining your lives." It shook its head, seemingly disappointed. "The nobility of Terestria . . . the 'light's virtues.' What a pitiful bunch of petty children."

"Fuck you!" Leo cursed as he withdrew his dagger.

The darkness laughed hoarsely. "This can't be Terestria's last hope! Honestly, I was itching for more of a challenge. But this one can't control a single emotion in his body, let alone his mouth."

"He's not the one you should be worried about," Lucia spat. "I am!" She sensed something different about this being. Its power was in fact growing. It drew its power from a source beyond that of what they knew. *The light's precious life . . . virtues of light?* Lucia thought. "I'm not afraid of you!"

"You lie so well." The beast laughed, sending his obvious horror into her.

The words sank into Lucia's body. There was no way she could respond. She had no words to say.

"Who . . . what are you?" Luzanna called out. She stepped over to Lucia and then ahead of Leo, near the edge of the patch. "Why are you here?" Her anger seemed to flare from the seas of her eyes like an underwater volcano as she placed logic to reason. "There is nothing here for you to destroy."

"You speak as if I need a purpose, as if I need a reason for existing. But that's where you're wrong, my dear. I exist everywhere, all at once, on the other side—and now here." It bellowed lowly, almost with maturity, but the glare of its eyes fixated on the light beneath Lucia's neck almost teasingly.

"You didn't answer my question," Luzanna said. "What *are* you?"

"Don't provoke me, little girl. I'm not like Wym or Lykorus. I'm something . . . much angrier." Its wings jumped, and like a shadowy star it shot from the sky.

Lucia's eyes widened as it darted forward, hitting her as it spun its wings around its body. She flew backward and tumbled as the demon brought itself to the ground.

Leo rushed to her side as Luzanna ran between them. "Luzanna, no!" he cried as the demon locked onto her green eyes.

Lucia's body ached as the Light Wings hung and sparkled

slightly. She watched the beast approach Luzanna. Lucia jumped up and, with her hands raised and crossed in front of her, started to pray. "Light Wings, please lend me your strength." From the wings came a light that clung to her arms. Like veins, it trailed up her hands, releasing a white aura that held a faint glow within the darkness of the fog. The fluid flowed onto her hands and then into her fingers.

Suddenly, there was a flash of light, and within her grasp the light turned solid like a large, finely cut gem. She held up a sword made of solid diamond. It was the length of her arm, and shimmered as the light of the Light Wings shined up from it. Lucia felt the light draw into it with power. It tingled in her fingertips. She saw the sharpness of the blade as she analyzed the cuts of the diamond.

"You monstrosity!" Lucia shouted.

The beast looked back to her and let forth a growl that left Luzanna falling back. Leo grabbed Luzanna as she shuddered, astounded.

"This just got interesting," the demon bellowed. "You dare to fight back to preserve your precious 'hope.'"

Lucia's eyes glared. She wasn't in any mood for games, not after everything good she'd felt tonight. She wasn't about to let this darkness control her life as much as her duty already did. She pointed the sword and yelled, "Why not?!"

Lucia let the light fill to the tip of her sword and into a single spark. A volley of spiraling white light shot from the point of the blade. It burst toward the beast, but it was too fast. It ascended into the air, sending the light into an endless journey through the fog. But Lucia wasn't ready to give up. With a swing of her sword, she sent waves of light into the sky, splitting the fog and revealing the moonlight. She took a deep breath as she drew the moonlight in and the stars themselves seemed to brighten. Lucia then remembered Luzanna's words. *Awakened with her song.* Immediately she focused, recalling her song's rhythm and letting it fill her head. She hummed as the Light Wings brightened. "No matter the fate, good or bad, this is where I stand!"

From her back, light traced the shape of wings that sent a pillar of multicolored sparks into the heavens. Slowly, the stars themselves seemed as if they plummeted, all heading toward the beast. Lucia allowed herself to stay connected and continued to sing. "So long, I've waited for the day! So long, I've waited for the faith and the hope I have yet to find."

The beast was caught by surprise, moving and dodging the rays of light as they showered down. It stopped, taking in the shadows beneath its feet, and with a gigantic push sent dark energy through the air, dissolving the light into nothing. The shadows ripped, and the aura grew as the light faded. The demons wings were charging, glowing with anti-light as their shadows were pulled from behind them. "Clever girl. You've discovered the source of your power—yet still underestimate the cost of using it." There was a crackling sound as its wings were covered in black lightning. "Where there is light, there is always darkness." The marshes were nearly solid as the terrain turned black. From it raised a pack of shadowy wolves, each of their bloodstone eyes focusing on the sword in Lucia's hand.

"Oh—" Lucia clenched her teeth as she readied the sword. Her fear raised bumps over her skin. *The wolves… the forest. It was him.*

"Get away from her!" Leo shouted, dashing forward. He leaped and, dagger in hand, plunged its blade into one of the wolves. The pack swarmed, running toward them as Leo struggled beneath the one he had stabbed. Snapping at his face, the wolf nearly subdued him just as Leo adjusted his hand atop the hilt of his dagger and twisted it to throw the wolf over his head. "Lucia, a little light please?"

Lucia nodded. She closed her eyes for a moment, continuing her hymn in her head. She held out her hand, and from it a sparkling blue light enveloped Leo, entering the blade of his knife. Charging forward, he slashed repeatedly as the wolves jumped at him. His moves were quick and deft, as the blade of his dagger melted through the ice-cold flesh of the beasts, causing them to explode into light.

Luzanna stood there, watching as Leo fought, scampering to think of a way she, too, could be useful. Her spear was lost in Aldric, and she was less adept at hand-to-hand combat than she was with her pointed polearm. But she could not let that deter her. She broke a large branch from a nearby tree and jumped in beside Leo, swinging it wildly just as she would one of the Carist-crafted lances. By the time Lucia's prayer reached the branch, it was taking on a new form, changing from the deep, dark oak into a stunning white marble staff. It was vibrating beneath Luzanna's hands as she danced around it and sent its edge into the shadow beasts.

The darkness growled as it hovered, watching as the three used their enchanted weapons to diminish the horde of beasts it sent after them. *These virtues—they have potential. They mustn't realize their true power.* With that thought, it dipped and brought itself close to the earth before gliding over the marsh and toward the trio.

"Lucia, here it comes!" Leo shouted as he fought off another wolf. "Look!"

Lucia saw the figure of the demon approaching in the distance, with its dark wings emitting their electrifying aura. She closed her eyes. *Focus. Let the words of your song empower you. Your prayer—it is enough. . . . I can't stop this feeling, not when the words keep coming. From deep inside, I hear it, the drumming of my conviction. To accept my fate with grace, even from within the darkest place, this is my conviction. Because even when I walk alone, it glows.*

Lucia opened her eyes just as the beast's claws reached for her face. She pivoted and maneuvered her sword between herself and its slashing claws. Her perception was too great. It was instinct. The edge of her diamond sword met the blades of the beast's gauntlets. Her reflexes were taking over, and her adrenaline-pumped body was thrust into a trancelike state. With each slash, she caught the monster's claws. In her head, she heard it whispering. There amongst the mess, the voice of light was accurately predicting the movements of the dark beast while waiting for an opening. "I'm going to rip you from existence," she said.

The beast chuckled as they faced off. "You say that with so much hate. Do you *hate* me, girl? Do you hate me,"—it shined a toothy grin as it charged its claw with dark energy—"*Lucia*?" It dropped its heavy hand and shattered her sword, surprising Lucia, who, with quick thinking, used the light to propel herself backward a good distance from the beast.

"You fool," it howled while sending its terrifying claws at her again. "How *dare* you challenge those who despise you? Hate leads to wrath. Wrath leads to violence. Hate kills . . . . Are you a killer?"

"I'm not a killer. Nor do I fear them. I don't hate them, even," Lucia said, shaking her head and summoning a new sword into her hand. "Do you want to know what I hate?" She brought her sword in front of her face. "Losing." And then with a step, enhanced with light, she bolted toward the monster, dodging under its right claw. Briskly with her left hand, she summoned a bright golden shield. She rose up and slammed it underneath the head of the demon before shattering it on the side of its face. *This is it,* she thought. *You're open.* As the demon was hunched sideways, Lucia sent her sword into its black torso. And with her diamond blade deep within the beast's tar-like flesh, she let go of the sword's hilt and flipped backward. With a light-filled kick, she thrust the sword deeper into the beast and brought the demon into the air as the sword exploded into shards of incandescence. She caught herself as the monster twisted and spun. Gravity was just about to bring him down before Lucia extended her hands and sent a powerful blast of golden light toward the monstrosity.

Consumed by the white flare, the beast snarled, burning with intense radiance. The trio covered their faces as the monster was enveloped in the light. The wolves dissipated, and the shadows retreated beneath their feet. The light beaconed before flashing into an array of sparks, revealing what was left of the demon. It fell to the ground, its anti-light and dark electricity inching about its body as it attempted to rise. Its wings were tattered, beaten. It let out an echoing cry as it fused its claws to its side. It knelt in the distance, glaring at Lucia intensely. "You're just a puppet . . . a tool!" it shouted in shock. "You think those wings will redeem you. You're wrong. They'll forsake you." The beast growled as it pulled in the shadows of the night to regenerate itself. "They'll forsake you all."

"Why are you still talking?" Leo spat. "You lost! So why don't you beat it before Lucia makes some target practice out of you? I mean, that is, if you'll fly again."

Lucia glanced toward Leo and then back to the demon. *Where did all that come from?* she thought. *Puppet?* She sensed something true about that word. She had never fought a day in her life, but today, all this came from somewhere. *I have to know why.* "What does the darkness really want? To destroy the world? The light? There has to be a goal. If I'm the light's puppet, so be it, as long as it rids the world of sin and rights the wrongs of the past. It intends on saving humanity, whereas you"—Lucia's voice rose—"intend to destroy it."

The demon released another growl, narrowing its bright scarlet eyes. "You mock me, but don't understand the light's true motives.

One cannot exist without the other. Our bond is eternal, regardless of the light's petty schemes. Don't underestimate our power, girl! Those wings hold nothing more than deception. It knows what was promised." It hesitated and then said with a disoriented chuckle, "And it will pay for what it has taken from us." And then, with a great push of its wings, the demon shot upward, flying high until it was out of sight.

The light of the moon and stars graced them as the brilliance of Leo's dagger dimmed and Luzanna's staff transformed back into a branch of oak.

"What was that?" Luzanna asked, stepping beside Lucia, her eyes fixed to the heavens.

"It was another sin. Hate, I presume. The sin that destroyed my home." Lucia's tone was solid. "I'm beginning to understand. I know why we were all brought together. The light—it needs the three of us. It spoke the names of the others: Wym. Lykorus. These sins—they're awful. But they're real, and we're the only ones who can stop them."

"We?" Leo asked, shocked by Lucia's words. Was she really saying this? Days ago, she'd felt the burden of the world lying solely on her shoulders. Today, she was confiding and placing her faith in them. "I mean, it was *your* light that saved us. That backflip was incredible!"

Lucia sighed. "Leo, you don't get it. It called us the 'light's virtues,' virtue being the opposite of sin. We all have a role to play in this. You, me, and Luzanna."

"Just as Stello predicted," Luzanna said, placing a knuckle to the beak of her mask as she thought. "He told my father that the light had an extraordinary destiny for me, but that'd I'd suffer greatly for it." She paused. "So you're saying the light is assembling its virtues."

Lucia smiled and nodded, "Precisely." She still felt it lingering.

Talon was right indeed—there was a connection, one she was at first unaware of. But now, as she tapped into it, everything started to fall into place. "There is a virtue for every sin, a counterpart destined to aid in its destruction."

"But we don't have powers. Whatever we did, *you* allowed us to do it. Aren't the Light Wings supposed to be the key to destroying the darkness?"

"Yes, in part. But when the beast was in the air, I read its thoughts. I know, it sounds odd, but there's truth to what it said about there being a bond. When I opened myself to the source of its power, I could feel it. The light and the darkness exist eternally, each bonded to the other within the same place. Except, now, the darkness is overpowering the light. How? I'm not sure, but the key to restoring the light's power is in awakening the powers within each of us."

"*Our* powers?"

"Yes. On the other side—where the light is, where the Light Wings and the sins are connected to. I'm almost positive that whatever we find in Remena is going to show us what we need to do to establish your connections, like I did with my song."

Leo pinched the bridge of his nose. "Look, I know a whole lot of crazy crap just went down, but I'm finding it hard to believe that we could create any sort of connection. Luzanna said only protectors could use the light's power. We're clearly not protectors."

"And neither am I," Lucia said.

"But you might be," Luzanna interjected. She followed with much skepticism. "I don't know. If I had any special connection, an intuition or spirit like yours, I'd know. My powers come from logic and reason. My nature is human, nothing more. What you're saying, it's just not viable. There is no evidence to support this."

"Does there have to be, though? Isn't that what faith's for? Let me ask you, Leo. Where does your power come from?" Lucia asked.

Leo hesitated. He didn't know exactly how to answer that. "I don't know. The only faith I've ever had was in myself and the choices I make."

"Well, I believe there is more to both of you than you're willing to accept. If you don't believe me, just remember. My intuition is never wrong. I know I'm right on this one." Lucia turned on her heel and started walking toward the forest in the distance.

"Lucia, where are you going?"

She stopped and glanced back, forgetting that they hadn't even rested. "Where do you think? Remena is this way. Come on!"

Luzanna and Leo looked at each other, bewildered by what their senses were telling them. *Virtues of light. The source of the light and darkness. The protectors.* It was all too much for their minds to take on at once. But the two knew they had no choice. What the Light Wings had demonstrated tonight only proved that Lucia was more powerful than they could have ever imagined. And even in those tight moments, fighting side by side, they were too. If they were blessed with power just as Lucia was, who was to say they couldn't save this dying world?

Little did they know, the answers to their questions were beyond that forest, waiting to open their eyes to a whole new world.

CHAPTER SIXTEEN

The Protectors' Promise

The vegetation was heavy as they walked through the ever-growing jungle. Luzanna was quick to explain how the jungle served as a border to this sacred realm where they soon hoped to discover the secrets of the Light Wings, and their plan to rid Terestria of the sins that plagued it.

With each new encounter, they'd learned more about the light's intentions, about their own roles, and about how they all fit into the grand design Stello had set in motion years ago when he left the Light Wings in Ara's care. The sky was thundering overhead, and a shower of rain came soon thereafter. Lucia sensed it. The Light Wings were pulling her, eagerly, toward their long-fated destination. They were ready—ready to go home.

"Remena is not far now," Luzanna said. "Once we cross the

forest border, we'll be there."

"Come on," Lucia mumbled as she pushed leaves from her face. "Just a little longer." The signs were growing all around them. The laws of nature, Terestria itself, called to her asking her to remember and discern the signs so she could redeem it. *I'm going to do it. I'm going to save the world. I will . . . I am.*

Lucia was determined. There was no other way. Her old life, who she was now, and everything she knew before was different. She had changed. Everything had changed. And she did not want to go back. No ounce of will in her body wanted to. There was a conviction building deep inside her, and oddly enough, the words her mother once so passionately spoke made all the more sense to her. *Duty above all else. That's my family's motto.* Lucia pressed forward, leading the way with glowing gold eyes. *Thank you, Mother, for teaching me all the right things. I'm sorry I ever doubted you.*

Eventually, Lucia stopped. She lowered her head noticing a pink rose. It tilted in the rain, pointing to her left. There, she saw roses of blue and yellow. Lucia followed them with her eyes, observing as they met a rose of violet and then another of pink and blue. "There's a trail this way. Look—the roses . . . ."

"I've never seen roses of violet or blue before. I actually never thought it to be empirically possible to produce roses such as these." Luzanna stated, fascinated with Lucia's discovery.

"Neither have I. But those colors—they repeat. I'm seeing them everywhere." Lucia sped along the path as the colored roses alternated and increased in number. "In my dreams, the stained glass window at home in the light of the pendant—these colors are connected to the light. They have to be." Lucia was catching on, learning the patterns. "Don't you see? We've been blind this whole time. Mankind has forgotten all about the things the light holds dear. They no longer believe or pay attention. They play with their politics and ploys for power, but they've forgotten about the one true source of all life. The knowledge was lost and kept secret, but to what end? Why? There has to be a reason."

"Lucia, are you feeling alright?" Leo was growing increasingly worried. Over the course of their journey, he had seen many sides to Lucia, but this one was intense and so unlike her. In a way, he was glad she was out of her head and focused on the mission, but in another, he felt like she was losing touch with who she was.

Lucia stopped to smile back at him. "I am. I think I'm finally starting to understand."

"And this . . . " Leo was trying not to sound skeptical. "This makes you happy?"

Lucia stepped back and took a moment to think. "No, not happy." She took two slow steps as she thought of how to explain how she was feeling. "But . . . content."

"Surely you've felt that way before," Luzanna said as they pressed forward.

"I really can't say so," Lucia said honestly. "My entire life, I lived in a cloud of doubt. I was never fond of my duty. I rejected it. I wanted nothing more than to be free, but now, even trapped in the midst of all this, I feel as if my *duty* is why I live. It's this purpose that makes me who I am."

"But, Lucia, you're more than that," Leo said touching her shoulder. "You're not just the high maiden of Moz or some virtue of light. You're still *you*, right?"

Lucia hesitated. She smiled again and nodded. "Of course."

Leo exhaled as a weight lifted off his shoulders. Maybe he was overreacting and overthinking the severity of the situation. Lucia was in no way the light's puppet. Why would the light enslave her and give her the exact opposite of what she always wanted? In the end, surely it intended to reward her and grant her many blessings. He hoped this was the case with each of them. Because he did not want to think of the light as such a force corrupted in its own intent. How could something that was meant to represent and embody all that was good in the world be capable of such evil?

It wasn't too much longer before they saw the light of dusk seeping through the edge of the forest, landing atop a white rose at the end of the heavy brush.

"This must be it," Luzanna said. "I don't know if I'm ready."

Lucia stopped and stood beside her. "Neither am I, but what other choice do we have?" She stepped ahead, exiting the forest with wide eyes, unsure of what she was expecting to see.

The sun was fading into the horizon beneath a gray-purplish sky. Though the light was dim, Lucia made out the details of a dormant city, which stood silently within the onslaught of vegetation that grew wildly from its border. Not a single person stood among its grounds. It was empty. Each of its buildings had been beautifully crafted, shaped into what looked like grand cathedrals and centuries-old pyramids. It was obvious that this place held many secrets. Its buildings were ancient, and the sacred energy fed into Lucia through the soles of her feet. But what was this place—if not dead?

"*This* is Remena?" Luzanna asked as she followed closely behind Lucia. She stepped ahead, squinting as she looked into the empty city. "This can't be right. This is nothing like what my father described." Immediately, her eyes were encapsulated. Worry filled them as she tried to recall her studies of the forgotten city. "Remena and the protectors, what has become of them?"

"There is life here," Lucia said, her tone hollow. " I can feel it nearby, but you're right, Luzanna. Something is definitely wrong."

"Do you think it was the darkness?" Leo asked. "Do you think the sins were responsible, I mean?"

"No. The darkness did not do this. The darkness is bound to the Light Wings. It could not destroy what it could not follow. The Light Wings are its only connection."

"But the protectors can commune with the light. What's to say they couldn't create the same connection you could?"

"Look around," Lucia said. "Does this place look destroyed to you? Every sin has brought destruction in its wake. Something else happened here. Nothing is ruined. It's just . . . unoccupied."

"So what are you saying? The protectors just vanished into thin air?"

"Maybe," Lucia said. "But not all of them." She placed a hand over the Light Wings, focusing on the whispers inside her head. A tingling came over her, moving through her body and into her fingertips. When she opened her eyes, her irises glistened as her vision shifted farther west. "This way."

Leo glanced toward Luzanna. She was breathing heavily with her head bowed—she felt it too, the shadowy truth. Surely, answers lay within this place. But were they the answers they hoped for? Something told Leo otherwise. Whatever truth they found here, whatever it might be, was going to be more dubious than they ever could have imagined.

They made their way through the city, deeper into the moss-covered buildings. There was something so familiar about this place, Lucia thought. It was almost as if she had been here before, though she knew she never had. But the memories of the Light Wings were there, deep within her psyche.

As they made their way through the city, a gripping cold tightened with every step. The chill ran down their spines, and the terror of what likely awaited them weighed heavily on their thoughts. Their salvation did not exist here. This dread they were feeling, this was their doom—because in reality, there was nothing more terrifying than the truth.

In the distance, Lucia saw it: a dimly lit window at the base of a large black tower. It was easily the tallest building in the city, standing so high that the top disappeared into the clouds. If it weren't for the window, Lucia might not have seen it at all, but she sensed it. She watched as the light flickered as if being made by the light of a candle or flame. "There." Lucia pointed.

"What is this place?" Luzanna asked.

"Well, whatever it is, I don't like it." Leo pulled his dagger from his sheath, perceiving the presence of something evil. He looked up at the hidden top, almost as if he knew someone or something up there was watching them, waiting. "It's here. The darkness, I mean."

Lucia sighed. "I know. I felt it as soon as we started walking toward this place."

"And it does nothing?" Luzanna asked. "Doesn't it know we're on the verge of learning of its own demise?"

"No," Leo said. "It knows we're on the verge of learning about our own."

"Leo," Lucia said softly as she made her way toward the tower, "shut up."

Leo's eyes softened as Luzanna followed Lucia toward the two large wooden doors in the distance. He shook off whatever he was feeling and followed.

Standing at the base of the large tower, examining the door, Lucia held out her hand, touching its bronze handle. With a deep breath, she gripped it and pulled, hearing the air as it rushed inside as if the door had not been opened for some time. *This is it,* she thought. *It's time to learn the truth.* As the door opened, she made out the details of the tower's entrance. With one cautious step, she moved through the threshold and into the candlelit citadel.

Luzanna and Leo followed. There was a loud echo as the door closed, seemingly signaling their arrival.

Lucia was quick in her thinking. "Hello?" she called out. "Is anyone here? We . . . we need your help." She looked around. Her breath shook as she stepped into the center of the vast room.

Ahead of them was an altar covered in large candles of four colors: magenta, violet, blue, and yellow—each alternating beneath an epitaph depicting what appeared to be the Light Wings. However, they were different than Lucia's Light Wings. One side was a wing of light, *feathered* like a dove, and the other was a wing of dark, *leathered* like a bat. At the center they met as a diamond within a sphere.

"I don't like this place," Leo whispered, touching Lucia's shoulder. "What if this is a trap?"

"Shhh." Lucia shook off his hand as her eyes trailed up toward the ceiling to a dome covered in frescoes, paintings of eight mystical beings. She could not make out the complete details of each one, but they were familiar.

"What has brought you here?" A woman's voice hovered in the air, shocking the trio as their eyes darted toward the staircase in the distance from where they heard it originate. The woman was dressed in a parted black gown with trimmings of purple-tinted silver lace. She stepped closer to them, walking into the candlelight to reveal herself. She was beautiful. Her skin was fair and her lips a bright red. Her eyes were dark but very familiar, shaped like autumn almonds beneath a layer of thick, dark lashes. Braids were tied back over her long dark hair with a silver bow, and her face held a distinct sense of purity, much like someone they all knew very well.

Lucia stared in shock and wonder. It was as if she were looking at an alternate, slightly older version of herself. The woman's eyes narrowed as she looked at Lucia and down to the Light Wings against her neck. "You're finally here."

"Finally?" Leo scoffed. "As if you knew she was coming? Who are you? Where is everyone?"

The woman tilted her head. "I can imagine," she said slowly, "you must have many questions. But as you can see, no one is here.

It's only me and one other. No one else."

"My father said the protectors lived here. Are you one of them?" Luzanna asked.

"Why, yes. I am one of the last of our kind." She looked down as she spoke. "Forgive me. My name is Emma, high priestess of the Remena citadel and the last survivor of the sacred line of Sarina."

"Sarina is your surname?" Lucia asked.

Emma nodded. "Yes. Everyone else has perished. It has been like this for some time. I believe it has been twenty years since the fall."

"The fall?"

"The fall of the protectors. Surely that is why you have come, isn't it? Because of the forces that have been unleashed on your world—*our* world." Emma blew out a breath. "I see that the Light Wings have chosen you as their savior. I'm not surprised—how do we look so much alike?"

"I'm glad I'm not the only one who noticed," Lucia said with a slight smile. "Emma, it seems you understand a lot more about what's happening than we do. So please tell us. What is the fall, and what is happening to Terestria?"

Emma nodded. She walked to the altar, took an incense, and lit it with one of the candles. She placed it into a holder before clasping her hands together. For a moment, she bowed her head, and the three stayed silent as she prayed. Soon, her head rose and she turned to them. She looked up toward the paintings overhead. "So it is true, then? The sins are waging war on the life that light created?"

"I wouldn't call it war. Each battle has been one-sided. They appear and massacre our people, wipe out entire cities and destroy lives. That doesn't sound like war to me. That sounds like genocide."

"But it *is* war, because *you* exist—the light's virtues, soldiers destined to take form and fight the sins of darkness."

"The light's virtues? So, the stories are true," Luzanna uttered. "My father—Talon, he knew about all this."

"Because he was destined to. The Renon line was designated by the light to be the keeper of secrets eons ago. They were to be the only connection Remena had to the outside world."

"But why?" Leo asked. "Why only them? Why keep all these secrets from the rest of the world? Why keep everyone else in the dark to place their faith in something they had no way of truly understanding?"

"The answer to that is simple: People fear what they don't understand. Your people underestimate knowledge and its power. The more one knows, the more cynical they become. If everyone knew the truth, if the stories weren't just stories, the people would live in fear and be difficult to control."

"So you keep them ignorant so that they can feel safe, without giving them the means to protect themselves. What about freedom of choice?" Leo asked.

"But they did have a means. The people had you—the royal families of Terestria and their runes. They were set in place for this distinct purpose—to destroy the sins and the darkness that created them."

"Runes? I don't understand." Luzanna blinked hard while she tried to think.

"At the time of the fall, the heirs of Terestria would be summoned to defend it. Their power relies solely on that of the Light Wings and the royal runes left behind by the creator."

"You speak as if we know what the hell you are talking about. Stop confusing us and get to the damn point already!" Leo was growing impatient.

"Leo!" Lucia yelled back at him. She turned again to Emma. "I apologize for his abrasiveness. Please go on."

"I apologize," Emma said. "I just anticipated that the Carist elder would have done a better job of explaining all this to you before you arrived."

"He died before he ever had the chance to. And he actually tried to have us killed right before the darkness came and blew Aldric to oblivion," Leo said with utmost sensitivity.

"I get bits and pieces," Lucia said. "The connection grows the more I use its power. It speaks to me, and I can just tell . . . when it's telling me the truth. We encountered a sin not long before coming here, and I could sense its fear of the virtues. I was able to hear the sins' names as well."

Emma approached Lucia. She leaned in closer, examining the Light Wings. "You know, I've never seen the Light Wings in person, even though they had remained here for thousands of years. I prayed for so long that they'd return. I thought that, when they did, so would everyone else return. But, of course they wouldn't. There is no escaping death once it has already claimed you. That much I know."

She put up a tough exterior, but visible within the young woman's eyes was a feeling of isolation and loneliness. Lucia felt it emanating from her. "Tell me about the fall. What is it, and how did it happen?"

Emma brought a finger to her lips. A deep sadness covered her face. "It's known that when the light created humans, it entrusted their lives to the protectors. In exchange for great power, the protectors made a promise. They were to use their powers to preserve the balance of nature by worshipping the light.

"We were to be servants devoted to protecting the delicate balance between our world and yours. If we were ever to break our promise, if we were to go against our promise and defy the light's wishes, the covenant that bound the forces of darkness from entering our world would be broken, and they would be free to take back what they created."

"And what was that promise?" Lucia asked.

"Every protector is born with a power, one distinctive to their own personality. Besides being able to commune with the light, these gifts were blessings of the light to be used altruistically for the good of humanity. If they were ever to be used for a purpose beyond that of virtue, the covenant would be broken. If the incorruptible were to become corruptible, the fall would be imminent."

"And this happened? One of your own turned against the light and used their power for something evil?" Lucia asked.

"I wouldn't say evil, necessarily, but something impure, something selfish." Emma took a deep breath before continuing. "It started with a bitter cold seeping through our land. Once sacred, this land became toxic and uninhabitable. Our crops would not grow, and our livestock died. There was famine and plague. One by one our people perished, leaving only Ralphoro, the highest of the light's clergy, and me. One would think it a blessing to be alive, but truly it's been a curse. I've been alone all my life. I was but an infant when it happened."

"Emma, I'm so sorry," Lucia said taking Emma's hand. "Who was it? Do you know?"

Emma looked away, trying to hide her tears. She nodded. "My brother."

"Emma, my dear . . . that's *enough*." The voice came from a figure descending from the staircase.

Emma stepped back, opening the way for him as he approached. He was an elderly man dressed in a robe of orange and green. His body was frail, and his hair was coarse and white, balding at the top. Lucia noticed his limp as he got closer.

Emma said, "Master, the virtues have arrived."

"Hmm," he said, studying the three visitors. He hunched over his cane as he got a closer view of the Light Wings then briefly scanned the trio. "I only see three of them. There's supposed to be four."

"I know, but I assume they simply haven't found the fourth yet."

"They will be useless without the fourth, whoever it is. Moz, Pinea, Aldric, and Argania—each is supposed to have an heir."

"Master Ralphoro, sir," Leo said awkwardly, "no one here has ever been to Argania. Argania has lived in isolation for centuries beyond the sea."

"Well I don't know what else to tell you, young sir. There are four virtues of light—and right now I only see three." He walked toward Luzanna, who cowered backward as he squinted and examined the stone on her forehead. "And what of the runes? Do you have them?"

"What runes? We don't understand," she said.

"My goodness. How unprepared are you? Your world is dying, and you have done so poorly assembling the tools for its salvation. I'm quite disappointed, to say the least."

"Oh, I'm sorry," Leo said sarcastically. "I was unaware that, for my entire life, our world has been on the tipping point of destruction because of some promise we were never told about. It's not our fault we didn't know what was going on. No one told us anything!"

"This is temperance, I assume? The mouth on that one surely needs work."

"Don't talk like I'm not standing in the room with you." Leo said with a wrinkle of his nose.

Lucia smiled, "Yes, Leo is quite impulsive at times. But temperance, you say?"

"Tell me your names. Hurry. All of you," the elder said.

"I'm Luzanna Renon, the new chieftess of the Carist tribe," Luzanna said gleefully.

"Leocadio Feral, sir of Pinea," Leo said before scoffing and looking away from the old man.

"I'm Lucia Sanoon, high maiden of Moz and—"

"Savior of the Light Wings." Ralphoro bowed his head. "Welcome to the Tower of Origin, High Maiden—the grand citadel of Remena. I'm sure your journey has been a long one, and rough to say the least. Emma, why don't you show these fine young people to a chamber where they can get some rest?"

"Rest?" Leo started up again. "There is too much to discuss. We don't have time for rest."

"Surely you do," Ralphoro replied. "Like I said, you are useless without the fourth heir. So, considering you are leagues away from the northern continent, you have plenty of time."

"And the sins? What of them? They follow us wherever we go," Leo said.

"Humph." Ralphoro turned from them, looking up to the dome above. "They wouldn't dare enter this place. Though our land has been corrupted since the time of the fall, it is still the promised land. It will always be the seat of light in Terestria. Your power is only stronger here, so you need not worry. You can rest easy tonight."

"So we'll wait to hear the rest of the story tomorrow, then?" Leo asked.

"Absolutely. You've heard enough for tonight. My poor Emma needs her rest also. Recounting the past weighs heavily on her conscience, and I would rather ease her mind from reliving the tragedy of the fall, since it has affected her so deeply. So, please, respect that."

Lucia nodded. "Of course. We understand." She looked over to Emma and smiled. "Thank you for your kindness and hospitality. A night's rest would be wonderful." She turned to her friends. "What do you think, everyone?"

Luzanna nodded. "Not to mention a bath."

"And a good meal," Leo said, rubbing his stomach.

Emma smiled, her eyes gleaming with excitement. "Well good, I can prepare something while you all get settled. We've never had company before, so it'd honestly be a pleasure. Right, Master?"

"Of course, my dear. These youths are here to right the wrongs of the past and restore the world back into prosperity." Ralphoro addressed the trio. "Now, off you go. Make yourselves at home here, virtues. You are among friends and servants of the light. It is our duty to assist you by any means necessary. So, please, don't hesitate to ask for anything." He coughed heavily into the side of his robe before instructing Emma, "Emma, show them to their quarters." He turned back to address them. "You will find each with its own bathing chambers. Once you've made yourselves comfortable, Emma will bring food to your rooms. Does that sound okay?"

"That sounds amazing," Luzanna answered.

"Great. Well go on. This old man has to turn in for the time being, but I look forward to getting to know each of you better in the morning."

"Thank you, Ralphoro. We are very grateful," Lucia said, bowing her head.

"There is no need to be. It is our duty. Now please, carry on, my children."

The three nodded as Ralphoro made his way back up the stairs. He was almost to the top when he stopped. "And once everyone is settled in, Emma, please see to it that everyone is off to their rooms and to bed. Though this place may be safe from your enemies, this tower has many secrets. Not to say I don't trust you all, but I don't need your bunch running amok and making a mess."

"Don't worry, Master. Everyone will be situated in the west wing."

Ralphoro nodded before turning on his heel and disappearing

out of sight.

Lucia knew this could not be the end to the misery they had seen. It was far from over—she knew that much. But she also finally felt like she had a moment to catch her breath.

"Follow me, everyone." Emma lit a lantern and walked toward the stairs. The three heirs followed behind her, eagerly anticipating the hospitality that was promised them.

Lucia thought it was all too good to be true, but then she remembered Ralphoro's words: *Duty,* she thought. With that word, she found comfort and felt her worries dissipate. They were closer than they ever had been to knowing the truth they longed for, and for the first time in a long time, she did feel safe. But despite it all, the familiar dread clung to her. She supposed there was no escaping it. It would always be there as long as the wings remained around her neck. But now, there was something to hope for. There was a resolution. Soon they would know the whole truth. It would be clear as day, and the war they spoke of would be over. Soon . . . she hoped.

CHAPTER SEVENTEEN

Depths of Darkness

mma gazed into a shimmering silver mirror, staring deeply into her own dark eyes. She watched herself, tracing the body within her soft silk gown. It hung loosely over her slender shoulders and hugged at her waist, where a silver-studded leather belt secured her dress in place. With the gentle touch of her fingers, she caressed the gracefully sculpted roses on the mirror's frame. They sparkled in the candlelight, emitting a bright yellow flow that refracted sparkles of violet, pink, and blue onto the redwood dressing table of her bedroom. She lowered her eyes, following the streams of light as they fell upon her many combs. Slowly, she took up her favorite, a comb of obsidian, and ran it through the ends of her raven-dark hair.

There was sadness in her eyes, a look of woe and grief that

stemmed from a memory of something her master had said some time ago. It must have only been yesterday when he told her the horrible truth: "I sense its presence in the world again. The darkness has come to claim what it's owed. Your brother—he has damned us all. Without the wings, we will surely perish." The voice of the old man echoed within her mind, circling around the feeling of dread and suffering unlike anything she had known before. Her intuition was strong, too. Somehow, she knew that something terrible was going to happen, sooner than they could have ever expected. Like a thief in the night it would come, for it hungered for the power of Light Wings. Her stomach turned as she envisioned the chaos, smelling the decay in her nostrils and feeling the heat on her face. There was fire, lightning, and even ice. Terestria's trials had only just begun. Soon, it would fully realize the consequences of its sin. As a protector, she had visions as a normality, but these were different. These visions were nightmares, and a reminder that the cost of her power was her duty as a protector—a duty she was never able to truly assume because the fall had happened so early in her life.

This duty was her life's purpose: to preserve the light and never stray from it, to protect and never to destroy. She was well aware of the promise her people had made. Darkness was her sworn enemy, as it should be, but she felt a troubling guilt inside. The protectors had been corrupted, and they had died; all but her and her master. *Why?* She thought she understood. All this time, she had felt like she'd always known, but when she saw those wings for the first time, she started to question whether or not she was truly worthy of the light's protection after what her people had done.

How long had it been since the world's corruption? *Twenty years,* she thought; shortly after her second birthday. She was to be the protectors' high priestess, to serve beside her brother, before he went into the crypts below the tower grounds and stole their sacred treasure all so he could follow that girl from beyond the forest. She wondered what had become of him, and if he knew of the grief he had caused her. Did he even think of her? And how could he have left the Light Wings in plain sight, for this innocent youth to find? The Light Wings had chosen her to fight—but why?

Emma's hand tightened around her comb, her grip clenching into a fist. Soon, there was a snap as the comb broke in half and cut into the palm of her hand. Blood dripped onto the table as Emma stared blankly into the mirror, her mind wandering. She tried to remember that part of herself that bound her to her duty as protector. She thought of the light of the moon and of the stars. She thought of the sun and the warmth it brought to a midsummer's day. She searched and searched, looking for that power she knew she held inside, the fragile incandescence that breathed life into the souls of man and the earth they inhabited. It was her duty to protect Terestria, to be the light that shined through the darkness. Yet, still, there was doubt within her mind. She refused to listen, shutting it out as she sprang from her seat. Her blood was *not* tainted. Her family, her lineage, could not be as dark as the truth perceived. This could not be her fault.

She grabbed her handkerchief and wiped the blood from her palm. Wrapping it, she rushed to the door of her bedroom. Quietly, she cracked the door open and looked outside, seeing nothing but the dim light of the moon shining through the stained glass of the hallway windows. She stepped out onto the carpet and shut the door behind her, trying hard not to let the sound of it closing echo through the hall. The last thing Emma wanted was to wake Ralphoro. In his old age, he had become stricter with her, and she could only imagine how he'd react if he found she had disobeyed him under the current circumstances. But she had this feeling brewing inside her. There was something she had to do. There was no waiting. She had to know the truth.

Emma glided through the hallway toward the chambers where she had put her visitors to rest. She had her eyes on the farthest one, where she knew the Light Wings waited. She approached the door, raising her fist to gently knock. She hesitated, wary still of Ralphoro sleeping down the hall. She took a deep breath before tapping on the door. It wasn't long before she heard a shuffle and some footsteps. Lucia opened the door.

"I'm sorry. Did I wake you?" Emma whispered before bringing a finger to her lips and watching her surroundings.

Lucia blinked before awkwardly replying. "No. I was praying to the light."

"Ah, I see," Emma said. "What were you praying for?"

"Uh, I don't know." Lucia blinked again, bringing a hand to the pendant. "I was saying the same prayer I say every night, praying for my family, my people, and Terestria's prosperity. But . . . " Lucia paused. She looked up, her expression changed. "This time, I prayed for answers. I'm tired of running, and it's been weeks since I've seen my mother. I must know what I can do to save her."

"So your mother—she's who you care about most?"

Lucia smiled. "I guess you can say that. Although, I've grown quite close with Luzanna and Leo. I don't know where I'd be without them."

Emma softened her gaze. "You are so fortunate to have such great friends by your side. And your mother, she sounds like she means the world to you. You must love her very much."

Lucia nodded as a surge of emotion built within her eyes. She cleared her throat, calming her thoughts so she could speak without falling into another one of her sobs. "What brings you here, Emma? Is something troubling you?"

Emma looked back again, watching the moonlight as it faded. "I was hoping we could talk. I know Ralphoro instructed us to wait until morning, but I'm afraid." She lowered her eyes. How could she be so deliberate? Defying her master's wishes. This was so unlike her. "I don't believe we have much time. There is someplace we must go, a place you have to see."

What was this? Lucia was confused. Emma was acting so strangely it caught her by surprise. When they'd first met, she seemed to be so composed and collected. Nothing seemed to faze her, but now it seemed as if she was sincerely afraid. Of what? Lucia wondered. She took a deep breath before smiling, trying not to look so alarmed. Putting on faces was her normal. There was something to gain from this, and at best, her curiosity was piqued. "Sure, shall I wake the others?"

"No," Emma said. "Ralphoro must not know about this, and I'm afraid the more people come, the easier it will be for him to find out. The place we're going is very sacred, and it's not meant to be visited by outsiders."

A sacred and secret place, Lucia thought. How odd was it that Emma would visit her in the middle of the night with such a request? Lucia sensed it in her core, a longing to go there, even though she had no idea where this place might be. What was it that was drawing her there? Her prayer for answers? The Light Wings themselves? She didn't think long on it and simply nodded.

Lucia looked outside to both ends of the hallway before stepping out into the moonlit corridor. She was wearing a brown leather vest layered over a light yellow blouse. Oddly enough, she was also wearing a fresh pair of ivory-colored boots that matched the silky white skirt that hung down below her waist.

"I never did thank you for the clothes. It feels so good to get into something fresh."

"It was no problem. After all, you're our guests. There's a long journey ahead of you, so I'm glad you're wearing your boots."

"Is it far, this place?" Lucia asked.

"Oh no," Emma said. "It's just not the most comfortable place to be."

This made Lucia's heart shudder. There it came, hovering over her like a silent rain, the dread of uncertainty that would continue to haunt her until she knew the truth. She took a breath, mentally preparing herself for whatever she might be walking herself into. "I'm ready," she said.

Emma, with a wave of her hand, started down toward the east wing, where they would find the entrance to the tower's catacombs—the home of the Light Wings.

* * *

Leo's face emerged through the crack of his door, the shadows beneath his sapphire eyes showing signs of his restlessness.

"Leo, are you awake?" Luzanna asked in a rush.

"No, not at all. Is something the matter?" Leo said as he wiped the sleep from his eyes. He turned his head to the other doors, noticing only his was open. "What are you doing here?"

"I couldn't sleep," Luzanna said before barging past Leo and into his room.

"Hey . . . h-hey!" Leo said, reaching for his shirt. "Could you just wait a minute? I'm not dressed."

Luzanna rolled her eyes before looking around the room.

Leo threw on a dark blue tunic. Tugging on a pair of black trousers, he tied a pair of silver-laced boots onto his feet.

"There is something about this place that strikes me as odd," Luzanna said as she turned back toward Leo, who was latching his dagger's sheath to his belt. "I have this terrible feeling."

"Well look at this place. It's ancient, musty, old—anyone would be spooked, sleeping in a place like this."

Luzanna crossed her arms. "Leo, that's not what I meant. There's something about us being here, something that I don't like. I can't explain it, but I feel like we could be in danger."

"Really? What danger? You heard Ralphoro. This place is

sacred. The darkness would not dare come into a place as holy as this. This is probably the safest place we could be right now."

Luzanna shook her head. "How can you be so certain or so trusting? These are the protectors—the same 'protectors' that supposedly corrupted the light's balance in the first place. Who's to say we didn't just fall into some sort of a trap?"

Leo pinched the bridge of his nose after he tightened one last strap on his vest. "Look, this has got to be the safest Lucia's felt in weeks. She needs a break. And if she's happy, I'm happy. So I don't see the problem here."

"Lucia? Safe? You don't say," Luzanna said with a sly bit of sarcasm. "Then tell me: where is she?" She squinted behind her mask.

"Sleeping in her room, of course," Leo said confidently.

"Nope, think again."

"What do you mean?" Leo felt a blow to the chest as uncertainty washed over him. "She's not in her room?"

"No, she's not. I went over to check on her before coming here. She's nowhere to be found."

As soon as he heard this, panic consumed his face and Leo's breathing became heavy. "We've got to go. We've got to find her!" He bolted toward the door, but Luzanna caught him by the arm.

"It's not that easy, Leo. This place is gigantic. She could be anywhere." Luzanna clenched her teeth. "Why would she go off on her own?"

"Maybe she's not on her own. What about Emma? Could she know where she is?"

"I went by her room and knocked. There was no answer. I assumed she was sleeping."

"No, she must be with Lucia. That could be the only explanation."

"Emma doesn't seem like the type to go against her master's wishes. I highly doubt that," Luzanna said.

"But, so. Lucia's the same. She wouldn't go off for no good reason, especially without telling us."

Luzanna lowered her eyes. She knew he was right even though she did not want to admit it. How much did they really know about Emma, Ralphoro, or the protectors? This could have all been a ploy to lower their guard and lead Lucia right into the darkness' grasp. "Okay, I think we're right to worry. But where would they go? There has to be something—a clue, or something they said, that could shed some light on where they could have gone."

"Ralphoro did leave very explicit instructions. He didn't want anyone wandering around the tower unsupervised."

"That's why Emma had us placed in the west wing, to keep us—"

"Away from whatever secret this tower is hiding," Leo finished for her.

"Lucia has to have gone east. She's more desperate for answers than any of us. Oh goodness, I hope she knows what she is getting herself into."

"She doesn't. She never does," Leo said, reaching for the brass handle of his chamber door and pulling it open. "We've got to get a move on. If we wait too long, Lucia might find herself in more trouble than she bargained for."

Luzanna nodded, stepping out of Leo's room. She looked at the angle of the moonlight. "The moon rises in the east, so we go opposite of the direction where the windows are pointed." She pointed to the light on the ground.

"Damn," Leo said, "you're smart."

Luzanna rolled her eyes again before stepping across the moonlit windows and toward the east wing of the grand tower. She hoped to her core that her intuition was right, that her theory was wrong, and that wherever they were headed was safer than she anticipated. But Luzanna could only think of the worst. There was a lingering sense of despair in the midst of that silent corridor.

Whatever secrets this tower was hiding, she wasn't at all sure Ralphoro was ready for them to realize the whole truth. Despite all he had told them, she held firmly on to this skepticism. Like they had been told: knowledge is power. But this was something Luzanna had grown up knowing all her life. So she knew it could be used to control those who lack it, just as Ralphoro had said. Whatever they knew now was only what the protectors wanted them to know—nothing more, nothing less. It was going to take more than some stories to convince Luzanna of the whole truth, that much was certain. But luckily for her, they were walking toward all the evidence she would ever need, for the east wing and the catacombs held all the answers they sought.

*   *   *

"I can't believe this place." Lucia gasped in admiration. The dim light of the lanterns hanging from the walls of the stronghold shined light on a place rich in artistic brilliance. It reminded her of her sanctuary in Moz, but on a greater scale. It held the same feeling, as if all the prayers spoken within the place were forever immortalized within its very walls.

As she followed right behind Emma, Lucia wondered if Emma wasn't too different from her. After all, they looked so much alike. The resemblance was uncanny. They could be sisters, or twins for that matter—doppelgangers. She smiled at the thought. It came as no surprise that their fate was intertwined like so. Two young women of faith caught in a struggle for balance, called to serve their lord and creator. It held a certain sense of poetry to it, and that made Lucia all the more eager to find what awaited her at the end of their journey across the Tower of Origin. "Who built this place?" Lucia asked.

"This tower has stood in Remena for eons, almost as long as time has existed," Emma said. "It's rumored that it was constructed by the light itself, but I have a hard time believing that to be so. Very few items are said to have come from the creators themselves. Most notably, that pendant you're wearing. It is what we call the 'master rune,' the rune that governs all the others."

"The royal runes. So there are others like the Light Wings?"

Emma nodded. "Yes, but none as powerful. Your friend—Luzanna, is it? She has the Heaven's Opal."

"You mean the Elder Stone? Her father gave that to her right before he died. Does that mean he always knew? Does it have powers like the Light Wings?" Lucia had so many questions. She was fascinated by the delicate nature their world was built upon.

"Of course it does. But it takes a very special kind of person to wield it. Obviously that person wasn't Talon. I can tell you now, if you hope to save Terestria, Luzanna will need to learn to use it. But I'm not sure how that'll work. Only those capable of Runespeech are able to use the runes." Emma let out a sigh of relief as the corridor split into two walkways. One headed right, into a hallway that looked similar to the one they were in at the moment. But the other was covered in a haze of shadow, with a stone threshold leading into it only a few feet from where they stood. Emma grabbed the unlit torch from its hoister on the right side of the door. She closed her eyes and, with a wave of her hand, circled the torch and brought about a bright orange flame from beneath her fingertips.

Lucia's mouth dropped in awe. "How did you—"

Emma looked back toward Lucia. "Runespeech."

Lucia followed Emma as they descended down a cramped and dark spiral staircase. The red carpet was changing beneath her feet, darkening as they moved farther down. Soon, there was no carpet at all. Only stone. "So—what is Runespeech?"

Emma smiled, glancing back at the Light Wings. The deeper they went, the brighter their light became. This was typical of the Light Wings when they ventured into dark places—she knew this, but to finally be able to see it with her own eyes made her feel honored. "Runespeech is not unlike what you call prayer. It's a communion between our world and theirs. However, it's not just how we *communicate* with the light—it is how we use its power."

"For good. For protection," Lucia asserted.

"As our name suggests," Emma said. "But how you seem to use it is quite puzzling. As far as I know, the gift of Runespeech was an ability granted only to the protectors. No one outside our realm has been capable of using it before."

"I see." Lucia bowed her head. Talon had mentioned this, and even Leo and Luzanna had their suspicions of why Lucia was able to use this power. She didn't have an answer, but it left her confused and worried about what the truth might be. "Talon said that I inherited the gift from my mother. She had used it during Frailty's War, to stop the darkness as it emerged in the final battle between Moz and Pinea."

"The sin manifested itself—and your mother harnessed the light's power on her own? Without a rune?" Emma asked skeptically.

"I mean, do *you* need a rune?"

"Actually, no. My powers are innate. I was born with them," Emma said. "As are yours."

The two eventually came upon another doorway, one that led into what looked to be only darkness. "What is this place?" Lucia asked.

Emma stepped forward, illuminating the walls around them. The air was filled with dust, and an earthy smell oozed up from beneath them, caught on an updraft caused by the fire. "Lucia, could you give me a hand and provide us some light?"

Lucia blinked as she stared at her hands. She nodded and focused her emotions into the tips of her fingers, lighting up the area around them. It didn't take long for her to realize where they were. The bones of bodies were laid upon stone shelves, and the stench she had smelled before was that of the death of hundreds of decaying bodies beneath the tower.

"This is where every protector who has ever lived is laid to rest after they have died. This is the most sacred place in all of Terestria. Only the protectors are allowed in here." Emma walked forward.

Lucia covered her mouth with her free hand, trying to keep the foul dust of the bodies from entering her mouth, but she found herself coughing anyway as she stared in disbelief at the amount of bones she was seeing. "But why am I here? Why would you bring me here?"

"Because, Lucia, you are the savior. And as savior, you deserve to know the truth about the fall. You need to know what really happened."

"So tell me," Lucia said while watching her steps carefully. The place wasn't as bright and pretty as the rest of the tower, to say the least, and she sensed something looming in the shadows. No matter how sacred this place may be, there was something ominous about it—something terrifying.

*   *   *

"She's got to be close," Leo said, using his left hand to cover his yawn. With a rough blink, he studied the hallways of the stronghold, examining them for clues as they approached the east wing.

"I'm not sure, but I have this feeling," Luzanna said wearily. She rushed ahead of Leo as her breathing became shaky. She couldn't explain it, but she perceived a connection. She sensed Lucia from where they were standing. Quickly, she looked to the ground. "They're below us, beneath the tower."

"You can't be serious. How do you know that?"

Luzanna knelt and touched the floor with her fingers. She closed her eyes as a trickle of energy collected at the center of her forehead. "The catacombs," she whispered.

"The what?" Leo asked, confused.

"We have to hurry. Lucia's in danger!"

*   *   *

"These catacombs are where it all began. The start of the fall, it all happened from within and beneath the most sacred of all places. You see, as time passed, it was only inevitable that our blessed blood would venture beyond the forest, but not in such a capacity that Runespeech would ever be attainable outside our tribe. The blood would have been diluted through generations. But in recent times, one person dared to venture outside the forest and leave Remena completely," Emma said.

As they proceeded deeper into the crypt, carvings and symbols of a language Lucia didn't recognize covered the walls. The tar-covered skeletons looked grim as they became denser within their bunks, and the stench became all the more unbearable.

"These carvings are prayers honoring the Light Wings. It is said that, when a protector dies, their power is never truly lost. That is why they are laid to rest here. Because if anything were ever to enter the catacombs or threaten the Light Wings, anyone with the smallest trace of blessed blood would be able to protect them."

"Protect the Light Wings?" Lucia asked.

"Yes, this is the home of the Light Wings—where they have been for all time, until the fall."

Lucia felt it, rippling to the surface. The truth she longed for, it was here, but it was not the truth she wanted. She should have known better, but now she was putting together the pieces of the wretched truth. "So the last protector to leave Remena, they took the Light Wings with them."

"Right. I must admit, Lucia, you are very intuitive," Emma said as they approached a crossroads in the catacombs. There were three paths ahead of them—one to the left, one to the right, and the last straight ahead. But at the center was a platform atop which an altar stood.

Lucia had not truly grasped how large the place was until she saw the dome above her head. As the paths around them stemmed toward unknown destinations, there at the center was the source of all of the light's power. Or so it seemed.

"Lucia, let me ask you something. Do you think the Light Wings chose you by mistake? Or do you think there was some divine connection in your meeting them?"

Lucia hesitated. She had always wondered why they had chosen her. It could have been anyone else but her, but the longer she traveled with them the more she understood—their motivations, their desires, their connection to her and who she was. "There is a *connection* between me and the Light Wings. It was no coincidence that I was chosen. They were given to me because they wanted to be. It was fate."

Emma climbed up the platform, approaching the altar, where two torch posts stood on each side. She took her torch and lit them both, illuminating the dome above them even more than it was before. "Correct. The Light Wings are not a senseless vessel, nor are they a puppet that serves one master. They are the light's manifestation on Terestria, its very essence in material form. They do not serve us or you; rather, we are subject to their design."

"What does that mean? I'm having a hard time understanding all of this. What does this have to do with the fall?"

"It's not a coincidence that the Light Wings chose you. Because there is a blood connection. You're the high maiden of Moz. You said it yourself, did you not? And that is precisely why they chose you, because of who *he* chose."

"Who?"

Emma placed her torch upon the altar and traced her fingers on the pedestal. "My brother. He stole the Light Wings and fled Remena decades ago to escape his birthright as high priest. At the time of the last Carist elder's coronation, Talon arrived here with two companions. They were of noble blood, betrothed to one another, and Talon's very best of friends. It's ironic that his daughter would now come with two companions, just as he did so many years ago. That was allowed, as long as the elder did not share the secrets learned within the Tower of Origin. But during their time here, my brother was taken with the woman Talon had come with, and though she was betrothed to another he longed for her. So much that he'd use his gifts to gain her affection." Emma paused for a few moments. "The woman was Ara Sanoon, your mother."

"What?" Lucia could hardly believe the words Emma spoke. Her heart was growing heavier with every beat. It couldn't be possible. "My mother never told me about this. It can't be true. She was never betrothed to anyone but my father. And my father, he was—"

"The man your mother was supposed to marry was Sigranole Feral. Familiar, isn't it? Do you see how you're all connected?"

"That's impossible. Pinea and Moz have hated each other for as long as I can remember. Their rivalry existed long before I was born."

"And you never wondered why? Why is it that so much chaos and war raged between the two nations? Over *what* did they fight? Is that a question you can answer?"

Lucia was at a loss. She couldn't answer the question, nor did she want to. She refused to accept the truth for what it was if it couldn't be the truth she was looking for. "If this is true, our parents withheld information from us. They lied when it mattered most. It's senseless. Destructive even. Why would they do that?"

"Perhaps to hide their shame or their sin? To not share blame in the darkness they breathed into our world."

Lucia's eyes tightened. She lowered her light and stepped onto the platform. "And my father's role in all this? That's where you're going, isn't it? You were going to tell me how he was the reason the fall happened in the first place."

Emma smiled. "It really is quite impressive how intuitive you are, Lucia. Your logic is pristine and crystal clear." She straightened before taking on an even more emboldened tone. "Your father's real name is Stello Sarina. He was my brother, and the rightful high priest of the Tower of Origin."

"My father . . . " Lucia's breath left her. "He was a protector?"

"And not just any protector. He was from the oldest of our families. The Sarina bloodline is descended from the first generation of protectors. They are the closest descendants of the light, the most powerful of the protectors."

"So my mother—she doesn't have any powers. It never came from *her*."

Emma shook her head. "No. At the time of your war, your mother must have been pregnant with you. That would explain how she used your power while you were in her womb."

"I can't believe this." Lucia barely managed to speak. Her voice shook as tears formed in her eyes.

Emma bowed her head. "I'm sorry, Lucia. I know this may come to you as a shock, but it means something more than you know. It means we're family, and the Light Wings chose you because they believe that all things must come full circle, and that promises are meant to be kept. You and your friends are examples of that—the descendants of those directly related to the fall, the noble youths of an entirely different generation of Terestrian rulers."

"I just don't understand. What did my father do that was so bad? It's not like he hurt anyone. He just fell in love."

"*That* he did, my dear." The voice echoed about the room, bellowing. Emma and Lucia looked around in confusion, unable to tell where it was coming from. The master slowly approached the platform dressed in a deep orange robe. He cleared his voice before speaking again, addressing Emma. "I told you to go straight to bed."

Emma bowed her head. "I'm sorry, Master. I just—"

"Enough! You've got the poor dear scared half to death, all the way down here telling her the story of your family. This is heartbreaking." Ralphoro shuddered and put a shaky palm to his face. "I thought I taught you better, but no, no. You couldn't resist telling your poor niece the truth. You just had to lay it on her all at once."

"But, Master, she deserved to know. After all, she's my family."

"*I'm* your family," Ralphoro bellowed. He turned to Lucia. "No offense, my dear, but I'm all sweet Emma has ever known. And your lot, you're the ones who caused all this. You and that stubborn father of yours."

"Excuse me, but my father did nothing wrong," Lucia defended. "I mean, sure, stealing the Light Wings. That was wrong, but you said the Light Wings are always in control. They serve no one, so in a way they were *trying* to find their way to me." Lucia's anxiety was soaring and her fear—and the tension—so dense that the stench of the catacombs was overwhelmed by a chill of repugnant disdain.

"You don't say?" Ralphoro chuckled. "Humph. Well that we can agree with . . . puppet."

"What?" Emma uttered, cowering backward. "Master, is something wrong?"

"Emma, don't pretend innocence. You know precisely why you brought her down here. It's not because she deserves the truth. It's because of what she did to your family!"

"What did I do?" Emma said, distraught. "No . . . I did nothing."

"Wrong!" Ralphoro shouted. "You did *everything* wrong. Your parents—they were fools, meddling with forces they couldn't possibly understand. But you, sweet, sweet Emma. *You* have always held this hatred, this thirst for something more. *She* took everything from you." Ralphoro pointed brashly toward Lucia. "And *she* was chosen to hold the light even after what Stello had done."

"Falling in love isn't a crime," Lucia cried.

"It is when it starts a war! People died because of him."

"No—it wasn't like that."

"Who'd have thought? Your very existence cost thousands of lives. Do you feel good about yourself? Sure, you have beauty, wealth, power—but are you truly complete?" Ralphoro looked toward Emma, who had tears streaming down her face. "How about *you*, my dear, do you feel satisfied?"

"Why are you acting like this? You've never spoken like this to me before."

"Oh no?" Ralphoro looked genuinely shocked. His mouth dropped as he fumbled his cane. He clenched at his chest. "You are my biggest disappointment. The best thing you've ever done is defy my wishes. And all it took was a little family reunion to get you to embrace the darkness within your heart."

Lucia interrupted, "What are you talking about? Emma's a protector. She loves the light. Don't you, Emma?" Lucia looked at Emma, who was staring blankly into the shadows.

CHAPTER EIGHTEEN

The Story of Origin

Emma stood silently beside the altar, her breathing shallow, her body catatonic.

What is happening to her? Lucia thought. "You see what you've done?" she said in anger to Ralphoro. "You've twisted the truth into some horrible nightmare, simply to—what, prove a point? And *you're* supposed to be some holy man."

"Do you see those images up there?" Ralphoro said calmly, pointing his cane toward the dome above them. Carved into it were two figures, joined at the center and fused into a magnificent gemstone that held stylized, luminous, almost sparkling fire beneath as if it were meant to signify a limitless power. From the sides stretched a total of four wings, parallel to one another. They curved with the dome and stood monumental to what lay below them.

Astonished, Lucia directed her gaze down to a vast crest etched into the floor of the wide room. It circled around the platform and rose with it, leading to the center and to an altar resting place that appeared to be for the Light Wings themselves. Surrounding the altar, in each compass direction, were four symbols that Lucia immediately recognized. She dropped to the floor and ran her hand against the curves and markings that stroked so gently against the stone. The symbols had been there—within her sanctuary window. Here they glistened beneath the gracious light. She examined the markings as they lay surrounding carved vines and roses cut in such high relief. It was beautiful and so familiar. How could she have overlooked this before?

"What are these symbols?" Lucia asked, pushing back her hair as her voice echoed near Ralphoro, who snickered in the glow of the torchlight.

"Those are the four virtues," he said, stroking a faint beard beneath his chin.

Lucia looked again at them, staring in amazement. "The light's virtues. Of course."

"Yes, the virtues of light." Ralphoro stared at the symbols with wide eyes.

"Four heirs destined to wage war against the sins that threaten Terestria," Lucia recalled.

Ralphoro nodded in the faint glow and gazed into the giant dome above. "Just as there are four virtues of light, there are four sins of darkness. But you already know that. After all, you've encountered, what, three of them by now?

"The darkness. When it first returned, the sins were concentrated within a single monstrosity that was fueled by a bloodlust, where all sin was existent—a war your father started when he took Moz's high maiden for himself. But a single prayer and unity among people, orchestrated by your selfish mother, protected them from the monstrosity. And it was *your* power that protected them."

Ralphoro let out an uneasy cough that brought about a dreadful chill. "Your father corrupted the balance, not because he fell in love with an outsider, but because he used his gift of prophecy as a weapon for the master of Moz. Rogan Sanoon, your grandfather, had initially held notions of establishing peace with his northern neighbors. But when Stello followed Ara back to Moz and used his powers to prove his worth to your grandfather and his court, your grandfather chose Stello, and called off your mother's betrothal to Sigranole. You can imagine that Sigranole was furious, so much that his hate and envy toward your father led to a military assault against your homeland. Within days, Pinea was on the attack, and Stello could foresee every move the Pinean armies made. In order to protect his love and his unborn child, he used his gifts to inform your grandfather's armies so that Rogan could destroy his enemies.

"Your father is in no way innocent, Lucia. His actions birthed the greatest evils Terestria had ever seen. And by the time the sins manifested themselves and entered our world, the rulers of both kingdoms had been slaughtered, their nations destroyed, and their people suffering. Until your mother's little act of peace—"

"How do you know all this? There's no way you could—"

"Well, because I was *there*." Ralphoro chuckled. His laughter increased louder and louder, distorting his voice. The air soon cooled, and Lucia's breath hung in the torchlight that was dimming by the second.

*　*　*

"In the beginning there were two forces, both equal in power and in nature, uncorrupted and pure, each one revolving around the other. The true origin of these forces remains a mystery, but it is known that they are the reason behind the very existence of our world and dimension."

Ralphoro went on, speaking rapidly. His face was twisted and changing, shifting constantly. "In the beginning there was only light and darkness. Both existed in a balance, like brothers, bonded and dependent upon one another. But there came an event that altered everything—the clash."

Who are you? Lucia thought to herself, stepping back, her fear overtaking her as she watched the man change into this crazed lunatic, a far cry from the simple and kind old man she'd met hours before. Emma stood still, her gaze blank.

"The forces merged at a point, creating a dimension where both could rule together in equal balance. The forces treasured this dimension as if it were a newly born child, and put priority on nurturing it. Even the darkness treasured its creation. The forces also worked together in creating a utopia for themselves, a home. Light took to the heavens, using energy and radiance to create the very sun and stars in the skies, blessing the dimension with warmth, while the terrain was materialized into the space that darkness had created, using matter to create mountain ranges that cast large shadows beneath the chasms and canyons of the earth.

"The light would rule the day, while the darkness would keep its equal place within the shadows created by the daylight. And when dark ruled the night, the light would hold its dominion within the heavens as the stars and moon. They were balanced and equal. The terrestrial world was composed of darkness. The celestial world was composed of light. But in unison—their creations were to be shared and ruled by both."

Ralphoro lifted a wrinkled hand and pointed to the dome as his skin tightened around his bones. "Though they had created this place together, it wasn't at all within terms of satisfaction. Light had taken to another creation of its own, one that would be blessed to live within its praise. It had taken the power of its radiance and breathed life into the oceans and placed them upon the land. Life was embedded with souls created of fragmented light—light that gave man the will to prosper as well as the morality and virtue that kept the early civilizations of the world together. These civilizations gave praise to their only creator, praising light for their very life and everything that its radiance had blessed them with. But this creation was not always appreciated.

"The conscious of darkness felt a deep resentment for the life its brother had created. It had grown too envious, feeling an intense hatred toward the praise that light had received when the bounty of the earth—that darkness had created—was the very foundation of the world. So darkness took to its own creations, something to rival those of its brother so that it, too, could remain powerful. These creations, however, would not be meant to bring about love or praise or worship, as life and virtue were. Their sole purpose would be to breed fear, death, and destruction among the life that darkness loathed.

"Envy, hate, pride, and greed—these four beasts were to be called Wym, Hatorium, Lykorus, and Ragium. The four sins of darkness. These beings were given one objective: to spread out upon the beings of light and taint their souls with corruption. Life would soon have to fall to the power of their sin, and ultimately lose the very will and right to live—leaving light no choice but to abandon its failed creation. Then it would be time for the darkness to take back Terestria. With the newly destroyed souls, tainted with the sins which had devoured them, darkness would be able to build enough power to destroy its rival, and take the whole of creation. The world would become a bed of darkness—lifeless, silent, and without radiance.

"But with light's precious creation at stake, it created a safeguard by making a covenant with the protectors. Their blood was blessed with the power of Runespeech, and the tribes of their world were given relics from the other world as a means to ward off the darkness. It was said that, if the protectors kept their faith and did not fall to the powers of destruction spread by the sins that darkness had created, all the souls of life would be spared. But only if the protectors remained untainted. The light believed, as long as its chosen people remained, that all life should be pardoned for the sins they'd fall victim to.

"But now, the world is corrupted and the balance is no more. Darkness can do as it pleases and corrupt the earth. There is but one failsafe, the light's last resort, crafted for the sole purpose that is to hold and collect what has been lost. When the power of the protectors becomes corrupted, and one of them lends their powers to the darkness, four virtues would be summoned to fight sin. These virtues would be born into the souls of four noble youths, each holding the power of a virtue strong enough to fight the darkness."

"As long as they hold a rune," Emma uttered, breaking from her trance.

"Right you are, my dear." Ralphoro nodded. "And last I checked, you only have one rune and the Light Wings." Ralphoro took up a torch and approached a relief opposite them, slowly illuminating it as the torch crossed over its shadows, exposing the relief's form in colors of faded rust. The curves of the cut stone formed four monstrous images, and beneath those were images of something more divine in appearance, surrounded by depictions of light that had been stylized onto each of the symbols that lay under them.

Lucia stepped closer to Ralphoro, aligning to his side and skimming her gloved fingers across the first of the images. It was something that seemed all too familiar, and as she looked deep into a pair of eyes that were cut and painted like bloodstones, memories of Aldric set a shroud over her. "This is the monster that attacked Aldric." She glanced over to Emma, who looked at the relief with provoked eyes.

"That is the sin of envy," Ralphoro said. "Wym, the serpent that corrupts and destroys through the power of jealousy."

Lucia touched her neck. "The hooded figure in Pinea. That was pride." She looked to Ralphoro for guidance.

"Why yes. Lykorus, the phantom. It has the ability to take on the forms of your greatest fears and can turn anyone into a coward. It's sadistic, that one. It really did a number on your boyfriend, didn't it? His pride is strong. Breaking him wasn't easy."

Lucia began to realize that Ralphoro wasn't who he said he was—it was all too obvious by now. He knew too much. The stories he spoke, the absolutes, they haunted her. He was trying to get into her head, and though she was scared, she tried her best to maintain her composure. She just hoped the others would find their way down to her before it was too late.

Ralphoro took a slow finger and placed it onto the figure of a beast that looked almost as if it did not have a form, but was portrayed as a hooded shroud of smoke mixed into a mass of many parts. It was a disturbing mixture of deformed life.

"So fitting for pride to prey on the fears of the weak," Lucia managed to say. Then she saw it there, the demon with its large wings, the one that destroyed her home. "Hatorium, I presume."

"Correct," Ralphoro said deviously.

"And this one?" Lucia placed a finger on a figure that assumed the form of a human with a handsome exterior. It was almost mistakenly good. But unlike the seraph shown in much of the virtue's reliefs, this figure had four batlike wings that sprang from its back, and horns on its head, signifying it was the opposite of the virtue above it.

"The sin of greed, Ragium, deception in its purest form. Some would call it a devil, but in reality, it's a Djinn—a being that promises you all the things your privilege warrants you . . . at a price. It knows no justice, no compassion, or need for balance. It feels only the thirst for more. It thrives on selfishness. Taken with its vanity, it consumes the souls of those it kills, taking their form whenever necessary." Ralphoro's shadowy eyes seemed to widen as his voice fell into a hoarse laugh.

Lucia grew more uncomfortable as the laughing continued. She had to think quickly. There was no telling if the others were anywhere close by, and if she acted too rashly and underestimated the power of the protectors, she could put herself into the most dangerous of situations. She asked another question, stalling. "What are the virtues?"

Ralphoro looked curiously toward Lucia. A wide grin stretched across his face. "I thought you'd never ask." He moved his hand to the reliefs above those of the sins.

Ralphoro pointed to a light with the image of a grand *phoenix* with tails made of clear magenta fire. "There is hope, the virtue of faith in all things good. They know no envy because they believe nothing is impossible and anything is achievable. They have unyielding, unwavering resolve in themselves and in those around them. Even more especially, in those they care about."

Beneath the next symbol was a gallant *buraq* draped in angelic armor, galloping gracefully beneath shimmering purple wings. "Of course, there is love, the virtue that knows the nature of true sacrifice. Loyal and to the utmost compassionate, they will do anything for those they care for."

Then there was an image of a courageous *lamassu*, releasing a beacon of shining blue light from its roar. "Temperance is the virtue of restraint. They are deliberate and act in moderation, perceptive of the outcomes of various choices. So they are not rash, but rather cool and collected, willing to accept responsibility for their actions."

Finally, Ralphoro pointed to the familiar image of the enchanting *seraph*, a jewel-like golden scale held within its gently carved fingers. "And lastly, there is justice, the virtue of balance. Justice acts only on reason, due to their incredible judgment. They separate truth from deception and will fight for what is right when no one else will."

Lucia's mouth dropped as she finally saw the truth. She placed her hand over the small diamond in the Light Wings, feeling its warmth as it emitted a still and soft misty glow. She bit her lip. Slightly disturbed, she said, "These are supposed to be us."

Ralphoro nodded and faced Lucia, beaming. Emma remained silent, her head bowed as she listened. Tears ran down her face as Ralphoro continued.

"A virtue's power is not fully realized until they have in their possession a rune derivative to their respective virtue. They must then self-actualize and align themselves with that virtue, and channel it through Runespeech, which only one of you knows how to do. To awaken the powers of each virtue, that virtue's strength must be at its fullest in order for the Light Wings to recognize its power and forge a link between them."

"But only protectors can use Runespeech." Lucia's hand shook as she placed it uneasily on the Light Wings. "How could the others do so, even with the rune in hand?"

"That's the big question, isn't it? Hmm. Maybe the light gave you an impossible task, knowing that it'd have no choice but to relinquish its creations to the darkness in the end. I'm afraid that is the one secret I can't share with you—because even I don't know."

"You're *lying*," Emma whispered, breaking her silence. "You know exactly how the other virtues will use Runespeech. You said it yourself."

"Pardon me, my sweet. I don't recall mentioning how the outsiders will use a power that's not their own."

"By forging the link with the Light Wings. Lucia, you've been able to lend your power to them in the past, right, fighting the sins? It was the same with your mother during Frailty's War. When they have awakened their virtue and forged the link, Lucia's power becomes their own. They will summon the virtues using the Light Wings."

Other than the sound of dripping off in the distance, there was silence. Ralphoro grunted and growled before raising his voice again. "Again, you *must* fail me, giving away all our secrets. How dare you betray me after all I've done for you?!"

Emma shook her head. "You are not the man who raised me. It took me a while, but I caught on. You like to talk, and flatter yourself by doing so. *You* are not Ralphoro. Ralphoro would never—"

"Do what? This!" Ralphoro hurled his torch at Emma, who shifted aside and let it clash against the wall behind her. A shadow ran between them as the flames of the torches flared into a heavy spiral, knocking Lucia backward and onto her back. Her head pounded as the flames disappeared.

"Lucia!" Emma's voice echoed around the void.

Lucia felt the damp stone floor of the catacombs beneath her. She touched her head, checking for blood. *That blast was too powerful,* she thought. *What was that?* Lucia felt nothing in the darkness. The faint glow of the Light Wings alone wasn't enough to reveal the vast room, not without the aid of the torchlight. She remembered the shadow as it dashed ahead of them. *Did the darkness set a trap?* Her blood surged through her veins. "Ralphoro," she whispered into the void as the damp air grew cold and stuck to her skin. She stood and took a step forward, trying to follow Emma's voice as she called out to Lucia. She tried to regain her senses, her head still stinging from her fall. As she took her next step, the screech of shadows moaned around her.

"Emma!" she cried, squinting in the darkness as her fear knotted into her muscles. The sound of scraping echoed in the distance along the stone walls of the catacombs. Lucia dashed around the darkness, frantically searching for Emma as the shadows collected around her.

Emma was quick to see the moving light. She hurried to help her, but Lucia was panicking and moving too fast. "Slow down!" Emma called.

Lucia could only hear the scraping in the distance. The sound of evil laughter intruded and distorted her mind. She screamed as a shadowy tentacle tightened around her legs, causing her to fall forward with a loud crash. "Help!" she shouted as she was dragged backward roughly. With another high-pitched scream, she released a bright light from the center of her chest causing the tentacles to wither backward in the pulsating light. Lucia felt the power of the Light Wings explode, filling her. She felt the hilt of her diamond sword as it formed in her gentle fingers, and with a loud grunt of anger turned her body and slashed at her feet, sending the shadows loose and into the darkness.

Emma tried to run as fast as she could toward the glowing light as she saw it rise, almost as dim as a firefly, jolting across and rushing toward a turn she couldn't see. "Lucia, come back!" Emma shouted, picking up her pace. But it was no use.

The screeching of the shadows consumed Lucia's senses, making it impossible for her to fully comprehend her surroundings. It was as if she were going insane. Every turn deceived her. The catacombs had become a labyrinth of despair.

A hoarse laugh echoed from behind, sending an eerie chill through the air, freezing any warmth from within the darkness. Lucia was distraught, her feet numb as she ran and thought only of escape. *I'm losing it.* The strength drained from her again as she held the diamond sword in her hand. The light was there, but she couldn't withdraw it from the abyss of this darkness, and with each second, the light drained her of her own life force. She sensed the shadows around her, hissing as the light hit them, and crawling from the crevasses of the tight corridor.

"Emma," she whispered to herself as panic shook through her body and her voice. The terror showed on her face as it grew along the edges of her skin. "Emma!" Lucia screamed, whipping around to stare into the face of a demonic serpent head with glowing, ruby-like eyes infused with fire. It jumped from the floor and snapped at her face, but Lucia's reflexes were too fast. With the help of the Light Wings, she sent out a starlike volley, shattering the beast into dark particles and a flash of sparkling dust. She looked around, holding out her sword, forcing it to glow as leech-like monsters crawled toward her from all directions. "Emma, where are you?" she cried, slashing at her feet as the monsters zipped around her on a furious circuit, sending her into a stomping fury.

Lucia suddenly remembered what Emma had said about the power of the dead protectors existing within the catacombs. As quickly as the thought presented itself, she began to pray, just as the tension of her breath rose in her chest like needles inside her throat. *I'm a protector. My father was a protector. I can do this*, she thought. "Ancestors, hear my plea. Lend me your strength. The Light Wings need you!"

A rumbling shook the walls around her. The moans of the dead rattled in the shadows. The Light Wings' light surged, shining so intensely that the entirety of her surroundings was now revealed. What she saw was nothing short of a terrible dream. The leeches flung toward her as she lost control of her body. Something burned inside her, forcing her to fight. "Back off, you fiends," she called, trying to get a grip on reality. "Stop!" She swiftly sent up her free hand with a blinded focus, pooling her power into a tightening orb. Lucia hurled her hand down, pushing her power into the earth, feeling the light absorb into it before sending out a shockwave into the vast radius ahead of her. "Emma!" she called out into the absence, exhausted. Lucia heard no response, only the escalating hiss of the dreadful serpents that outnumbered her easily as they emerged from where the light had first destroyed them. "This is not happening," she whispered to herself, cold sweat running like ice down her soft forehead. "I'm trapped."

It was nearly impossible to think clearly, alone within the hostile and damp shadows of the catacombs. A chill ran down her prickling skin, sharply stinging the joints of her body with fear. She jolted up to her feet, sending a flash of white glowing mist around her with a graceful wave of her hand. It pulsed through the air, dissolving the dark matter around her, but the power of the light was weakening. She called out to the protectors. "Please, don't leave me. We need you!" But Lucia felt the Light Wings slowly dimming, like a flickering candle. Even the tips of her fingers sparked out like a depleted fuse. There was not much else she could do. Her fear was consuming her, tightening over her chest as the Light Wings slowly faded.

"Lucia, run!" she heard from behind as the hiss of a large leech vibrated at her feet. Like a falling star, the tip of her sword cut down, slicing the beast just as it lunged at her. Lucia's feet took action, stomping against the damp ground beneath in long strides. Her feet were in overdrive, powered by not only the terror that embodied her but also the sensation that magnified each time she used her power. This thirst for light had begun to possess her every movement. It drained her body of its own energy and took control, as if she were a mere vessel, as the thirst for survival tightened around her neck, nearly choking her.

Lucia stared blankly as she thought, *What am I doing?* She whispered to herself within the slow vision of her own reality. The hunger wasn't weakening her as it had before, but instead became more a drive that she had never fully realized, fueled by the protector's devotion to the Light Wings. Even as she had grown with the Light Wings, her resistance to its will had thinned as she found diligence within the ability of the wings. But she was tired—so, so tired. "Why," echoed forth from her lips as she slowly released crystal-like tears from her eyes, "don't I just . . . " Flinging her arms to her side, she stopped and let out the next words, her final will: "give in."

And with a flash, as she almost stumbled forward, diamond wings sprouted from a misty aura behind her, glowing bright gold within the cuts of heavenly stone. They burst into a shower of sparkling dust, darting into the swarms of dark fiends that had started to collect into masses of deep black, tainted crimson. The shards of the wings danced around the army of malformed shadows, shattering and blasting them into a brilliant cloud of sparkling dust, a storm of light that eventually condensed into a single shining orb as small as the tiny pendant around Lucia's neck. The orb shot back to Lucia, whose body came to a sudden stop as the light circled upward, filling the wings around her neck, revitalizing her. The Light Wings now shined with a vibrant radiance, returning the energy Lucia felt had been drained from her by the darkness.

Lucia touched a fragile shaking hand to the pendant, feeling the warmth of light cross the gaps between her fingers. She sighed, not understanding why the Light Wings had spared her yet again this time. They always acted as a last resort. Must she suffer until they felt she was worthy? Hadn't she been through enough, by now, that they should know she would be seeing this mission through till the end?

Her mind was faint, but Lucia still sensed the evil in the air. Though the dark swarm had quieted back into the emptiness, she felt the tingling cold of fear. Something powerful lurked within the catacombs of the protectors. The spirits of the dead seemed to whisper it to her, calling to their redeemer.

Slowly she turned around, facing the way she had just come. "Emma," She thought of pulling her blade into her free hand. She held it close as it began to shine simultaneously with the pendant with the same sparkling stream of light that came from nowhere.

*   *   *

"Lucia!" Emma struggled to consciousness, pushing herself upward in a daze, feeling the rising alertness of her mind. She looked up immediately and touched the damp hair stuck to her cheeks, as she reached around her body. Her head was fuzzy. She had taken a hard hit, and she could not remember any of the events leading up to it. The last she remembered was chasing after Lucia from within the darkness as the shadows emerged, but after that it all went blank.

Emma hunted for a glow in the darkness of the void. Lucia was nowhere in sight. She had lost her. She feared the worst as she clenched her throat, trying to cope with the tensions of her own sobs. This was all her fault. If she hadn't felt compelled to tell Lucia the truth, if she had not led her into the catacombs, if she'd only realized sooner that Ralphoro was a demon, none of this would have ever happened. The anxiety built as it blurred her eyes, so strained by the lack of light. Then she saw a slim figure materialize as someone reached toward her. "Lucia," she gasped, watching as the flowing strands of blonde hair fell ahead of the light. "Lucia," she called again before looking up into the face of Luzanna's beautifully crafted mask.

"It's Emma!" Luzanna cried, falling beside her. Leo quickly walked to Emma's side as Luzanna brought a lantern closer. She assessed her body, examining Emma's wounds. "Are you alright?"

Emma struggled to speak. "Lucia, she's . . . she's gone. It was the shadows. They are here too. The sins, they can seep through here. It is not safe. She has to be somewhere. Ralphoro is gone too."

"Ralphoro was here?" Luzanna asked with a tone of urgency. "He did this?"

"He must have!" Leo roared, ripping his dagger from his sheath, feeling the weight of Lucia's absence crush his body.

"No," Emma said, "it wasn't Ralphoro. It's one of the sins. It's taken the form of Ralphoro's body because it killed him!" Emma cried in grief, realizing for the first time that her master was dead. "I'm sorry . . . I led Lucia down here. I felt she deserved to know the truth about the fall, about her father, my brother, and our family." Emma paused before looking up at them. "She's my niece."

"Oh, wow. That is . . . ." Leo took a deep breath at the thought. "Well, I can't say I didn't see that coming."

"Leo, this is not the time to act smug. Emma is hurt, and Lucia is in real danger! We have to hurry," Luzanna said. "Emma, can you stand?"

Emma's dark eyes widened as she clapped a hand to her mouth. She closed her eyes with a soft turn of her head, as if she was ashamed of this danger she had so naively put them in. "I think so. I'm so sorry. I would never do anything to hurt Lucia. She's my family. I wouldn't."

"I understand, and I trust you. But now you have to trust me, okay? Now, help me get you up." Luzanna hoisted Emma's arm around her right shoulder. "Leo, a hand?"

Leo shook his head, trying to regain his composure. "Right. I'm sorry." It was as if his mind was in two places at once. He was there in body, but the longer he and Lucia were separated, the more his mind drifted. He had to find her. He hurried and helped Luzanna bring Emma to her feet. "Where could Lucia be?"

Emma hesitated as she wiped the tears from her face. "I don't know. The spirits are calling to her. I can sense that much, meaning she must still be alive. But Ralphoro—I don't know where he might be."

"Well, he's here. We can be certain of that. Stay on guard. This is going to be a long night." Luzanna's eyes hardened. "I know you've already been through a lot, Emma, but you're a protector. Can you use your power to fight?"

Emma bowed and shook her head. "The protectors aren't allowed to use their powers for destructive purposes. They are only supposed to use them for protection."

"The covenant is already broken! Emma, does it count if it's self-defense?"

"I . . . I don't know. I just know I can't."

Leo shrugged. "Leave her be." He gave Emma a careful look. "You don't have to fight if you don't want to, but if you could use your power to shield us in any way, can you do that?"

Emma lifted her head up and stared into Leo's calm blue eyes. She nodded.

Leo smiled. "Good. Now come on. We've got you."

Emma blinked, looking at Leo's dagger and then at Luzanna. "How are you going to fight? You don't have a weapon."

Luzanna brought her fist in front of her face. "I don't need one. I'll fight any way I have to."

Emma grinned at Luzanna's answer. "You believe nothing is impossible, do you?"

Luzanna nodded. "You can do anything you put your mind to. If you believe it, it can be so. Mind over matter."

Emma reached out and touched the side of Luzanna's mask. "Please remember that when you're fighting."

Like a phoenix with a fire of determination in its eyes, Luzanna said, "I will. Thank you, Emma."

*　*　*

Lucia walked through the tunnels as the darkness surrounded her, confusing her. She heard the cries around her—crying out for forgiveness, it seemed.

"Help us! Forgive us! Please, redeem our fears. Set us free," they called out.

Lucia felt the pain as the voices rose in agony within her head, louder than even her own thoughts. Was this why she had lost their power? Had their power long since been corrupted by the folly of her own father? The pain they were in couldn't be his fault—but it was. If only she had known.

A heavy sense of burden fell on her slender shoulders, and her heart thickened with sadness and guilt. There was injustice in their restlessness, for these souls could not be at peace while their blood failed to protect the world that had been blessed unto them. She tried to ignore the voices, tried not to let them faze her as the sins of her parents tormented her. She had gotten the message, but these spirits held no sense of an end, not to this misery. They continued to moan and scream from within the shadows, in distorted pleas.

Her fear was multiplying as she ran through the catacombs, with no idea where she was going. And then, suddenly, as if by a mistake of fate, her foot slipped on some sort of glass that must have broken there before. Lucia fell numbly to her knees, the voices overtaking her mind, breaking her focus. Her sword slipped from her fingers and flashed as it hit a distant wall and shattered into light dust. She held her head, tightening her grip as the voices seemed to turn into a single deep, demonic laugh. "Stop!" Lucia screamed, clenching her head as she stretched upward from the ground. "Leave me alone!" She let gravity pull her fists down as she cradled her head between them. She looked beneath her body, seeing a familiar symbol reveal itself within the light of her pendant. The symbol seemed to curve around her hand as she stared at the circular stroke. She had found her way back, hadn't she? The vastness of the room swallowed her shallow light in the abyss of the endless emptiness of her desperation.

Quick footsteps fluttered not far from her. A clang of metal against a hard surface sent a chill up her spine. She quieted her breath as she tried desperately to distinguish what she could see, but the darkness was impossible. "Emma," she whispered, sitting up and thinking positively as the gripping cold wrapped around her damp clothing. She inhaled deeply, catching her breath as she heard the distortion of another laugh. She hesitated, taking in yet another slow breath, trying to calm her already-edgy nerves into words. "Ralphoro," Lucia whispered before a sudden and fiery pain pierced through the center of her body.

Lucia choked as her warm blood leaked from her body and spread across the floor. She stared at the scarlet flow, unable to comprehend where it all even came from as it rose into her throat and from her mouth. Her head felt faint and her body tightened into shock as she watched a silver blade withdraw from her body, lifting her a bit before she slid off its tip and fell hard onto the floor. Blinded by the blossoming pain, she felt her sight slip away and her thoughts fade from her mind as if she were drifting into a silent hell, and into a storm of complete agony. She fell back to the floor, feeling her blood flow past her outstretched arm, leaving it to sparkle in the light of a lantern that emerged in the distance.

"Lucia!" Leo cried out. His eyes immediately filled with tears as he noticed the blood flowing from her body.

Lucia looked up, struggling to breath, reaching out to Leo with the last of her strength before her head collapsed to the floor again. Leo stood in shock as his companions behind him screamed at the sight of Lucia's waving hair floating in the dark mass beneath her. They watched helpless as a blade hovered above her body, now bathed in the light of the lantern.

Light's Lament

The scream that left Luzanna's lips was absolutely mortifying and filled with an anguish none should live to hear. It struck fear in its shaking echo, sending a tempest of terror through the moist air around them. Tearing off her mask, Luzanna released one last cry before bringing a quivering hand to her face. The sight before her was the revelation of her greatest fear: the death of whatever hope she had left.

Emma's shock was written all over her face, and surprisingly, her heart felt nothing. It knew only silence as its beat fell beneath the clatter of her own teeth. She watched as Lucia's blood slowly dripped into the spreading puddle from the tip of a shining blade, long and slender. The light of the lantern exposed the shape of the old man, Ralphoro, bearing a wide grin, the wrinkles of his face stretching so far they were showing the bone beneath them. His skin had turned a ghastly pale, like a corpse, the color of pale green ashes. "Ralphoro, what have you done?"

"Naive girl," he whispered into the echo of Emma's voice. "Why do you still deny it? The fate of your master should already be known to you. Do you still refuse to acknowledge the truth?"

Emma's throat swelled as her mind flooded with memories of her true master's image. "You killed him!" she shouted, sobbing as she stepped back into the shadows. "You tainted this holy place," she said softly, her body trembling. The air cooled as the lantern light dimmed. A sharp chill blew from behind Ralphoro out of the nothingness around him.

"Did I?" asked the imposter, looking genuinely confused. "I don't recall killing anyone. I mean, not tonight. Actually, I don't really know how long it's been."

Emma gasped, placing both of her hands over her mouth. Could it have been *him* this entire time?

"No. Impossible. Ralphoro was here. He greeted all of us," Luzanna cried. "You're a liar!"

The shape chuckled. "I see that my reputation precedes me, but I guarantee you, Ralphoro has been long dead."

"So it's been you this entire time," Emma said between hiccups. "Ralphoro never lived past the plague, did he?"

"No. He didn't," the imposter replied. "I must say, the corruption of Remena was among my most impressive work. It didn't take much to turn this land toxic. After all, the darkness created the earth. It is the very source of our power. Easy, it was."

"You killed everyone," Emma shuddered.

"Everyone"—the imposter stepped forward, pointing the dripping blade at Emma—"except you."

"What do you want from her, you freak?!" Leo shouted, drawing his blade. "I'm going to kill you!"

"Ah, ah, ah!" The old man pointed the sword down to Lucia's limp body, still bleeding on the floor. "She's alive for now." He snickered. "Don't tempt me. I'm not like the others, blindly following orders in order to bring about the eternal's grand scheme. I will gladly put an end to her life and this prophecy once and for all!"

"Then why don't you?" Luzanna asked, her voice bold. "While you have your enemy within your grasp—are you a coward?"

"On the contrary, beautiful. Though powerful, I too, am a servant just like you. But my will is the very core of my being. It is who *I* am!"

"Who are you?" Emma asked, her voice quivering.

"The better question is, who are *you*?" Ralphoro's skin was growing more twisted as he spoke, darkening around his eyes as they glowed a bright red. "After all this time, why is it that I chose to keep you alive?"

"Shut up!" Luzanna cried. "Don't listen to him, Emma. He's trying to deceive you."

Emma looked down at Lucia with her tears still fresh on her face. "It was my family. We corrupted the balance."

The man grinned yet again. "Right," he snarled. "Your blood is marked, tainted by the sins of your cowardly brother. What better vessel could we choose to harbor our power?"

"Harbor your power?" Emma asked faintly.

"The light chose its vessel—a weak one, I admit. It chose her, your niece, but also the heir to the Sanoon bloodline. If I had to bet, I'd say the light's the losing side. Its precious savior is cursed, too, but of no use to us four. But you, my dear, your blood has no link to the light. It never has."

"What?" Luzanna shouted, grabbing hold of Emma's arm. "No, Emma, that's a lie. You're a protector. Your duty is to the light."

"It was. But now, she's ours. For years I've watched you grow, Emma. I taught you how to control your powers—but did you really think your powers came from the light? After what your family had done?" Fangs extended from his grin as he spoke, his voice becoming more distorted as Emma attempted to shield herself from the words he spewed.

"If what you say is true, then Lucia, too, would be cut off from the light. How am I to believe you?" Emma asked.

"Have you not heard a word I said? The girl is a Sanoon. The light could not ever truly abandon her. Her bloodline was destined to hold one of its precious virtues. You, however—the light has forsaken you. The more you use your powers, the more attuned to the darkness you become."

She was shaking, her breath coarse. Could he be telling the truth?

"But trust me, her blood makes her weak. The cursed protector's blood makes it harder for the light to consume her. We have the advantage."

Emma's eyes widened as the curve of Ralphoro's thin, wrinkled lips formed into an evil snare. "Grasp onto your destiny, my dear, and accept the protector's fate."

Emma flinched backward, keeping her hands close to the warmth of her body as Leo's hand seized the hilt of his dagger. Emma was confused. His words were baseless, cold, and relentlessly shocking, but they repeated over and over inside her head. Something told her, something whispered—what exactly was Ralphoro, or whatever he was, up to? Emma glanced toward Lucia as her breathing slowed. She watched Lucia squirm in anguish, trying to fight through the indescribable pain that consumed her.

"If I do, will you let her go?" The question came with two sad tears, one streaming from each of Emma's eyes. "Will you give her a chance to challenge us?"

"Emma, what are you saying? Stop it now!" Leo demanded.

The evil turned its gaze toward him. "She's made her choice, and well she has chosen." Ralphoro sent his sword plummeting down once again into Lucia. She wheezed deeply as her body was pulled upward, until she slipped hard off the blade.

"Bastard!" Leo screamed, lunging at the old man. Leo shoved his blade forward, but it wasn't enough. Ralphoro raised his hand and Leo felt a gripping force surrounding him, piercing him from every direction as if his entire body were suddenly afflicted by frostbite. He froze midair. The hilt of his dagger frosted over, and the air grew dense as he was lifted into the air and thrown backward. His body collided with the far wall, cracking the bone beneath his bruising muscles before tumbling forward to land in Lucia's blood. Leo struggled to rise, but he collapsed as his breath left his body.

"Challenge us, she will. But first, you must swear to me your allegiance. Reject your calling to the light and swear fealty to the darkness. Only then will I release them."

Emma's eyes were quivering. In her heart, she knew this was wrong. Her duty to the light, her calling as a protector, couldn't all be a lie. But there was something deep down that believed him. All her life, she had been alone, isolated, and raised among sin. It was the sins of her family, her blood, that bound her to this fate, this dreadful punishment. She stepped forward, away from the light of the lantern, and faced Ralphoro, her eyes still on Lucia's squirming body. "A promise is a promise. I was damned the day Stello chose corruption. And it is now my duty to face the consequences. Leo, Luzanna . . . " Emma released two more sad tears. Slowly, she approached Ralphoro before kneeling down in front of Lucia's body. "Lucia, please forgive me," she whispered.

Ralphoro smiled, seemingly in agreement, as his body floated into the dark background of the catacombs. The shadows drifted from the walls, swarming around his body. His voice distorted as he roared. Dark matter seeped from the boils in his skin, circling and spiraling around his body, latching onto it as he transformed.

The air swirled upward into an icy gust as he spoke. "We accept your terms, Emma. And now you shall know who I truly am." From the darkness emerged large batlike wings, sharp to the tip with bladed edges. The wings sprouted from the back of a tall, dark-haired, humanlike being, only his torso was covered with a shimmering black cloth made of tar. His hands sprouted long claws covered with gauntlets made of thick demonic onyx, cut into sharp jagged edges. Horns climbed up over a handsome face with narrow scarlet eyes and long, thick lashes. His crimson irises held pupils slit like serpent eyes, and from his lips hung two razor-sharp fangs.

"Ragium," Emma whispered as she closed her eyes.

"Yes," the devil said. "You have much to learn, my sweet. You've only just begun to quench your thirst for power. Tonight, you will be reborn as a mistress of sin."

"Emma, don't." Luzanna reached out toward her, mind racing. The final sin, greed, stood before them, finally revealing itself. "There is still hope. No one is irredeemable. There is so much good in you. I *know* there is."

"Redemption is for the weak. Emma—rise and accept your new power," Ragium directed with a claw at Emma's chin.

Emma took a step, raising her body. Her gown was covered in the blood of her niece as she gaped into the eyes of the beast.

Ragium sneered. "With your power, the world will cower at your reckoning. You're Terestria's new queen."

"But what if I don't want to be," Emma cried quietly.

"Oh . . ." Ragium brushed Emma's cheek with the side of his cold, bladed fingers. His eyes were tense, almost worried. "Like you have a choice." He opened his hand, and from it a spark of anti-light formed a small violet sphere. The amethyst orb floated beneath Emma's neck as she was pulled toward it with an incredible force. The orb flashed in a thick dark mist, relinquishing a thin iron wire that wrapped around her neck and ornately shaped itself into a chain. The orb jolted with anti-light again, sending Emma into a shriek as her body tightened.

An unknown force exploded within her, filling her body with emotions that were not her own. *Envy. Hate. Pride. Greed.* The dark matter shaped around the orb, stretching the fabric of time and space around her. The object pulled, absorbing the light as a black hole would a star. All was drawn into the orb as it condensed and vibrated. A powerful wave pulsated from it as a pair of horned black wings sprouted from the sides of what was now a teardrop-shaped pendant. The wings were demonic, emitting an ominous evil as they pulsed with dark energy.

Emma felt the power oozing from her fingertips. Her eyes darkened, changing into a blood red as her veins filled with a rage she could not contain. All she could sense were voices, deep distortions within her mind, ripping at whatever humanity she had left.

Ragium grinned, raising his sword high above his head in triumph. "And thus, the Dark Wings have chosen their protector! Here is our savior of darkness—Emma Sarina, our dark eminence."

"Emma, you can't be. You simply can't!" Luzanna cried out, losing her breath. There was a rift that had just opened, far within the chasms of Luzanna's mind, as she collected the images in front of her. Forces struggled to separate. "This is impossible!" Was this fate's cruel design to have evil claim another innocent soul? A power of its own?

"And so the tables have turned," greed jested. "To think, you thought your precious savior would never meet her match."

Emma turned toward them, her eyes blank. She tilted her head, blinking softly. "I can feel it. The power. Has it been here all this time?"

"Yes, child." Ragium growled. "Let the darkness consume your soul."

Emma lifted her palms to where she could see them. She

watched as anti-light sparked between her fingers. "I've never felt so strong."

"It's all a façade," Luzanna called out, stepping toward Emma. "The darkness could never marvel to be as powerful as the light. It may seem impossible right now, but in my heart I know this to be true. With darkness may come fear, but as long as there is light, there is hope!"

It was those words that suddenly drew air into Lucia's lungs. Silent whispers echoed from beneath her pain, sprouting into bursts of power. Weakly, she lifted her head. In the haze of her blurred vision, she saw a glow under Luzanna's fingertips. The opal was emitting an odd glimmer only she could see. Lucia, breathing heavily, held out a trembling hand. "Lu . . . Luz . . . anna," she called out with all her strength. "P-put on . . . your . . . mask."

With a swift kick, Ragium struck Lucia, who grunted in anguish. "Shut up! Can't you see we're having a moment?"

"And so are we," Luzanna said, her eyes glowing with a fiery determination. She raised her mask to her face and closed her eyes.

Lucia started her prayer, remembering Luzanna's words as they drifted between them. Lucia felt the emotion buried beneath, the lingering light lost on a field among a cliff. "Hope," she uttered as the Light Wings glowed a bright pink. Her glove filled with the magenta light, and from it shot a beam that bound to the opal stone in Luzanna's mask. Lucia collapsed just as a symbol traced under Luzanna's feet.

"No!" Ragium roared. "Not now!"

Streams of light cloaked over Luzanna as her mask brightened, the light intensifying as it wrapped around her face. Leo dragged himself up, captivated by the blinding light that illuminated her body.

A bright magenta radiance surrounded Luzanna, as a misty aura of white light expanded her glowing armor. From her mask gigantic feathers blossomed, blazing, as enormous wings of stylized platinum sprouted from her back, sharp to the tips of detailed feathers. Her mask expanded into a long veil that draped backward over the waves of her golden hair. Magenta ribbons flowed from her waist as platinum feathers formed around her torso and over her thighs. Her hands were covered by light armlets, while an emblem was burned into the skin of her palm in the form of the symbol that radiated beneath her.

"Luzanna, you're glowing," Leo said softly. "You're actually glowing."

Luzanna's body filled with power as her hope tightened within her. It was real, tangible, and unbreakable—the darkness would not win, not as long as she held on to this faith. She held out her hand as it was enwrapped by a bright pink flame. It exploded, letting out a bright white smoke as she traced a beam of light into the air with a finger. She grabbed hold of the light and spun it in her hands as a glowing spear formed, made of the same shining opal as the Elder Stone. "Leo, get Lucia—and leave *him* to me." Luzanna shot forward, her wings propelling her with incredible speed. She gripped her spear as Leo dashed toward Lucia.

Ragium brought himself upward, flying into the dome overhead just as the tip of Luzanna's spear missed by a mere second. "Emma, destroy her now! Use the power of the protectors and bury them within the catacombs!"

Luzanna pushed herself upward, spinning within her wings before sending her spear flying toward Ragium.

He dissipated into the shadows around them as the spear burst into light against the rock of the dome. The crust absorbed the force and sent a large crack toward the surface. Rocks began to fall from the dome as Ragium's voice echoed in the air. "Emma, use the darkness. Bury them with it!"

"Emma, don't!" Luzanna called out as she floated down.

"Please, Emma, you must resist it," Leo said as he brought Lucia into his lap. She clung to him as her strength left her.

Lucia's breath was shallow, but she managed to speak. "Emma, please."

Emma shook her head. "Indeed. I'm impressed. The power of the virtues. It's remarkable. But I'm now bound. There is no escaping fate. Surely you would know this by now." She clenched her teeth as her eyes turned from soft to hard and filled with rage. "The Light Wings chose you, and the Dark Wings chose me. It's that simple, Lucia. One's virtue is another's sin—and I will not let my brother go unpunished." She held up a hand and felt the heat of a rising fire mix with the darkness within it, creating a deep, dark blue flame that sent the room into an even darker inferno. Two tears splashed down Emma's face as she uttered an apology. "I'm sorry, Lucia."

Luzanna's eyes widened as Leo held Lucia close. Luzanna threw herself over the two, using her wings to shield them from the falling debris. As Emma's power pulsed through the catacombs, it sent the entire labyrinth into a quake. The walls crumbled around them as the dome above cracked and caved inward. Death was almost certain, an inevitable doom they should have expected. Luzanna held on to her hope, using it to calm the air around them and shield them from the fire now spreading through the cracks of crumbling earth.

The sounds of crashing stone were overshadowed by the deep demented laugh of Ragium, as he appeared and took Emma up in his arms. Emma was emotionless, her dark eyes now void of humanity. With a wave of her hand, she shot a ray of darkness toward them.

Leo closed his eyes, hearing his words cry within him with a final effort. He looked at Lucia's gentle face, with tears flowing, as he stared and admired her beauty once more as he always had.

"I'm sorry I failed to protect you, Lucia. Please forgive me."

Suddenly, as the world began to fall apart around them and Emma's blast depleted the last of Luzanna's hope shield, a ripple of light shot from beneath them, filling the markings of the crests around the altar. The Light Wings pushed up from under Lucia, sending a bountiful warm radiance around them. And just as Ragium looked in disgust at the light, shocked at how Lucia managed to raise her head to say a final prayer with the very last ounce of her strength, the light dissolved the trio into nothing. The catacombs fell into the shadows, sending the three virtues into another dimension tucked safe within a deep and relieving sleep, while Ragium and Emma disappeared into the darkness that created them.

CHAPTER TWENTY

The Awakening

There was an emptiness, a silence that shrouded Lucia's thoughts. She wallowed in it, floating within the painlessness of this space far from the world she knew. Her spirit was flickering, beating like a pulsating star in the far reaches of space. Slowly, her spirit became brighter as it connected with her body, causing her consciousness to pull her awake.

Where am I? It was only then that she felt the prickling of water against her skin. Her eyelids lifted as she regained feeling in her hand. Wearily, she dug her fingertips into the mud beneath her. A huge influx of air entered her body as if she were an infant drawing breath for the very first time. She coughed as rain continued to pour over her, purple thunder flashing overhead. Lucia was on the surface of a grassy terrain within a vast empty field—alone. And for the first time in a very long time, she could feel again.

An inferno raged inside her, a burning anxious panic, as she pulled herself up from her side. The storm was amplifying as the wind blew toward it in the distance. Her eyes quivered, and she wiped the mud from her face with her hands. *Leo. Luzanna.* She thought, *Where are they? How did I get here?* She analyzed her surroundings, hoping to find her companions somewhere close by, but she was alone. Even the Light Wings around her neck told her so. She felt no life within a reasonable distance. The pit in her stomach hardened as her anxiety ripped at her torso, where the blade had—*wait.* Lucia jolted up, moving her hand toward where Ragium had dealt the mortal blow. Miraculously, the wound was gone. Not even a scar remained.

How am I alive? Lucia looked up at the darkening sky. Though she lived, she knew very well that she was not safe. The world had changed, becoming something unfamiliar and distorted, a shell of its former self caught in the grip of darkness' conquest. It was as if the world had been cast into an eternal tempest filled with winds of sorrow and pain. And she could hear them, Terestria's cries, as its light was seeping away and dimming beneath the storms of purple and gray. Not a single ray of light could penetrate through the overcast that shrouded the land in shadow; not an ounce of mercy left. There was no time, only an endless night. Terestria had fallen into ruin because life had played its hand into the sins the darkness had created, leaving her world corrupted. There was nothing left to preserve—or so she thought.

Lucia shot upward, reaching painfully to grasp the Light Wings. "Light, I need you now. Please speak to me. Guide me. Tell me what I must do," she whispered. She scoured her mind, hoping to find a glimmer of truth beneath the confusion, doubt, and fear. She waited, listened, and continued to pray. "My light, my salvation, I must go. I must find my friends. I have to finish our mission. I can still fight. By your will, I am alive. So I must fight until the end. Dear light, please hear me. I need you. Please."

In that moment, her mind cleared. A tingle hovered over the

back of her head as a comforting chill covered her body. "I am alive because I know. *I* am the scales of justice. I am your sword. My purpose is yours, and yours alone. Light, I know this. It is all clear to me now. Your will, your glory—it shall be yours."

Lucia brought herself to her feet as the roaring of thunder intensified. She looked toward the storm. The wind was blustering from behind her, ripping through her hair as the Light Wings glowed. "There," she said, looking across the mountain range ahead of her where the storm loomed. There was something familiar about this scene. It was as if she had seen it somewhere before. *Could it be?* she thought as she remembered. "One of my father's landscapes." The image flashed within her mind, its colors fresh and vibrant as she stared off in the distance. Her heart fluttered. *Home. I've got to find the others,* she thought. *I can't.*

"But you must," they whispered. "They are there. They need you."

"My mother," Lucia uttered. "She needs me." She strode toward the storm, her steps quickening to a run. There was no stopping her. Her mind was made up. The Light Wings had directed her, so she followed. Rarely did the Light Wings ever grant her wishes. Rarely had they validated anything she ever felt. But this was what she desired most: to go home, to see her mother again, and to leave the rest of the world behind—was this now what she wanted? More than anything, was this how she truly felt?

"The world is a wretched place. It's dark and scary. It's no place for a girl like you."

"But how do you know, Mama? The world's so beautiful from way up here. I want to see more."

"I know, child. I know."

"Papa's out there too. I want to see him, Mama. I've got to ask him something."

"Ask him what, Lucy?"

"Why did he leave me? Why did he leave both of us?"

She always knew, didn't she? The truth. This entire time, she knew. She knew who he was and why he left. She merely refused to tell me.

"But would you understand? How could you? How could any-one? The truth had been lost."

Yet, Talon knew, and still denied it! My father left his family to die, not once but twice. How could anyone ever forgive that . . . ? Emma. Lucia remembered the moment Emma gave in during those last moments in the catacombs. She had given up everything due to her father's sin, for the corruption he had wrought. And how could Lucia blame her? *His selfishness, his lust, and his sin caused all this. He stole the Light Wings and then used his powers to do the very thing he swore never to do! He betrayed his duty and his family.*

"All to protect you."

"Shut up!" Lucia shouted. A clap of thunder echoed over her like a sonic boom. Her anger was swelling inside her. She did not know how to feel about everything she now knew. She was a pro-tector chosen by light. Emma was her aunt, a protector chosen by darkness, with wings like her own. Her closest allies were vir-tues, vessels of light destined to fight the sins of darkness. And her father—he was the protector who started it all, the one who broke the balance because he fell in love with someone he never should have.

"My birth," Lucia said to herself. "It was a mistake. I should have never . . . ." Her tears fell alongside the rain as she ran. Her thoughts scurrying still, she could not relieve herself of the guilt or self-hatred. Her entire life had been a lie, a life she did not deserve. Even though a faint voice inside her told her not to believe this to be true, she couldn't change how she felt. She was a child of sin, and hardly the savior of virtue Terestria called her to be.

There was but one glimmer of truth that seemed to break through the darkest of her thoughts, though—a sensible determination she could never rid herself of. *I must save Moz at all costs. I won't let it see the destruction that Pinea or Aldric did. Never.* She hurried her pace, dashing into the storm as the rain turned to sleet and then to hail and heavy snow. The cold was piercing as the winds tore at her clothing. Shivering, she finally made it to the base of the Mozian mountain valley. The snow was thick beneath her boots, piling high over her feet.

This was the first time Lucia had touched snow. The climate of Terestria's southernmost continent remained fairly warm year round. Even during its winters, crops would die beneath chills of cold air, but never would ice pile as high as this, not at the base of the mountains. Lucia stepped deeper into the range, following the path until she found herself approaching the grand gates of her marble city.

She took two deep breaths before continuing. She had no way of telling how long she had been gone, nor could she predict what had befallen the city since her departure. She continued, though she was wary of what she might discover. As she came upon the gate, she stared in awe, watching how the icicles still glistened beneath the archway despite the heavy fog. Oddly enough, there were no guards. She could only wonder why. She placed a hand on the gate and released a warm glow from her fingertips. The ice around the gate began to melt, and the icicles dripped as steam rose from beneath. The doors loosened, and slowly, Lucia pushed, frightened of what she might see.

As she pressed through, she saw only buildings of marble and glass covered in snow, untouched by anything but a drastically changed climate. Lucia stepped through and onto the streets, peeking around while her heart pounded inside her chest. *Am I really home?* She heard the sound of bells in the distance coming from the center of the city, where Sky University stood. "I remember," she whispered, stepping toward it. "It must be midday. The bells always rang at noo—" She stopped, watching as her people poured into the streets. *Wait, why are the bells still ringing?* Groups turned to mobs, scurrying from their homes, terror in their eyes as they hurried, grabbing hold of their possessions and weapons. Lucia's dread rose as her skin prickled in the sharp chill of the air. She glanced upward into the storm as it darkened. "No," she whispered. *Did it follow me?*

Lucia darted forward into the crowds of people as they ran toward the university in a panicked frenzy. She kept her sights focused, trying to see past them so that she might recognize where she was. But before she could truly grasp it, a sense of white-hot fire burned below her face. The Light Wings brightened intensely, pulsating, as a towering shadow stretched over her. Lucia's breath grew cold as she attempted to hold her composure. She blocked out the noise, the clambering of their footsteps, their screams. Lucia tried to hold on to every beautiful memory she once had of this place, before turning to face it. She clenched her eyes shut as she heard the sound of its horrible hiss.

"People of Moz," it bellowed beneath its high-pitched screech, "your high maiden is home!"

Without hesitation, Lucia lifted her arms and summoned forth her diamond sword. From her back sprouted sparkling wings of golden crystal. Her eyes opened and locked on the serpent.

Its tentacles were wrapping around the marble buildings as its body moved through the outskirts and toward the city's center. "We have been expecting you," it said from the mist of its shadowy nest of bladed vipers.

"Leave here at once, Wym! I won't allow you to take this city. It belongs to me!" Lucia roared, holding out her sword. "These are my people!"

Wym chuckled. "Hatorium warned us that you had grown more accustomed to your power, but he said nothing of how arrogant you've become."

"Arrogant? No, this is not arrogance. This is rage. You killed Talon. You slaughtered thousands of innocent Carists. You destroyed Luzanna's life. This isn't arrogance. This is justice!"

"Justice?" the black snake slithered. "Don't you now know the truth? This is our *revenge*. Not your pathetic justice."

"The sons of Terestria will not pay for sins of their fathers. You will not punish one generation for the sins of the former. That's not justice. That's corruption."

"That was not part of the deal!" Wym shouted in anger as it agilely positioned its face yards away from Lucia's. Its tentacles pressed down against the exteriors of the buildings, causing them to crumble. "Terestria is corrupted and ours for the taking. Life had its chance. We're taking what was promised to us."

Lucia shook her head. "Not today." With a swift slash, she sent a wave of light through the air. It collided into the beast, causing it to wail and fall into the buildings behind it. The people slowed down, watching as Lucia lifted her feet from the ground with a flap of her wings. She turned to them. "Run, now—to the university, all of you!" she said, her voice filled with power as her eyes shone a vibrant yellow.

The people nodded and started to run yet again, but not before Wym's tentacles sprouted from the shadows and took the innocent within its grasps. Men, women, and children were crushed by the tightening black bodies of snakelike tentacles.

Lucia flew upward, watching as clouds of red puffed up in all areas of the city. The north, the south, the east, the west—all were under attack simultaneously. She covered her mouth, failing to hold back her tears, as Wym let out a loud roar.

"Their blood is on your hands, Savior. Your light alone can't save them."

"I don't care," Lucia cried as she poured her sadness into her wings. They pulsed vibrantly, changing from pale yellow to vibrant magenta. From the tips of their delicately stylized feathers shot glimmering shards of pink crystals that rained into the blood-soaked streets. The light tore into the flesh of the monsters, freeing many of their victims before more lives could be taken, and into the soil, charging it. Lucia held out her free hand, palm down. She then clenched it as her anger swelled. From the earth shot a pillar of light that entered the sky, parting the clouds and exposing the sun. "I will destroy the darkness. I will take back *our* world. I will break *you*!" And with that war cry, Lucia pointed her sword up. "Now die!" She slashed it downward, and from the sky rained a shower of stars.

* * *

"Madame. The bells are ringing. The people are making their way to the university now."

Lady Ara was sitting atop a decorative bed, her face pale and ghastly, her amber eyes darkened by the circles beneath them. It looked as if she hadn't slept in weeks. She coughed as she tried to rise.

"Milady, please. You must rest." A knight clad in scarlet armor came to her side and held her shoulders.

"I'm quite alright, Lieutenant Sarf. Thank you."

Angelo Sarf nodded, retreating as Ara made her way toward a window at the far side of the room.

She said, "I can see it coming. The darkness is approaching as quickly as I remember."

"It won't take the university, milady. Moz's finest are out by the thousands, guarding the grounds."

"And the others? Where are they?"

"Leo is commanding the eastern battalion, Luzanna the west. Are you sure they can handle this?" Angelo asked. "They're merely children."

"If what they say is true, they are also our only hope," Ara whispered sadly.

"I suppose you're right, madame."

Amelia emerged from the doorway. She rushed toward Ara, her eyes wide and filled with tears. "The monster, it's already taking lives in the south side. Some are saying it can reach as far as the northern district." Amelia wiped her eyes, trying to remain calm. "Lady Ara, no one is safe."

Ara clenched her eyes as a faintness came over her. "Lieutenant, ready the northern and southern troops. Take Sebastien Bono with you and send him to warn Luzanna."

Angelo nodded. "Yes, milady." He turned on his heel and pushed past the door.

"But, milady," Amelia started, her voice quivering.

Ara tried to regain her composure, swallowing hard as her head dizzied. "Y-yes? Amelia, what is it?"

"There have been sightings . . . sightings of a girl with a diamond sword and wings protecting the city."

Tears formed in Ara's weary eyes. "You don't say," she whispered, bringing her fingers to her lips as she smiled. "My Lucia has returned. She's home."

*　*　*

"Gather round, people! This is not a drill." Luzanna stood proudly in front of a row of what appeared to be a hundred men dressed in golden armor. She embodied the natural sense of a leader, speaking with authority as her aqua green eyes hardened with devotion. "Protect the university at all costs. You hear me? There are innocent people out there. Mothers, fathers, sons, daughters—people not unlike you and me. It is our duty to save them. Every life matters. So stay alert. Stay focused. The fate of Moz and Terestria depends on each and every single one of you." Luzanna lowered her gaze. "Disband."

"Yes, sir!"

"Lady Luzanna!" called another voice from right behind her.

Luzanna turned from her men to face a blond fellow carrying a scroll. "What is it now, Sebastien? We're preparing for an attack." She picked up a platinum spear and placed it through a loop in her armor.

"Come on, love. With all this talk of life and death, you'd think you'd show me a little more compassion." Bono licked his lips as he grinned. His face was pouty and sweet.

Despite Bono having the handsome features of a strong jawline and piercing, powder-blue eyes, Luzanna remained unfazed. The city was under attack. She had no time for Bono's foolish ploys of attraction. She blinked. "And that is precisely why I don't take you seriously."

Bono gasped. "Come on, you're not gonna tell me that didn't work. Not even a little."

Luzanna said nothing.

"Humph." Bono sighed. "Geez, you're tougher than steel root." He shrugged. "I'm sorry. I was just trying to make light of the situation, ya know? This might have been my last shot."

"You humor me, Sebastien." Luzanna rolled her eyes. "What did the commander say? Any news from Lady Ara?"

Bono shook his head, holding out the scroll. "You're gonna wanna read this. Apparently, there is a lotta commotion going on in the city. A girl matching the description of the high maiden has been spotted on the south side."

Lucia, Luzanna thought. It had been three months since she last saw her long-lost friend. "You can't be serious. Is it really her?" An odd sensation filled her as she touched her palm with her fingertips. Slowly, she clenched her fist over the symbol burned into it.

"It has to be, right? She was spotted flying with a diamond

sword. You can see the lights even from here. Look!"

Luzanna turned to look up into the sky, noticing only then that the storm had been parted. Streaks of shooting stars fell within the twilight. "Oh my, the grace of the light! It is her!" Luzanna cried. At that moment, she sensed it rising from within her as surely as the sun would rise on a summer's day. As she stared into the sky, the stone in her mask glistened.

*　*　*

"Master Leo!"

Leo was scurrying through pages and pages of books, scavenging for answers. *Where could she be? She can't be gone. She's not . . .* He was panting, his long hair matted. He wasn't himself, and it was quite clear he hadn't been for some time. As the chill in the air sharpened, his panic only heightened.

"Are you listening to me?" Angelo approached him at the center of the library, where a mess of dusty books, parchments, and ancient scrolls covered a long table.

"Yes, Angelo. Can't you see I'm busy?" he snapped, turning his head.

"This is urgent. You're needed at your station. The city is under attack."

Leo's eyes clamped shut. "What's the point? She's gone. We can't defend ourselves without her. She's the key to everything. Don't you see? In all of Stello's notes, the Light Wings were the key to sealing the darkness away and awakening the virtues. Without them, we can't close the link to the other world."

"Master, control yourself," Angelo said. "Hear me out, please." He rested a hand on his friend's shoulder. "I sent Sebastien to inform Luzanna. Troops are reporting sightings of a winged girl fighting the sin in the southern district." Leo's sapphire eyes widened, and Angelo knew his words were music to Leo's ears. "There may be hope after all."

"Lucia," Leo uttered under his breath. "She's back. I've . . . I've got . . . " He paced back and forth, tapping his finger against his lips. "I've got to go!" He bolted past Angelo and toward the library door before Angelo could stop him.

"Leo, wait," Angelo said. From his back, he removed a shield. On its face was the Feral coat of arms. The chained lion was engraved in silver atop a shining blue surface. "Ara instructed me to give this to you. This was your father's. After they were betrothed, the two had exchanged heirlooms. She described it to be her greatest shame not having the chance to return it to him herself. She wants you to take it and use it as your father proudly would."

Leo took the shield into his hands and touched the surface. Immediately, he began to cry. *Protect her,* Leo remembered as he caught his breath. "Thank you, Angelo. Tell the lady, on behalf of house Feral, all is forgiven. I'll be seeing her soon."

"As you wish. Please take care of yourself out there."

"You too, Angelo. You too."

Angelo nodded, leaving the library.

A strange calm came over Leo. Since his father had died, something within him had broken. But now, with this shield in hand, his spirit started to mend. Like the roar of a lion proud and true, his determination shined within his sapphire gaze, reflecting back at him off the surface of the shield and into his soul, where his virtue lay dormant.

*   *   *

The darkness was rising up as Lucia flew past geysers of shadows and blades, with dark puddles of ooze beneath them trapping people as they tried to flee. Lucia tried her best to dissolve the tar with blasts of light, but the ooze spread too quickly. It was hard to hold them all off at once. She sent a stream of light volleys into the air as the serpent's tails swiped at her. She dodged each blade swiftly, using the light to divert their attacks. She formed a diamond shield with her free hand and slammed it into the tip of one of the serpent's blades, sending a shock wave through the air as the shield shattered and filled the air with divine light. The mass of tentacles dissolved in the light, freeing people from their grasp.

Lucia let out a breath of relief before another wave of serpents rallied before her. She propelled herself forward, spinning as she tackled the monsters. She charged light into her wings and let them shatter into shards of multicolored sparks, the beasts squirming as they were obliterated within white flames. Lucia caught herself on the ground with her hands, and with a quick flip, new wings formed from her back before she again took flight.

How did this become so easy? She remembered a time when the powers of the Light Wings frightened her more than anything, but now they were a part of her, as natural as any other part of her body. Lucia looked at the center of the city, where Wym rose high above the buildings. She heard the cries of her people as it moved toward the university. The beast let out a cry and shot a beam of anti-light north, incinerating the buildings with its cosmic breath. Sweat ran down Lucia's face. Her teeth were clenching. *I have to do something. But how? I can't kill it.* She took a deep breath, collecting herself before flying toward the university. *I have to find Mother. Leo and Luzanna are here too. I can feel them. Luzanna— her virtue. It's close by.*

Tremors shook the foundations of the city as Lucia made it to the university, where hundreds of troops were preparing to fire cannons at the beast as it roared and shot beams of anti-light into the air. Lucia held out a hand, filling the cannons with light as the troops lit their fuses. Beams of sparkling light catapulted from the cannons, tearing through Wym's onyx scales.

Despite the horror and bloodshed she witnessed within her own city, Lucia was determined to eradicate this menace once and for all. Something inside her was illuminating, becoming stronger as she focused, as her emotions surged to provide her with new power. She closed her eyes, listening. With her mind, she called out to them. *Virtues, please. Come to my side. Aid me in this redemption.*

"You have no one. Can't you see, Savior? You're all alone, and your people are weak! You can't save them all," Wym hissed.

Lucia shook her head. "You are mistaken. I am stronger than you could ever know! With the blood of Sanoon and Sarina combined, I will bring glory to our names once again. Shining is the light of justice in life and in death. I won't fear sin."

Wym roared as its patience wore thin. "Your anger is futile when confronting darkness. Darkness is fueled by anger!" it cried as it threw a tentacle upward.

Lucia, quick with her senses, attempted to dodge. But the scaly grip of the tentacle hit the base of her legs, sending her flying through the air and out of control. She landed hard, feeling her wings shatter as they collided with the earth and dissipated into light. She tried to catch her breath, rising up weakly as she watched the base of the sin.

The nest of its body lay directly ahead of her, in front of the university, standing still, almost as if it was waiting for her to rise. Wym let out a distorted roar of laughter beneath a crescendo of purple lightning. Its scarlet-red eyes illuminated as it sent a cosmic blast toward the west, turning what was left of the district into a violet inferno.

The stench of death and decay filled the air, sending another sharp chill down Lucia's spine. *I can't . . . give up . . . hope.* She had to think fast. She jumped to her feet and dashed toward the university. Something drew her to the place. Somehow, she always knew there would be knowledge there that she'd need. So, naturally, it was the one place in all of Moz worth protecting if they ever hoped to truly defeat the darkness. She thought of Luzanna, who had always dreamed of attending it. *If only she were here. Is she here?*

Wym let out a devilish laugh as it sent forth a shower of tentacles. Each one was like hundreds of bladed leeches, each racing to impale Lucia first.

Lucia couldn't bear to look, but she had nowhere else to go. She had to face Wym despite all her fears. Remembering her words, she thought, *I mustn't fear sin, nor death.* She summoned her sword as the blades came down. She closed her eyes, waiting and listening to the sharp sound of the air as blades whipped toward her.

Moments before they were to strike, a flash of pink light shot across the sky, slicing through the tentacles. They burst as the light incinerated them. Lucia's heart raced as she searched for the source of the light. *That wasn't—* And there, to her right, she saw a bright pink phoenix flying overhead.

It cried out and flapped its wings, dropping feathers that exploded into magenta flames as they hit the ground. The phoenix hovered over the beast, glaring with its bright eyes of clear aquamarine.

"Is that," Lucia said in awe, "Luzanna?"

A familiar voice echoed from behind her. "Close, but not quite."

Lucia turned from the scene to see her friend smiling, ear to ear, with the Elder Stone still shining in her mask. "You were kicking ass out there. What happened?"

Lucia touched her head, feeling blood drip from its side. "I don't know," she grinned. "I must have pissed it off." She turned back, watching as Wym's head took snaps at the phoenix with its sharp teeth. The phoenix descended upon the sin, latching onto the base of its head before pecking at its flesh with its beak. "What is that?"

Luzanna laughed. "You've been gone too long."

There was a pause as their eyes met. But by the time the tears formed in both of their eyes, they were in each other's arms.

"We've missed you so much."

"You still didn't tell me what that was. Is that yours?"

Luzanna nodded as they parted. "It's hope, the virtue's true form."

"Just like the sins, the virtues have physical manifestations," Lucia revelated, her intuition as sharp as ever.

"Exactly. Leo and I discovered how to summon it while researching the virtues here at Sky University."

"How long have you guys been here?"

"Well"—Luzanna put a finger to her beak, as if she were thinking of the right way to explain everything—"Leo arrived first. I didn't return until a couple weeks after he did, but we both appeared about a mile from here. I assume you did too, from the same place. We're not sure where we might have been this entire time. Leo's been driving himself mad trying to figure it out, but the point is that you're back now. It's been three months, from what I remember. It's winter now."

"Obviously," Lucia said, pointing at the snow. "But how did you summon the phoenix?"

Luzanna's eyes hardened. "I'd love to tell you, but there's no time to explain. We've got to get moving. I'm not sure my phoenix will be able to hold Wym for much longer. We need to regroup with the others." She helped Lucia to her feet.

As the two made their way back, they heard the screech of the phoenix as a ray of anti-light exploded beneath it. It fell from the sky, dissolving into a flash of magenta flames before hitting the ground.

"*You,*" Wym hissed as it caught a glimpse of Luzanna. "Carist— how do you like the destruction I've wrought? Doesn't it remind you of all you've lost? Of all you don't have?"

"I don't dwell on the past, nor do I succumb to sinful wishes, envy," Luzanna said flatly. "I hope—"

"Hope? Your hope is as fragile as that bird," Wym mocked, positioning itself beneath the darkening sky.

"No, my hope is strong!"

"Hope"—the beast chuckled—"is a meek and weak emotion. Real power comes to those who take what they want."

"You'd like to think so," Luzanna whispered. She nudged Lucia to the side. "You want to know how I summoned my virtue, right?" she said to her. "Just watch!" She closed her eyes just as Leo came running up from a good distance behind them.

With his shield and dagger in hand, Leo bolted from the doors of the university and roared, "Lucia!"

At that moment, Lucia noticed his eyes. His sapphire gaze glowed as the shield started to shine a bright blue. Streaks of blue trailed beneath his feet, and a light rose up from the growing pool. The form of a lion's head emerged, using its claws to rise from the now-hallowed ground that became marked by a glowing symbol of temperance. It pulled itself through the light and stood tall behind Leo with its shackles and broken chains. From its back sprouted large wings of sparkling sapphire.

"Leo!" Lucia cried as she ran toward him, astounded by the sight of his virtue emerging from the light behind him. As they collided, she brought her golden gloved hands to Leo's face. She planted her lips on his.

Leo held her close, locking her into a passionate embrace, his senses returning to him in a full sweep. They parted, studying each other's eyes as they smiled. Leo's eyes were still burning.

"You're hot," Lucia said, as she noticed the length of his hair and moved it from his eyes.

"So are you," Leo said with a smirk.

"No," Lucia shouted, trying hard not to laugh, but missing his wit. "You're burning up."

"What?" Leo said, looking at his body as he stepped backward. Whether or not he'd noticed his transformation was uncertain, but as the lamassu of temperance approached him from behind, light poured from his shield, climbing up his arm and encasing him in a bright blue aura. His clothing changed, turning from silk into shining plates of cobalt. His armor was traced with silver as a cloak sprouted from his back. His dagger metamorphosed into a mythril dual-bladed sword, while the symbol of temperance burned into the flesh of his left palm.

"You've awakened," Lucia whispered as the lamassu lowered its head beside them.

"H-hey buddy," Leo said, touching the fur on its glowing, bright blue head.

"It has your eyes," Lucia joked as she petted it. Its purr was loud as it nudged Leo forward.

In his revelation, Leo's power surged. His emotions intensified, and instinctively it was as if he and the lamassu became one. He was in control again. His emotions were finally where he wanted them "Lucia, look—"

Lucia stopped him, touching the sides of his face. "You don't have to say anything. We've got a job to do." She lowered her eyes before glancing back toward Luzanna. "Duty above all else."

They watched as a magenta light shot from Luzanna's head. As it lurched backward, pink ribbons wrapped around her body, changing her armor and enhancing her spear to a sparkling weapon of bright pink quartz. The magenta orb floated in the air, charging into a large sphere, and from it burst the phoenix in a pink inferno.

Lucia was impressed, as Luzanna turned to look back to her.

The phoenix glided downward and landed behind Luzanna. "Virtues, rise!" she shouted proudly.

Leo was beaming as he roared, "Let's kill the bastard!"

Lucia nodded, "We can do this."

Wym growled, watching as three of the light's virtues came together for the first time.

Lucia summoned forth her wings and sword as Leo climbed onto the back of his lamassu. Luzanna sprouted wings of her own, made of platinum and sharp to the tip.

Wym hissed, not finding any pleasure in what it was watching. "Easy prey—I'll kill each and every one of you."

For the first time, within the monster's gaze Lucia sensed genuine anger. This battle would not be like the last. She shook her head as a golden devotion hovered within the irises of her yellow eyes. "We'll see about that. Let's fly!"

CHAPTER TWENTY-ONE

Conviction

Dusk came quickly as the city turned into a fiery frenzy. Ara watched from her window as pillars of lights rose high into the evening sky. Her vision was fading, blurring as her tears formed.

Amelia came to her side. "Lady Ara, please rest. The high maiden will certainly save the city. I'm sure of it. It will be just as Stello predicted."

"Stello," Ara whispered, coughing into the sleeve of her scarlet robe before lying down in her bed. Her breath was shallow as flashes of light seeped through the window and covered the walls in many colors. "He always knew—I knew—she would be so powerful."

"As did I, milady." Amelia tucked Ara in. "Now rest. Save your strength for when Lucia returns." Amelia rose from the bed as Ara held her wrist. Ara's skin was pale, sweaty, and cold to the touch. She tightened her grip.

"Amelia, you must tell her." Ara closed her eyes as she tried hard to recall the memories she had long since forgotten. "Tell Lucia the truth."

Amelia's eyes widened. "No, Lady Ara. *You* will. You must."

Ara shook her head. "No, you misunderstand me." She coughed. "Lucia, she is Moz's—no, Terestria's salvation. She need not forget her birthright. As a Sanoon or as a Sarina, she has always been a protector of light. Please, Amelia. Remind her of who she is. More than the high maiden of Moz or the girl I raised. Remind her. She's a child of the light, blessed by the graces of its will, deserving of so much more than I could have ever given her."

"Milady," Amelia whispered, grasping her best friend's hand, "don't speak. Save your strength and fight this. Fight like you always have."

Ara smiled. "This is my fate. Just as the Light Wings are Lucia's." She closed her eyes, releasing sad streams of sparkles. "Tell Lucia to remember . . . to remember . . . " Ara's breathing fell softer as she uttered, "her song."

*   *   *

There was a roar as the thunder summoned a shower of rain. Shadows were forming into large vipers, turning on the soldiers as they stormed into the fray.

Angelo cried out, "For the glory of Moz and the high maiden! No holding back!" He unsheathed his broadsword, launched himself forward, and slashed into the masses of shadows.

Lucia flew over the army, imbuing their weapons with light, while Luzanna and her phoenix worked side by side using their wings to knock and crush the vipers into the marble walls of the buildings where they sprouted from underneath.

Leo, atop his lamassu, took to the streets below. With his sword, he cut through the serpent at the lion's feet. The lion snarled as it pounced. "Get him, Temp!" The lion latched onto Wym's neck, sinking its teeth into dark flesh. Leo climbed up the back of the lamassu, and Wym turned its attention toward him. Leo saw every single one of its sharp teeth as it charged a beam in its mouth.

"I don't think so!" Leo shouted, holding his shield over his face.

Wym let out a high-pitched scream as it shot a ray toward Leo. But the cosmic blast minimized as it was drawn into his shield, causing it to radiate with a bright blue light. And then, with a forceful swing, Leo knocked back the light, reflecting the power back at the serpent in the form of a large blue chain.

Telekinetically, Leo used the shield to trace and guide the chain, wrapping it around Wym's extremities. Wym's skin sizzled as the chain tightened around its horns and neck. Its cries were no longer those of rage or intimidation, but pain, as the lighted chains bound Wym to its own tentacles and blades. Leo's lamassu withdrew itself backward and landed a few yards from the monster, as if to admire the work its master had created.

"Not so tough now, huh?" Leo held out his hand as his lion roared. From the cracking earth of the war-torn streets sprouted more chains that continued to bind the sin to Leo's royal blue light.

Wym cried out, "Damn you. Damn you all!" It emitted a beam of anti-light into the storm, filling the sky with purple lightning. Within moments, anti-light stretched and sparked inside the clouds.

"Shit," Leo whispered as purple lightning descended upon the city, sending a shock wave through the buildings. The earth quaked, crumbling the buildings while simultaneously setting them ablaze with shadowy fire. The chains Leo had summoned shattered into sparkling dust as the ground rumbled.

The lightning continued to pour as Wym snarled, releasing a distorted roar as it chuckled. It moved its scarlet eyes, focusing on its prey, arching back its head as if it were ready to snap.

Leo shouted, "Let's go!" as blades sprouted from behind him.

The lion propelled itself into the air, using its large wings to send a blast of light from its back as it took flight. The light covered the ground, destroying the tentacles as Wym shot beams toward Leo.

The lion tried its best to dodge the blasts, but it was not as fast as Lucia or the phoenix. It struggled as one of its wings was caught by a falling piece of purple lightning. The lion cried as its body began to shatter, dissipating as it fell. Leo was freefalling from hundreds of feet in the air, on the verge of panic, watching as the streets turned red. He was screaming as he came crashing to the ground. There was a large flash as he collided into the earth encased within a bright pink sphere. He caught his breath as the sphere dissolved, revealing Luzanna flying overhead.

"Thank you," Leo said, seemingly embarrassed. "I'm new at this." He shrugged.

Luzanna rolled her eyes before summoning a quartz spear into her hand. She sent it flying through the air as she summoned another and darted forward, with the phoenix coming in from the left. The phoenix cried out as it circled overhead, surrounding Wym in flames of hot pink. Luzanna landed on the back of Wym's head as the phoenix clawed at one of its many arms. Wym cried out in pain as it attempted to shake her off. She held one of its horns with her free hand as her flying spear landed into the base of Wym's neck, causing it to cry out in agony.

Leo pushed forward, past the vipers, slashing as his shield bashed one of Wym's blades, and used its power to summon a chain of light. With it, he immobilized Wym's head. "Luzanna, now!"

Luzanna held her spear high above her head with both hands. With an echoing war cry, she thrust the spear into the head of the beast between its blood-red eyes. It roared loudly as Luzanna jumped backward and used her wings to shoot platinum feathers of light into the sin's flesh.

The monstrosity continued to cry as Lucia slowly descended from the sky. "It's over," she said, powerfully charging her wings with golden light. The light was so strong it brought the night into day. Lucia let go of her sword, letting it float between her golden hands.

Blinded, Wym shot blasts mindlessly through the sky, its cries filled with terror.

"This is justice," Lucia said. "No mercy." Her sword absorbed the light as it poured from her wings. It became a glowing orb, growing as the light of the stars and moon stretched toward her. A pillar of light sprouted from the ground and filled the air as it hit the orb. At that moment, the orb changed, transforming into gigantic seraph wings. The wings opened, revealing the blinding flash form of a beautiful golden woman. Her eyes were covered by a golden sash as she held up a set of golden scales. The glowing symbol of justice formed beneath her. Her movements mimicked Lucia's. Lucia closed her eyes as her body floated toward her virtue. She then merged with it, becoming one as it held up its free hand, summoning a diamond greatsword.

"No, impossible! It can't be . . . ." Wym said.

The woman spoke, her heavenly voice singing. "Your reign ends here, envy. No longer shall you hold dominion over Terestria." Her voice echoed, unworldly, causing the running people below to stop and stare into her radiance. The shadows cowered backward, unable to move beneath the bright beams of the seraph's scales of justice.

"The girl, she could not—she knows no justice!" Wym roared.

"She does now," said the seraph as she, with one swift strike, sliced the head of the serpent off its body of nested vipers.

The serpent's glowing red eyes hardened, turning gray as it fell to the ground, crackling as its body turned from black to gray, shriveling as its extremities retreated into the mass. Holding up her scales and pointing her sword at the center of the nest, the seraph shot a beam of light into the serpent, and from within it was torn apart by a blaze of golden fire, incinerated into a heap of sparkling ash. Wym's head crumbled, changing to stone as it weathered and disappeared into the smoke of justice's fire. The seraph lowered her sword as it dissolved with a flash of light, releasing Lucia.

Lucia floated downward, reverting back into her true form. Leo and Luzanna rushed toward her. Luzanna's form changed, as well, as she glided to Lucia's side. Leo transformed as he took Lucia into his arms. The survivors cheered.

"Lucia, you did it!" Leo exclaimed.

"*We* did it," Lucia said, burying her face into Leo's chest. She sobbed, overwhelmed by emotion. She was crying as the spirit of light filled her. Her faith had saved them. It had saved her home. Moz had survived.

"I can't believe it," Luzanna said, embracing her friends as she let out tears of her own. "We destroyed it." They held each other for what seemed to be forever, taking in the moment. The three of them, together, had achieved the impossible. Combining their strengths, facing their fears, and realizing their destinies had given their lives new purpose—purpose they found in each other.

As the three dispersed, the armies and the people of Moz surrounded them. Angelo Sarf emerged, followed by Sebastien Bono, both covered in soot and blood. Angelo kneeled before them, and slowly everyone else did as well. "To our virtues of light—the mighty altruists of Terestria."

The air filled with warmth as tears covered Lucia's face. These were *her* people, bowing before her, loving her. She remembered that fateful day, which seemed like ages ago, when she had been afraid of someday knowing what her people truly felt about her. But now she knew. *I can rule.*

"Lieutenant," Lucia said shakily, still trying to grasp the shock of all that had happened. "Where is my mother? Can you take me to her?"

Angelo rose. "Of course. She's taken refuge within Sky University. I can take you to her now."

Angelo turned to Bono. "Take the men and attend to the wounded. I'm going to take the high maiden to see Lady Ara."

Bono nodded. "Yes, sir!" The people clapped and cheered as Lucia, Leo, and Luzanna were escorted by Angelo Sarf to the grounds of Sky University.

*　*　*

The city was still burning as they approached the doors of the university's main building. Angelo held the doors open for the trio, who, despite their victory, remained heavy of heart and exhausted from their plight.

"This way, High Maiden," Angelo said, leading them to a staircase that ascended high up into the building's western wing.

Like her home, the university walls were made of marble with high windows of stained glass. It reminded Lucia of the sanctuary that was now gone. The entire place was everything she had missed this entire time. For a time, it had been all she wanted to escape her duty as high maiden. She'd longed to see the world and to be free to experience life how she wanted. But now in the halls of the university, she questioned that. As they made their way past elegantly carved statues and gracefully flowing tapestries, Lucia wondered about the very things she missed most of all.

"Lucia, are you okay?" Leo asked, holding her hand. "You're quiet."

"I'm fine. I'm just taking this all in. I haven't been home in ages. I'd almost forgotten what home looked like."

They came to the end of the corridor, at the base of a large archway where two large ruby-colored doors stood. Angelo stepped to the side. "Your mother is inside. I'll give you both a moment." He looked to the others.

Luzanna nodded. "We'll see you in a minute," she said, pulling Leo's arm. "Let's go."

Leo kissed Lucia on the forehead before parting from her and following Angelo and Luzanna toward the university entrance.

Lucia looked back at the threshold. She couldn't help but be reminded of that feeling as she reached for the brass handles of the ruby-colored doors. *That dread,* she thought as she pushed the door open. Candlelight seeped into her eyes as she walked through the door. At the foot of the bed sat Amelia, who immediately stood up, wiping away her tears.

"Lucia, I'm so happy to see you." Amelia whimpered as she attempted to hold herself together. She rushed to Lucia and took her hands.

"Amelia, what's wrong? I've never seen you so . . ." Lucia felt it, coming up from its burrow and clasping her heart with its wretched grip. "No."

"I'm afraid . . ." Amelia cried. "I'm afraid you're too late." She raised her hands to cover her face. "She's gone."

"Who's gone?" Lucia asked as tears flooded her face, refusing to believe the words she'd just heard. Her heart was racing as she rushed toward the bed. She saw her then, with her graceful face, pale and seemingly asleep in the candlelight, dressed still in her favorite color. "No," Lucia cried, dropping to the side of the bed. She touched the side of her mother's face, feeling the cold beneath her touch. "No, no, no. Mother. It's me. It's Lucia. Your daughter, Lucy. I'm here. I'm home," she called out, but there was no response. "Mother, please. Say something!" Lucia buried her face into Ara's robe. "I'm sorry I never listened. I'm sorry I didn't believe enough. I'm sorry I wasn't . . ." The Light Wings glimmered as she remembered. *If you stay, she will die.* "I didn't have a choice. You were supposed to live." She whispered, "I was trying to save you."

"My dear, I'm so sorry," Amelia said. "She grew ill after you disappeared. It was a mysterious sickness, unlike anything anyone had seen. There was no way of treating it. No doctor or scholar could describe what was happening. Many others in Moz are afflicted. It's a plague."

Lucia swallowed hard, rising from the bed as her tears hit the top of her mother's hands. She placed her cheek within her mother's palm, rubbing it gently against her pale thin skin, trying hard to remember, to believe that her mother was alive, stroking her face. Lucia sniffled as she lifted her head and held onto her mother's hand. "Just like Remena—the same thing happened to Emma and her people." She faced Amelia. "*My* people." She turned back to her mother. "Life cannot live without the light that created it. People are going to continue to die if we do not restore it."

"What are you going to do?" Amelia asked. "Moz needs you, now that your mother is gone."

Lucia shook her head. "This is bigger than Moz, Amelia. Terestria needs me. There are three more of those things out there, and there is one more virtue we need to find before we can fix all this."

Amelia lowered her head. "I understand, but . . . " She continued to cry. "What are we supposed to do?"

Lucia's face felt numb. Her expression was stoic despite the constant outpouring of tears from her eyes. "Let's start by doing the only thing we can do right now. Let's bury my mother."

*　*　*

In the following days, a tomb was constructed atop what was once the grounds of Sanoon Manor. The people of Moz had started to rebuild with the help of Leo, his friend Sebastien Bono, and Lieutenant Angelo Sarf. At Sky University, its scholars and

Luzanna were hard at work within its many libraries searching for a cure to the mysterious sickness sweeping through the city. And Lucia, the newly named lady of Moz, waited.

The day the tomb was finally finished, the people of Moz gathered. The city's inhabitants, who once came by the thousands to these very grounds to catch a glimpse of whatever festivities the nobles had planned, now came by the hundreds, reduced to a mere fraction of what they once were.

The day was the brightest Moz had seen in the weeks since the virtues had arrived. It was as if the world was in some way healing, but Lucia knew that was not the case. Even if Moz was healing, Aldric was gone, and no one had any way of telling whether Pinea had survived Lykorus's attack, or if the Pineans still believed Leo murdered his own father. These were the consequences of Stello's corruption—time and life lost, lives ruined.

And still, three remained: hate, pride, and greed—each with now even more reason to despise light and its creations, with envy's death.

It was a victory, yes. That much was true. But in the face of all they had lost up till then, they were still on the losing side. Emma was now a slave to the darkness, serving the sins to see that Stello's plans to redeem Terestria would fail. And they still lacked the final virtue they needed if they ever hoped to defeat the darkness.

These things were on Lucia's mind as she watched Moz's royal guard bring her mother's body into the newly constructed tomb of marble and glass. The people of Moz had decorated her coffin with makeshift flowers of different types of linen and ribbons. The flowers of the Pinean hills to the north had long since stopped growing. Winter had come, making it harder for any of their crops to grow. Famine was almost imminent; but with the reduction of Moz's populace, rationing what was left per household was much easier. Yet, it hurt Lucia very much to see her people continue to suffer this way.

Alongside Ara, the families of Moz laid to rest their loved ones as well on the grounds of Sanoon Manor, turning it into a resting place and memorial for all those who'd lost their lives that day. Lucia tried her best to find the right words to say as she took the podium. This was only her second public address, but her first officially as lady. She held her breath, watching as the people, clothed in black, cried amongst themselves. She recalled something her mother had once said. *I believe now that you are ready to show the province and the world what you really are inside.*

Lucia sighed as Leo and Luzanna gazed up at her from the crowd with tears in their eyes, too. She collected herself, searching deep within for that strength her mother so boldly spoke of. "People of Moz, I come before you today, not as a noble, or a savior of any kind, but as your equal, as someone who, like you, knows grief. Grief is such a powerful emotion. It rivals only one other—love. And like love, it can consume you. But you see, no matter what, we must always remember, in the face of our pain, our suffering, our fears, and our doubts, that despite whatever we may be feeling, it's in knowing grief that we truly know what love is.

"And without fear, we'd know no courage. Without suffering, we'd know no reward. Without pain, no relief. Without doubt, no certainty. I come to you today, tormented by the same grief that consumes us all. But I've also come to tell you that this torment, this despair, it will not be the end of us. Because despite our differences, or our loss, we now know what love truly is—because we've faced evil, because we've faced death and survived.

"So let us grieve and remember those we loved. Use that love to rebuild your homes, your families, and to rely on one another. Because it's with our love, our faith, and our light that we will be able to overcome and conquer anything. In life and in death, with love, darkness cannot destroy us. With darkness may come fear, but as long as there is love, there will always be light.

"Today, I'd like for you to listen and join me in this song as we remember those who have fallen. Let our voices ring as we sing. Call to the heavens and pray that those we've loved and lost will now know the true grace and love of the light."

Slowly, Lucia brought a hum up from within her throat. With it, like an angel, she started her melody, her devout hymn:

> *I travel far and alone, seeking peace and simple bliss.*
> *But I have found myself in the darkest space.*
> *Still, I long to feel it:*
> *The essence of home, a place to call my refuge.*
>
> *Yet still, I must accomplish an unknown task.*
> *Will I find it here, or is it there?*
> *I do not know.*
> *So why must I go?*
> *Why should I walk this path alone?*
> *Is there truly something here for me?*
>
> *In the darkest depth, I must admit.*
> *This is where I belong.*
> *It's as if I fight for no reason.*
> *For this is my conviction.*
> *There is something I must fight for.*
> *A revelation . . .*
>
> *This is not what I had planned for,*
> *But this is my contribution.*
> *This is my conviction.*
> *Because even when I lose, I win.*
> *This is fate conspiring.*
> *There is something guiding me.*

I must follow this feeling.
Because with it, my heart sings.
I can't stop fighting this feeling,
Not when these words keep coming.
From deep inside, I can hear it,
The drumming of my conviction.
To accept my fate with light's grace,
Even from within the darkest place,
This is my conviction.
Because when I walk alone, it glows.
Those who are led by the light,
Must go where they are needed most.
Into places where they can fight,
Into places where their conviction can shine bright.

A crack of thunder broke through the echoes of Lucia's voice as her song came to a close. Her golden eyes were frozen as the rain slated over them. She looked outward into the darkening overcast of the northern sky, as the Light Wings began to beat with a vibrant violet light. With a deep breath, Lucia closed her eyes and listened to its voice as it whispered. "Into shadows, you must go . . ." Lucia's eyes opened beneath the orbs of sparkling water collecting on her long lashes. She turned her head, watching as her people prayed silently beneath the patter of rain, locked within the memories of her soft hymn. As she surveyed the crowed, her eyes were met by those of Luzanna and Leo, whose transcendent hope and shining temperance glistened within walls of sapphire and aquamarine. Lucia smiled faintly, blinking as she released the pendant from her grasp. Surely, the trials ahead would continue to test them. There was no cause to deny that the Light Wings would not continue to do so. However, Lucia could not absolve the lingering intuition—the same intuition that had plagued her from the day she first came into contact with the Light Wings.

The familiar dread of uncertainty hovered over her as she strived to cling her spirit to the virtues they had discovered.

358

Acknowledgments

First and foremost, I'd like to thank the many people who have supported me throughout the many years of *Dutybound* and Light Wings composition, family and friends alike. I'm incredibly grateful to the mentors and peers who encouraged me to write and to NEW Apprenticeship (formerly the Digital Creative Institute), who provided me with the incredible opportunity to pursue a career as a content writer and digital marketer in San Antonio, Texas. Without you, I would not have chosen this path for myself. So, much credit to NEW Apprenticeship and its CEO Brad Voeller for taking a leap of faith and bringing me aboard.

I'd also like to thank my line editor Audra Gerber at Creative Detail in Austin, Texas, for being the first to read my novel and provide me with insights that would eventually lead to its publication. You helped make *Dutybound* so much better. To the people at JKS Communications, thank you for making my boyhood dream a reality with your brilliant polish, editing & publishing expertise. This is definitively a dream come true, so sincerely thank you.

To my team at Light Wings Promotions, thank you for everything you do to keep our company thriving and in supporting the Light Wings brand name. And one last special acknowledgment I'd like to share is to my dear, sweet Big Momo, Esther Lopez, who passed this last Thanksgiving. The portfolio you gave me for my 11th birthday, to this day, still holds all the original handwritten stories I used as source material for *Dutybound*. I wish you could be here to read it in its completion. Among all my supporters, you were always my biggest fan. With love, I so humbly thank you all for this achievement. From here on forth, I shall remain *Dutybound*.